ABOUT THE AUTHOR

© Ibbitson Photography

Fiona Keating is a journalist and editor, covering world news, travel and current affairs as well as history and archaeology. She has worked for ITN, *IBTimes*, *SKY*, the *Independent*, and the *Guardian*. She was born in Penang, Malaysia, is from Chinese/Irish heritage and has lived in London since she was two years old. She completed the Crime Writing MA at City University and lives in Greenwich with her partner. *Smoke and Silk* is her first novel.

SMOKE AND SILK

Fiona Keating

First published in 2025 by Mountain Leopard Press
An Imprint of HEADLINE PUBLISHING GROUP LIMITED

This paperback edition published in 2025

1

Cataloguing in Publication Data is available from the British Library

ISBN 978 1 0354 1832 9 (Paperback)

Typeset in Adobe Garamond by CC Book Production

Printed and bound in Great Britain by Clays Ltd, Elcograf S.p.A.

Headline's policy is to use papers that are natural, renewable and recyclable products and made from wood grown in well-managed forests and other controlled sources. The logging and manufacturing processes are expected to conform to the environmental regulations of the country of origin.

Headline Publishing Group Limited
An Hachette UK Company
Carmelite House
50 Victoria Embankment
London EC4Y 0DZ

The authorised representative in the EEA is Hachette Ireland,
8 Castlecourt Centre, Dublin 15, D15 XTP3, Ireland
(email: info@hbgi.ie)

www.headline.co.uk
www.hachette.co.uk

For Angela

JUNE

1

Limehouse, London,
1st June 1888

Smoke curled from the chimney pots in lazy swirls, too lethargic in the heat of the summer to rise any higher. Instead heavy layers of dense grey hovered over the moss-covered slates of tenement buildings.

Pearl coughed, her lungs filling with the gritty, grimy London air. She walked along the crooked edges of the road to avoid walking under the eaves of the rickety old warehouses that lined Wapping High Street, in case some of the slates came loose and crashed to the cobblestones. She was going home. Dread was seeping into her chest, forcing her to take short little breaths.

The journey had been long and uncomfortable. Her back ached after sitting on the hard wooden seats; the train from Portsmouth had rattled incessantly, screeching to halts, twisting and turning, then fading into darkness as they traversed through tunnels. Her bones still felt every jolt of the third-class carriage.

The day was stifling; her scalp prickled with sweat, and the strings of her bonnet cut uncomfortably into her neck, making it difficult to swallow. During the journey, a travelling salesman in a battered stovepipe hat had tried to engage her in conversation, beginning the moment they had left Portsmouth. His thigh had pressed hard against hers whenever the carriage took a violent lurch to the left or the right, or even when there was no lurch at all. In frustration, she had gripped her umbrella tightly and brought it down with some force on his foot. He gave a slight gasp and – thankfully – retreated. Pearl settled back more comfortably then, her head against the window, and closed her eyes.

Upon reaching London, in her haste to avoid the grubby hand he had held out as she'd disembarked from the train, she had stepped into a sludgy mound of horse dung. She'd forgotten how much there was of it here, compared to Portsmouth.

Taking a moment to shake off the muck from her boots, she glanced around, looking from left to right as she crossed the road, careful to dodge the carts and hackney carriages that clattered by. She wound her way through street after street, heading in the direction of East India Road. As she grew closer, the streets became more and more rundown, the alleyways dark and sinister. Her father had always warned her to avoid the blind courtyards where policemen would only venture down in pairs, if at all. Her father. She swallowed painfully.

Looking to her right, there was a yard full of shrieking children, mostly barefoot, their hard little feet encrusted with dirt. A couple of the lucky ones had boots, but they were in such a pitiful condition, with huge holes in the toes, soles flapping, and precariously tied up with fraying string. A baby was bawling on a doorstep, dangling from the arm of a girl barely past five years old.

The path ahead was littered with potato peelings and vegetable detritus. A group of young scavengers were carefully picking their way through the heaps, although it was doubtful that anything was edible.

After seven years in Portsmouth, she was back home.

Pearl walked faster and faster along the Limehouse streets, until finally, in the fading light of the sunset, she stopped in front of The Sailor's Arms.

She held her sides, lungs raw. Was she too late?

Pearl took a few steps back, staring up at the façade of the waterman's tavern. It looked much the same, the faded gold lettering on the wooden panelling above the windows spelling out:

The Sailor's Arms
Proprietor: Patrick O'Dwyer

But something was awry. The familiar painted sign of a tea clipper was squeaking in protest at the lack of oiling and hanging down at a lopsided angle.

Littered around the entryway were piles of broken bottles, stacks of crates and, to Pearl's horror, a dead dog, flies buzzing around its innards. Her father always used to get one of the pot boys to sweep down the front of the pub every morning as one of the first chores of the day.

Pearl frowned, wondering why The Sailor's Arms was in such a sorry state. She raised a hand to push open the frosted glass door but hesitated on the threshold. Could she just turn and go back now, evade her old life? No, she wouldn't run away again, not this time.

The noise hit her first as she opened the doors and tumbled back into a world she had thought never to see again. Roars of hoarse laughter, two dockers arguing over whose round it was, pint glasses shattering on the slate flagstones, the sound slightly muffled by the sawdust. A toothless man was thumping out *The Wilting Banshee* jig on the pianoforte, the middle C still sticking. She was surprised to find herself smiling at the faded memories the sound conjured.

And then the smell hit her. Beer, burnt sausages, tobacco smoke and the stink of stale bodies enveloped her.

The main saloon bar was as she remembered, though perhaps smaller and more drab. The room had seemed enormous to her as a child. The embroidered damask curtains were torn and ragged at the edges. Surely they were a more brilliant red during her teenage years? The gas lamps sputtered and flickered, casting a greenish glow over everything, while the ebony cabinet that stocked her father's favourite tipples was now tilted to one side, a leaning Tower of Pisa right here in Limehouse.

She could still list the names, reciting them like Hail Marys on a rosary: James Buchanan's Special Reserve Scotch whisky, Martell's Three Star Brandy, Royal Lochnagar, and of course Jameson's, her father's favourite. He'd pour himself a generous measure from his favourite shot glass, the one with a four-leaf clover on it, as the evening wound to a close, only a few stragglers left in the pub. Downing it in one, he'd smack his lips and put an arm around Pearl. She always dreaded those maudlin moments.

'There's nothing finer than a sup of this Irish nectar – only the lovely face of Jai Li, your beloved mother, God rest her soul.' PJ would have a faraway look in his eye. He'd wipe his nose with the back of his hand, clear his throat, then cast an eagle eye across the saloon and deliver some vicious thumps to a few sailors trying to pilfer some bottles from behind the bar.

Pearl leant back against a wall, still unobserved. She looked at the portrait of Queen Victoria hanging on the wall to the left, so ingrained with the smoke from a thousand pipes its picture frame could be mistaken for ebony. A handlebar moustache was drawn on the royal's upper lip and a pirate's patch covered one imperious eye.

'I'll clean that off when she gives Ireland back to the Irish,' Pearl's father had said.

Pearl ducked as a footstool whistled past her head, her reflexes still as sharp as ever. A fight had broken out amongst a group of sailors on shore leave, who were trying to gouge each other's eyes out. No Queensberry rules here. Biting, scratching, a swift knee to the groin. Their female companions were screaming and egging them on. A woman was dancing on a table, kicking up her legs and bawling out *The Good Ship Venus.* Pearl silently sang along with the words she had first heard at the age of six.

'The captain's daughter Charlotte
'Was born and bred a harlot
'Her thighs at night
'Were lily white
'By morning they were scarlet.'

A high-pitched, grating voice cut through the din. 'Well, if it ain't the return of the prodigal daughter.' A blousy woman was pushing through the crowd, a majestic ship cutting through stormy seas. Pearl took in the floor-length paisley-patterned dress, edged with a filthy lace frill, revealing plump shoulders. The old-fashioned bustle swayed as she moved in time to the melody of a rollicking Irish jig played by the toothless man, still bouncing up and down on the music stool.

Pearl had been Betty Sullivan's punch bag since she could remember. The corners of Betty's thin lips drooped into a sour smile.

'Took your time getting here. Think you could waltz in like the grieving daughter and all's forgiven? Me and Mr Matthews have been working our fingers to the bone since you buggered off.'

A ginger-haired man behind the bar who was polishing glasses winked at Pearl.

'Now you leave her be, Betty. She's only just got here. Lovely to see you, darlin'.'

Pearl smiled at Mr Matthews, then turned to face Betty again, grinding her teeth, determined not to let the other woman rile her. 'I rushed back as soon as I got the telegram from Uncle Peter. How is Pa?'

'PJ is still with us, but only just. And what do you care? Broke your father's heart, you running off with that scoundrel, Tommy Fitzgerald. But I've been looking after your Pa ever since. You've got me to thank he's still alive and kicking, with you gone these past seven years.'

'That's my business,' Pearl shot back. 'You're not my mother. I had every right to wed Tommy and go wherever we wanted.'

Betty grinned. Pearl noticed she had lost many more teeth since she had seen her last. 'I heard about Tommy. Drowned, didn't he? And you bereaved at such a tender age.'

The blood drained from Pearl's face. She forced herself to breathe slowly, and then fixed a smile on her face.

'Thanks for your commiserations. Tommy died where he loved to be. And yes, I am a sailor's widow, that's my lot in life. And so lovely to see you, too, Betty. I must say, how frugal of you to be wearing the same dress I remember from childhood. But you'll need to take a needle and thread to it. You're busting out of the sides.'

'Your manners ain't improved much. Shouldn't be speaking like that to your elders, especially me that's been with your Pa all these years.'

Pearl sighed. They'd had this conversation so many times before, and she wasn't in any mood for sparring with Betty. 'I've got to see my Pa,' she said abruptly.

'PJ don't want to see you. Never spoke your name again once

you'd scarpered. He had me and that's what mattered to him. Couldn't get enough of me. Know what I mean?' Betty raised an eyebrow and sniggered. Pearl suppressed a shudder.

'Get out of my way, Betty. I need to see him.' Pearl shoved past Betty, moving rapidly along the bar and up the stairs at the end of the pub, taking two steps at a time. Betty screamed after her, 'You're even worse than when you were a nipper. Always cheeking me. You always was a wrong 'un. It's your mother's Oriental bad blood running through your veins. You don't belong here.'

The brass doorknob to her father's bedroom was icy cold to the touch. Pearl took a tentative step inside. At first, she couldn't see anything. The curtains were closed and in the dim light, Pearl could only make out indistinct shapes. She closed the door quietly, crossed the room and moved to the bed where her father lay. His chest was moving slightly, his breathing laborious. A votive candle flickered on the bedside table – a picture of the Baby Jesus on the side of the glass, the candlelight casting mellifluous shadows on the walls – next to a bible and a bottle of holy water in the shape of the Virgin Mary. The frankincense was pungent; the scent to some extent masked the sulphurous smell of decay. Pearl breathed through her mouth.

'Oh, Pa. Always hoping for a miracle to make things better,' she said softly. Pearl remembered the time she'd fallen and hit her head on a rock. He had prayed so fervently and offered up so many rosaries for her recovery, only for him to berate her for playing out on the foreshore once she'd recovered consciousness, and keep her indoors for two weeks.

Pearl held the candle aloft and gazed down at her father. His brow was furrowed with pain, his cheeks a latticework of deep lines. His mouth sagged open and a line of saliva traced its way down his beard, like the trail of a snail's slime. When had her father's beard transformed from auburn to white? The double chin was also gone, replaced by a mass of loose wrinkles, resembling a turkey's neck.

The man had aged so much in the time since she'd been gone. Where was the tyrant of her childhood? He'd been such a strong, strapping man, with a huge belly, voluminous trousers held up with a belt and thick braces. Never again would he chase her around the pub, giving her a good clout when she'd dropped a glass. He'd not done it out of anger, but so she would remember the cost of replacing things. Always the publican.

Pearl took his hand. It was still warm. Hope rose and she wondered whether there might be a chance he would recover, that she would have one final conversation with him, to talk to him honestly. But he would never understand the reasons why she had left. She squeezed his hand harder and he groaned softly. Tears coursed down her cheeks.

2

'Pearl! Get your lazy arse down here!' The dulcet tones of Betty were clear and sharp enough to travel up two flights of stairs to the attic bedroom.

Pearl groaned. Her back and neck were stiff from sitting up with her father until the small hours.

She'd crept into her bedroom to get a few hours' sleep. In the blurry light of daybreak, the bedroom looked like a rag and bone man's treasure trove. She turned on her side, realising she'd been using a man's unwashed long johns as a pillow. She scrambled off the bed.

Pearl stretched and yawned, peering out of the dirt-encrusted windows. She rubbed the glass panes vigorously with her sleeve, looking down on Wapping Old Stairs and onto the Thames foreshore. Her father's gravelly voice came back to her. He loved regaling his punters with gory tales of Limehouse. 'Of course, this place has a fearful history.' PJ took a sip of his Jameson's, leaning heavily on the bar.

'This was where Execution Dock was, where sailors, pirates and smugglers were hanged for offences committed on the water.'

There were horrified murmurs from the pub crowd.

'Well, no one really knows the exact site of the executions; it could have been anywhere along here,' a waterman said as he shrugged his shoulders dismissively.

PJ glared at him. 'D'you know more than me? My family have been here for generations. Stories passed down from father to son.'

The waterman looked sheepish, wiping his nose.

'As I was saying, this is where many ne'er-do-wells were hanged or gibbeted. They were taken from Marshalsea Prison in Southwark and brought down the river here to Wapping. They died in agony, after a long suffocation, twisting and turning in the wind. That's why they called it the Marshal's dance.'

A woman screeched, making several people in the crowd jump.

Pearl's father nodded with grim satisfaction, sucking his teeth. 'But I'll tell you something worse,' he whispered, making them all lean further forward to hear his words.

'Those hanged criminals were kept there until three tides had submerged their bodies. Thousands of people would come and stare at their swollen corpses, all green and bloated.'

Betty's shrill voice cut into Pearl's thoughts. 'Oy, Mrs Fancy Pants. Come down and make yourself useful.'

Pearl leaned out of the window and closed her eyes, listening to the sounds drifting in from the Thames. A pleasure boat cruise, with its passengers singing and dancing on the deck, chugged its way past, edging closely by some small fishing boats. The tide was out, the pebbles on the riverbank glistening green with moss and thick strands of seaweed. The sun was shining brightly, not a single cloud marring the duck-egg blue sky.

'It's five o'clock already and we're late for opening. You've had your lie in.' There was Betty's grating voice again. Reluctantly, Pearl left the nostalgic sanctuary of her bedroom and trudged down the stairs, for a moment tempted to slide down the oak banister as she had done as a child.

The saloon bar was a mess. Piles of unwashed tankards and glasses were on the bar counter. The washing up should have been done last night, but who was there to do it? Clearly not Betty. The sawdust floor was piled in wet clumps, puddles of stale beer under the tables. Pearl walked to the back of the pub and into the kitchen. Seated at a large table was Betty, tucking into a hearty cooked breakfast. Biting into an enormous slice of buttered bread, Betty gestured to the front of the pub with a fork. 'Have you seen the shambles out there?' she said with her mouth full. 'Get the bucket and mop, there's a good girl. You know the drill. Been doin' it since the age of six, ain't you?' Betty laughed and chomped on a slice of black pudding.

'Who do you think you are? I don't work for you,' Pearl snarled back. 'I'm only here because of my father. And if he doesn't recover, things are going to change around here.'

Betty tutted. 'You're in for a big surprise, with your airs and graces. You have no idea what's coming.'

'I'll help out in the pub, but I will do it my way. The proper way my father taught me. This place is going to rack and ruin; all the barrels need refilling. We need to bring up crates of porter, Guinness and Murphy's from the basement. And where is the Jameson's? PJ would have a fit if that wasn't in stock.' Reluctantly, Pearl had quickly fallen back into her old life.

A heaviness descended on her as she trudged to the cellar. She pulled open the trap door with more force than was necessary, and walked down the basement stairs, careful to miss the rickety fifth step, which always creaked ominously. Despite the musty smell and cobwebs, this was one of her favourite places to hide.

With her best friend Tommy, she'd come down here when they were children, chattering excitedly of the adventures they would have as grown-ups, away from interfering parents. Already, the first signs of darkening clouds on the horizon had been closing in, PJ talking about the future, when his daughter would take on the responsibilities of running the pub with him.

Pearl sighed, leaning against a dusty wall, breathing in the powdery dankness. She thought she'd escaped Limehouse forever, only to be back here again. There was nothing for it except to wait out her father's illness, and see if he would recover.

She hefted a crate of Rogers' Light Bitter Pale Ale onto her shoulder, staggering slightly. The bottles rattled and tinkled as she walked back up the stairs.

Pearl set down the beer crate behind the bar, breathing hard. She was out of practice, but a few more days like this and she'd be able to fetch and carry from dawn until dusk without any trouble, as she had done as a young teenager.

She quickly put all the glasses and tankards in the sink to wash them and wiped down the bar. Stretching out her back, she stood in front of the cracked glass mirror panels that lined the back of the saloon bar, giving them a quick swipe with a cloth.

In the mirror's reflection, a scene of unexpected romance was unfolding in the far corner of the bar. Mr Matthews was holding Betty in a close embrace, lips glued to one another. So that's what the two of them had been up to! How long had this clandestine affair been going on, with her father barely clinging on to life? She wondered if it had started before Pa took ill. Did her father know? Pearl rubbed her forehead, feeling outraged and amused in equal parts.

Pearl watched the smooching couple a moment longer, then turned away. She needed to get ready for the customers who were already forming a line outside, some of the more eager ones pressing their faces against the windows, clouding the panes with their breath.

Mr Matthews strolled up to Pearl from the back of the bar,

smoothing down his hair, which was standing up in wiry tufts. He gave her a cheery 'halloo' as he walked over to unlock the front door. Pearl nodded back, thinking how little she knew of this man and his intentions.

'Ain't you forgetting somethin'?' Betty had crept up behind Pearl. She was looking very perky.

Pearl frowned. 'What are you talking about?'

'Got to look respectable when you're serving punters. Your old dress is still upstairs in your bedroom wardrobe. Just where you left it.' Betty smiled maliciously. She looked at Pearl's drab brown dress, creased and dishevelled from the long train journey. 'Can't have you wearing that. The Sailor's Arms is a salubrious establishment.'

Pearl snorted. She'd heard the tavern called many things but never that. She did, however, concede that Betty was right. Pa always insisted on her looking presentable as the proprietor's daughter and future landlady. Reluctantly, she made her way back up the two flights of stairs to her bedroom. Rummaging in the wardrobe, she found the frock that her father had made especially for her. A neat black dress with a white lace collar. Pearl scowled at herself in the full-length looking glass. It was much tighter than the last time she'd worn it, with a few moth holes ventilating the armpits. She was back in the uniform of the barmaid. The only thing out of place were her muddy boots, but standing behind the bar, no one would ever notice. Besides, being on her feet all day, there was no way she'd survive in heels.

The first hour passed in a blur. Pearl pulled pint after pint of porter, stout, ale and Guinness. She was just making up a Sherry Cobbler when she became aware of the eyes of a man staring at her. It felt different from the men who were trying to catch her attention for another round of drinks.

A Chinese man wedged in amongst much taller bodies in the middle of the bar was calling and beckoning to her. He was of small stature, perhaps five feet in height. The front and sides of his head were shaved, his hair scraped back in a pigtail, a skullcap of black silk perched on the back of his head. His shy, encouraging smile caused a flicker of recognition.

It was her old friend and unofficial tutor. 'Xianfan! How good to see you. Glad to meet up with at least one friendly face here.' Pearl grinned at him.

He nodded his head, bowing low. He had shrunk with age, and Pearl guessed he was now in his forties. His eyes were slightly glazed and unfocused. He smiled happily. A special bliss that Pearl knew the source of. So he was still enjoying a pipe of opium in the evenings.

'Miss Pearl, I have been expecting you. So sorry to hear about your father. It is a good thing you came back home. I hope you are keeping up with your Cantonese.' He looked into the far distance and spoke in a mellifluous voice:

'床前明月光,
'疑是地上霜。
'举头望明月,
'低头思故乡。'

It was one of the last poems they had worked on together. She closed her eyes, trying to remember the translation, then spoke haltingly:

'Moonlight reflects off the front of my bed.
'Could it actually be the frost on the ground?
'I look up to view the bright moon,
'And look down to reminisce about my hometown.'

The poem, by Li Bai, was a classic from the Tang dynasty. Years ago, Xianfan had explained to Pearl that it expressed loneliness and homesickness in its elegant phrasing.

Pearl excused herself from him, promising to be back later. She couldn't ignore the clamorous calls for more pints and there was a bitterness at the back of her throat. Well, it might express Xianfan's own feelings about China, but Pearl hadn't thought twice about Limehouse as she and Tommy ran laughing with delight through the dark streets on their way to the train station all those years ago. They were youngsters back then, full of hope, their future bright.

Pearl's shoulders sagged as she looked around the tavern now, rubbing the back of her neck. The tables needed swabbing down again. She ran a cloth under the cold tap, squeezing it hard in her fist. It was still gritty and slimy with strands of pork scratchings and tobacco.

Xianfan was calling to her again. Going over to him, he whispered in her ear, 'I have some beautiful black spice. I hid it in the hollow soles of my sandals when I came in from Shanghai last time,' he winked. 'Come round later. You still like?'

Pearl brightened. She remembered many happy evenings as a teenager when Xianfan would read poetry out to her, while sucking deeply on his opium pipe. Pearl would beg him for a puff or two, the spicy, flowery scent sending her off into a delicious drowse. Her opium-laced slumbers were the only time Pearl dreamt of her mother. Jai Li holding her close, humming a lullaby. Pearl would awaken shivering in the mornings, the tears cold on her pillow.

She hadn't had any black spice for a long time, and it would certainly take the edge off her morose mood, but she had promised never again to be under the influence of the drug. She was frightened of the power it had over her, and needed to keep her wits about her, especially with her father in his present condition and Betty snapping at her heels.

Reluctantly, she shook her head. 'No thanks, Xianfan, I'd better not. But perhaps we could read some poetry together, just like the old times?'

Lifting her chin, she forced a wide smile on her lips as she served a rowdy group of watermen who swayed and rocked from side to side, wolf whistling at her tight dress. Pearl made a mental note to let out the seams later that evening, or whatever it took so she could breathe more easily.

'You don't know what's been happening here since you've been gone.' Mr Matthews was beside Pearl, rubbing down the bar stools vigorously.

Betty nodded. 'Few months ago, on Easter bank holiday Monday, a friend of mine got killed. Emma Smith. We had a whip round for her plank suit. She wasn't no angel, had to go on the streets to earn money for her gin and lodgings, but she was a good laugh. Poor Emma often came in here with a black eye some fella had given her. Then there was that time she got thrown out of a window.'

Pearl commiserated. 'It's not an easy life; the streets have never been safe for women around here.'

'But this was something else.' Betty's eyes had widened, and for once she looked nervous. 'They think she got attacked only three hundred yards from her lodging house. You know the one, on George Street in Spitalfields. The injuries she had . . . Terrible. There's talk of a madman going round ripping up tarts. Them poor gals lost to the drink and sleeping on the streets don't deserve to be cut up like pigs in an abattoir.'

'Who would do such a thing?' The blood was singing in Pearl's ears. 'If I ever come across the bastard, he'll pay for it. Have they caught him?'

'Don't you go getting yourself in trouble,' Mr Matthews warned.

'Nah. Peelers never got 'im. Slipped away in the night. The killer was wearing dark clothing and a white handkerchief around his neck.'

Pearl shook her head. 'Not much of a description. The police are probably up to their usual poor efficiency,' she said, before adding hastily: 'Apart from my Uncle Peter, of course. And where is he? He hasn't come in today.' Her uncle had saved Pearl from many scrapes when she was a youngster, and had reasoned with PJ to let her go on the occasional outing.

Mr Matthews breathed hard into a glass and polished it. He and Betty exchanged a look, but said nothing. Pearl was desperate to know what had kept her uncle away, but stopped herself from asking. She wasn't going to give Betty the satisfaction of keeping secrets from her. Pearl would find out another way.

'Worst thing was it affected our trade.' Betty sniffed, helping herself to a large brandy. 'Coppers in here night after night, questioning all the sailors on shore leave, and all the dockers. None of 'em would come back here once the mutton shunters sat on their fat behinds here. And they all expected free drinks.' Betty took another large gulp of brandy and then topped up the glass.

'I'm surprised there were any profits left. We'll have to get more bottles of brandy in. You're finishing off our last one.' Pearl jutted her chin at Betty's nearly empty glass.

'None of your cheek. I'm grieving for your Pa.' Betty glared at Pearl. 'Besides, don't forget your place here. PJ left me in charge of The Sailor's Arms – not you.'

Pearl turned her back on Betty, determined not to get into a war of words. She needed more time to find out what was going on here.

* * *

Pearl awoke with a start, heart pounding. There was a shout from downstairs. 'Jai Li! Jai Li! Come back.' Her father was calling out for Pearl's long-dead mother. She rushed down a flight of stairs, nearly stumbling in the pale early dawn. She opened her father's bedroom door. Betty was at his side, shaking him by the shoulders. 'PJ, it's me, Betty, *I'm* your wife. Talk to me.' He made no more sound and turned his face to the wall.

'What are you doing, Betty?'

Betty twisted round to face Pearl. 'Leave us be!' she snarled. 'I'm with him now. He don't need nobody else, least of all you.'

Pearl looked from Betty to her father. Her head was pounding. 'What do you mean, his wife?' Her voice was low and calm.

'Because that is exactly what I am. We got wed, him and me, soon as you left here.' Betty's voice sounded distant and far away.

'I don't believe you. That can't be true. He wouldn't do that.'

Pearl winced at Betty's shrill laugh. 'Did you really think you were the apple of his eye? I made him forget about you. After all, a man has needs.'

'Stop talking! I don't want to hear it.'

'As you wish. But I will tell you this. He never mentioned your name again. Never talked about you. You were dead to him. And this pub is mine.'

This time Pearl laughed. 'You've been supping at the brandy far too much. It's addled your brain. My father always wanted me to have this pub – and I will decide what to do with it. You can stay for a while, but you need to be moving on soon.'

'Oh no. I'm his lawful wedded wife, so The Sailor's Arms is mine if he pops his clogs. Now, I'm a generous woman. I would never turn you out. You can stay. We need a barmaid who can do ten hours a day, seven days a week, and you've had the training since you were a nipper. I don't want to train no newcomer. What do you say?'

'You've got a nerve. I saw you with Mr Matthews, carrying on like lovesick teenagers. Carrying on with two men? You'll not get a penny from my father.'

Betty smirked. 'I'll deny it. It's your word against mine. You're the one who left, while I've been here all this time. And I'm not a filthy half-caste like you. Folk round here won't believe you. You know how they feel about your lot. Evil Chinkies. People only put up with you because of your father. Without him, you're nothing.'

Pearl grabbed hold of Betty's shoulders and shoved her off the bed. 'Don't you ever talk to me like that again or you'll regret it.' She loomed over Betty, who was still smirking. Pearl dearly wanted to slap that look off her face.

Clenching her hands, Pearl took a step forward. 'We'll settle this one way or the other. But I'll tell you this. You will be on your way out soon, whether my father recovers or not.'

3

The stench of the river took her by surprise. Pearl had forgotten that potent mix of night soil and stagnant seaweed in the years she had been away. The Thames was a convenient dumping place for rotting fish, garbage and of course the suicides. As a child, she had grown used to the stink. She wondered how long it would take for that all-pervasive aroma to become familiar again.

Today, the river was a lively hubbub of noise and movement, with its constant stream of schooners, clippers, barges and lighters, coming in from the four corners of the globe. There were the familiar sounds of shouting and quarrelling of the river workers, nimbly running up and down the ships laden with cargo of every description, from wine to turpentine, tallow, furs and skins. Pearl hummed a music-hall song, enjoying watching the world go by, trying to forget Betty's taunts for a moment.

A man carrying a tray bumped her arm as he passed. ''Ot peas! 'Ot peas! Fill your bellies and warm your 'ands – on'y a ha'penny!' Pearl's stomach rumbled. A small girl was pushing a cart with crisp brown fish sizzling on it. Pearl beckoned to her. The fish seller grasped her fork like a harpoon and speared a penny's worth into some wrapping paper. Savouring tasty little bites of fish, Pearl walked down Wapping High Street, where the market sellers were out in force. She might as well pick up some supplies while she was here. They needed onions, carrots, cabbage and turnips. The pantry at The Sailor's Arms was bare; Pearl cursed the bone-idle Betty.

Standing at the watercress seller's stand was a woman with sleek midnight-black hair, smoothed back in a tight bun. A Chinese woman in Limehouse was a rare sight. Even more unusual was her apparel. A sleeveless red silk dress, with a golden phoenix coiling itself around her body. It was beautifully cut, hugging her lean figure. As the woman reached over to pay for the watercress, Pearl noticed the taut muscles in her arms and shoulders. She moved with fluidity and ease, like a dancer.

As the woman disappeared into the crowd, Pearl continued staring after her. She sighed, thinking of the grinding chores waiting for her at The Sailor's Arms. Instead of pushing through the frosted glass doors, Pearl walked along the right-hand side of the building, to the narrow alley leading to Wapping Old Stairs. A special place was calling, where she had once felt happy and carefree.

The steps leading down to the foreshore were steep and slick with moss. They were worn away in the middle, from the tread of a thousand people and a thousand tides. She jumped down the last two stairs, as she and Tommy always did when they were young, landing with a satisfying crunch on the pebbles.

Breathing in the briny tang of the Thames, she walked towards the water's edge, and heard as if from far away, the sound of children's voices.

A memory came to Pearl, unbidden: three children scampering and shouting along the foreshore, wild and eager for adventure. Pearl could hear that familiar voice, high and shrill, as if it were yesterday; 'Pearl! Wait for me!'

A young girl, around eight years old, came running towards her. Wild and unruly bright red hair, the green eyes brimming with tears.

'Don't worry, Lizzy, I've got you. But keep up with us.'

'I fell over.' The girl's lower lip trembled. 'You were going too fast.'

A boy came running over. 'You're holding us up.' He turned to Pearl. 'I told you she shouldn't come.' He tugged at the peak of a sailor's cap, pulling it more firmly down on his thick, curly hair.

'Leave her be, Tommy. We agreed. The three of us stick together.'

Tommy had nodded at her grudgingly, and now Pearl remembered that feeling of fearlessness. Together, they were invincible, and with the help of her friends, she was going to sail to China. Their dreams would come true, but only if they stayed loyal.

As she pondered on the past, a slight movement caught her eye at the river's edge. Some long, cylindrical object, perhaps a seal, was lying half in and half out of the water. The animal was moaning piteously. The sounds of distress grew louder as Pearl scrambled over layers of broken bricks and rusty nails down to the shore.

But it wasn't a seal. It was a man, lying on the pebbles, the incoming tide remorselessly creeping up his motionless body. A Chinese man; his cheeks smooth apart from a scar that ran deep from eye to jaw. Embroidered on the front of his padded jacket was the Chinese zodiac sign of the monkey. He moved suddenly, convulsing. The large gash on his head pulsed blood. He moved again, and as his jacket fell open, the hilt of a dagger protruded, the blade stuck deep in his belly.

There was a pool of liquid at the side of his body. It was an eerie, glowing, greenish colour. Pearl leaned forward to inspect it more closely, but before she could make out what it was, the man's eyes flickered and he let out a low, guttural moan. He was still barely clinging on to life.

Pearl knelt by his side, heedless that her long skirts and boots were being soaked by the incoming tide. She cradled him in her arms. He was trying to say something. 'Mei, Mei . . .' he murmured. The man was calling for a woman. 'I'm sorry. Forgive me, Mei,' he said in Cantonese.

Pearl gently stroked his cheek, trying not to gag as blood continued pumping out of the deep wound in his stomach. She spoke in his mother tongue. 'There, there. Hold on to me. Who did this to you?'

His hands gripped Pearl's arm as he looked into her eyes, then a shudder wracked his body, his grasp slackened and he breathed no more. A lone seagull screamed above them. For a long moment, Pearl looked into his sightless eyes.

'Halloo there, Miss! What's going on here?'

Pearl jumped, her heart beating fast, as a young policeman came running up from the back of the wharves. He pulled out a whistle and blew loudly to alert the river police to his location.

'Thank God you're here. Please help, this man has been attacked!'

The policeman adjusted the chin strap of his helmet, as the visor was obscuring his vision. He peered down at the man and tutted. 'He's a goner. Not much we can do for him. We got the alarm just now. Some lightermen spotted the body from their boat.'

He looked at Pearl, taking in her drenched skirt and boots. 'Miss, you'd best get up, otherwise you'll be catching a terrible chill from the water.'

She realised she was still holding on to the dead man. Gently, as if tending a slumbering baby, Pearl laid his head on the ground. Reaching up for the policeman's proffered arm, she staggered to her feet, shivering from head to toe.

There were shouts from the water as riverboat police from Thames Police Station arrived. Two men jumped out of the boat, one with a waddling gait, the other as round as a barrel. They nodded at the policeman. 'What's the story here, Bill?'

'Looks like a dead Chinaman. Stabbed in the belly. This young lady found him.'

All three men turned to stare at Pearl, taking in the front of her dress, smeared with blood and river mud.

The squat policeman cleared his throat. 'Did you know him?' He peered at her more closely. 'Relative of yours?'

Pearl shook her head. 'No, I've never seen him before.'

'Then you'd best stand back, Miss. Not a nice sight for a lady. Get yourself indoors and have a stiff drink to warm yourself. Might be summer, but the water's still perishing cold.'

'If it's alright with you, Sir, I'd like to stay and see if I can help. This poor man died in my arms.' A tremble crept unbidden into her voice.

'Nothing you can do for him now. Leave it to us.'

Chastened, Pearl retreated a little from the dead man but was still reluctant to go. 'Yes, you're right. But the man was killed on my property. I'm the landlady at The Sailor's Arms just here.' She gestured towards the pub, surprising herself by claiming ownership, but surely it would be hers before long.

'My punters will be asking me what's going on. Otherwise they'll make up all sorts of scare stories about a killer on the loose. You don't want grief from the locals. And what about a few tots of whisky to warm yourselves?'

The policeman looked at the pub behind him, involuntarily licking his lips. Before he could refuse, Pearl said quickly: 'As my guests, of course. Drinks on the house, Constable, or may I call you Bill, since we are now acquainted over this terrible incident?' She smiled up at him.

'Make it two pints and a tot of rum for each of us. Then you can stay as long as you want.'

'My pleasure.' She stood back a respectful distance to watch Bill and the river policemen begin their grisly work. They dragged the corpse none too gently by the heels towards the boat. The dead man was still wearing a black felt slipper on one foot, but the other was bare. His toes looked so vulnerable, ghostly pale and wrinkled from the briny water. Pearl put a hand to her mouth, bile threatening to rise. It seemed like the Grim Reaper was stalking her.

Bill knelt and rifled through the dead man's pockets, but there was nothing of value to be had. Pearl could see them inspecting the dagger, admiring its workmanship, before Bill put it in his jacket pocket.

It took all three policemen to lift the corpse. Bill lifted the dead man's head by his pigtail and then let it drop heavily back down on the pebbles. Finally, they managed to throw the body into the boat, the head smacking the side of the vessel with a loud thud.

'Take more care with him, please! Show some respect, gentlemen.'

They looked at her with surprise. 'He can't feel it now,' Bill said. 'Besides, you Orientals don't suffer the same way us English folk do. That's what my sergeant told me. You're different.'

'I can assure you that we feel just the same amount of pain as you,' she replied, her voice tight with anger.

The policemen looked at each other and rolled their eyes.

A scream rang out from behind them. 'Murder! Murder!' A group of people were gathering at the top of the steps, craning their necks for a better view.

Moments later, Betty threw open the first-floor window of The Sailor's Arms. 'Pearl! What you doing down there?'

'A man's been killed on the foreshore, just here. I tried to help him, but he died,' Pearl shouted up to her.

'That's just like you to get mixed up in trouble. Peelers don't need you meddling. You come back in. The outhouse wants a good cleaning.'

'Thought you owned the pub,' Bill muttered, disappointed that the offer of free beer was fading.

Pearl pointed to the crowd that had gathered at the top of Wapping Old Stairs. 'You don't have time for drinking now. Perhaps one of them has seen something.'

He gave her a sour look and moved towards the gathering.

Some mudlarks, barefoot and covered in rags and tatters, were chattering, craning their necks. A rosy-cheeked cigar seller, with a garland of flowers in her hair, was doing brisk business. The men around Pearl puffed away, clouds of smoke swirling above them, nodding at one another as they conjectured over what had taken place. More people were gathering, standing on tiptoe, trying to peer down the alleyway, hoping to see where the victim had met his violent end.

A man had managed to slip past the policemen and make his way down to the foreshore, cackling and rubbing his hands together. Pearl recognised him and waved, a familiar figure since childhood. He loped over to her, his white hair standing up in bristles, like a chimney sweep's brush.

'I wondered when you'd show up, Old Jake. Did you see anything? Were you there, down on the foreshore?' He was Tommy's uncle and one of her father's best friends.

'Heard you was back, Pearl. Not been the best of times for you, what with Tommy lost at sea and now your father so poorly.' He removed his cap. 'And now this. Not surprised to see you at the centre of things.'

'You as well,' she teased. The old rascal had a way of knowing everything that was going on in Limehouse. If there was a bootleg shipment of rum coming in from the West India Docks, he was first on the scene.

'So what's the local gossip since I've been gone? Perhaps I'll ask my old man to stand you a pint.'

'Don't think PJ will be standing any time soon, darlin'.' A shrewd look came into his eye. 'I might know something but I'm fair parched. Need something to wet my whistle.' Pearl wondered how many tots of rum she'd need to pour down his gullet in order for him to spill his secrets.

He looked up at her, a dark smile dancing on his lips. 'I'll tell you this. I bet someone got real angry with that Chinaman. Filthy foreigners coming in, working for half the wages of us locals. Big trouble in Limehouse. There's more drugs coming in, rival gangs making noise. Lots of heads bashed in.'

Old Jake was rarely wrong when it came to local disputes and who was behind them. Pearl was just about to press him on a likely suspect when she was distracted by a sharp whistle from Bill. His shoulders were back and he was standing to attention.

He saluted a tall, stately man, slim as a reed, shouldering his way through the crowd. Fair haired, his beard was neatly trimmed and just beginning to grey; a long-stemmed pipe was clenched between his teeth, smoke billowing out of his mouth. He walked slowly up to the dead body lying at the bottom of the boat where the police had left him, and stared down at it for a long time, tilting his head this way and that, scrutinising the corpse. After a brief glance up and down the foreshore, he turned to Bill and the river policemen, speaking in quiet, measured tones.

They jutted their chins at Pearl. She held the stranger's gaze as he approached, and saw that he was younger than he had first appeared, perhaps in his early thirties. A vain man, she thought, with his dapper, woollen waistcoat and chequered suit that fitted him snugly, showing off his trim figure, although the beginnings of a paunch was curving his outline. His nostrils quivered, as if catching a scent in the air, like a greyhound.

'Good morning, Madam. I believe you were first on the scene. Can you tell me what you saw?' He was softly spoken with a faint Dorset accent.

'Good morning, Sir. My name is Mrs Pearl Fitzgerald. Yes, I found the poor man on the foreshore, just in front of my father's pub. He was barely alive and died soon after I tended to him. If there is anything at all I can do to help, do let me know.'

He nodded. 'Pleased to make your acquaintance, Mrs Fitzgerald. Inspector Crowley, Thames Police Station. Did you see anyone about? Anyone who attacked the man?'

Pearl shook her head. 'I didn't see anyone.'

He pursed his lips, disappointed in her reply.

'Many thanks for your assistance.' He turned on his heel. She was peeved at being dismissed so quickly, wanting to tell him about the luminous green liquid next to the body. But even to her ears, it sounded far-fetched. Could she have imagined it?

If only she could detain him a while longer, perhaps she could be of assistance in other ways. 'The Sailor's Arms is at your disposal as a place for your men to meet, since it is so near to the murder scene. I expect you will want me to make a statement as an eyewitness . . .'

'We will be in touch with you soon. Until then.' He bowed slightly and looked at her pointedly until she reluctantly joined the crowd who were still milling around, hoping for further revelations. But even the most ghoulish of gawkers realised that there would be no more sightings of the corpse and headed for the pub; a flock of black crows, squawking and pecking over the little scraps of information they had gleaned or imagined. The pub was so full that several of the onlookers had to stand in the doorway. Brief flares from their lucifer matches illuminated faces as they smoked cigarette after cigarette, taking deep draughts from their beer tankards. Pearl pushed past them to help Mr Matthews behind the bar.

'Not safe around here and getting worse,' said one man in a tattered and frayed pea coat. 'Strangers coming in from foreign parts, don't even speak English. Heard the yellow devil was slit from ear to ear and his entrails hangin' out for all to see. Probably killed by one of his own.'

A sea captain shook his head. 'I heard from sailors down on the docks it was some fella they called "the Blue Man". Got a vicious temper. They reckon he killed that woman down in Spitalfields as well. Very handy with a knife.'

'Rot and balderdash!' sneered Old Jake who had remained silent until now. 'Making up stories, whether it's a hobgoblin or the Bogeyman. I reckon it's someone much closer to home. Someone you'd never expect.' He nodded, chortling to himself as if at some private joke.

Pearl listened to their chatter, wondering which of them was correct. Her father always had an opinion on local matters, holding forth on politics, the price of beer and the latest antics of the Prince Regent, while vigorously polishing the countertop. What would he think about having such a violent attack so close to the pub? He'd certainly appreciate the extra takings with all the punters clamouring for pints. Murder was a thirsty business.

But he was upstairs, oblivious of what was happening around him. She really should go and check on him, but her heart shrank at the thought.

The incessant chatter was deafening. She could scarcely breathe. Hoping no one would notice her absence, she quietly slipped out of the pub.

4

She looked out across the river and breathed a long sigh, limbs heavy. Pearl had always loved the meandering flow of the Thames, its rippled surface and greyish-green hues that changed with the seasons. The barges were steadily making their way to the London docks, just as they had always done.

She wrapped her arms tightly around herself, shivering. Who was the dead man on the foreshore? Why had he asked for forgiveness? Pearl shook her head. Perhaps she would never find out.

Back in Limehouse. A place she had wished never to return to. Pearl bit her lip and looked longingly at a tall ship powering by. If only she could board a vessel and travel far away to see for herself the Sahara Desert or climb mountains so high their peaks disappeared into the clouds. The furthest she'd made it away from Limehouse was to Portsmouth. She smiled ruefully. Her dreams of becoming a high-seas adventurer had come to nought.

There was still an unexplored world out there she was longing to see. Most of all, a yearning to cross the oceans and set foot in China, the land of smoke and silk, the land where her parents had met. Pearl wondered about the dead man, and what part of China he had come from. He might even have been a relative of her mother's.

She'd often asked PJ if she resembled her mother. He frequently brushed off the questions but one time he relented, sitting her down on a beer barrel and telling her of Jai Li, a seamstress he'd met when he was working in a Shanghai bar. PJ had somehow ended up there after a long sea voyage and decided his days as a sailor were over.

'The shape of your face is just the same, her eyes, and the way you tilt your head.' PJ's voice cracked. Then he laughed. 'You've her fiery temper. I first saw your mother when she was giving a telling-off to some boys who were taunting a young girl on crutches. She was whacking them with her broom. Such a firecracker! You remind me of her, with your hot-headed ways. Jai Li, she was my precious water lily, my one true sweetheart,' he'd said, a far-off look in his eye.

They'd married quickly, filled with optimism and romantic dreams. PJ wanted to return to England with Jai Li and raise a family, but his new wife didn't survive the arduous journey, slipping from life while giving birth to Pearl on the ship.

'But do I look like her?' Pearl had persisted.

PJ looked at his daughter and smiled. 'You have inherited her spirit.' Then he wiped his nose with an oilcloth. He cleared his throat and said gruffly: 'No time to be moping about. I've got customers to serve, so you get on with slopping out the yard.'

Pearl stared out at the river, watching the flecks of white foam on the waves. A log of wood rolled over in the water. As it came closer to shore, she saw it wasn't a length of timber at all but the decaying carcass of a whale, washed in from the North Sea.

Death was stalking her. Pearl's thoughts turned once again to the murdered man. She shuddered at an unbidden image of his face, his mouth wide open in agony, reaching out to her. Who was Mei, the woman he had called out for? And what was the pool of glowing green liquid near the body?

She shook her head. Today, the river was of no solace to her. She walked past Thames Police Station and wondered if Inspector Crowley was there. She curled her lip, recalling her abrupt dismissal by that imperious man. Those mutton shunters really seemed a hopeless bunch. They couldn't catch a shoal of fish in a barrel.

She headed towards the narrow lanes of Limehouse Causeway. Pearl was distracted from her morbid thoughts by the cry of the fish seller. 'Three a penny, Yarmouth bloaters! Now's your time! Bag of whelks, still fresh.' The fish seller was holding out his hands beseechingly. Not to be outdone, the apple woman joined in. 'Penny a lot for sweet Pippins!' Their cries grew fainter as Pearl crossed into a side road, trying to remember her way around the labyrinthine alleyways she had skipped down as a child. On and on she walked, coming to Garford Street and then into King Street. Pearl had always loved going out on her own. But whenever Pearl slipped away for solitary walks along the river, or even worse with Tommy, PJ's face had creased with concern.

'Keep away from that Fitzgerald boy. He's trouble. Caught him trying to lift some crates of my best Jameson's out the back.'

Her father had always disliked Tommy. When she turned thirteen, his animosity grew stronger, the rules increasingly strict. Pearl was surprised when Tommy declared his love for her and began talking of engagement. They'd grown up together and she'd not thought of him in that way before. But their increasingly secretive meetings away from PJ were an adventure in themselves, and climbing out of the bedroom window to meet Tommy for moonlight walks in the shadows of the West India Docks was so exhilarating.

They would scamper down to the pebbled shore and Tommy would put his coat around Pearl, pointing out to her the constellations in the sky. His face lit up under the light of the stars, his cap far back on his thick, brown curls.

'See that one? That's the North Star. Since the first mariners sailed the oceans, the North Star has always guided them home. Seafarers can easily find true north by its location. It will always guide me back to you when I'm away at sea.' His arms tightened around her. 'We'll show everyone we're a force to be reckoned with. Just you wait and see.'

Pearl had nodded, buoyed by his enthusiasm and imagining the good times ahead, the voyages that awaited them. 'One day I will be captain of the finest ship to sail the seven seas. We'll be best mates forever,' she said.

'You will be my lovely wife, and *I* will be captain, bringing you jewels from the four corners of the world,' Tommy had said. He kissed her softly, and Pearl wriggled out of his embrace, laughing. 'Catch me if you can,' she shouted, and then ran ahead of him down the wharves.

Such foolish dreams. Seven years in Portsmouth, and five of them spent alone, after Tommy went down with his ship in the Indian Ocean. For the first few months, Pearl had never felt so desolate. And then fear set in. She had no money, how would she survive? She went from shop to shop, begging for work. It was only when she fainted from hunger at Mr Fortescue's grocery shop that he took pity on her and offered her a few days' work. But he soon realised his good fortune when Pearl offered to do his books, something she had done for years at The Sailor's Arms. She was honest, with a good head for numbers.

Life after that had slowly picked up, and a familiar routine of working at Mr Fortescue's, visits to the music hall and reading Cantonese poetry, helped lessen the anguish at Tommy's disappearance.

But now back in Limehouse, she felt like a stranger once more. She shivered, looking around her. She had always felt safe here as everyone knew her as PJ's daughter. But it was a dangerous place for those unfamiliar with these byways and back streets; easy to be caught unawares by thieves looking for hapless victims to rob. Lost in thought, she hadn't kept track of where she was going, and now peered around a dank, unfamiliar back street.

The light was fading and a shadowy figure scurried across the lane behind her and disappeared through a doorway. The hairs on the back of Pearl's neck prickled as she whirled around to catch a glimpse of the stranger. But then she chided herself for even thinking that someone could be following her. The merry sounds of children playing up ahead was comforting, and she began to relax. Dressed in rags and barefoot, their toys were pieces of wood, bones and oyster shells. Happily playing with old bits of rope, they scampered up and down the alleyway, without a care in the world.

Pearl watched, entranced, as they chased each other, nimble-footed and avoiding the sharp slivers of broken glass on the uneven ground. She was so busy admiring their agility that she didn't notice the loose cobblestones in front of her. She pitched forward, her head hitting the ground with a thud. She tried to get up, but feeling dizzy, staggered sideways and fell heavily, twisting her ankle.

Pearl lay there for a while, trying to breathe through the pain. She was aware of a tickling sensation on her scalp. She winced at the throbbing, and realised blood was dripping from a cut on her forehead.

Someone was tugging at her clothes. Her hem was being lifted up slowly and carefully, hands probing, reaching into pockets, searching and seeking with a quiet urgency. Voices whispered, the sound of giggling. Pearl groggily opened her eyes and looked into the faces of the children she had watched playing so innocently in the muddy puddles. One was removing her silk handkerchief, another deftly extracting a drawstring purse. Another was cutting off the lace on her sleeves with a knife.

Years of slapping pilfering hands away from the pub till had honed Pearl's fast reflexes, and instinctively she reached out to grab a scrawny wrist, giving it a sharp twist. The little boy, who was barely ten years old, wailed in agony, a pitiful look on his face. Looking at the fury in Pearl's face, he quickly realised that sympathy was not her strong suit, and swiftly changed his demeanour, cursing loudly. 'Geroff me, you old trollop, you're gonna break my arm!'

'Stop struggling, you little bugger.' Pearl tried to hold on to him, catching at his other arm. His comrades in thievery had come to the boy's aid, and joined in the fray, kicking and punching her with their hard little feet and fists.

She curled up into a foetal position to protect her face and chest from the blows, hoping they would tire of their sport and leave. She was coming in and out of consciousness, the light turning a sparkling grey.

'Leave her be, you little varmints. Off you go before I take a switch to you. Scarper!' Firm, warm hands helped Pearl sit upright. A woman's concerned face came blurrily into vision. Clucking sympathetically, she said: 'Will you look at that bump on your head? And there'll be quite a shiner in the morning.'

A bushy mop of salt-and-pepper hair was winning the fight for independence from a bonnet with a stuffed bird perched on the side. Suddenly, the most enormous bosom swam into Pearl's vision. It started from just under the woman's collar bone and ended somewhere around her stomach. In fact, her entire middle section seemed to be composed of bosoms. *I must be hallucinating*, Pearl thought.

'Come on, dearie, let me help you up. Time to rise and shine, my little plum pudding. Put your arm around my shoulder.' The woman hefted Pearl up from the ground and guided the way across the street to a ramshackle, two-storey tenement building on Pennyfields, opposite the Silver Lion pub. The rickety front door had large gaps in its panels, clumsily nailed over with several wooden struts, while the broken windows were patched over with sodden newspaper.

Pushing open the door, the old woman brought Pearl down a short corridor that led to a parlour. Pearl hobbled over to a sofa and sank into it gratefully.

The woman squinted closely at Pearl. 'Why, it's PJ O'Dwyer's daughter, ain't it? Not seen you in a while.'

Pearl looked at the woman more closely, her gaze beginning to focus. That bulbous nose and bushy eyebrows looked familiar. It was Ma Jennings, the mother of Lizzy, her childhood friend. 'So good to see you again! I can't thank you enough. Those vicious little brats took me by surprise. Which swell mob do they belong to – the Millwallers, the Golden-lane Gang or the Lambeth Lads?' The woman still had some bright ginger in her hair, amid the grey. So reminiscent of Lizzy's fiery curls.

'Been a long time since you were round here; those little buggers running riot don't belong to anyone. They get precious little to eat, so I give them the occasional scrap of food, but I've not enough money to feed them every day. Makes 'em turn to other ways to survive. Can't blame the wee mites.'

Ma coughed awkwardly. 'Sorry to hear your pa was taken ill, may the saints preserve him.'

'I arrived back just in time to see him. He looks awful; not like himself at all.'

Mrs Jennings crossed herself, lips moving as she silently mouthed a Hail Mary.

A lump rose in Pearl's throat. She didn't want to think about her father anymore. 'How's Lizzy? Haven't seen her in such an age.'

Pearl fondly remembered playing with Lizzy and Tommy on the foreshore at Wapping Old Stairs. One day, when searching for sailor's loot, as they often did, they'd whooped with joy at discovering a few gold nuggets buried underneath an old boat. Pearl smiled at Lizzy's wish to use her third of the winnings on having currant buns every day, and when she was grown, Champagne, too. Pearl had planned to sail away to Canton to learn about the land her mother came from. Tommy wanted to be a pirate on the high seas. A sliver of sadness pierced Pearl's heart now; their lives had turned out so very differently to their dreams.

The old woman grew thoughtful at Pearl's question about Lizzy. 'You and my daughter were thick as thieves once upon a time. Sad that you drifted apart.'

'Does Lizzy still live local?'

'Oh, yes. She's done very well for herself, my Lizzy. Hitched to a Chinaman now, these four years. Created a lot of nasty gossip at the time. I didn't mind, but a lot of the neighbours kicked up a fuss, saying how could she marry a yellow devil, and being twenty years older than her. Mind you, everyone happily stuffed their faces at the wedding reception. Lizzy and Soo Chow own The Dragon Inn restaurant on Castor Street, and a laundry on the corner of Turners Buildings. They're doing really good. She's so busy. Doesn't have the time to come and see me very often.' Ma sighed, a flicker of sadness behind her eyes.

Pearl was taken aback at news of Lizzy. The scrawny little girl she once knew had made a success of herself. Ma mistook Pearl's pensive look for hunger pangs. 'You're looking peaky. Let me fetch you something to eat.'

She returned with two large pieces of hot, buttered toast and a generous mound of glistening blackcurrant jam on the side. Pearl's stomach rumbled in anticipation. Taking a large bite out of the warm bread, she curled up on the sofa, curious to find out how Ma had been. She looked around the room, taking in the cracks in the ceiling, the sparsely patched wallpaper. At some point, there had been an effort to do some repairs. One wall was painted bright yellow, although the sloppy paintwork pointed to an inexpert or lazy hand.

Ten tables were tightly packed together, covered with red-and-white chequered cloths. Each was neatly laid out with chopsticks. This place should have been alive with the sounds of sailors and dock workers speaking in Chinese, Mandarin and Hokkien dialects, and yet there was an unsettling silence.

'So how long have you had this lodging house? You and Lizzy used to live down Bird Street.'

'We moved a year after you left with Tommy. I got together with the owner of this place, but he died soon after.' Ma Jennings shook her head mournfully. 'Business has been right bad. Fewer ships coming in from Canton means fewer lodgers for me. The place is nigh on empty. And to be honest,' Ma looked around her, 'it could do with a touch-up. Ah Sim, my handyman, lives here. A lovely lad, but he'll go off and I don't set eyes on him for days at a time. He's not much of a worker, to be honest, but he's company.'

The older woman fussed around with the teapot, clattering cups and gathering Pearl's empty plate. 'Maybe it'll pick up. Times are tough.'

Pearl had the feeling there was something Mrs Jennings wasn't telling her but didn't want to intrude as the older woman had been so kind.

Ma watched Pearl limp tentatively around the room. 'Ah Sim and his sister are quite the lively pair. She's busy working all the hours at Lizzy's laundry but comes here to cook Ah Sim his favourite dishes from back home.'

The pain in her ankle had lessened, so Pearl tested putting more weight on her foot. 'I should be getting back to Pa. I didn't mean to stay out this long. I'd love to come back and visit though.'

'Of course. Anytime. And don't worry about those little rascals bothering you again. They'll feel the back of my hand if they do.'

Ma Jennings waved a cheery goodbye from the door, and Pearl hobbled back along Brewhouse Lane, and after a few false turns, soon found herself back at The Sailor's Arms.

As soon as she opened the door, Betty's tear-streaked face loomed in front of her. 'Where the hell have you been?' Betty demanded, a black handkerchief clasped under her nose. 'Your father's stone cold dead and you off gallivanting the streets without a care in the world.'

5

The wake had pulled in a rowdy throng. The mourners' thirst was insatiable as pint after pint was gulped down with a ravening intensity.

'He was a good man, was Patrick O'Dwyer. The best friend I ever had. A regular saint. He did no harm to anyone and had the sweetest nature, God rest his soul.' Old Jake's head was bowed low, apparently in respect, but Pearl thought it more likely he was casting his eye around the floor to spot the odd farthing.

Jake was thumping on the bar with his fist. 'What's a man gotta do to get a drink round here?' he demanded. He nodded when Mr Matthews put a full tankard in front of him. The old man caressed Pearl's arm, his gnarled fingers fastened on to her in a grip she couldn't shake off.

'Generous with his drinks, 'twas PJ. Always remembered his pals,' Jake murmured.

In reality, PJ O'Dwyer had been the toughest, meanest landlord in Limehouse, who would beat seven bells out of anyone who had the temerity to leave without paying. But she decided not to argue the point with her father's old mate. At least on the day of the wake, she should try and control her temper. 'You're very kind. He was a force to be reckoned with and we'll all miss him.'

Her father was dead. The words kept repeating in Pearl's head as she tried to make sense of it all. He was never coming back. She'd never see his face again, hear him shouting for her, or chastising her. When she was a child, her father's eyes would follow Pearl wherever she went, a silent pleading that she would never leave him.

One of his favourite bedtime tales was the story of how Pearl's mother had died. Night after night, Pearl had fallen asleep to the sounds of her father's voice describing the ship caught in a storm and Jai Li, the blood pouring out of her, as she gave birth to Pearl. It had given Pearl nightmares, but she clung to any information about her mother, who was shrouded in mystery – even this childbirth scene, which ended in Jai Li's gruesome death.

She wondered if her father ever blamed her for causing her mother's untimely demise. But it had made PJ even more devoted to her. 'You've only got me now, and I've only got you. So I have to love you twice as much,' her father would say. 'When you're grown up, you'll stand beside me, the landlady here. We'll be together, always.'

She shivered now at the memory. Her whole life mapped out for her. At times, his love and protection seemed all that she had needed. It had been enough. And then it was more than she could bear.

Old Jake was speaking again, and she forced herself to concentrate. 'Your father looks so peaceful now.' Jake had tried to smooth down his tufts of white hair with nasal-searing pomade. He dabbed his eyes as he looked in the coffin and at the garlands of flowers surrounding it. Pearl realised that before long Pa would be taken away and she'd never see him again.

She stared into the open casket. Her father's cheeks had always been ruddy, but she couldn't recall them ever being this scarlet. And those vermilion lips! The undertaker must have taken a few too many swigs of laudanum. Her father now looked like one of the female impersonators Pearl loved to watch at the music hall. He had hated them with a virulence. It offended his sense of what was the correct order in the world. 'Men have got to be men. Can't see why they would want to prance around in skirts like that.'

She reached out to touch her father's hand. It was ice cold, like a marble baptismal font in January.

If PJ could sit up and speak, she wondered what he'd say. She imagined his raspy chuckle, gloating at her failure to build a new life for herself. 'See, my darling? Thought you'd got away from me, running off with that good-for-nothing Fitzgerald boy. But here you are, back in Limehouse where you belong.'

An unfamiliar reflection in the mirrored wall behind the bar stared back at her. The skin puckered around the eyes in a pained stare. Pearl looked gaunt, her skin sallow. She turned away, pacing to and fro, unable to settle, tracing the wood-panelled dado with burgundy-coloured walls, digging her fingers into every groove and indentation.

Low down on the far corner of the wall, leading out to the back door, was a faint inscription. Pearl put a hand out to touch it.

Pearl, Lizzy and Tommy. Friends forever

It all seemed so long ago, when the promises and pledges of youth were sacred. It was only later that the desire to escape grew stronger.

Lizzy had stayed on Pearl's mind since she'd visited Ma Jennings. Their childhood delight at finding gold nuggets on the foreshore had soured into despair. Years later, she'd discovered that Tommy had kept Lizzy's share of the spoils, using the cash from the pawned gold to pay for their elopement and his gambling debts. It was the first of their big arguments as newlyweds, but it wasn't the first time they had kept secrets from Lizzy.

By the time they were thirteen, Pearl and Tommy had grown close; their relationship was turning more intimate, very different from the friendship they had with Lizzy. As the three became a two, Pearl was conflicted between spending more time with Tommy, who captivated her imagination with tales of adventures and freedom, and guilt at not being with Lizzy. Her young friend was increasingly moody, a silent plea in her eyes. Often, Pearl would tell Lizzy she had to work late in the pub. In reality, she was sneaking out to meet Tommy at West India Docks, sharing kisses, watching the opium shipments being smuggled in from the boats and imagining a life together on the high seas.

Pearl was lost in her thoughts as she cleaned the pub. But despite all the time she'd spent wiping and dusting, the cluttered chaos continued. The tables and chairs had seen better days, some of the footstools were missing a leg. The floor was filthy; the surface sticky with spilt beer and wads of tobacco, chewed and spat out by sailors and stevedores. She'd have to fix a few things here.

But what was she thinking? There was no need, she wasn't staying for long. Selling up and using the money to buy a place in Portsmouth was what she longed to do, moving out of that soulless rented room she and Tommy had set up home in. She'd have more funds to go to music halls, no longer scrimping and saving for the cheapest seats. Her heart lifted slightly at the thought of watching the gay girls singing their hearts out, getting the chance to leave this humdrum world and enter a world of imagination inhabited by ventriloquists, comic duets, snake charmers and magicians.

Pearl caught sight of Old Jake sidling up to a lighterman who was snoring in a chair. With nimble fingers he reached into the slumbering man's pocket. Pearl knew what he was up to. 'Oh no you don't.' She put the barge worker's wallet back into his pocket and steered Old Jake away.

'Just for once, put your thieving ways to one side. Let's have some respect here,' she said.

Jake sneered. 'Changed your ways, ain't you? I was the one who taught you how to pick a pocket. You were a quick learner. And I was the one who showed you how to look after yourself on the streets.' He thumped a wooden stick against the table. Pearl looked at it, frowning.

'What happened to your other walking cane?' Pearl recalled the black-lacquered beechwood cane, with the bulbous head of a bulldog on its silver handle. She had never seen Old Jake without it.

He shrugged. 'Oh, can't remember where it is. Think I lost it,' he said, shaking his head. 'Now let's see if you can keep up with a few of Old Jake's moves.' He feinted to punch her on the shoulder. Pearl grabbed his wrist and twisted it round his back.

He gave a sharp wince of pain. 'That's my girl! Haven't lost your touch.'

Pearl gave a slight bow before walking over to help Mr Matthews behind the bar, who smiled gratefully for the assistance.

'Why isn't my Uncle Peter here? He must have known about the wake. Practically everyone in Limehouse has come.'

Mr Matthews frowned. 'There was bad blood between your pa and uncle. Came to blows one night, and PJ was lucky not to have been banged up for hitting a copper. But Peter hushed it up, didn't want his brother in the nick. Not been here for a long while now.' He placed a comforting hand on the small of Pearl's back. 'I know all this is hard, love. But don't worry yourself. Me and Betty will be more than happy to look after the pub.'

Pearl looked at him, pursing her lips.

'You two lovebirds break it up now.' Betty elbowed Pearl sharply in the ribs.

She pointed an accusing finger at Pearl. 'It's your duty to help me here. It's what your father wanted.'

'Don't tell me what my father wanted! You've got no business here.'

'You don't know what's coming to you, my girl. I'm in charge now. No more lah-di-dah manners, with your nose in a book. You need to keep indoors or you could end up like that Chinaman.'

They squared up to each other, but before Pearl could hurl another insult at Betty, she was pulled into a dance by Old Jake, his whiskery face rasped against her cheek. The music growing wilder, a raucous tempo built up. 'Come and have a dance with one of the Wild Eyed Boys,' growled Jake.

'A wild what?' Pearl asked as she was dragged around the crowded floor careening into other dancing couples. 'We are the kings, little Pearl, and there's changes coming to Limehouse!' Pearl was swung under Jake's arm and back into his grasp. She concentrated on avoiding her feet being trampled. 'Not so much a wild boy but a clumsy oaf,' she muttered.

A fast Irish jig struck up, encouraging more whirling couples. Until now, the musicians had been playing mournful laments as befitted the occasion of a wake, but as the evening wore on and the drink flowed, the tunes became increasingly faster.

A crowd had gathered around the pianoforte and were bellowing out PJ's favourite ballad. Her father used to croon the melody to Pearl with a catch in his voice. Such a sentimental old fool when the mood took him. Pearl managed to extricate herself from Old Jake and held on to the edge of the bar. Tears leaked from beneath her eyelids as the words echoed around the pub.

'Her eyes they shone like diamonds
'They called her the queen of the land
'And her hair hung over her shoulder
'Tied up with a black velvet band.'

Pearl couldn't take any more. She climbed the stairs and with a sigh of relief closed the door to her attic bedroom; the pounding in her temples lessened. Pearl looked again at the poster of Maude Kingsley with those come-hither eyes.

Memories came flooding back of seeing Maude for the first time in real life, four years ago at the Portsmouth Theatre. Pearl had paid dearly for a front row seat in the gallery; the six pence was well worth it, even though she had no money for dinner that night. Maude was so vivacious, belting out tune after tune, winking and waving to the gallery.

Pearl had waited two hours at the stage door in the freezing cold before Maude came out. As the door opened, Pearl plucked up her courage and walked towards the singer, holding out a wilting red rose with numb fingers.

'Miss Kingsley, that was so wonderful. Your singing and dancing were perfection. You have the most beautiful voice I ever heard.'

Pearl blurted out those words, feeling reckless and giddy with excitement. Ready to risk everything for a moment with Maude.

The music-hall singer squinted at Pearl through a haze of cigarette smoke, her eyes taking in Pearl's scarlet cheeks. 'Thanks, sweetheart. Quite a lively crowd for a Portsmouth theatre on a wet Wednesday. I saw you tonight, you were at the front of the gods, straining so far forward I thought you'd pitch over into the stalls!' Maude laughed softly and a queer look came into her eyes, making Pearl shiver.

The singer hesitated, then took a final drag on her cigarette and ground it into the dirt with her dainty slipper. 'Are you free this evening? Keep me company. I've no friends in this godforsaken town. You look like a lively kind of gal.' Pearl didn't leave Maude's side for the remainder of the singer's two-week Portsmouth engagement.

She continued staring at the poster, of Maude frozen in time. So different from the flesh and blood woman that Pearl had come to know, teaching her the ways of love and desire.

With a sinking heart, Pearl walked down a flight of stairs and crossed the landing into her father's bedroom. How empty it seemed now that his powerful presence had vanished. She opened the corner dresser and tugged open a drawer, which squealed in protest. The top drawer contained all the letters, Christmas and birthday cards she had written to her father over the years. She blinked rapidly, blowing out her cheeks. So he hadn't forgotten her.

There was a shout from the wake downstairs.

'Pearl, come down here and join us! We got something to show you,' Betty's voice boomed out. By the slur in her words, Mr Matthews had given her the Boodles gin. Betty was tight as a boiled owl.

With a forefinger, Pearl traced the outline of a jolly sailor on the last birthday card she had sent her father. *Oh, Pa, why did you never write to me?* She carefully put away the cards and letters, closing the drawer. Pearl walked slowly down the staircase, but almost ran back up at the commotion in the saloon bar.

A crowd had gathered around her father's coffin. Pearl stood stock still at the foot of the stairs, aghast. Old Jake was twisting her father's pinkie finger, attempting to remove the large gold signet ring with his initials engraved on it. Betty had shoved a cigar between the corpse's lips and was trying to light it.

'Let's give him one last dance!' Betty shouted. The crowd roared approval as Old Jake tugged at the dead man, pulling him upright in the coffin.

A flush rose from Pearl's chest to her face as she watched in horror as her father's body flip-flopped about like a rag doll, as three men heaved him out of the casket.

'He needs a drink!' Betty said, raising her own glass. Old Jake clapped his hands with glee and poured a pint of bitter over PJ's head. His make-up, so painstakingly applied by the undertaker, was dissolving. The mascara began to run, causing streaky black tears to cascade down his face.

Pearl was furious. They'd never have dared treat him like this when he was alive. 'Stop it!' she shouted. But that made them laugh even harder.

'Come on, ole fella, we know you'd love a waltz with your lovely daughter,' Betty said to the corpse. She pushed Pearl forward. 'That's right. Give your Pa a cuddle.'

Everyone clapped in time and stamped their feet, the macabre Ceilidh growing wilder by the minute. Rough hands took hold of Pearl and pushed her onto PJ. She struggled to keep him upright, the heaviness and closeness of his body making her legs buckle. The smell of formaldehyde stung her nostrils. As if in slow motion, she toppled backwards and crashed onto the ground, arms around her dead father. All the air was sucked out of her lungs and she landed with a thud on her back. She couldn't move. 'Get him off me!' she screamed as a deafening cheer went round the pub.

Giggling and wheezing, Old Jake rolled the corpse off Pearl and helped her up. Two brawny sailors hefted PJ onto their shoulders and slung him back into the coffin.

'Don't fret so, darlin'. A bit of merriment is the best way to chase away the grief,' Betty laughed.

Pearl brushed down her dress, now covered in filthy sawdust and drenched in beer. She choked back tears, flooded with humiliation.

There was only one thing for it. She had kept off the liquor tonight to keep her wits about her. But now all bets were off. Reaching for a bottle of absinthe, she poured a double measure of the aniseed-flavoured green spirit and gulped it down in one, sighing as the burning rasp hit her stomach. She poured another.

'You're all on your own now, with your father and husband gone.' Old Jake had sidled up to her.

Pearl held tightly on to the absinthe bottle, taking grim satisfaction in not passing it to him. She looked at him fiercely, feeling the effects of the absinthe. 'I can look after myself.'

The old man cupped Pearl's elbow. 'You'll be missing a man to look after you, now that you're on your lonesome. I am at your service.'

'Quite the sauce box, ain't you? First flirting with Mr Matthews and now Old Jake. Think you're better than all of us.' Betty was itching for a fight.

'I think you've had enough to drink. And start thinking about another place to stay, now that my father's gone. You've no place here.'

Betty moved even closer, a triumphant smile on her face. 'This is my home now. PJ left The Sailor's Arms to me. I'm his wife. He wanted me to have it. Not you.' Pearl gaped at her. The room was spinning.

'You're a liar! My father always wanted me to take over the pub, ever since I was a nipper.'

'I'm the second Mrs O'Dwyer. Everyone knows that. Like I said, we got wed the week you left.'

'Prove it. Show me the marriage certificate.'

'Why should I? Miss snooty pants, coming back here, trying to lord it over me, like bleedin' Queen Victoria.' Betty looked around the room, nodding at the eavesdroppers who were sniggering.

'I'm his next of kin. There's no way you're stealing the pub from me.' Pearl's voice was a jagged whisper. She'd die rather than see Betty steal The Sailor's Arms from her.

'Filthy half-breed. You're a freak of nature.'

Pearl struck Betty hard across the face. Then she picked up a bottle of gin and hurled it against the wall. She threw bottle after bottle, showering her father's bar with myriads of glass shards. An oil painting of the *Cutty Sark* turned sepia as a wash of brandy soaked it. The crowd fell silent as they all turned to stare at Pearl.

'The Sailor's Arms is mine and always will be. Now clear off, the lot of you, the wake is over. Get out!'

Betty wiped the droplets of gin from her face and licked her fingers. She glared at Pearl, a large welt blooming scarlet on her cheek. 'This ain't over. I'll be back with *my* name above the door.'

6

The shrill clang of a ferry startled Pearl from feverish dreams. It was still dark. She could sense her father's presence. The deserted bar smelt of an acrid body odour, tobacco and furniture polish. It was him. Perspiration beaded her upper lip. He was here. She half-hoped, half-dreaded that her father's ghostly apparition would materialise. He would have chastised her for the waste – all those expensive bottles of spirits she'd hurled around the pub. Pearl's head ached from too much absinthe.

Maude once told her that in Paris they called it *la fée verte*, the Green Fairy, rumoured to cause hallucinations. It was the first time Pearl had tried absinthe, and they had finished off a bottle between them, singing loudly, their arms around one another. It was then that Maude kissed her softly, just behind the ear.

A bottle crashed to the floor. Pearl swung round wildly, looking into the gloom.

'Show yourself!' she called out. 'Pa!' she tried again, her voice faltering.

But nothing happened; there was no sign of him. He was gone. Pearl crossed to the end of the pub and opened a door to the left. In the snug, she found what she was looking for. There it was, a figurine of Mazu, perched on a high shelf. The goddess was worshipped by Chinese seafarers and sailors, hoping for a safe journey. Legend had it that she protected believers through miraculous interventions. In another myth, she drowned after a failed attempt at finding her lost father. PJ had said the statue looked exactly like Pearl's mother.

'What will become of me?' she asked the goddess. But Mazu wasn't able to come up with an answer; her perfect porcelain face stayed frozen in a serene smile.

Dispirited, Pearl trudged back to the main bar. Smashed bottles littered the marble counter, while tables and chairs lay scattered on their sides. Her eyes avoided the oak coffin, containing her father's body, now thankfully covered over with a cloth. The surrounding lilies were giving off a cloying smell.

The grandfather clock ticked irregularly. Five bells sounded. Her limbs were heavy, as if the tidal Thames was sucking her under. She felt hot and sticky, perspiration collecting underneath the tight collar of her black taffeta mourning dress.

She doubled over and hugged herself. There was no one in Limehouse who could assuage her loneliness. Pearl grabbed her purse, lunging for the front door. She'd suddenly thought of Ma Jennings. It surprised her that the person to draw comfort from was a woman, down on her luck, who ran an empty lodging house.

Pearl knocked on the door. After waiting for several minutes, she knocked again, harder. Finally, she could hear shuffling behind the door. After much rattling of bolts and locks, Ma Jennings peered out. She quickly turned her head from left to right, peering down the street, her eyes wide and fearful.

'My goodness, Pearl! What brings you out so early? Come in quickly. Best not to hang about at the door.' Ma Jennings' eyes were watery and red. She looked ten years older.

'What's wrong? Has something happened?' Pearl asked.

'Oh Pearl, I've had such a dreadful shock. My handyman Ah

Sim . . . he's dead. Murdered! I can scarcely believe it. He was so young and full of life.'

Pearl frowned. Could this be the man she had found close to death on the foreshore at Wapping Old Stairs? She gently steered Ma Jennings to the kitchen table and started preparations for making tea, thinking this through. She lit a fire to take the chill off the room. Once the tea was ready, Pearl added a drop of laudanum from a bottle on the Welsh dresser to Ma's cup.

'Mei, Ah Sim's sister, came with news yesterday evening that he'd been found dead near the river on Wapping Old Stairs,' Ma's voice was trembling. 'The poor girl was in an awful state. Said he'd been killed.'

Pearl sat down next to Ma, clutching her ice-cold hand. 'I found a Chinese man on the foreshore there, just in front of The Sailor's Arms,' she said. 'He had a deep scar on his face and was wearing a jacket with a monkey embroidered on it. It must have been Ah Sim. He was barely alive, but with his last words he asked for someone called Mei. So she is his sister.'

Ma's mouth sagged open. 'Yes! He always wore that jacket. You found him? Please tell me he didn't suffer.'

Pearl remembered his last tortured breaths, the blood pouring out of the large wound in his belly, the terror in his eyes. How much could she tell Ma about it? At the pleading look in Ma's eyes, Pearl hesitated, then decided it was best to keep the worst from the dead man's landlady. She shook her head and spoke softly. 'No, I'm sure he went quickly.'

Ma Jennings nodded her head and sighed. 'Thank goodness. My poor, poor boy. Mei will be so comforted to hear that. And to know that someone was with him at the end.'

Pearl smiled at Ma. 'Come, drink your tea, it's getting cold.' She wondered about the deceased, comforted that at least two people had cared for him. 'Ah Sim,' she murmured. 'I'm glad to know who he was.'

A sharp rap at the front door made them both start. Ma groaned. 'I'm not fit to see anyone today.' She heaved herself up and shuffled to the door. Her reluctance gave way to a cry of welcome upon seeing the visitor.

A woman came into the kitchen. Her jet-black hair was oiled and smoothed back in a bun, gleaming in the flickering gaslight. She wore a red sleeveless dress with an embroidered phoenix coiled tightly around her body. Pearl stared, her mouth suddenly dry. It was the Chinese woman Pearl had seen in the market.

'This is Mei Tan, Ah Sim's sister,' said Ma, gesturing to the stranger. 'And this is Mrs Pearl Fitzgerald. She found Ah Sim on the foreshore!'

Mei's eyes, deep pools of obsidian, brimmed with tears. She gazed at Pearl, drawing in her breath sharply. 'You found my brother?'

'Yes, at Wapping Old Stairs. I stayed with him until he passed.'

'Did you see who killed him?' Mei reached out a hand. Pearl's skin prickled.

'I'm afraid not. But he was able to speak a little; he wanted you to know he was sorry. Those were his last words.' Again, Pearl decided to spare Mei's feelings and not reveal the gruesome way her brother had been killed.

'What would he have to apologise for?' Mei blinked rapidly. She took her hand from Pearl. 'I'm so glad you found him, Mrs Fitzgerald. So pleased he did not die alone.'

The woman turned back to Ma. 'I must be going soon. I just wanted to let you know what happened at the police station.' Mei spoke fluent English with a Cantonese accent. Pearl found it charming. She wondered if she could ask Mei to read Tang dynasty poetry with her. Perhaps a new teacher, apart from Xianfan.

'Don't rush off, pet, fresh brew coming up.' Ma Jennings put the kettle on the stove.

Pearl struggled for something to say. 'I'm so sorry for your brother's passing. My sincere condolences.' Her words sounded stilted and awkward. 'That's a beautiful gown. Was it made in China?'

'Thank you. Yes, the silk is from Shanghai, but Liz, I mean Mrs Soo Chow, had it made for me. I work for her in the laundry,' Mei replied stiffly. 'The police were very rude; when I went to the station asking questions about Ah Sim, the sergeant and constable couldn't tell me anything – just stared at me the whole time.'

Pearl wasn't surprised. She doubted those peelers had seen anything like Mei or indeed this gown before in Limehouse. It was hand-made and must have cost Lizzy a pretty penny, fitting Mei's lithe figure as snug as a sealskin glove. It was unusual for an employer to spend so much on a laundry worker, but these thoughts dissolved as Pearl looked in wonder at the skilful needlework; golden thread made the phoenix sparkle and shimmer, its limbs and claws curving around Mei's breasts, shoulders and neck. No wonder the coppers had gawped. Pearl was also finding it hard to take her eyes off Mei.

Mei paced up and down. 'They said some very coarse things and then told me to go home.' She twisted the handkerchief in her hands as she turned to Ma Jennings. 'I need to get back to work at the laundry. Mrs Soo Chow doesn't like it when I am away too long.'

'Don't mind Lizzy. I'm sure she understands how upset you are.' Ma handed her a cup of strong tea.

'I'm not sure what to do. The police won't let me see my brother's body. I need to arrange the funeral.'

Pearl spoke quickly. 'I may be able to offer some assistance. My father died recently, so I could help with the arrangements. Also, my uncle is a policeman. Perhaps I could enquire on your behalf, if you would like me to. I also need to give a statement to the inspector in charge of the case, so I might be able to find out more.'

Mei nodded eagerly. 'That would be very kind of you.'

Ma Jennings smiled in agreement. 'Let Pearl help. She knows folk round here.'

Pearl was pleased to be of some succour to Mei. 'No trouble at all. Anything I can do. Anything at all.' She held Mei's gaze.

'I would be so grateful if you spoke to the police. They might listen to you more.' Mei's words rushed out, revealing more of what had happened to her at the station. 'I overheard them talk. What do they mean, about the Yellow Peril? They believe that Ah Sim was killed by one of his own kind, a Chinese thug, they said. But it's not true. My brother didn't have any enemies.'

'Most peelers are ignorant swine. I'll do what I can.' Pearl held out her hand. 'Once again, my condolences for your loss.' Mei's grip was strong. A ripple of heat ran up Pearl's arm.

JULY

7

The kitchen window at the lodging house was slightly ajar, ruffling Pearl's hair with a sharp breeze. It was an unseasonably cold day for mid-summer. Ma Jennings had gone to the local market and Pearl wanted to get the place ship-shape while Ma was out of the way. A rush of resentment came over her as she plunged her hands into scalding soapy suds.

A week after the wake, PJ's funeral was held. Following the burial, there had been a big reception at The Sailor's Arms for the hundred-plus mourners. To Pearl's intense annoyance, Betty acted like the grieving widow, crying and wailing, accepting commiserations from all the mourners with great gulping sobs.

Ah Sim's funeral, on the other hand, was a sad little affair, attended only by Mei, Ma Jennings and Pearl. The three women had silently looked down on his grave in St Anne's Churchyard, a simple plot, marked only by his name written in Chinese characters. Pearl was unsure how to comfort Mei. She had put a tentative hand on the other woman's shoulder, feeling the muscles tense at her touch. Pearl had wondered again if Mei was a dancer.

Pearl scrubbed down the sink and mulled over the situation with Betty. Her father's lady friend was determined to make Pearl's life as unpleasant as possible, with continual jibes and threats that she – and not Pearl – was the rightful owner of The Sailor's Arms.

Could it be really true that Betty had married her father? The priest at the funeral mass had addressed Betty as Mrs O'Dwyer, but he could have fallen for her lies and obfuscation.

Pearl was spending increasing amounts of time at the lodging house. She felt more relaxed here than at the pub, and was worried about Ma Jennings, who was fraught about how she was going to cope without a handyman. Added to that, a murder was not good for business. Looking around, Pearl knew that the lodging house was failing badly, rather than just needing a little spruce-up here and there, as Ma had described it. This looked like a long-standing problem. Very few lodgers, which meant very little income.

The front door slammed and in came an exhausted-looking Ma Jennings. 'It's so good of you to stop with me, Pearl. You're such a godsend. I just don't know what I'd do without you.'

Pearl had made tea, and handed Ma a cup, adding four sugars. 'Here, drink this. You're looking a bit peaky.'

'Why don't you fetch down that brandy bottle and we both get blootered?' she said hopefully.

Pearl shook her head. 'Not for me. Otherwise I'll be asleep before lunchtime.'

'You sure? Well, I'll just have a small one.' Ma added a generous splash of brandy to the cup.

Pearl hesitated before saying: 'How are you managing these days – without Ah Sim, I mean?'

Ma took a large gulp of her tea, then wiped her mouth with a dusting cloth.

'I miss him helping out around here. This place used to be a very nice little earner. The sailors loved my food.' Pearl wondered about this. She had tasted Ma's greasy suet pudding. After one mouthful, she had quietly given the remainder of her dinner to the little gang of children outside. They had devoured it with relish.

'Best boarders are most definitely the Chinese. Well, you'd know about that,' Ma said, looking fondly at Pearl. 'Where did you say your mother hailed from?'

'Shawan Village in the Guangzhou Province. I hope to visit one day.'

'Oh yes, to see where you came from. But it's such a long journey, Pearl. And very different from here.' Ma took another large gulp of her tea and burped quietly.

Pearl laughed. 'It would be wonderful to visit China instead of just reading about it in books.'

Ma exhaled heavily. 'My nerves are a'fright, what with Ah Sim being done in. It's getting more dangerous, I swear. And you don't need me to tell you how people round here treat foreigners. You must have had it all your life, poor love. I can't understand why the locals believe that all Chinese are evil fiends who smoke opium and sell white women into slavery. Making up such stories. Well, they do love their opium pipes. But nothing wrong with that. Better than a skinful of beer, that brings out the fight in 'em. At least the poppy don't make 'em mean and nasty.' Ma picked at the stains on the front of her apron. 'I'm thinking this place is too much for me. I'm old and tired. I just don't have the energy no more. I should go and live with my sister in Ramsgate for a while. Get me strength back.'

'Can't you talk to Lizzy? Surely she can help you.'

Ma shook her head, picking at a thread on her shawl. 'She's far too busy with the restaurant and her husband to take care of me.'

Pearl tried to lighten the older woman's blue funk. 'Do you remember when Lizzy sobbed for hours when her pet mouse got trodden on by a drayman's horse?'

Ma Jennings cackled, then grimaced. 'She's changed a lot, Pearl. I've not seen her cry since she was a child. Quite the fancy lady.

She likes mixing with the West End crowd. They all come to her restaurant.'

Pearl wondered about Lizzy. The woman she had grown into seemed so different to the girl she once knew. Lizzy had been so naïve when they were younger – her greatest wish was a life filled with currant buns and Champagne – but as they grew older, with Pearl and Tommy growing closer, Lizzy had changed. And when Pearl did see Lizzy, she was irritable, wanting to stay the night with Pearl at The Sailor's Arms and refusing to say why she didn't want to go home. Lizzy would have terrible nightmares, waking up screaming, eyes wide in terror. Pearl had an uneasy feeling, wanting to ask more, but at the haunted look on Lizzy's face, thought better of it.

'Probably helping out at Ma Jennings' card parties,' Tommy used to say. 'They go on all night. All sorts going on.' Pearl had shut her ears and eyes to the gossip. But surely if Lizzy was successful now, everything must have turned out well for her.

'I could stay here with you at the lodging house for a while and help out.' The words were out of Pearl's mouth before she could stop them. 'Just some time to think about my future. I had a terrible row with Betty who says she got wed to Pa and now owns The Sailor's Arms. It's unbearable staying under the same roof as her.'

Ma Jennings looked doubtful. 'Now, don't you be pulling my leg, girlie. An old woman can only stand so much teasing.'

'We'd be helping each other out.' Pearl felt a rush of excitement.

'We can split the profits, what little there is,' Ma said slowly. 'But it don't amount to much these days.'

Pearl's impulsive gesture had come from a mixture of restlessness, pity and fury, a need to get away from Betty. And the thought lessened an ache in her chest.

'I had only intended to stay in Limehouse briefly, but there's nothing in Portsmouth that I urgently need to get back to. Just my job at the grocer's with Mr Fortescue. And he said to take as long as I needed. Perhaps I'll remain for a while longer until the matter with The Sailor's Arms is sorted. I can muck in here for the time being.'

So it was decided. Pearl now spent her days traversing up and down Pennyfields, from the West India Dock Road, and along to Poplar High Street, completing errands for Ma Jennings. She talked to tradesmen and haggled for the cheapest timber needed to repair the window frames and the front door of the lodging house. It kept her mind busy, with Pearl realising she didn't know the slightest thing about being a lodging house landlady. There were times she regretted ever suggesting this venture as she would never have guessed that Ma Jennings was such a slave driver.

Pearl struggled to concentrate while Ma Jennings was barking out instructions. The older woman seemed to have twice the energy, now that she had Pearl at her beck and call.

'For breakfast, you need to serve them a mug of hot coffee and two slices of bread and butter for a penny. Of an evening, they love a currant and meat pudding, a real belt tightener, we call it. Charge 'em a couple of pence for that. See how the money adds up?' She winked at Pearl and rubbed her hands.

Ma began ticking off on her fingers everything a lodging house proprietor should know, from being on good terms with the butcher for the cheapest cuts of meats, to charging for extra blankets. 'Sometimes the lodgers will pay more for use of a razor and another halfpenny for hot water. But if you're feeling generous, then give it 'em for free occasionally,' Ma advised.

The kitchen was in need of a good clear-out. Dust and cobwebs clung to every surface. The cooking-pots, ladles and toasting forks looked like they hadn't been used in months. The clinker fireplace was lifeless, a great, black, yawning mouth instead of a red-hot furnace, which needed a cauldron of bubbling stew at its centre. A yellowing sign on the kitchen wall announced to all lodgers that hot water was currently unavailable on the premises until further notice.

Pearl's friend Xianfan was the only long-term lodger in the place. He had just come back from a job stoking coal on a ship that was delivering wool to Newcastle. He sat in the corner of the parlour, eating from a pail of pickled winkles, seasoned with vinegar and pepper, that he had bought at the end of the day from a street seller down on King Henry's Pier. From the smell of them, they were well past being fit for human consumption, but Xianfan daintily ate them one by one, humming the refrain of a Chinese opera. Pearl recognised it as *The Dancing Singing Woman*, about a wife battered by her drunken husband. Pearl laughed and said they could see that any night of the week on Flower and Dean Street. She and Xianfan spent a delightful evening discussing the finer points of the opera; Pearl listening with wonder when her old tutor explained that the performance was usually performed by a man dressed as a woman.

Getting the lodging house back in a decent state of repair was slow and arduous, but extra help was at hand. The wily old Ma Jennings had enlisted the help of the matchgirls who lived on Ropemaker Fields, to assist with washing and scrubbing down the lodging house. They were also given the task of tending the fires, sweeping the yard and making the beds – not that many needed changing.

'Poor mites,' Ma Jennings whispered to Pearl, nodding at the young girls washing down the walls. Two sisters, Rose and Polly Duffy, and their friend Gerty Connolly, had all gone on strike at the Bryant & May match factory on Fairfax Road in Bow.

'They don't see a piece of meat from one year to the next. They'll scrub the floors and shine the silver all night for a decent bit of mutton.' Pearl nodded but didn't see any evidence of silverware that needed polishing in the lodging house.

Rose Duffy's moon-shaped face looked mournful. She kept her eyes downcast as she timidly asked: 'Anything else you want cleaning, Miss?'

'If you could scour down the floors next, that would be wonderful, Rose.' The girl looked about sixteen, but careworn, a melancholy air clinging to her.

Rose's sister Polly was a tiny, frail girl, around thirteen years of age. She kept her head bent down and a scarf around her face partially hid the large gaping wound in her cheek, the flesh around it greenish in colour. A putrid odour clung to her and Pearl wondered about giving Polly some rose toilet water to disguise the smell.

'Phossy jaw,' Ma Jennings said in a whisper that travelled the length and breadth of the room. 'The matchgirls don't have no separate eating area, so they've got that nasty phosphorus on their hands all day long. Rots their teeth and gets into their bones.'

But Ma wasn't all sympathy. Her sharp eye caught Rose staring into space.

'Rose! What's the matter with you? Don't just stand there dreaming. That dustpan and brush got a purpose. You used to be such a good worker. Get lively now, or there won't be any mutton stew for you.'

The girl started, embarrassed at being caught idle, and hurriedly began brushing down the stairs.

'What's it like at Bryant & May's?' Pearl asked Gerty, who was vigorously scrubbing a pot covered with thick layers of black grease. She had heard the working conditions at the match factory were amongst the worst in London.

Gerty wiped her brow. 'It's pretty tough, but what else can we do? Start at 6.30 in the morning for a fourteen-hour shift. And that's a hard graft for some of the little 'uns like Polly. She ain't strong.'

'I do alright.' Polly had joined them to help with the washing up. 'But things are changing.' Then she said in a hushed tone: 'We're not going back to work at the match factory until we get what we want.' Her swollen jaw pouted forward defiantly, and she dabbed the pus away with her sleeve.

Gerty nodded. 'We've got more support this time. People know what we're going through. That article by Mrs Besant in *The Link* newspaper did good for us.'

'If there is anything I can do to help, do let me know.' Pearl was impressed that the matchgirls were keen to fight back against their bosses. 'I would have thought William Bryant and Francis May, being Quakers, would be better employers, but they seem just as bad as any other.'

Mei came into the kitchen then with a bag of cabbage, leeks, rice and various bottles of condiments. 'I thought I'd make us all some lunch,' she said, smiling at the matchgirls. Pearl felt a rush of pleasure at seeing her.

Rose was also staring at Mei. '*Mhgòi*,' Rose said shyly. '*Wǒ xǐhuān zhōngguó cài*.' She bobbed her head.

'You speak Cantonese!' Pearl was surprised at Rose thanking Mei in her native tongue and saying how much she liked Chinese food.

'I know a few phrases.' Rose was still looking at Mei, a haunted look in her eye.

'You speak it well, with a good accent. Who was your teacher?' Mei asked.

Rose started to say something but her mouth trembled. She turned a chalky white, burst into tears and ran out of the boarding house.

Pearl looked at the front door in astonishment. She took Polly to the far corner of the room and whispered, 'Whatever's up with Rose?'

Polly bit her lip. 'Her man got murdered. Taken it right badly.' She said it so quietly that Pearl barely made out what she was saying.

'Poor girl. Who was he?' But Polly just shook her head.

Pearl watched Rose running down the street. Could the matchgirl have been stepping out with Ah Sim? Following her down Poplar High Street, Pearl called out: 'Rose! Wait up a minute.'

But Rose didn't look round. She started walking faster, then picked up her skirts and ran as fast as she could down the street. Pearl decided not to give chase as the matchgirl was so distraught. She'd have to wait until Rose was in a better frame of mind. Pearl thought about sharing what she'd found out with Mei, even though it was a slim excuse to talk to her again, but perhaps they could visit Rose together and see if the matchgirl would say anything more.

They were now ready to take in lodgers. Pearl lay with her eyes closed on the divan, utterly exhausted. Ma Jennings gave Pearl a sharp poke in the stomach with a feather duster. 'Look sharp now. We've got to hurry. Just heard that some ships from Foochow are coming into East India Docks, chock full of sailors looking for a place to kip. I've told the quartermaster this place is under new management and that a nice, respectable half-Chinese lady is taking over here and offering a good price for board and lodging. So no more lounging around, Duchess.'

With a pang, Pearl realised again that she hadn't yet seen her Uncle Peter, and she missed his high-pitched chuckle, so out of step with his burly frame. He had kept away from The Sailor's

Arms because of some feud with her father while she was away. He also hadn't been to the wake or the funeral. Pearl was very fond of him, and he was now her only living relative in the world. She wondered if he would be pleased to see her, or furious with her for leaving Limehouse without saying goodbye. Besides wanting to see him, as a copper on the streets, Sergeant O'Dwyer might have some information on Ah Sim's murder.

Ah Sim often intruded upon Pearl's thoughts. He was in her dreams, looking up at her with such pain in his eyes, his life slowly ebbing away. She thought again of the glowing green liquid beside his body. The memory was growing hazy; perhaps it was nothing more than a trick of reflection, the greenish sheen of a gaslight illuminating a puddle. Pushing aside these doubts, she shook her head. She had definitely seen it.

'Hello?' a voice cut into Pearl's thoughts. Mei was standing at the kitchen door, the afternoon sun turning her face golden. She was holding some freshly laundered sheets. 'Ma asked me to bring these back. Of course, she asked for a cheap deal – even from her own daughter.' Mei gave a slight smile.

Pearl smoothed back her tangled hair. Had she washed her face that morning? 'Thank you for bringing them. They look so white and clean!' She cursed herself for such inane chatter. Couldn't she have thought of something witty and intelligent to say?

'I can help put them on the beds, and perhaps you can tell me if you've found anything out from the police.' She looked at Pearl hopefully.

Mei leant over the beds, smoothing down the sheets and tucking in the corners with deft, expert hands. Today, she was dressed very differently from when Pearl had first met her. Mei wore laundry work clothes, a black smock tied in at the waist, and loose, flowing trousers. A scarf covered her hair.

'So have you found out anything more from the police?'

Pearl shook her head. 'To be honest, I haven't had time, it's been so busy getting this place in order. I do intend to pay a visit to Inspector Crowley at the station, although it's really up to the police now.'

Mei's shoulders sagged. Pearl bit her lip, wishing she had more positive news. Wanting to keep Mei at the lodging house a while longer, she said: 'Please stay and have a brew.'

Collecting crockery in the kitchen, she brushed past Mei, breathing in a scent of sandalwood perfume. A cup slipped through Pearl's fingers, smashing on the floor. Under Mei's curious stare, Pearl's face grew scarlet. Mei's pensive expression lifted as her mouth twitched. 'So clumsy,' she teased. 'What is making you so – how do you say – butterfingers?'

'I've no idea,' Pearl said, stammering. The two women looked at each other for a long moment. Mei broke their gaze first.

Pearl unclenched her hands and started to pick up the broken crockery from the floor. Trying to think of something to salvage her reputation in Mei's eyes, Pearl said: 'By the way, this might be nothing at all, but the matchgirl Rose Duffy could have known your brother, possibly she was close to him. I thought perhaps we could visit her together, tomorrow if you are free, once you have finished at the laundry. Rose might be inclined to say more if you were there. She seemed to take a shine to you.'

Mei's smile faded, her mouth turning down at the corners. 'Is this true? Ah Sim never mentioned Rose.'

'They might have been keeping it a secret. White women get a lot of trouble if they go with foreigners.'

'If Rose knows anything at all, we must see her.' Mei gathered her belongings quickly. 'I must be going.'

Pearl watched from the kitchen window, admiring Mei's graceful figure running back towards the laundry.

In the morning, Pearl wondered if she could heat up enough hot water for a bath before she met up with Mei, and tried to decide which of her dresses was most presentable. None of them, she surmised with a sinking heart. While putting on her cleanest frock, she resolved to do more in asking about the progress of the police investigation.

The resourceful Ma Jennings had commandeered Xianfan's friends to help out around the lodging house. They helped to fix the rotted window frames and loose slates on the roof. Pearl watched, terrified that they would lose their balance and fall off, especially Xianfan who was not in the prime of youth. But he waved down at her and laughed, fearless as he replaced missing roof tiles, clambering about as if he was on a ship's rigging.

'Thank you so much for helping. We have very little money to pay you, but is there anything else we can offer?'

Xianfan thought for a moment. 'There is one thing that would make Chinese lodgers happy.'

She looked at him, hoping he wasn't going to ask for a cheaper room rate. 'If we could have some congee or chicken rice broth for breakfast?'

Pearl tried not to laugh. 'I could make my braised Mandarin fish and honey roast pork. Do you remember when the Chinese cook on *The Sunrise* came to visit at The Sailor's Arms?'

Xianfan's eyes danced with delight. 'Then every seaman from Quanzhou to Kowloon will come here straight from the docks, you can be sure of that.' He scurried off to fix the pump in the yard, a renewed sense of purpose in his step.

There were sheets drying on the line, billowing in the wind. The honeysuckle Mei had planted in the garden was in flower. Pearl inhaled deeply, taking in the scented breeze. Turning to Ma, she said: 'I think we'll rename this place The Fragrant Blossoms.'

Ma winked at her and said: 'That's a lovely idea to rustle up some new customers.'

That evening, Pearl and Mei met up on Pennyfields and walked together towards Rose's lodgings in Ropemaker Fields. Mei was wearing her red dress, embroidered with a phoenix, and Pearl thought again how fine she looked.

On the corner of Castor Street, they passed a young woman who was rattling a tin. It was Gerty Connolly. She waved at them. 'Just been to see Rose and Polly, and now I'm going round collecting for the matchgirls. If you can spare any coppers . . .' She looked at them pointedly.

Pearl dug in her purse and dropped a few pennies into the tin. 'How's the strike going?'

'We get shouted at in the street to go back to work, but some folks understand what we are going through. We won't give up so easy.' Gerty's lips set in a determined line.

The matchgirl was wearing an enormous feathered hat. The turquoise, red and yellow ostrich feathers quivered with every step she took. It added at least another six inches to her height. She looked like a fierce bird of paradise.

'That's a gorgeous hat,' Pearl said, wondering where Gerty had purchased such an extraordinary bonnet. She wondered about buying one, and if it would impress Mei.

The matchgirl preened. 'It's my turn to wear it today. Several of us girls clubbed together and saved our pennies to buy it. I dropped by to see if Rose and Polly want to come to the boxing match at Sebright Hall down in Hackney some time. Rose is looking pretty glum these days; that girl needs cheering up.' Gerty's eyes were dancing. 'Polly's favourite, Ching Hook, is in town. He's fighting Bob Dunbar, the one-eyed Welsh champion.'

'Oh, is there a Chinese boxer?' Pearl thought she might go along.

'Nah. He's really from the West Indies, a black gentleman. The ladies love him. Some journalist from the *Sporting Life* called him "the Sable Chinaman", thought he looked a bit Chinese, and the name Ching Hook stuck. You know what journalists are like, never let the truth get in the way of a good story.'

Pearl thought back. Her father and Old Jake often went to see the boxing at The Oriental Hotel in Blackfriars. They'd arrive home, describing the bouts, the knock-out blows from vicious left hooks and criticising boxers well past their glory days.

'The Sapphire Stevedore is on the bill as well. He's always a big draw.'

Pearl frowned. 'What's special about him?'

'He's completely covered in blue tattoos. A mystery man who wears a mask, so no one knows who he is.' Gerty shook her head. 'Dirty fighter. Been banned a few times. The last match he got caught with lead weights in his padded gloves. Then he lost his temper, started kicking, gouging, head-butting and biting. They were all declared fouls.'

Pearl's mind was racing. She remembered now that the locals gathered at The Sailor's Arms after the murder had said the Blue Man might be Ah Sim's killer. Could they have been describing someone with a torso covered in tattoos?

'I'd love to come along with you to see Ching Hook. What about the Sapphire Stevedore? Do you know where his lodgings are or what pubs he frequents?'

Gerty tittered. 'You keen on him? Fighters get their fair share of lady admirers. I'm not sure where the Sapphire Stevedore stays. Boxers lay their head here, there and everywhere.'

Polly answered the front door, her eyes darting. 'Rose isn't feeling well. Can you come back another day?'

'We just want to see her for a few minutes. Please,' Pearl said.

After looking at Mei's beseeching look, Polly relented. She led the way up three flights of stairs and into a small room. There was a strong smell of damp, large patches of black mould on every wall. The only furniture in the room was a table and chair.

Rose was curled up on the small bed, sobbing quietly.

'I'm so sorry to disturb you.' Pearl felt terrible for intruding on the girl. 'You remember Mei, Ah Sim's sister? He was killed on Wapping Old Stairs.' Rose looked at Mei with something akin to fear in her eyes.

'I need to ask you something, and forgive me if this is indelicate, but did you know Ah Sim? Perhaps you were friends?' Pearl's words echoed around the room. Rose opened her mouth several times to speak, but no sound came out.

'Please leave her be,' Polly entreated. 'She's not herself.'

'You are upset, forgive us for this intrusion,' Mei spoke for the first time. 'I can bring you some won ton broth. It will make you feel better.' She moved forward and touched Rose's hand.

Pearl tried again. 'We dearly want to find out what happened to Ah Sim. As you can imagine, Mei is devastated by the loss of her brother. If there is anything you know, please tell us. We won't tell anyone.'

Rose hid her face in the pillow. 'Yes, I knew him,' came the muffled reply. 'Ah Sim loved won ton broth. He used to bring me some from the kitchens at The Dragon Inn.'

'What can you tell us?' Pearl kept her voice soft. 'Do you have any idea who might have done this to Ah Sim?'

'No. I can't tell you no more.' Rose pulled the covers over her head and turned away from them.

Mei put a hand on Rose's back. 'Perhaps when you feel better, you will talk to us again. Please. We need your help.'

There was no reply except for Polly shuffling impatiently in the background. It was time for them to leave. As they closed the door to the sisters' garret room, Rose said in a small voice, 'I loved him very much.'

'Rose knows more than she is telling us,' Pearl said as they walked towards Pigott Street on the way back to Pennyfields.

'Perhaps, but there is no point in us scaring her even more. I will make her my special broth.'

'Yes, gain her trust. By the way, have the police been in contact with you?'

Mei bit her lip. 'No. I've been to the police station several times. They sent me away saying they would contact me if they had any news.'

'I'll go to the station tomorrow and see what I can find out. I'll try and track down my uncle – he's a sergeant. Perhaps he can help. The police can be confounded dunces at the best of times. I heard from the butcher's boy that the latest recruit lasted two days on the job. Found passed out in a doorway. He'd been on a huge bender. And the rest of them are dealing with those dreadful murders; George-yard Building, I think it was. So the coppers have their hands full with that.'

Mei shivered. 'Do you think it could be related to Ah Sim's murder?'

Pearl shrugged. 'Could be. I'll ask Inspector Crowley down at the station. They still haven't got in touch with me for my statement, and it's been weeks.'

'Would you?' Mei impulsively drew Pearl into a hug. 'I'd be most grateful,' she whispered, her breath warm on Pearl's ear.

AUGUST

8

Running up the wide stairs at the police station on Wapping High Street, Pearl held up her long skirts, inadvertently revealing none too clean petticoats.

The waiting area was crowded. On a long wooden bench opposite the sergeant's desk sat a cluster of women, bedraggled and forlorn. Each with a bawling baby in their arms. They were there to see if their errant husbands had been locked up for the night and had any coins for dinner.

The police station held little fear for her. The last time she had been in this nick was eight years ago, to fetch her uncle, Sergeant Peter O'Dwyer, to come round for Christmas dinner at The Sailor's Arms.

To her disappointment, he was proving very elusive and difficult to track down. Pearl walked up to the front enquiry desk. 'Excuse me, Constable, I would like to see Inspector Crowley. It's about the murder of the Chinese man on Wapping Old Stairs in June. I have come to make an eyewitness statement and have important information to offer. I'd be obliged if you let him know I am here.'

The policeman looked up from his newspaper, peering at her over his spectacles. He had carefully rearranged a few strands of hair in a misguided attempt to hide a shiny bald patch. 'The inspector is a very busy man; he can't be disturbed at present. You can leave a message with me, Miss. And it's Sergeant Knox.'

Suppressing an urge to snatch his paper away, Pèarl beamed at him. 'Don't worry, I can wait all day if necessary.' On his desk was yesterday's *Evening News*. She had a quick glance at the front page.

A WHITECHAPEL HORROR

Tuesday 7th August 1888

> A woman, now lying unidentified at the mortuary, Whitechapel, was ferociously stabbed to death this morning, between two and four o'clock, on the landing of a stone staircase in George's-buildings, Whitechapel.
>
> George's-buildings are tenements occupied by the poor labouring class.
>
> A lodger going early to his work found the body.
>
> Another lodger says the murder was not committed before he returned home about two o'clock.
>
> The woman was stabbed in 20 places. No weapon was found near her, and her murderer has left no trace. She is of middle age and height, has black hair and a large, round face, and apparently belonged to the lowest class.

'This is terrible! Let's hope you catch him soon. Do you think this is connected to the Chinese man who was killed on Wapping Old Stairs, Sergeant Knox?'

'Who?' The policeman was scouring the racing pages.

Pearl sighed. 'The murder just by The Sailor's Arms. I've already told you that. I want to see Inspector Crowley. I haven't given him my statement yet.'

'You need to sit down over there and wait.' The sergeant licked a pudgy finger and turned a page of his newspaper.

Pearl started to walk back to the long bench but then sharply turned on her heel and headed towards a corridor to the right of the enquiry desk, pushing through a glass-fronted double door.

'Hey! You can't go barging in there!' The sergeant heaved himself up, but just then there was a scream from the front door; a woman staggered through, blood gushing from her mouth. Distracted, the sergeant moved from his desk to help the wounded woman, leaving Pearl to continue unimpeded.

The corridor's wooden parquet flooring was highly polished, smelling of beeswax, the soles of her boots slipping on the fine sheen. She followed the curve of the wall, with a long row of police commissioner portraits, their solemn faces watching her disapprovingly. Even though it was bright sunshine outside, the gaslights were lit, emitting a dullish glow and hissing noisily. She passed door after door, each with the name of their occupant engraved on a brass sign: Franklin, Wright, Porter, Crowley.

She knocked tentatively on the last door. There was no response, and after waiting for a few more moments, she knocked again, this time louder. Still no answer. Undeterred, Pearl opened the door. Sitting behind a large mahogany desk was the man she recognised from Wapping Old Stairs. Crowley had his eyes closed, a large bible in front of him, hands clasped in prayer.

At the sound of the door, he opened his eyes, his demeanour sharp with annoyance. Pearl raised her hand in apology and smiled in a friendly fashion.

Keeping a brightness in her words, she said: 'My dear Inspector Crowley, do forgive this intrusion. Perhaps you don't remember me. I am Mrs Pearl Fitzgerald who found the Chinese fellow who was murdered. I'm happy to make a statement to you now. If you have time, of course.'

'Very kind of you to take the trouble, Mrs Fitzgerald. But you should have waited until we called on you.' His slight Dorset accent was gentle and lilting, but his eyes lacked warmth.

Pearl pressed on. 'It was Sergeant O'Dwyer, my uncle, who encouraged me to see you immediately. He said you were the most intelligent detective he had ever worked with.' She hoped these little falsehoods would flatter the policeman's ego and delay the moment she was dismissed.

The inspector considered this, then gestured to a chair. 'Please, take a seat. I was unaware that you had relatives on the police force. Sergeant O'Dwyer is most kind.'

'I wanted to ask if there is any news on the Ah Sim murder. Do you have any suspects?'

He frowned and Pearl cursed herself for being too impulsive.

'We are following some leads but I really can't tell you anything more at this time,' Crowley said.

There were two small spots of colour on his cheekbones and he ran a finger under his starched white collar. Pearl noticed there was a slight smear of blood on his jawline where he had cut himself shaving. His dark brown Harris tweed suit was thick and expensive. But it also looked uncomfortable and itchy. The rash on the side of his neck from contact with the coarse material confirmed her suspicions.

He took out some note paper and a fountain pen from his desk drawer. 'As you are here, let's begin your statement. Tell me exactly what you saw.'

'I was walking along the wharves, just by The Sailor's Arms when I saw a man lying on the foreshore at Wapping Old Stairs. I went to see if I could help, but he was in a terrible way.' Pearl tried to keep her voice steady. 'He had a dagger stuck in his belly and a serious head wound. I held him in my arms until he died.'

Crowley was writing this all down, head bent in concentration. 'Did he say anything to you?'

'He asked for his sister, but that was all.'

'Did you see anyone around?'

'No one.'

'Was there anything unusual you saw at the scene?'

Pearl hesitated as the luminous green liquid beside Ah Sim's body came into her head. She thought Crowley would never take her seriously if she told him, so shook her head. It sounded odd, even to her ears. Pearl resolved to think on it further. Once she could find a logical explanation, she would tell the inspector.

Crowley scratched his signature on the statement, then gave her the paper to sign. 'Thank you for coming in to the station.' He stood up and pulled a watch out of his waistcoat pocket.

Pearl remained seated.

'I understand you can't give me any specific information, but is there any at all I can give to his relatives? The sister of the deceased, Miss Mei Tan, requested that I come and find out if there are any developments in his case. As you can imagine, she is beside herself with worry.'

'No doubt. But I promise you, Mrs Fitzgerald, we are doing everything we can.' His grey eyes were flinty.

'Surely you must have a number of suspects,' Pearl persisted.

'It is still very early days in the murder investigation. But let me assure you. We will catch the culprit.'

'If there is anything I can do to help with your enquiries, please do let me know.'

He smiled thinly, looking again at his watch. 'The police have this under control. Now, I really must be getting on, so if you will excuse me, Mrs Fitzgerald.'

He stood up and opened the door to his office. As she got up to leave, Pearl shot a final question: 'Do you think he was killed because he was Chinese? The locals are suspicious of foreigners or anyone new in the area.'

He bared his teeth in the semblance of a smile. 'We are treating the murder of this Chinese fellow very seriously. But we do have many other crimes to attend to. Drug gangs, robberies, drunkenness, vice. And of course the Whitechapel killings are taking up a lot of my men's time.'

'Surely every murder needs your equal attention, Inspector. I would hate to talk to the *East London Advertiser* about this. I'm sure you know the police are often the butt of jokes. The newspapers are calling you incompetent fools. There was a picture of a blindfolded copper surrounded by a group of villains.'

'I wouldn't advise saying anything to the press. You will be making it harder to catch the person who did this. Just because the victim, a . . . Mr Wong . . .' He quickly scanned the desk for his notes.

'His name is Ah Sim Tan,' prompted Pearl.

'I beg your pardon. I have many cases that I'm working on,' he snapped. 'I understand that Mr Sim was a foreigner, but that doesn't mean we are not giving it our full attention. As you well know,' he held her gaze, 'the Chinese community is very secretive. They don't help themselves, what with not speaking English, and we have no interpreters to help us.'

'I could ask around at The Sailor's Arms. People often have information they want to keep from the police, and I know there's been talk of suspects. It may even have been a local that murdered him.'

'That's not necessary. We have our own leads to follow, men undercover and police informants in the area.' He leaned in close to Pearl. 'You'd do well not to interfere in police business. I would warn you to be very careful and stay indoors after dark. There's a foul fiend, a dangerous killer, on the streets of Limehouse. I wouldn't want you to be his next victim.'

9

The next day, Pearl was so lost in reverie on her walk back from the butcher's on Cable Street, that she collided with a woman coming in the opposite direction. Turning to apologise, Pearl's pulse quickened as she recognised the sleek dark head. 'Why, Miss Tan. Good evening.'

At Mei's forlorn look, Pearl put a tentative hand on her shoulder, but then withdrew it, unsure whether the gesture would be welcome. 'Would you like to come over to the Fragrant Blossoms? You might want to sort through some of Ah Sim's belongings.'

Mei wavered, then shook her head. 'I'm afraid I can't. I am already behind with my laundry deliveries.'

Disappointed, Pearl said: 'Of course. I had wanted to tell you what I found out at the police station but if you are busy, then perhaps another time.'

Mei's head went up. 'I might have a little time to spare. I think Mrs Chow will understand me being a little late. I very much want to hear anything you know. I could come for a little while. Thank you, Mrs Fitzgerald, for going to the police station on my behalf.'

Pearl smiled at Mei. 'You must call me Pearl.'

'And please call me Mei.' The two women walked along the river, with Pearl pointing out the places where she used to play as a child, with Tommy and Lizzy.

Mei took it all in, eyes wide. 'How nice it must be for you to come back to your home.'

'There's good and bad memories. It's strange being back in Limehouse, after so many years.' Pearl caught Mei's wistful look and wondered whether she was homesick.

'Do you miss China?'

Mei touched the jade necklace at her throat. 'I miss the countryside and the waterfalls. I have no friends here. And I have no one close, now that Ah Sim is dead.'

I could be close, if you let me near. The words lodged in Pearl's throat.

She forced a cheeriness in her voice. 'Come, let's have something to eat back at the lodging house.' She slipped her arm through Mei's.

The congee soup for the lodgers' evening meal was boiling over, spilling onto the stove. It was sizzling and spitting as Pearl hurriedly tidied around the kitchen.

'Here, let me help with that.' Mei moved the pot off the fire and picked up a ladle, stirring the congee.

'Ma's just gone to buy some milk and bread for our tea. I'm afraid we've run out. I also asked her to mention the Blue Man to locals. See if they know anything more. He might be a suspect in Ah Sim's killing. She might tell us more when she gets back.'

Mei's eyes widened. 'Do you think this Blue Man is the killer?'

Pearl shrugged. 'I don't know. There's a lot of chatter, but that's all. No one seems to know who or where he is.'

Mei paced restlessly around the kitchen, her eyes finally resting on the large cast-iron pot suspended above the fireplace. 'I just can't believe I will never make chicken noodle broth for Ah Sim ever again. We used to cook together when we were in the Shanghai circus. He said it would make me strong and supple in my limbs for the high wire.'

'Were you an acrobat? I had guessed that you were a dancer from your build.'

'Being a high-wire artiste is much more difficult than being a dancer. You need to be very strong in your arms and legs to climb and land properly. It was what I was born to do.' Mei tasted some congee before adding more pepper to the pot. 'My teacher said I could have been one of the best. But since I arrived in London, I've not had time to practise. Working at Liz's – I mean Mrs Chow's – laundry doesn't leave me much time.'

Pearl nodded. 'I hope Lizzy treats you well. She and I were close once. Once, long ago.'

Mei looked away. Pearl thought she looked nervous and wondered why. 'Yes, of course she is very good to me. I am grateful to her for the job and the lodgings above the laundry on Turners Corner. Work is difficult to find, especially if you are not from here.' Mei's brief moment of warmth had vanished, instead her expression was guarded.

'Yes, I understand how hard that must be for you. Although I am only half Chinese, I have also been at the receiving end of insults. I've always felt different.'

Mei considered this. 'You belong here and yet you don't. But think of it this way, you are from two different worlds, so you are doubly rich.'

'That's a good way of looking at it. I've always thought of myself as doubly cursed.'

'Are you always this gloomy?' Mei's mouth curled with amusement.

'Perhaps you could cheer me up with tales of the circus. And I can show you around Limehouse, when you have a day off.'

'I would like to know more of the ways here, if this is to be my home.' Mei looked thoughtful.

'I'm happy to oblige.' Pearl was glad to have found something to interest Mei. 'And I have some Cantonese poetry books. We could read them together, if you like.'

They smiled at each other and moved into the parlour, to lay out the tables for the evening meal.

'What was Ah Sim like?' Pearl was curious about Mei's brother.

Mei's demeanour lifted. It was the first time Pearl heard her laugh out loud.

'He was such a funny boy. Always joking with me. But he was naughty, too. Up to mischief. But when I scolded him, he would tease me, so I was never cross with him for long.'

'I wish I'd met him; he sounds very jolly. What kind of work did he do?'

'Anything and everything he could to make money. Work on the docks, carrying and loading from the ships. There were odd jobs for Liz, bringing food stuffs to the restaurant. Our family knew Mrs Chow's husband from Canton. Life was difficult when our parents died. Soo Chow became our guardian and we had to leave the circus. There was a job waiting for me at the laundry.'

'I've always wanted to go to China and watch the circus. My lodgers say it's the most wonderful spectacle to watch,' Pearl said, her eyes shining.

'There's no feeling like it in the world. Imagine flying. I trained since I was five years old to perfect the moves. Let me introduce you to the human Jack-in-the-Box!' Mei flexed her arms, then flipped over in a somersault.

Pearl clapped her hands in admiration. 'You must have been the star of the acrobatic troupe! I've never seen anyone so graceful.' Pearl stared at the ground, worried she had said too much.

Mei glanced at her briefly, then smoothed down the wrinkled tablecloths.

Pearl placed the chopsticks next to the bowls on each table. 'Do you know why Ah Sim was at Wapping Old Stairs so early in the morning? Was he meeting someone?'

'Ah Sim was a good boy,' Mei said, firmly straightening the corners of the tablecloths. 'I need you to know that. He had no enemies.'

'Of course not,' Pearl said hastily. 'I'm just trying to help. Forgive me if I am asking impertinent questions and causing you pain. It's the last thing I would want to do.'

'Will we ever find out who killed him?' Mei's voice was ragged.

'I promise I will find out what happened. I can never forget his eyes looking into mine when he died. I owe him something. His last thoughts were of you, and I'm sure he loved you very much.'

'You're very kind.' A tear trickled down Mei's face.

Pearl gently touched Mei's cheek and pushed back a lock of hair that had fallen in front of her eyes. They looked at each other. Pearl wondered if Mei's heart was racing like hers.

The front door slammed shut and they quickly jumped apart. Pearl rubbed her hands down the side of her dress. Ma Jennings stomped into the parlour and grunted as she sat down on a chair, wiping her brow. 'You wouldn't believe the price of milk and bread these days. Just been having a row with the grocer, so he gave us some buns for free.' She beamed at Pearl and Mei. 'Look at you two! Getting on like a house on fire. Pearl, did you find out any more from the police?'

'I've been waiting until you got here. They tried to fob me off. Especially that arrogant Inspector Crowley. He told me they have suspects, but wouldn't say any more. I think the locals know a lot more than the police. They usually do. Did you hear anything about this Blue Man at the shops?'

The old lady blew her cheeks out. 'Heard it down at the coal yard. Blokes muttering about this new villain in town.'

'What did they say?' Pearl moved closer to Ma.

'Just he was a nasty piece of work. The Blue Man likes using a dagger.'

'Perhaps they will find this Blue gentleman and arrest him.' Mei stood up, ready to leave. She smiled at Pearl, taking her hand. 'Thank you so much for talking to the police on my behalf.'

'Of course.' Pearl's skin was warm where Mei had touched it. 'To be honest, the police are bumbling idiots. They have no sense of urgency.'

'You're a real treasure, Pearl,' Ma cooed. 'Now, before I forget, that chimney sweep is in for a right telling off.' She hurried out of the room.

'You haven't had any tea yet, Mei. Let me get you some now.' Pearl cursed herself for being a poor hostess.

'I would like to, but I must be getting back.'

'Yes, of course, I'm sure you're very busy.'

'You have been a great help. The police have suspects, and hopefully will catch this Blue Man. You have done more than enough.'

'My pleasure. I could keep asking questions around town.'

'I don't want you to get in trouble with the police.'

'It's no trouble. But we can try and find out more.'

'Of course, I only meant this is a dangerous business. There are some terrible people around here. Look what they did to my brother.'

From the window, Pearl watched Mei Tan walk down the street, a strange yearning welling up in her. Was Mei holding something back, and why wouldn't she confide in Pearl?

10

In search of her uncle, Pearl tried the Blue Coat Boy on Dorset Street, a favourite with the local coppers. She spied one of O'Dwyer's pals propping up the bar and greeted him like a long-lost friend. After much cajoling and several brandies later, he agreed to divulge the name of the pub where Sergeant O'Dwyer was, but swore her to secrecy. 'He's on special orders, can't say more than that,' he'd muttered, looking around nervously.

The Ten Bells was on the corner of Fournier Street. She felt jittery about coming to Spitalfields, away from the familiarity of Limehouse. The Sailor's Arms felt as grand as the Café Royal in Piccadilly, compared to this drinking den. Only the most desperate would darken its doors. 'Get all kinds of lowlife there. Some very strange folk skulking around. Don't want you anywhere near them,' her father had said.

Pearl settled herself at a table and waited, uncomfortable in her clothes, which were drenched from the sudden downpour that evening. She thought of Mei's eyes, dark as the ocean's depths. An image came to her of Mei's smiling face, whispering: 'Is there anything I can do for you, to show my gratitude in bringing Ah Sim's killer to justice?'

A roar interrupted Pearl's reverie, and two men started throwing punches at each other. Pearl only just avoided being caught by a blow, as they crashed on top of the table she was sitting at. Steam was coming off their damp overcoats. Pearl decided to move further into the pub, but caught the attention of some men, who eyed her up and down, and began calling to her.

A woman approached, shoving Pearl so hard that she stumbled backwards. 'Piss off out of my patch. Don't need no more gals here offering a three-penny upright.'

'I'm not here for business, just here to see a friend. I'll be on my way soon.'

Mollified, the woman nodded 'Alright, darlin'. Can't have my regulars deciding to go with someone a bit younger.' The woman was emaciated, just under five feet in height, and Pearl thought she must be at least fifty years old. Her face was grey, etched with wrinkles, dirt embedded in the folds of sagging skin. She was joined by another woman, who had just rushed in. She was taking in deep, rasping breaths. 'God help me. It's not safe out there tonight. A friend of mine's just been knifed. If the human devil who murdered all these women isn't caught soon, why, I might be next! It makes my blood run cold.'

While the women were discussing the bizarre tastes and fetishes of their regular punters, Pearl slipped away and moved further into the recesses of the Ten Bells. She tried to make herself as inconspicuous as possible by leaning back against the glazed tiles on the back wall, decorated with scenes of Old Spitalfields and Flemish weavers. The minutes ticked by and still no sign of O'Dwyer. There was a copy of the *Evening News* on the counter. Pearl picked it up for a quick read to pass the time before she moved on to another pub.

HORRIBLE MURDER IN EAST LONDON

Friday 31st August 1888

Scarcely has the horror and sensation caused by the discovery of the murdered woman in Whitechapel some short time ago had time to abate, when another discovery is made, which, for the brutality exercised on the victim, is even more shocking, and will no doubt create as great a sensation in the vicinity as its predecessor.

The affair up to the present is enveloped in complete mystery, and the police have as yet no evidence to trace the perpetrators of the horrible deed.

The facts are that as Constable John Neil was walking down Bucks-row, Thomas-street, Whitechapel, about a quarter to four o'clock this morning, he discovered a woman between thirty-five and forty years of age lying at the side of the street with her throat cut right open from ear to ear, the instrument with which the deed was done tracing the throat from left to right.

The wound was an inch wide, and blood was flowing profusely.

She was immediately conveyed to the Whitechapel Mortuary, when it was found that besides the wound in the throat the lower part of her abdomen was completely ripped open, with the bowels protruding.

No wonder the local women were terrified. The East End was one of the poorest districts in London, with a reputation for violent crime. Ewer Street was so dangerous that the police wouldn't dare venture there. But this level of ferocity was shocking even for Limehouse.

Pearl heard a familiar, high-pitched chuckle. At last – she'd found him. O'Dwyer was talking to a couple of porters, accompanied by some good-time gals. She tapped him on the shoulder. 'Hello, Uncle Peter. It's been an age. Why haven't you been to see me?'

His eyes widened as he cocked his head to one side, then leered: 'Alright darlin'. Let's go out to the yard,' he said gruffly. His companions cheered.

Before Pearl could say another word, O'Dwyer grabbed her hand and they made their way out of a side door. He ignored her howl of protest until they were in the darkness of the backyard. She could just make out his angry scowl.

'That's a nice welcome, Uncle Peter. Besides, what are you doing out of uniform? Surely you'll get in trouble for that. And what have you grown that ridiculous beard for?' Pearl eyed the luxurious facial hair that now covered most of the policeman's face.

Her uncle said sternly: 'Never mind me. What are you doing here? You'll get taken for a dollymop if you hang around the Ten Bells. Your Pa would be turning in his grave.'

'Are you on secret police business? No one would tell me where you were.'

'Just make yourself scarce. This is no place for you to be.'

Pearl chuckled at O'Dwyer's clothes. He wore a scarlet jacket that had seen better days, and a bright yellow kerchief was tied around his neck. 'Quite the dandy. Why are you dressed up like a cardsharp down on his luck?'

O'Dwyer made a shushing motion. 'Watch your mouth! Folk don't know me round here. I'm undercover, trying to get the local chatter on the Whitechapel murders, and what local crims won't tell police. Keep it down or you'll blow my disguise.'

'Sorry, Uncle Peter, but I've been trying everywhere to find you. Now I understand why no one would tell me.'

The policeman grunted. 'Been assigned to keep close to the pubs and catch any talk on Saucy Jack. Orders from the Metropolitan Police's Criminal Investigation department.' He puffed out his chest.

'I hope you find him,' Pearl said fervently, 'but I came here to ask for your help, Uncle Peter. A man was killed at Wapping Old Stairs. He died in my arms and I'm trying to find out who done him in.'

'Heard about that. Chinese, wasn't he? But ah, no. Can't go meddling.'

'You know how foreigners are treated. Remember how you used to stop people having a go at me? Please, for the sake of my father. We missed you at his wake and funeral.'

O'Dwyer removed his tattered bowler hat and tugged at his hair. 'There was bad blood between me and PJ. It happened just after you left. Fought over a woman. Can't say I'm proud of it. My condolences to you, sweetheart. Anyways, you're now the new landlady at The Sailor's Arms.' He beamed at her.

Pearl winced. 'Don't tell me you fought over Betty?'

Her uncle looked sheepish. 'What can I say? I was a fool in love. Then I found out she was only after money. I tried telling PJ, but he wouldn't listen.'

'She's out for everything last penny and farthing. Betty says she got wed to Pa. Did you know they were married?'

O'Dwyer wrinkled his brow. 'I don't know, but that woman won't stop at nothing. You've got to fight for that pub or you could lose it. Go and talk to a lawyer about inheritance, get someone official on it. Know where you stand.'

'That may be, but Betty's not budging from the pub, and I'm not staying under the same roof as her. I'm stopping with Ma Jennings – you know, Lizzy's mum – at the lodging house on Pennyfields, until I can find a way to kick Betty out.'

Raised voices nearby made her uncle look behind him sharply.

'Best you were off, I've got work to do. Be careful. Don't want you ending up as the next poor girl ripped wide open, your bowels hanging out.'

'Please, Uncle Peter. My father always said to turn to you if I was in trouble. If you could keep an ear out for me, if there's any word about the dead man on Wapping Old Stairs . . . His name was Ah Sim. I heard local talk that there's someone called the Blue Man, who might have done it. Have you heard of him?'

The policeman chewed at the ends of his moustache. 'Yes, that name's come up, but we don't know who he is. Annoying, really. I'm supposed to be looking for this Whitechapel killer, but all I'm hearing about is this Blue Man.'

'Do you think the killings could be done by the same man?'

'Possibly. But my gut is telling me it's two different culprits. I think the Whitechapel suspect only kills women. Nasty.'

'Have you heard any other talk or anyone else who might know something? Please, Uncle Peter. I've made the acquaintance of the dead man's sister. She's distraught and I'm the only one helping her.'

'I'll see what I can do. If you need me, I'll be in the Three Crowns tomorrow. That's my new spot for a while.'

'Is there anything else you can tell me?'

O'Dwyer took in Pearl's strained expression and stroked his beard. 'I do have one suggestion, but you won't like it.'

'I'm all ears.'

'You might want to talk to your old pal Lizzy. She's got her finger in every racket around here. Her husband's a Chinaman so he'd know the local gossip with his lot. We think Lizzy's running the opium business here. We're keeping an eye on her, but we've got no proof yet, and she's paid most of the coppers round the West India Docks to look the other way.'

'Really? Lizzy mixed up in drugs? I would never have thought it. She gave Ah Sim odd jobs occasionally and Mei works at her laundry. So she might well know something. Do you think Ah Sim was mixed up with the drug smuggling?'

'Aye, could be. Where there's drugs, there's danger, and plenty would kill for the money.'

Pearl hesitated. 'I didn't leave here on the best of terms with Lizzy. She might not want to see me.' With a shudder, Pearl thought back to the last time she had set eyes on her childhood friend.

Lizzy had coiled a lock of bright ginger around her forefinger. 'I've got something to tell you,' she giggled, prancing around Pearl's attic bedroom. 'It's about Tommy. I'm sweet on him. Fallen for him something rotten.' Lizzy laughed again, exultant.

'Oh, no, Lizzy . . .' Pearl was about to say more, that she and Tommy were eloping that night, Portsmouth bound, but Lizzy rushed on. 'I know he's a wrong 'un, but I understand him. We're alike, we two.' Pearl just didn't have the heart to break the news to Lizzy about her impending departure. She took the coward's way out and disappeared without a backward look, so desperate for a new life.

But it didn't take long for wedded bliss in Portsmouth to wither into disappointment. 'What are you doing here?' Pearl had yelled at Tommy after spotting her husband outside the Derby Tavern, laughing with a disreputable gaggle of dockers. 'I thought you were going down to the docks to see if there were any ships leaving tomorrow.'

Tommy was unsuccessfully trying to hide a pint of porter behind his back. 'Wife! Go back home and put my dinner on.' He shot a glance at his mates who sniggered into their beers. A woman staggered out of the pub, looked around, then honed in on Tommy.

'There you are, Treasure. You promised me another drink before we go upstairs.'

Without a word, Pearl turned on her heel. She was halfway up Angerstein Road when a voice called out to her: 'Wait up a bit!' She continued walking until Tommy caught hold of her arm. 'Pearl, let me explain, it's not how it looks.'

'I don't want to hear your excuses. I'm tired of them.'

'Hear me out, my lovely Peking Pearl.' He started singing in his rich baritone: *'Ah, give me the girl with the bonny brown hair. Your hair of brown is the talk of the town.'* Tommy went down on one knee in front of her, clutching his heart.

Pearl laughed in spite of herself, and then sighed. 'What's your story this time?'

'Those men I was talking to, they want me in on a real money maker.'

'Well, what is it?'

'Cock fighting!'

'Oh no, Tommy . . .'

'This is the big time, my love. I'm going to be rich.'

'You are the most foolish man I have ever met.' A red mist was forming in front of her eyes. 'What happened to us? You promised me we would travel the world, visit China. Instead I'm working three nights a week at The Golden Eagle, just to make ends meet. I'm back in a pub! And I won't ask you about that woman.'

'Pearl, I love you. I've got no idea who she is, must be some mistake.'

Torn between tears and fury, Pearl rounded on him. 'I don't care. I wish I'd never married you.'

11

Some street urchins had set fire to a broken-down cart and tossed the carcass of an old nag onto the pyre. She wondered if they were intending to devour it. A cloud of smoke from the blaze enveloped her as she crossed West India Dock Road and turned left onto Castor Street, eyes smarting, the smell of horse meat nauseating.

At the corner of Oriental Street and Morant Street, she stopped in front of a double-fronted shop. The billboard above the cornice was in the design of a Chinese blue willow pattern. Pearl looked up at it closely; a man in a boat, with two birds fluttering in the sky. Above the billboard were Chinese characters traced in gold, red and black: 龍門客棧餐廳. Underneath was the English translation: *The Dragon Inn restaurant*.

The windows were misty with condensation, but Pearl could just make out the scurrying, blurry figures of waiters, holding large platters of food above their heads.

There was the sound of laughter and faint melodies of a Chinese opera. Pearl stood in front of the ebony-panelled door, admiring its brass door knocker, a sinuous, snarling dragon. Surely this couldn't be Lizzy's restaurant? Pearl had been curious to see how her old friend was doing these days. But now that she had arrived, she wasn't feeling so bold. She was suddenly nervous of Lizzy's reaction at seeing her.

The door opened, and a man, probably around sixty years of age, peered out, squinting at her. He wore a yellow and red satin shirt. Perched on top of his head was a black silk skullcap.

He smiled. 'Welcome to The Dragon Inn. Best Peking duck in London.'

Pearl stood on the threshold, drinking it all in. Lizzy's establishment was certainly fancy. The room was packed with West End swells, not an East End accent among them, decked out in white tie and tails. Waiters scurried between tables, carrying silver platters piled high with mounds of steamed rice, stir-fried egg noodles, vegetables, honey roast pork and steamed monkfish. Her mouth watered; the food looked delicious.

A high-pitched shriek cut through the rumble of conversations in the restaurant. Pearl closed her eyes. Lizzy's laugh.

As a young girl, her childhood friend's piercing cackle turned the heads of road sweepers and organ grinders, who stopped what they were doing to see what that fearful racket was. But it had been one of the loveliest sounds in Pearl's childhood. She had heard it every day, right up until her sixteenth birthday, and then she heard it no more.

And here Lizzy was, those incredible ginger curls unmistakable, blazing as a glorious summer sunset. Lizzy moved through the tables, twisting this way and that, her silk turquoise gown cinched in tight at the waist. Lizzy chatted to a gentleman, placing a hand lightly on his shoulder. A thick gold ring on the third finger of her left hand caught the light, with a large diamond engagement ring next to it. It looked extremely expensive.

Lizzy laughed again, but it had shifted to a more coquettish giggle, as she toyed with the curls at the back of her neck. She was still talking away to the gentleman who continued to spoon rice into his mouth; some of it had not reached its target, the little white grains embedded in his beard.

Her childhood friend was wearing a gown cut daringly low. A stark difference from the young girl who was so modest that she was always bundled up from head to toe in scarves and thick stockings. Where was the bashful teenager who stayed in the shadows and clung on to Pearl? Who would often hide out at The Sailor's Arms, chalk-white and clutching her belly, wincing with pain. The Lizzy in front of her now was a completely different person, and Pearl marvelled at her ease in these surroundings. 'Bring out the roast lobster for the honourable duke.' Lizzy snapped her fingers at the nearest waiter. She turned to beam again at the gentleman. 'It's the finest you'll ever eat, My Lord, I promise you. I paid a pretty penny for Shanghai's best chef to work in my kitchen.'

Lizzy turned to a man standing next to her, who was much shorter; his red silk jacket stretching at the seams, tightly buttoned up to his thick neck. She put an arm round his shoulder. 'My husband Soo Chow brought him back personally.'

Her voice, once as high-pitched as a choir boy, was now transformed into a husky contralto. Lizzy was all grown up. Pearl had pushed memories of Lizzy to the furthest corners of her mind during the years in Portsmouth, but now, confronted with the confident Lizzy of today, suddenly felt shy. She was seized with a temptation to turn tail and run.

But there was Mei. Pearl had promised to help. Otherwise, Ah Sim would be just another dead foreigner to the police, unmourned and unloved by his adopted town, who didn't want him here in the first place.

Lizzy was in full throttle, telling an amusing anecdote to the duke, her arms waving around like windmills. Then she stopped suddenly in mid-sentence, frozen, like a waxwork model. She had caught sight of Pearl. Pearl waved at her, like a passenger on a ferry boat, greeting a friend on the docks, feeling slightly foolish.

Lizzy reddened slightly, eyes narrowing as she stared at Pearl, her jaw muscles tensing. Then she grinned, revealing sharp little canines. And in Lizzy's mocking grin, Pearl knew she was taking in her drab, unkempt clothes.

Pearl's boots were caked with mud, a small hole evident where her big toe had worked its way through the leather. Lizzy's boots were a shining gold; high-buttoned and sharply pointed at the tips with a dainty high heel. As she walked, pretty little bells on the tassels jingled mellifluously.

Lizzy walked towards Pearl, a strident step, hands on hips. She stood so close that Pearl nearly took a step back, but she held her ground.

'Well, look what the cat dragged in,' Lizzy said in a raspy whisper.

'Hello, Lizzy. You're looking very well.'

Lizzy narrowed her eyes. 'I wondered whether you'd be back. Heard your Pa died. The old bastard finally hopped the twig.'

'Oh, he wasn't so bad.'

'Since when?' Lizzy raised her eyebrows. 'You were always out on the riverfront wanting to get away from his prying eyes.'

Pearl looked away. 'That was a long time ago, I can hardly remember.'

'I remember everything.' Lizzy twisted a curl behind her ear. 'And how's Tommy, your dear husband?' The question was spat out, like an insult.

'He drowned. Went down with his ship in the Indian Ocean.'

'Yes, I did know that. Just wanted to see your face when I asked you.' Lizzy's lips pressed together, white.

'Oh, Lizzy, can't we just forget what happened all those years ago? Tommy and I were young and selfish.'

Lizzy moved closer. 'You're right, it was a long time ago. Best thing you ever did was leave here. Meant I wasn't walking in your shadow. Just look at me now.' Lizzy jerked her thumb at the crowded restaurant.

'All mine. I'm rich, I've got a husband who adores me, and two businesses that bring in a mint. See these boots?' Lizzy pointed her toe like a ballet dancer. The little bells trilled. 'Soo Chow bought them for me. Made in Italy with the finest leather and workmanship. That's real gold leaf. You won't find another pair like 'em in Limehouse, or probably in all of London.' Her eyes gleamed, staring at the missing buttons on Pearl's coat. 'Looks like the years haven't treated you so well.' But then she looked at Pearl suspiciously.

'What did you really come here for? Surely not to talk about the good old days of childhood.'

'While I was in town, I thought I'd see you. To be honest, I was intrigued to see how things turned out, and to apologise for leaving that night without telling you. It's been seven long years. It's good to see you, Lizzy.' Pearl smiled. But was that true? The adult Lizzy had lost her softness, there was only bitterness and boasting. Cruelty, even.

A small part of Pearl had wondered if they could rekindle their friendship, but this now seemed an impossibility. They were more like strangers. Besides, she reminded herself, she was really here to gather more information, to find out what kind of work Ah Sim had been doing for Lizzy.

Lizzy's eyes bored into Pearl, trying to read her thoughts. 'Nice of you to drop in, but there's really nothing more we have to say to each other. You've had a gander, now go.'

As Lizzy turned away, Pearl called after her: 'You've done so well for yourself. This place is wonderful. And you married! When we were young, do you remember telling me your dream about owning a restaurant and inviting dukes and duchesses? Looks like you've accomplished that. Did you also get your diamonds and emeralds?'

Slowly, Lizzy turned back. 'Yes, I have, more than I dreamt possible. My office is like an Aladdin's cave, filled with jewels and gold, and a few extra delights.'

'I'd love to see them.' Pearl made a face, looking down at her own clothes. 'I've not done so well since Tommy died.' Pearl held her breath, wondering if she had overdone the poor widow act.

Lizzy hesitated, her mouth twisted into a thin line.

'Do you remember a promise you made to me when we were nippers? You said you would drink Champagne every day, twice on Saturdays. Will you not keep your promise now with me?'

Lizzy shrugged, keeping her eyes on Pearl. 'I did indeed. Come on then, I'll show you how much I've achieved since we were running barefoot on the foreshore.'

Leading the way through the tables, Lizzy walked up the first flight of stairs and gestured to Pearl to follow her along the corridor. The second door along the hallway had red and gold panelling and was flanked by two men. Pearl was surprised to see that one of them was Xianfan, her favourite lodger and tutor. She was about to greet him, but he looked away and wouldn't meet her gaze. What was he up to?

After the din of the restaurant, the office was quiet, the noise muffled by walls covered in a deep maroon damask wallpaper. A large tapestry decorated with a multi-coloured phoenix emerging from flames covered one wall.

'This is wonderful.' Pearl took in a long breath. It was one of the most lavishly decorated rooms she had ever seen.

Lizzy patted the curls at the back of her head. 'Taken a lot of hard work. It's been worth it, though.'

'There was something I wanted to ask you,' Pearl said quietly.

Lizzy snorted. 'I knew there was something else. Never straight, were you, Pearl? What is it – money? A job?'

'It's not for me, but for a friend, the sister of Ah Sim. He was killed down by The Sailor's Arms. I heard that he and Mei were working for you.'

Lizzy's eyes narrowed slightly. She moved to her desk and lit a cigarette.

'Do you know anything about what happened? Was Ah Sim in trouble? Mei is terribly upset.'

Lizzy took a long draw on her cigarette. 'Yes, Mei is a lovely girl. But her brother didn't work for me.'

'Really?'

'I don't know where you got that information from,' replied Lizzy, tapping ash into the large crystal ashtray.

'If there is anything you know, or find out, please do tell me.'

'I've no idea what happened. Probably a drunken fight. Never a night when someone doesn't get clobbered. You know how it is round here. Or maybe you've forgotten, although Portsmouth's pretty rough, I hear.'

'Yes, of course I remember.' Pearl laughed mirthlessly. 'Looks like you know everyone. But if you could ask around, we might get closer to knowing what happened to Ah Sim.'

Lizzy savagely ground out her cigarette. 'Not sure there's much I can do.'

'Just thought I'd ask. Now what about that Champagne you promised me, and then I'll be on my way.'

'I'll fetch a bottle of Krug Grande Cuvée Brut from the cellar. You couldn't afford anything like it. I keep it under lock and key. It's only for my best customers, old friends and enemies.'

Once Lizzy had left, Pearl scanned the room. The walls were

covered from floor to ceiling with paintings of seascapes and idyllic English countryside scenes. Every surface had knick-knacks, gewgaws and huge vases overflowing with flowers. She walked to Lizzy's desk by the window and opened a leather-bound ledger. Flicking through the pages, Pearl realised it was a detailed record of all her business transactions.

There were neat stacks of papers and trays piled in rows, each labelled in large, sprawling handwriting: butcher, brewery, fishmonger, furniture, candles, ironmonger, vegetable merchant, baker. Lizzy was very organised, keeping meticulous files and accounts of everything.

Pearl wondered what else she could find in this office. Lizzy had lied about not employing Ah Sim, and this was an opportunity to do some snooping. She didn't know what for, exactly, but she looked around, hoping for inspiration. Her eye was drawn to a black lacquer chest of drawers on the wall opposite Lizzy's desk. She ran her hands over the front, fingers tracing a Chinese emperor's hunting scene, inlaid with mother-of-pearl. She opened all the drawers one by one and looked inside. There was nothing that looked out of place, mainly more bills and expenditure concerning the running of the restaurant. She pulled at the bottom drawer, but it was locked. Pearl tutted in frustration. Lizzy could be back any minute.

Then she remembered a trick Xianfan had told her about. His mother once worked in the kitchens of the imperial household at the Forbidden City in Peking. Some of the servants knew about secret compartments in furniture used to hide money or jewellery. Pearl knelt in front of the chest of drawers and felt underneath it.

There was a small lever right at the back. She reached in and pulled hard: the bottom drawer sprung open. With trembling fingers, Pearl leafed through an accounts ledger. Each page had a title in red ink, followed by a row of numbers, dates and names: police payments, Mah Jong gambling takings, monies ascribed to the dockmaster. Her uncle was right, Lizzy was involved in some very dubious payoffs to various officials in Limehouse.

As Pearl shuffled the papers around, she found a tiny, gold key inscribed with 福, the Chinese symbol for good luck. But there was no clue what the key was for, and still absolutely nothing about Ah Sim.

She moved to the large wardrobe to the right of the door, which was filled with fur wraps, dresses, shoes and hats. She rifled through coat pockets, opened the hat boxes, but uncovered nothing of note. Lizzy had spent a fortune on her finery; there was enough here to feed at least six families for several months.

The office kept tight hold of its secrets. Pearl looked around the room once again. Her eyes lingered over the brilliant colours of the tapestry. She stood in front of it, touching its lush surface, admiring the skilful embroidery. The phoenix's feathers glimmered golden. Its aquamarine wings were spread wide, emerging from the incandescent flames. Was this how Lizzy saw herself, rising from the ashes to be reborn into the woman she always wanted to be?

As a child, Lizzy had a favourite hiding place; a secret alcove in her bedroom, hidden behind a poster of Eugene Sandow, the Amazing Muscleman. Perhaps . . . Pearl pushed the tapestry to one side. There was a small strong box in a wall recess. Pearl turned the handle, hoping against hope it would open. But it remained firmly locked. She ran back to the chest of drawers to grab hold of the golden key inscribed with the good luck symbol.

It fit snugly into the strong box keyhole. As the little door sprung open, Pearl inhaled a sweet, fragrant scent. She breathed in deeply, again and again. She caressed the packages, fingertips lightly skimming the silk fabric they were wrapped in. Opium.

Her nepenthe, her joy; the drug of forgetfulness and oblivion. How she had missed it!

There were so many packets, perhaps up to twenty, all wrapped in a distinctive orange cloth. A huge amount of money, worth stealing or perhaps even killing someone for.

Pearl's fingers twitched. She took one package and quickly slipped it into her coat pocket. She thrust her hand further into the secret compartment, checking if there was anything else worth looking at. There were bundles of envelopes, again each with a name written on the front. She shook her head. Lizzy's scrupulous bookkeeping would be her downfall. Pearl went through each of them. The third one she opened had money in it. There was a note in a beautiful script on the front. Where had Lizzy picked up such wonderful penmanship?

Wapping Old Stairs shipment, Ah Sim to collect and deliver 鸦片*. Fee – one sovereign.*

Pearl recognised the Chinese symbol for opium. Ah Sim had been working for Lizzy in some very nefarious business. Her childhood pal knew much more than she was letting on. Pearl slipped this in her pocket as well. A thought bubbled up. Why was Lizzy hiding the fact that she had employed Ah Sim, and could she know something about his murder on Wapping Old Stairs? Pearl could scarcely believe it, but the change in Lizzy was remarkable. Who knew what she was now capable of.

Pearl's heart constricted at the thought of Mei's reaction to news that her brother had been involved in delivering opium. But then Mei could have been keeping this from Pearl to protect his reputation. Pearl had to admit it, getting Mei to reveal her secrets was like prising open an oyster shell.

A loud crash echoed out in the corridor, and Lizzy was screaming insults at a waiter who had dropped some plates and glasses. Pearl hastily closed and locked the strong box door, rearranged the tapestry and returned the golden key to the chest of drawers. The packet of opium felt heavy in her pocket.

There was a soft tread of footsteps outside the door. Pearl quickly flung herself onto a chaise longue in the corner of the room just as Lizzy came in, carrying a Champagne bottle and two glasses.

'Such gorgeous upholstery.' Pearl ran a hand over the fabric. 'You have excellent taste.'

'I have nothing but the finest. The chaise you are sitting on cost me two guineas, imported it all the way from France.' Lizzy was in high spirits as she popped the cork with a practised hand. The Champagne fizzled as it was poured into the crystal glasses.

'A toast. To romance, heartache and the dear departed. My condolences for losing the two men closest to you.' Lizzy's eyes were glinting.

Pearl sucked in her breath; Lizzy's barbs had hit their mark. But she inclined her head. 'You really shouldn't hold on to old grudges. It's not good for your complexion.'

Lizzy gave a half shrug and clinked glasses with Pearl. The Champagne was smooth, with a kick. A pleasant, slow burn started in Pearl's stomach. She felt light-headed and giddy. Lizzy splashed out another glass of Champagne for herself, but didn't refill Pearl's proffered glass. 'You took me for a fool.' A mottled pink flush was creeping up Lizzy's décolletage.

'You were my best friend. For the life of me, I never understood why Tommy preferred you to me. And I knew you didn't really care for him. You were just using him to get away from your father. I tried telling him that, but he wouldn't listen. You – his Peking Pearl. That's what he used to call you.' Lizzy took a swig from the bottle.

Pearl opened her mouth to reply but the bitterness continued pouring forth from her former friend. 'I know what you are.' Lizzy jabbed a talon-like nail at Pearl. 'It took me years to understand. Why you wanted to sneak off to the penny gaffes and watch chorus girls kicking up their legs, singing bawdy songs.'

Pearl longed to get away from Lizzy's knowing, jeering laugh. The opium was pulsing, throbbing in her pocket and she was worried Lizzy would suspect her papers had been rifled through.

She tried to appear unruffled. 'You've become bitter, Lizzy. It's ugly, your behaviour is ugly, and all this finery can't hide that.' Pearl got up to leave. 'I'll see myself out.' She slammed the office door, running as quickly as she could down the stairs and out of The Dragon Inn.

SEPTEMBER

12

There was a jumble of boxes and suitcases filling the hallway of the Fragrant Blossoms. 'Are you sure your sister's house is big enough for all of this stuff? You're only going for a few weeks.' Pearl's shoulders were aching from carrying down Ma Jennings' possessions.

'Plenty of room in those Ramsgate houses. Be lovely to stay with my sister. She says the sea air will be good for my lungs after all this Limehouse smog.' Ma coughed and held a handkerchief to her mouth.

Xianfan stood at the door. 'Take care and try not to sit in a draught on the coach. Safe journey.'

'There's a pet. All the best to you, Xianfan. Look out for Pearl. I'll be back before you know it.'

There was a rumble of hooves clattering outside the front door. 'You'd best be off. Goodbye, Ma. My best to your sister. I'll write. Don't be gone too long now.' Pearl's throat was constricting. She'd grown very fond of Ma.

Ma gave a wheezy chuckle. 'If you don't send me news on how you're getting on, I'll be on the first stagecoach back from Ramsgate quicker than a minnow can swim a dipper!'

A hazy mist hovered over the water and the sun made its way above the horizon as Pearl gazed out of her bedroom window.

There was so much to do at the lodging house. Pearl spread her arms wide; she was looking forward to being in sole charge while Ma Jennings was in Ramsgate. But she would also miss her friend's throaty laugh and ready jokes. And the old woman's cough was getting worse; everyone agreed that the sea air would do her the world of good.

Nebulous shapes shimmered above the rippling surface of the tide. With a jolt, Pearl thought of Ah Sim prone on the foreshore, the water immersing his body. Would she ever discover the truth about what happened to him? Uncovering what he was involved in meant revealing unpleasant truths. She wasn't looking forward to having a conversation with Mei about Ah Sim's involvement with Lizzy's opium business. How much did his sister really know about what her brother was up to? Pearl didn't want to be the bearer of bad tidings to Mei.

But perhaps she was reading more into the situation than it warranted. Ah Sim might just have been an innocent bystander, caught in the wrong place at the wrong time. But no, she had a gnawing feeling there was something sinister lurking in Limehouse.

Pearl yawned and rubbed her eyes. By dawn's early light, she slowly felt her way down the stairs and lit the gas lamps, which protested and sputtered into life. It was early still, and she loved this time of quiet, just before her lodgers stirred. She felt like the only person awake in the world.

Pearl lit the fire and placed a large pot of mutton broth on the stove. It steamed and bubbled as she stirred it slowly, adding ginger and fresh watercress.

She tasted the congee, making sure it was hot and spicy, and she started to hear the shuffling footsteps of her lodgers upstairs, preparing for the day of work ahead at the docks.

By five o'clock in the morning, the parlour was a blur of noise and bustle, her lodgers chattering in a mixture of Cantonese, Hokkien and Mandarin. Pearl listened to snippets of their conversation, complaining about their poor wages, which were much lower than the Irish dockers, about their aching backs and then talking about girls back home in China. There was a mention of Mei, the Chinese girl in town. They giggled and nudged each other, waggling their eyebrows. She moved closer to hear more, and caught the scent of opium. Her mouth watered and a sudden craving entered her body. Such a vanilla-sweet aroma, and so deeply delicious.

The lodgers had taken their morning pipe. Pearl watched them enviously. That's why they were all so animated so early in the day, their eyes bright with feverish energy. If only she could have a pipe! Pearl closed her eyes, her body aching for that sweet lassitude, the forgetfulness of all troubles and the delicious bubble of joy that the haze of opium brought. But she knew where that dark, meandering road would lead, and didn't want to end up there ever again. She had sworn off the poppy and would do her damnedest to keep away from its siren call. The opium taken from Lizzy's office was just to test herself – to prove that she could truly do without it – and never fall down that well again. It was also evidence of what Lizzy was up to and her connection with Ah Sim. She decided to wait until she had more information on what exactly was going on before telling Mei.

Pearl nodded to Yat San, a skinny young boy of seventeen. He was growing so quickly that his trousers only reached to his calves. Xianfan had told Pearl that Yat San had worked in the boiler room of a ship on the Canton to London route.

When Yat San fainted because of long hours working in front of the fiery heat of the coal furnace, he was badly beaten by the engineer. 'So he decided to jump ship in London and I found him sleeping in a doorway near the docks,' Xianfan confided in Pearl.

Since then, the young boy had followed Xianfan around like a devoted puppy. Pearl looked fondly at the smooth-cheeked youth, refilling his bowl of congee. He ate greedily.

Xianfan sighed deeply. Pearl looked at him, concerned. 'Is anything the matter, *baakfuh*?' He smiled, clearly touched by her calling him 'uncle'. They hadn't spoken since seeing one another at Limehouse Lizzy's. Pearl had wanted to talk about it, but Xianfan seemed intent on pretending it had never happened. Times were tough, and Pearl guessed that Xianfan was doing whatever it took to earn a few pennies.

'The dockmaster is keeping back two days' wages from Xianfan for being late. But it is a lie,' Yat San blurted out.

Xianfan shushed the young boy, his brow creased with deep furrows. 'No need to trouble Mrs Fitzgerald, I will have money to pay rent.'

Pearl knew that dockmasters routinely tried to cheat Chinese sailors out of their money, thinking, often correctly, that they had no one to turn to for help. 'I could come down and vouch for you if that would help?' Pearl offered, trying to protect Xianfan's dignity. 'Sometimes a well-placed entreaty from a lady can't be refused.'

'Miss Pearl, I would be most grateful.' His face, weathered by sun and rain, creased into a thousand wrinkles as he grinned, showing his gums.

'Let's go to the West India Docks now to speak with the old rascal, and while we're walking there, can we continue with our lessons?' Xianfan had resumed teaching Pearl the classics of Chinese literature, pleased that she had kept up her studies while in Portsmouth.

As they left the lodging house, Xianfan began to recite *The Dream of the Red Chamber*. 'You must listen to the rhythm and then you will truly understand such great writing.'

At the junction just east of St Anne's Church and into Commercial Road, Xianfan began talking in earnest. '*The Dream of the Red Chamber*' is most eloquent and the human characters are so true to nature, being neither wholly good nor bad. The story shows it is possible to step beyond your humble beginnings. Take the character of Xiangyun. She was orphaned in infancy and her aunt treats her with great unkindness. But Xiangyun remains of noble heart. She is also admired for her striking looks, and fondness for dressing in men's clothing.'

Pearl listened with keen interest. 'I am an orphan now, similar to Xiangyun.' How would her life have been different, had her mother lived? Even a vague memory of a maternal presence, kind and comforting, would have been something to hold on to, but there was nothing. At times, she keenly felt the lack of a guiding presence, especially growing from childhood to becoming a woman. Her father had been no help at all.

Xianfan continued. 'But Xiangyun has many faults. She is forthright and tactless, but means well. Often becoming involved in other people's business. Her husband dies shortly after their marriage. Tragedy follows her at every turn, and she remains a dutiful widow for the rest of her days.'

Pearl said nothing, but wondered if Xianfan was sending her a veiled message.

It was still early when they arrived at West India Docks, but already hundreds of men, many of them Irish, plus a few Indians, Chinese and West Indians, were shuffling along on the walkways, spitting chewing tobacco into the river and hawking up great yellowish-green gobbets of phlegm. Pearl also recognised a few of her lodgers waiting for the daily Call On, anxiously hoping to be chosen as the lucky few for work on the ships.

She could see a crowd of white men glaring at her lodgers.

No, it wasn't her imagination, they were definitely looking at the Chinese men with hate-filled eyes. 'Bloody foreigners coming into our country and stealing our livelihoods,' said one fellow in a loud voice.

Xianfan shuffled beside her, looking down at his shoes. He kept his head bent, shoulders slumped, trying to make himself as small as possible. Pearl's thoughts drifted to Mei, wondering if she had experienced such hostility since arriving in Limehouse. If she had, it was no surprise Mei was cautious and distant. Pearl wondered what she could do to break through that curtain of reserve, but perhaps her offer of friendship was undesired. That familiar mantle of loneliness settled on her shoulders.

'Xianfan! Over here, matey!' Pearl looked round to see who had called her lodger. Just by the tobacco warehouse stood a group of men, set apart from the rest. They were dressed in blue linen outfits, including their shirts, trousers and caps. In fact, from head to toe, they imbued the very essence of blue.

Xianfan waved back, then turned to Pearl. 'The indigo dye men are my friends. They must be finished with loading carts from the Jewry Street warehouse and come to collect their wages.'

Pearl cocked her head to one side, like a fox terrier picking up a scent in the air. She had seen the indigo dye men once before as a child, when her father took her to the docks. Pearl's mind was whirling. Why hadn't she thought of them before? Could one of the indigo dye labourers be the Blue Man that the locals and Uncle Peter had spoken about?

'Let's talk to them,' Pearl said, her breath coming quick and fast.

A man came forward and shook Xianfan's hand vigorously. Her lodger greeted him warmly and turned to Pearl. 'This is Jeremiah, who loves a good game of Blackjack. A wily player and wins often.' Xianfan laughed ruefully.

'Pleased to make your acquaintance,' Pearl said. She needed to get to know this man better. She took in his powerful, stocky build, the pronounced stoop to his shoulders, bowed from years of lifting heavy indigo dye sacks. It wouldn't take much effort for him to have won a fight with Ah Sim.

Jeremiah noticed Pearl staring at him, thinking she was interested in his unusual appearance. She looked away hastily, but he laughed. 'We are from a noble profession, and keep to ourselves, apart from the other dock workers. And there are people like us all over the world. The Tuareg tribe are called the Blue Men of the Sahara Desert. They smear the indigo colour on their skins to protect them from the hot sun. They also say it protects them from evil spirits. I saw them with my own eyes when I sailed to Africa.'

A ripple went through the crowd and in an instant, the atmosphere had changed from apprehension to agitated animation. 'Must be half past seven. Time for the Call On,' Jeremiah said.

A rumble of deep, baritone voices grew louder, with a top note of anxiety, as a huge throng of men pushed forward towards the ships. The entire area of the docks was filled with writhing bodies, standing closely together, shoulder butting shoulder, pushing and shoving to get a better vantage point. A rope held them back, otherwise they would have rushed forward and boarded the ships.

A frantic scramble broke out amongst the men. 'Don't think you're getting ahead of me! I've got seven kiddies and a wife to feed,' shouted one man. He was small, perhaps five foot two, but his fists were quick and lethal. Several men stepped out of his path, but then six more threw themselves on him and pounded him to the floor without mercy.

A man in a bright green coat swaggered along the walkway beside one of the ships. Portly he may have been, but he was agile as a monkey, pulling himself up onto the bridge of the ship. 'It's the calling foreman,' Jeremiah said. 'Everyone wants to catch his attention.'

The crowd of men started thrusting their hands high in the hair, waving and beckoning. They called the foreman by name: 'Ned! Neddie! Over here, my son.'

The wheedling, pleading and whistling kept on for some time. When that didn't work, the men started jumping on the backs of their fellows to lift themselves above the crowd. But the foreman ignored them all and after asking for quiet, started shouting out names from a book. As time went on, the remaining men became more frantic, realising that the chances of them being called for a day's hire were receding. And with that, the chance of a meal.

Xianfan also waved his hand in the air and called out, but someone kicked his leg from behind while another forced his arm down. A third gave him a swift punch in the stomach. Winded, he fell to the ground, curling up into a ball to protect himself. Pearl bent down to help Xianfan up, while Jeremiah shook his head. 'It's a rough business. Those hooligans are handy with their fists, especially if it means they can knock a foreigner down. Always ready for a fight.'

The voice of the foreman said briskly: 'That's it for today, we've got enough now. Off you go.' There were whoops and cheers from the men who had been successful. She saw the distraught faces of those who had not been chosen, the glares of anger and disappointment.

The leftover men turned their fury upon the foreman, who they previously had been entreating as if he was their best and dearest friend.

'God damn and blast the filthy cur! It's not a fair place to look for work when the fellows who are picked have already given the jumped-up bastard of a foreman a few bob,' one man growled. 'If I ever see him on a dark night, he'll get a real battering from me.'

The unlucky ones slowly walked away from the wharves, their heads bowed in defeat. They moved menacingly towards Xianfan, and were also eyeing up Pearl. 'Come on,' she said quickly. 'Let's go and find the dockmaster so you can get paid.'

Pearl turned to Jeremiah. 'I don't know my way around the docks very well. Would you mind accompanying us to the dockmaster's office? I'd be most grateful.'

He nodded. 'Happy to oblige a friend of Xianfan's. Follow me, it's the largest building near the gates.'

Pearl knocked loudly on the dockmaster's door. After a few minutes, she banged harder again with her fist. 'Mr Armstrong! Are you really going to ignore the pleas of a sailor's widow?' Pearl shouted as loudly as she could. It had the desired effect, as several Jack Tars on leave turned to look at her with sympathetic looks. 'Shame!' they called out. 'Can't trust that blasted dockmaster further than you can throw him.'

The door opened slightly and a man with a stained napkin round his neck peered at Pearl. Seizing her chance, Pearl pushed the door wider and slipped past him into the room, quickly followed by Xianfan and Jeremiah.

'Really, my dear lady. I must protest,' the dockmaster said.

'My dear Mr Armstrong, I apologise for disturbing you from your breakfast. But I am here on important business. I believe you owe this gentleman two days' wages. It would be wonderful to settle this matter now. He has rent to pay me, and I am tired of waiting,' Pearl said.

Xianfan was looking at the floor. Anywhere but at Armstrong. Jeremiah was enjoying the discomfiture of the dockmaster, and looking at Pearl with increasing respect.

Armstrong had retreated to safety behind his desk, scattered with the remains of his meal: bacon, sausages, eggs, potatoes, a large jug of beer and a plum pudding. The cramped room had book ledgers stacked against one wall, which looked close to falling on top of the dockmaster.

'This man has a record for tardiness. That's why his wages were docked.'

'Come now, Mr Armstrong.' Pearl walked towards him, stepping on papers littering the floor. 'You know that Xianfan is the most reliable of workers. He has been here on the docks for a long while now.'

Armstrong hesitated. 'Yes, he has, but I can't make exceptions. Otherwise everyone will be coming to me with their hard luck story.'

Pearl laughed derisively. 'I run a lodging house for Chinese sailors. This is affecting my business. If you don't pay them, they can't pay me. So, it's me you're cheating. I'm not afraid to go to the port authorities to complain about this. You might be able to pick on a poor docker, but I have connections here. Your superiors will be breathing down your neck before you can finish that fine breakfast of yours, looking at every detail of your accounts.' Pearl paused, letting her words sink in. 'I'm sure you wouldn't want that.'

Armstrong licked his lips nervously. 'Now steady on, young lady. Just this once I will settle the claim. There's no need to make such a fuss.' He fumbled around for a key in his pocket and unlocked a mahogany chest on the corner of the desk.

Pearl, Xianfan and Jeremiah suppressed their laughter until they were several yards from the dockmaster's office.

'You have quite the persuasive way, Miss Pearl. Can you always get people to do what you want?' Jeremiah asked.

'Quite often, but not always.' Pearl wished she had the same effect on Mei.

Having accomplished her mission of retrieving Xianfan's overdue wages, Pearl asked Jeremiah to take her around the docks. 'You must know so much about this place, I could listen to you for hours. I find it so fascinating.'

As they walked back along the wharves, Jeremiah recalled heart-rending tales of the men who, out of desperation, came here to find work on the quays. 'You get all sorts a-labouring here. Those that have fallen on hard times. The bankrupt butchers, publicans, grocers, old soldiers, old sailors, pensioners and thieves.'

Of particular interest to Pearl were the courtyards and alleyways around the docks, which Jeremiah told her were crammed with lodging houses where dock labourers, sack-makers and watermen stayed. She looked at the indigo dye man. 'Maybe you could ask around here if anyone wants to board at the Fragrant Blossoms lodging house. We've still got a few rooms to let,' she said.

They strolled past shops selling gear for ships and sailors. Pearl gazed into the windows, which were filled with brass sextants, chronometers and mariners' compasses, and her eyes grew wide as Jeremiah told her what they were used for and how much each item was worth in the pawn shop. They stopped at an art shop selling vividly coloured posters and paintings. One was of a Chinese circus act, an aerialist hanging upside down from a trapeze. Pearl's thoughts strayed yet again to Mei. How she would love to have seen her high-wire act.

They passed some wooden cages filled with screeching green parakeets. Pearl thought about purchasing one and sending it by mail cart to keep Ma Jennings company in Ramsgate.

'A life on the water is a good life, if you've got work,' Jeremiah was saying. 'With money jingling in your pocket, you can kit yourself out with new boots at the sailor's cheap shoe-mart, some canvas trousers, and a smart pilot coat. An oilskin nor'wester jacket on your back to keep you dry in a howling gale.'

Despite her initial misgivings about Jeremiah, Pearl was beginning to take to the indigo dye man, who had such a fascinating store of stories about life on the docks. But she needed to keep her guard up. They walked further along the wharves until they came upon a row of food shops. At the grocer's, Xianfan's stomach growled upon seeing the cases of meat and biscuits spread out invitingly in the windows. The butcher in his bloody apron walked briskly past, shouldering a brisket of beef on a tray.

A group of Jeremiah's friends were calling to them. They ambled over to the indigo dye men who were outside a warehouse, puffing on their clay pipes. They were standing around a beer barrel, which served as a table for their game of cards. Their skin, powdered with indigo pigment, gave them an eerie otherworldliness. She thought they looked majestic.

Xianfan greeted the men warmly.

'You old rascal, Xianfan. Are you in funds? Come and join the game,' they called.

To Pearl's dismay, her lodger pulled out the coins he had just been given by the dockmaster. There was a swagger to his shoulders. 'I will join you, I've plenty of money.'

Pearl was annoyed that Xianfan could be so foolish as to spend his wages just minutes after he had been given them, but knew it was not her place to say anything. He, however, sensed the disapproval.

'Maybe we play later,' he said, looking like a mournful basset hound.

'Maybe you think your luck won't hold. You Chinamen will spend your last penny on gambling, even if it gets you into trouble,' Jeremiah teased.

'Ah Sim was the worst. Such a bad player. Do you remember all the times he lost to you? He owed you so much money!' Xianfan was laughing heartily. He stopped suddenly, becoming aware that Jeremiah was glaring at him.

'I, I didn't mean . . .'

'Did Ah Sim play cards with you?' Pearl was on alert. 'So you knew him?'

Jeremiah's jaw was clenching and unclenching. After a long moment, he inclined his head. 'Yes, Ah Sim played cards with us, although I did not know him well.'

'But he was in debt to you,' Pearl insisted.

'It was really a trifling sum.'

Pearl looked at Xianfan. 'Is this true?' She knew her tutor was terrible at lying.

Xianfan's mouth trembled and he avoided Pearl's eye.

'Jeremiah, I only ask as I would be more than happy to pay Ah Sim's debt,' Pearl said. 'I know his sister and she would not want his honour besmirched.'

The indigo dye man hesitated, and looked out at the ships, their sails billowing in the wind. 'It is not good to speak ill of the dead.'

'That's very generous of you, but times are hard and I'm sure you could do with the return of what he owed you. It's only fair.'

Jeremiah inclined his head. 'True, and very generous of you. Ah Sim owed me near on sixteen shillings.'

Pearl raised an eyebrow. That was more than a month's wages for a dock worker. Was that enough to kill for? She'd known drag-down fights and fisticuffs at The Sailor's Arms kicking off for much less.

'I will find a way to pay you back. I am low on funds at the present but will pay you when I can.'

'That's very kind of you, Miss.' Jeremiah inclined his head to one side.

'Do you know if Ah Sim was in trouble? Was anyone angry

enough to kill him?' Pearl thought she might as well see if she could get anything out of him.

Jeremiah held up his hands as if to fend off the question. 'That's not my business. We played whist a few times, that's all.'

'Do you think Ah Sim was attacked because of his gambling?' Pearl persisted.

Jeremiah's demeanour altered to a forbidding chill. She had pushed too far and too quickly.

'If you know what's good for you, best not to ask such questions. As I said, don't go poking your nose where it don't belong. Could be dangerous for a woman alone.'

Xianfan patted Jeremiah gently on the arm in a conciliatory gesture. 'Now, now. Miss Pearl means no harm. Just upset about Ah Sim. She runs a lodging house where he stayed. His murder is bad for her business. No more Chinese workers means no more rent.'

A shrill whistle from one of the indigo dye men made everyone jump. 'Look lively, boys! Watchmen coming round the corner. Let's make ourselves scarce.'

The blue men silently picked up their playing cards and turned into the alleyways adjacent to the warehouses. Jeremiah gave Pearl a hard stare before slipping away.

Pearl was annoyed that Xianfan had not been more forthcoming. 'You knew Ah Sim had gambling debts and that he worked for Lizzy,' she said accusingly on their walk back to the lodging house. 'Was Jeremiah the only one Ah Sim owed money to?'

Xianfan kept his head bowed low, eyes focused on the cobblestones, saying nothing until they reached the Fragrant Blossoms. Finally he replied: 'As far as I know, yes. I say this for your safety. They had a quarrel and I heard Jeremiah threaten to kill Ah Sim if he didn't pay him the money he owed. Stay away from Jeremiah. It is not safe to see him on your own. He has done some very bad things.'

13

Pearl laced up her boots with a tight double knot; the heels were worn down nearly to the leather, and the hole at the big toe was getting bigger; they wouldn't last another winter. She scowled at herself in the full-length bedroom mirror, adjusting her hat so it sat more securely on her head, skewering in two hat pins. Not even a gale-force wind would dislodge it. A dark grey shawl was wrapped around her shoulders, so she could blend into the night.

Pearl's excitement at seeing Mei again was building. She was early for their meeting and now paced up and down the foreshore impatiently, scanning for a first sight of her. They had agreed to meet at Wapping Old Stairs as Mei wanted to see where her brother had been killed. She felt ready to pay her last respects. Pearl wanted to search the murder scene again for anything the police might have missed, even though the incident had occurred months ago. She looked out at the river; the tide was low, with clouds scudding in from the horizon. The early evening was still warm, but tempered with gusts of wind. In the far distance, she could make out the mudlarks nimbly picking their way along the treacherous shore, studded with broken glass and crockery, searching the stinking mud on the banks of the river for wood, metal, rope or coal from passing ships.

Pearl knew practically every single nook, cranny and hiding

place on Wapping Old Stairs. If anything was hidden here, she was sure she could find it.

She broke into a wide smile as Mei approached, and they looked at each other shyly. Leading the way, Pearl slowly and carefully walked down the moss-covered steps. Mei nearly slipped and was only prevented from tumbling by Pearl putting an arm around her waist. They gripped each other, laughing nervously. *If only you knew what I felt,* thought Pearl. *I'd like to keep my arms around you, at least for a little while longer. Would you mind?*

It was dusk, Pearl's favourite time of the day; light drizzle was making the pebbles shine as if they had been lightly varnished. A faint glow shone down on the steps from the windows of The Sailor's Arms behind them. There was a shrill scream, the sound of glasses smashing, followed by gales of laughter. Just another night at The Sailor's Arms.

Pearl had brought a lantern with her and the pale yellow circle guided them along the foreshore. 'I grew up in these byways, so keep close to me.' Pearl reached out a hand to Mei. She was well aware of the dangers lurking in the shadows.

As they looked out on the foreshore, the lights of ferries and skiffs bobbing in the waves, Mei asked: 'Is there anything else you can remember from that morning?'

'I haven't told anyone this, for fear of them not believing me, but I saw something very strange. There was a pool of a greenish liquid that glowed, beside Ah Sim's body. It was most peculiar, and I tried to get a closer look, but then the police came.' Pearl immediately regretted saying it out loud. 'Do you believe me?'

'Of course. Perhaps it was a spirit.' Mei's voice was hushed. 'It might have been supernatural, an aura, perhaps of Ah Sim's soul leaving his body.'

Pearl was relieved at Mei's trust in her, so looked around, hoping against hope to see remnants of the luminescence. Of course it would have been washed away by the tides.

They approached the spot on the foreshore where Ah Sim was killed. 'This is where your brother died.'

Mei knelt on the ground, placing both hands on the pebbles, her shoulders shaking with grief. The sobbing twisted at Pearl's heart. She pulled Mei up from the wet mud and held her tightly as she wept. It began to drizzle, dampening their clothes and making them shiver. In spite of the cold, Pearl could feel the heat of Mei's body pressed close to hers.

After a while, she reluctantly let go, moving back several yards to give Mei some privacy, so she could bid a final goodbye to her brother. It was nearly dark now, the lantern casting a halo of light as Pearl walked around the area, dislodging pebbles and broken bricks, in search of something, anything, that might help. The ground was littered with old beer barrels and fishing nets, their catch of yesteryear long since filleted and consumed. Pearl knelt down, crawling on her hands and knees to feel around the slimy pebbles and seaweed. She drew back hastily as her fingers closed around the slippery carcass of an eel, its innards wriggling with worms.

There was a sparkle of silver in the lantern light, something deep inside one of the beer barrels. Overcoming her repugnance at the rotting eel, she held her breath and crawled further inside to retrieve it.

Mei came over to her. 'Did you find anything?' Her voice was a crackled whisper.

Pearl stood up, a thick black cane with the head of a bulldog on its silver handle in her hand. 'I think I know who this belongs to.' She was about to say more when the baritone bark of male voices came closer.

'Quick!' she whispered to Mei, 'let's get behind these old beer barrels.' The two women crouched behind the splintered wooden containers, trying to make themselves as small and inconspicuous as possible. Pearl guessed they were sailors on shore leave by their talk, and hoped the men would be too drunk to notice them, but they were getting closer, their shouting louder and cruder. Any minute now and they would be discovered.

Pearl remembered the rotting eel; she felt around on the ground for it until her hand touched the clammy carcass. She hurled it at the sailors. It landed with a wet smack over a tar's back, making him shout with shock.

'What the blazes did you do that for?' he shouted at his mates. 'I'm covered in this filth!' The sailor ran at his companions, flinging the remains of the rotting eel at them as they ran in the direction of the pub, laughing and hollering.

Pearl looked at Mei, who was holding her hand over her mouth trying not to laugh. When the sailors were no longer in sight, the two women looked at each other, wide-eyed with relief. 'I can't believe you picked that disgusting thing up!' Mei said.

'Yes, but it worked.'

'But your hand.' Mei grimaced.

Pearl smelt her palm and pulled a face. 'Come on, let's hurry. We don't want to get caught again.' They were both laughing, on the edge of hysteria, as they clambered over sinews of old ropes and broken shards of pottery. Mei was still smiling, dancing and sliding between the pebbles and patches of moss.

Suddenly, a blow caught the side of Pearl's face and she fell to the ground, winded. Mei was shouting in Cantonese: 'Look out – he's got a knife!'

Pearl rolled over as a blade slashed through the air. She kicked out hard. 'Try that again and I'll break your leg.' Her early training at the pub came back instinctively.

A familiar voice broke through the gloom. 'Is that Pearl Fitzgerald? Damn and blast! What you doing a-creeping round Wapping Old Stairs on your own?'

'Old Jake?' Pearl croaked, rubbing her temple. 'My father would skillet you alive if he knew you'd laid a hand on me.'

'I didn't know it was you. Saw two figures coming towards me. Thought you was a thief. Startled me, right enough. Can't be too careful with a killer on the loose.' He sounded scared but indignant.

Mei crept from behind the remains of an old cart, her face glowing in the lantern light, which now lay crookedly on its side.

'Pearl, you know it's not safe for you to go gadding about unchaperoned. There's more thieves and vagabonds in Limehouse now, and much bolder now that PJ's no longer here to carry out his kind of justice. Especially with these Whitechapel killings. Not safe at all. Friend of yours?' Old Jake jerked his head over at Mei.

'This is Miss Mei Tan. She's the sister of Ah Sim, who was murdered here. I'm sure you remember that.'

'Yes, I sure do. I've heard talk about you, Miss Tan. Work for Limehouse Lizzy, don'tcha?' He licked his lips. 'Not often you see a young Chinese lady here.'

Mei crossed her arms, nodding slightly.

'Terribly sorry for your loss.' Old Jake removed his cap.

'We came here to see if the police missed anything. They don't seem in any hurry to find out who killed Miss Tan's brother,' Pearl said. 'What brings you out here?'

'Me? I'm just looking for pieces of scrimshaw to whittle away on a quiet night, as I often do. Slim pickings this evening.'

Pearl frowned. 'By the way, I found something of yours just here.'

Running back to the broken-down beer barrels, she retrieved the walking stick.

Old Jake gave a quick chuckle. 'Why, thank you, my dear. Don't know when I lost it. Someone must have stolen it from me.'

Pearl thought he looked extremely shifty. Her eye was throbbing. He was nearing seventy, but could still pack a punch. Tonight, he was lurking around at the murder scene, and for what reason? To retrieve his silver cane, perhaps, from the morning Mei's brother died? Old Jake was certainly capable of inflicting that terrible blow to his head.

'You never answered me that evening, when Ah Sim was killed. Were you there?'

His eyes narrowed. 'What are you accusing me of?'

'I'm simply piecing together what happened. You know everything that goes on round here. If there is anything at all . . . I'm sure you'd want to help Mei find her brother's killer.'

He scratched his whiskery chin. 'Come to think of it now, must have slipped my mind, but I was in The Sailor's Arms that morning. Went for a piss out the back, and I saw a woman running away mighty quick. I remember because she was wearing lovely gold boots. They had little bells on the side. I'm partial to a well-turned out ankle.' He winked.

Pearl's mind started racing. Was he implicating Lizzy?

Old Jake's eyes narrowed as he leaned in closer. 'Now let me give you some fatherly advice.' His voice lowered to a harsh whisper. 'This is no place for respectable ladies. That murder, your brother I mean,' he nodded towards Mei, 'probably two Chinkies fighting over an opium pipe. No offence to you both, but there's no changing the nature of Oriental folk.'

Mei stared straight at him, eyes blazing. 'We are hard-working people, just the same as everybody else.'

Jake's eyes glinted. 'No disrespect meant, my dear. Now then, I'm walking back as far as Butcher Row. Can I escort you ladies to the main thoroughfare?' He waved his cap with a flourish and bowed.

Both women shook their heads, anxious for him to leave.

'As you wish. And apologies for my rough treatment of you, Pearl. Didn't know it was you. I'd never do anything to hurt the daughter of PJ O'Dwyer, may he rest in peace. But you see what could happen? You just scared the living daylights out of me. Good evening to you ladies. Have a safe journey home.'

Pearl let out a sigh of relief as Old Jake walked away from them and clambered up the steps. She hesitated, wondering whether to ask Mei more about her brother. 'Is there any possibility that Ah Sim was involved in opium smuggling, and got into an argument, like Old Jake said?' she said in a rush.

Mei turned on her, eyes flashing. 'He would never have anything to do with opium. We have seen too many people waste their lives on the poppy. It is for weak people who have no willpower.'

'For some, opium is a way to cope with the hardships of life. It affords a little joy and escape from the pain of daily life. There's nothing wrong with that.'

Mei looked unimpressed, so Pearl changed the subject. 'We need to focus on Old Jake. That rascal's up to no good.'

They walked back towards the Fragrant Blossoms, each absorbed in their own thoughts. Pearl wondered about her father's old pal. His story made no sense whatsoever. Old Jake had never carved a piece of scrimshaw in his life, she was sure of that. Beating bargemen over the heads with his walking stick and robbing them was more like it.

Pearl cast her mind back, and it occurred to her that Old Jake hadn't had his trusty silver-topped walking stick with him since she had found Ah Sim on the foreshore. He was never without it. She remembered that at her father's wake, he had a wooden club with him instead.

Tonight, he had used his fists and a knife on her, rather than his 'Sailor's Priest', as he fondly called it, which had saved him from many a life-threatening encounter.

There were so many childhood memories of Old Jake expertly wielding that weapon, the silver top flashing in a mighty arc, knocking seven bells out of anyone who crossed him. Suspicion crawled up and down her spine like fire ants. He was involved somehow. And why was Old Jake casting suspicion on Lizzy, mentioning a woman in gold boots running away from the scene of the crime? Maybe to turn attention away from himself. They could even be involved in the murder together. She closed her eyes, trying to find connections between the two of them.

'Let's get back to the Fragrant Blossoms,' Pearl said reluctantly, then tentatively touched her temple. 'I've a powerful headache. Old Jake can still pack a punch!'

The lodgers who were still awake looked curiously at the two women, who were caked in mud, but asked nothing. Yat San enquired about the morning's breakfast and then murmured good night. Yawning, the lodgers trudged up to bed.

In the kitchen, Mei applied a bread poultice to Pearl's head; a bruise was blossoming just above her eyebrow. 'I hope it doesn't leave a permanent mark,' Mei said.

'I'm not worried. There's no man in Limehouse that will look at me anyway with my lack of genteel manners.' She was conscious of Mei being so close and would gladly have been punched again if it kept her closer.

'That's where you're wrong. You have very striking features. I can see both the east and the west in you. It's lovely.'

Pearl felt her face grow hot. 'I don't belong anywhere.'

'You belong everywhere.' Mei smiled. Then she added: 'Perhaps you should find a new husband. Someone who will look after you.'

'I don't need anyone to look out for me.' Pearl was vexed at Mei's remark. 'I do very well for myself. What about you? Do you have a sweetheart?'

Mei looked away. 'I have no time for such things.'

The silence between them lengthened. Glowing embers from the fireplace created undulating shadows on the walls. Every time Pearl asked Mei personal questions, there was that closed expression.

Pearl walked over to the pantry. 'Let's eat.'

Mei's face brightened at the suggestion. 'I've missed cooking so much. What do you have in the cupboard?'

'Everything you need. My lodgers come with spices and condiments from China. They get very homesick for their favourite dishes.'

Mei opened the pantry door and gave a murmur of satisfaction. She quickly pulled out dried red chilli pepper, star anise, five spice powder, turmeric powder, preserved plums and pickles of cabbage, radishes and cucumbers.

'Ahh, lap cheong! I haven't tasted that since I left China. I can make fried rice and sausage with sweet soy sauce.'

After dinner, Mei stoked the fire until the flames roared. 'I had a dream last night. The spirits of my ancestors were calling. They warned me about a man on the river who would do harm to someone close to me. It might have been a warning about Old Jake.'

'Are you sure?' Pearl asked.

'It must be. Ah Sim was also in my dream. His spirit cannot rest until I have avenged his honour. He will lead me to his killer from the other side, I'm sure of that. But please, I don't want to put you in any more danger; you have already been hurt on my behalf. I couldn't bear it if your face is scarred because of me.'

Pearl fought an impulse to caress Mei's cheek, to hold her in the warmth of the firelight. 'I wish I could take you back to The Sailor's Arms and offer you a sweet sherry. But it looks like my father gave the pub to Betty. She claims he married her and shouts at me like the devil incarnate any time I go back. I've lost my inheritance.'

Mei's brow wrinkled. 'That pub is worth much money. You should fight for what's yours. It was your father's and is your birth right.'

Pearl felt lighter. It was good to have someone on her side. 'Yes, I shouldn't just give up. My uncle suggested getting in touch with a lawyer to see where I stand legally. But first we need to find out what Old Jake was doing on Wapping Old Stairs.'

She thought back to their encounter with that scheming scoundrel on the foreshore. 'Old Jake might lead us to finding out more. His walking stick was at the murder scene. I think we should follow him and see where he goes. There's no time to waste.'

14

Old Jake was standing with a group of sailors, their dark grey guernseys stained with oil and tar. The two women had caught up with him in the New Globe on the Mile End Road. Mei had been reluctant to venture out again so late, but fortified by their dinner and Pearl's encouragement to keep on Old Jake's trail, they had walked the streets, peering through the windows of hostelries around Limehouse.

'Come on, while he's here, let's go to his lodgings and see what we can find.'

The church bells of St Mary-Le-Bow had just rung out two bells as the women made their way past tenement buildings and rookeries. They passed a side alley, where a group of sailors were urinating.

Pearl and Mei quickened their pace and turned into a courtyard, hoping to get away unseen. But like hyenas sensing the blood of a wounded animal, the men had followed, silently forming a circle around the women.

'Looks like we've found our fun for tonight, boys,' one of the men said. Another grunted. The sailors inched closer.

Pearl stood in front of Mei. 'My dear gentlemen,' she said in a voice slightly higher than its usual register. 'I beg your forgiveness, but we are new to the area, so please let us pass. I appeal to you to remember your sainted mothers.'

At this, the gang laughed loudly. 'Our mothers were whores and bawds who gave us gin instead of breast milk. Do you think we'd give up such sport as you pretty ladies? Our dear mamas would look on and cheer,' said one, his bell-bottom trousers flapping in the wind. He loped towards them, his eyes devoid of emotion.

'As we are gents, we'll let you go home after we're done with you,' said another while his mates nodded in approval. 'Besides, you shouldn't be out so late at night if you was respectable ladies. For all you know, I might be Saucy Jack that goes around cutting up whores for my jollies. I'd be on the front pages of the *Illustrated Police News*.'

Pearl's legs were trembling. 'If you leave us be, I have money in my lodgings for you. There's plenty. Enough for several nights of drinking,' she said, willing her voice to stay strong and calm.

The runt of the gang, who was shorter than Pearl, whistled through his teeth. 'Listen to this one talk! Tell you what, my lady. I'll take you front, back and sideways. Then I'll walk you home for your money. Now that's what I call a good bargain.'

Pearl tried to remember all the things her father had taught her about fighting. First, don't fight fair, but go in for the attack. But at The Sailor's Arms, she had only tackled one drunken lout at a time in the pub, rather than a group of four.

While the men were laughing and joshing each other, she bent low and charged. Her target was the first man who had spoken. He sidestepped Pearl easily and pushed her to the ground. And then he was astride her, ripping at undergarments.

His hands were now pulling up her dress. His weight had squeezed all the breath out of her. Pearl tried to scream but he put a hand over her mouth. She could feel his calloused palm scraping her skin raw.

She struggled for breath. There was a sudden hissing noise, like an angry snake, beside her. Pearl wrenched her head to one side and saw that Mei had leapt forward, turning a cartwheel, followed by a somersault. Then Mei started walking on her hands towards the men. She began singing the chorus of a Chinese opera in an ear-splitting voice.

It was an unfamiliar sound to the Limehouse sailors. The fellows had stopped dead in their tracks, disconcerted by this strange virago emitting unearthly shrieks. Their hesitation gave Mei the advantage she needed. Swinging her leg around in a wide arc, her boot made contact with two of the men, toppling them like ninepins at the Old Royal Naval College's Skittle Alley.

As soon as the men were prone, her leg came down hard, the heel of her boot making contact with the tallest man's nose, which crunched on contact. Mei aimed a kick at another man who was creeping towards her, but missed. She gave another ear-splitting howl and charged forward again.

Pearl's assailant had looked up to see what the commotion was and she headbutted him in the throat. He rolled off her, coughing and spluttering. She sprang up and kicked him in the small of his back.

The men were sprawled on the ground, writhing in pain and groaning. Pearl held out a shaky hand to Mei. They picked up their skirts and dashed towards the main thoroughfare and on to safety. When they were close to King Street, their pace slowed. Breathing heavily, Pearl looked at Mei. 'That was incredible! Where on earth did you learn to do that?'

'My circus master taught me the ancient martial art of *Shǒubó* when I was an acrobat in Shanghai. You never forget the training. Very strong muscles in the legs.'

Pearl wiped her brow. 'If I'm ever in trouble again, I'll be calling on you. And what on earth made you sing that Mandarin opera? It frightened the living daylights out of them.'

Mei hesitated before asking: 'So you are familiar with the opera, you knew it was a love song?'

Pearl smiled, now getting her breath back. 'It's one of my favourites. A woman dressed as a male warlord is singing to her lover, a beautiful princess, saying that she has captured her heart.' She glanced at Mei. 'It's a love song that has always touched me very deeply. Whenever melancholy strikes, I often think of this opera. Love will always shine through, even when you believe there is no hope. Don't you believe that?'

'Life does not always allow you to find true love. It's never that simple.' Mei's voice was brisk. 'Come on, we're losing time. We must search Old Jake's room before he returns.'

The two women hurried forward, still looking nervously from side to side, shadows dancing on the cobblestones like genies released from their Jinn bottles. They both flinched at the sounds of the night, starting when they heard doors slamming, the noise echoing against walls, amplifying the sound.

Pearl stopped momentarily to get her bearings, then she nodded and led Mei down a maze of alleyways. They walked down Butcher Row before stopping opposite a tall tenement building, which leant precariously to one side, defying the laws of gravity.

'Old Jake lives at the top.' They looked up; it was four storeys high. Pearl remembered how much her young legs ached from climbing the flights of stairs when she had accompanied her father on a visit to Old Jake. PJ had come to collect a debt. A small amount, perhaps a shilling, but her father was not one to let anyone avoid paying him monies due, whether friend or foe.

She considered the problem of how they were going to get into Old Jake's room. She thought about looking for a ladder, but there was no way to gain entry without drawing attention to themselves. The door looked solid. She shook her head and gently took Mei's arm. 'I'm sorry for dragging you here. There's nothing more we can do tonight. Let's go home and come up with a new plan tomorrow.'

'You don't think I'm going to stop now, do you?' Mei pulled away from her. Before Pearl could argue, Mei was walking towards the tenement building. She looked around to make sure the streets were deserted, then tucked in her long skirts. She started to climb up the drainpipe.

'Come back! Mei!' Pearl whispered, fearing her voice would cause a disturbance. But the words went unheeded as Mei effortlessly shinned up the side of the building. At one point, she looked back and gave Pearl an exultant wave, as if to the crowds at the Shanghai circus. Pearl could see the acrobat Mei once was, fearless and joyful in her natural habitat of the big tent.

Pearl was about to raise her hand in salutation, when she saw the figure of Old Jake tottering towards them, being held up by a couple of his drinking companions. Horrified, Pearl whistled up to Mei. 'He's coming back!' she mouthed, and nipped into a doorway to hide in the shadows.

At the windowsill of the fourth floor, Mei waited. With sure hands and feet, she clung on to the drainpipe, silent as a cat. From the doorway opposite, Pearl could see Old Jake at the door of his lodgings. He was weaving side to side. 'And nothing gets past me in Limehouse,' he slurred. 'These young whippersnappers think they rule the roost, but I know everyone's secrets.' His friends clapped him on the back and bade him farewell.

After several minutes, a flicker of candlelight illuminated the top window, and the shadow of Old Jake moved across the room.

The drainpipe started to make a creaking noise and dislodged slightly from the wall. Mei was tipped back and hung on by her fingertips. Pearl shut her eyes tight, half expecting to hear the thud of Mei's body falling on the cobblestones. But there was just the metallic squeak, squeak, squeak of the rainwater pipe, swaying precariously from side to side. Pearl opened one eye and saw Mei swing one leg up onto the ledge of the window. She clung on, gripping the sides of the wall.

After what seemed like hours, the candlelight in the room finally sputtered out and there was darkness. Mei waited for a long time before pushing up the window frame several inches and slipping in. Pearl drew out a shaky breath, teeth aching from clenching her jaw.

A light rain was falling, becoming heavier and heavier. Water dribbled down the back of Pearl's neck. Her boots were letting in rainwater from the puddle she was standing in, toes beginning to freeze. The enthusiasm with which she had started this caper was beginning to dampen along with the weather. A group of carousers was coming towards her. She crouched into the doorway, making herself as small as possible. She stayed like this for some time, waiting for the ruckus to pass. The enormity of the task was beginning to dawn on her. She had put Mei in danger.

As the minutes dragged on, Pearl grew more concerned. A picture came unbidden into her mind of Mei walking on her hands towards those ruffians who had cornered them. How brave and fearless she was. But these thoughts were replaced with unwelcome images of Old Jake, his gnarled hands choking the life out of Mei. If she didn't come out soon, Pearl would have to find a way to go in after her.

A terrible dread was numbing Pearl's limbs when the front door to the tenement building opened a crack, a thin line of light illuminating the street. Mei's face peeped out.

The stairs leading up to Old Jake's room were littered with broken bottles, discarded boxes and rotting food. Walking carefully around them, Pearl's footsteps echoed on the steps, even though she tried to be as light and nimble footed as Mei, who stood practically dancing at the top of the fourth floor.

'I don't know how you managed to hang on to that drainpipe.'

'It's easy when you know how,' Mei whispered. Pearl wanted to hug Mei, but controlled herself. All this excitement was making her giddy.

'He's fast asleep,' Mei said. 'But tread carefully so we don't wake him.'

'I'll go in alone. I don't want to put you in danger.'

But Mei was not easily dissuaded. 'You're not going in without me.'

Gingerly, they opened the door to Old Jake's room and Pearl involuntarily recoiled upon inhaling a stench of sour urine. Holding their shawls in front of their noses, they crept in. The attic was dark, but the missing roof slates were letting in shards of moonlight. Old Jake was lying under a bundle of rags on the floor in the corner of the room. At least the man had a tiny attic to himself, but noise from the other occupants was coming up through the floorboards, almost drowning out Old Jake's snores. She remembered her father's words about sleeping in these tenement buildings. 'You need to get half-drunk, or your money for your bed is wasted because of the bugs and bad air.'

Peering around the room in the semi-darkness, there were few pieces of furniture to search through. She crept over to a sideboard and pulled open the top drawer. It creaked loudly, unwilling to give up its contents without protest. Old Jake shifted slightly and moaned. Pearl held her breath, standing as motionless as a Madame Tussauds waxwork.

After several minutes, Old Jake continued his snoring. Hoping he was now in a deep slumber, Pearl opened the bottom drawer of the sideboard. A ripped pair of trousers, a filthy grey vest, several broken clay pipes, a harmonica and a woman's whalebone corset. She closed the drawer, disheartened at the paltry contents. Pearl looked across at Mei who was bending over the supine figure of Old Jake.

With a gossamer light touch, Mei rifled through his pockets. *This woman is made of stern stuff,* Pearl thought, as she watched Mei methodically going through the ex-sailor's lice-infested clothes.

But her admiration turned to concern, as Mei's face contorted with horror. She had pulled out a large handkerchief from the old man's trousers. All pretence of stealth and quiet had gone as Mei pummelled the old man's chest, shrieking at him in Cantonese. Old Jake blinked open his eyes. A claw-like hand reached out for Mei's neck. Stunned for a moment, Pearl grabbed the nearest thing at hand – the chamber pot – and smashed it over Old Jake's head. A deluge of urine and pottery shards cascaded everywhere. He slumped to one side, groaning. But the fight was not out of him yet, as he called out: 'Help! Murderers! Thieves!'

'Quick,' said Pearl. 'Let's get out of here.' She pushed Mei out of the room. They ran down the stairs, hurtling down the high street until their lungs and legs gave out.

At Amoy Place, they stopped, hands on knees. There was a stitch in Pearl's side. 'What on earth were you shouting about? I've never seen you in such a rage. I thought you would kill him!'

Mei's eyes were blazing as she unfurled her fingers, revealing a blood-spattered handkerchief with Chinese characters on the edge of the cloth. 'I think that man did something terrible to Ah Sim. Look at this, I embroidered my brother's initials on it. I'd know it anywhere. Mrs Soo Chow offered me some handkerchiefs, and I gave this one to Ah Sim for his birthday. They are made of the finest Belgian linen.'

Pearl closed her eyes, scarcely believing what they'd found. She'd known Old Jake since childhood; he'd taught her how to fight, helped her escape from Limehouse with Tommy. She clutched on to Mei's shoulder for support.

'This is evidence we can bring to the police. You're a marvel. I would never have found it without you.' Pearl drew Mei into a hug, but then drew back, laughing. 'You need a good bath,' she teased. 'We got a good dowsing with Old Jake's piss and the Lord knows what else.'

'You don't smell so good, either,' Mei replied. 'Come back to my room, I've still got work to do at the laundry and I can wash our clothes while we're there.' The two women linked arms, drawing close to each other, jumping like jack rabbits at fleeting figures that darted along the alleyways. Pearl's pulse quickened at the thought of being inside Mei's room. What would she find there?

15

Mei bustled around, filling large vats with boiling water. The laundry room had long wooden racks attached to the ceiling, each one with white bed sheets hanging over them, drying in the stiflingly hot room. There was a strong smell of bleach.

Mei pushed a damp lock of hair out of her eyes. Pearl wondered how Mei managed the back-breaking work in this sweltering heat. 'I'll go and see Inspector Crowley tomorrow. He won't be able to dismiss me so easily this time. Old Jake could have taken Ah Sim's handkerchief after killing him. The police should question him about this and whether he is an accomplice of the Blue Man. Or perhaps he is the Blue Man.'

'Now, there's just one thing you need to do tonight,' Mei said, frowning.

'What's that?'

'You need to come to my bedroom and remove your clothes.'

Pearl blushed. 'What for?'

'If you want to get rid of that stink, you need to let me wash all of your garments.'

The two women undressed in Mei's room, Pearl bashful and nervous, while Mei readily took off all her clothes, without any embarrassment. Naked now, the taut body of an acrobat was uncovered.

Pearl's gaze was drawn to a small mole above Mei's left breast. She longed to trace the curve of her nipple, but she dared not move.

Mei walked over to a cupboard and put on a brilliantly coloured turquoise dressing gown. She rifled further inside and selected a purple dress, handing it to Pearl. 'This will suit you very well,' Mei said, her voice soft.

It was a beautiful silk taffeta gown. Mei helped her button the dress at the back. It was too small, fitting her very snugly, so different from Pearl's usual attire. She could feel Mei's eyes on her.

In the silence, Pearl laughed awkwardly. 'What a wonderful frock. I'm not used to wearing anything so close fitting. Anything with lots of room to stride about in suits me.'

'You have a lovely figure.' Mei's eyes appraised Pearl's body.

Pearl awkwardly smoothed down the sides of her dress. She cast around for something to say. 'Where did you get this frock? It would cost more than a month's stay at the lodging house.' She regretted the words as soon as they were out of her mouth. It sounded so accusing when said aloud. Mei turned quickly away from her.

'Mrs Soo Chow gave it to me. She said it was an old dress and I might as well have it,' she said in a rush. 'She was going to send it to the second-hand clothes market in Petticoat Lane.'

'I'm sorry, I didn't mean to pry. That was very good of Lizzy.'

Mei tightened the belt of her dressing gown. 'Nothing is for free.' She gestured towards the door. Her eyes avoided Pearl's. 'It's very late. Be careful on your way home.'

Pearl knew it was time to go, but she wanted to stay with Mei a little longer. Perhaps they could talk about Ah Sim. She spoke gently, hoping to encourage Mei into revealing more about her brother. 'I need to ask some questions that may hurt. But if we are to find out who killed Ah Sim, you might need to face some difficult truths.'

Mei nodded reluctantly. 'I'm beginning to see that he didn't tell me everything.'

'Everybody keeps secrets. Do you know someone called Jeremiah? I found out that Ah Sim owed him a gambling debt. Quite a lot of money.'

Mei's mouth pressed into a thin line. 'Who have you been talking to? Ah Sim was a good boy. I never saw him gamble. He wouldn't do something like that.'

'I'm just asking,' Pearl said gently. 'All I'm saying is that Ah Sim might have been involved in some dangerous activities that got him into trouble.'

'Don't speak about my brother like that! You must go now.'

There was that anger again, which had flared at Old Jake's lodgings. Mei pushed Pearl towards the door, her face rigid with fury. Mei's grief had unleashed a surge of powerful emotions. Pearl gripped Mei's shoulders to comfort her, but was roughly shoved away. They struggled briefly but as their eyes locked, they both froze.

Pearl slowly raised a hand to Mei's face. 'You're so beautiful.'

She looked at Mei's mouth and kissed her. It just happened. Their tongues touched, tentatively at first. Mei gave a low moan and Pearl's stomach swooped, a throbbing, pulsing sensation spreading in her loins.

She looked into Mei's half-closed eyes, wanting to find out what caresses gave the most pleasure. She wanted to taste Mei all over, to undress her slowly. She teased Mei with her tongue, probing deeper and deeper.

'Stop.'

Mei wrenched herself out of their embrace. She knotted the belt of her dressing gown more tightly around the waist, breathing hard. 'This was not meant to happen.' She seemed to be talking to herself.

Pearl took a step towards Mei.

'You must never do that again. Your washed garments will be by the door tomorrow.' Mei's voice was distant and cold. 'Leave now.'

'Please don't send me away.'

Mei stared at the floor, saying nothing. She walked Pearl to the front door.

It closed with an icy click. Pearl stood in the doorway and groaned. She wondered if she could change Mei's mind and was tempted to knock on the door and beg for forgiveness.

Standing on the laundry's front step, she looked up at the Milky Way, which twinkled and glittered in the heavens. Perhaps she had taken liberties, but Mei had responded. Pearl could feel it when they had embraced. She had wanted it, too. It was unmistakable. So then, why had Mei stopped so abruptly?

Pearl sighed. She yearned for someone to hold close and kiss on warm evenings, arms clasped tight around each other, whispering loving endearments.

She wanted someone to share her life with, to look up at the sky with; to feel someone's warm cheek next to hers, and marvel at the constellations in the heavens. Pearl had once thought it possible with Tommy, swept along by his declarations of love.

They had eloped the night she turned sixteen. Slipping out of the pub to meet her fiancé in the churchyard of St Anne's, she had been met by a bloodied and bruised Tommy, cowering behind a gravestone.

'Have you been in a fight again?'

Tommy had shaken his head slowly. 'Don't worry, but we have to get out of here now. They're after me. People I owe money to.'

Pearl pressed her lips together to stop a torrent of accusations that were threatening to spill out. This was supposed to be romantic, the promise of a new life. She had been tempted to leave a note for Lizzy, who would be heartbroken and betrayed, left alone in Limehouse to fend for herself. What would she do without Pearl and Tommy? But the fear of being discovered had stayed Pearl's hand. She couldn't risk her escape plans being found out. The urge to get away from The Sailor's Arms and to start a new life was too strong. First, Portsmouth, and then she would finally set out for the home of her mother – China!

16

It was nearly dawn when Pearl passed a group of flower sellers who were singing their way to Covent Garden. One of them stopped to admire Pearl's dark purple dress. Pearl was reminded of Mei's searching look when she'd first put the dress on, but pushed the thought away.

The West India Dock Road was crowded with people rushing to work or back from an evening's entertainment. A poster plastered on a hoarding outside Limehouse Town Hall caught her eye:

THE ALHAMBRA, LEICESTER SQUARE

Miss Maude Kingsley, Canning Town's Canary

The Lorenz Svengali Trio

Meister Glee Sisters

Randy and Dandy

Twice Daily at 2 and 8

A Grand, Gorgeous, Glorious, Glittering and Unique Entertainment

She savoured the drawing of Maude Kingsley, her blonde hair cascading around bare shoulders, strumming a lute; mouth wide open in song. It was a delight to see the singer on such a huge poster, dressed in a diaphanous peignoir. Maude had managed to climb her way out of the provincial music halls and into West End success.

And yet, a viscous tang of disappointment and jealousy flooded Pearl's mouth. She hadn't amounted to much herself; in fact, she had come back to the place she had sworn never to return to.

She chided herself for feeling envious as she stood in front of Maude's beguiling face. 'So you finally made top billing, just like you whispered to me that you would, all those nights ago in Portsmouth. I wonder if you remember me. You said you'd always keep me in your heart.'

Pearl recalled the night she first met Maude. The night everything changed. She'd cheered herself up after Tommy's death, spending money she could ill afford to see Maude at the New Theatre Royal. Ellen Terry and Sarah Bernhardt were coming to the music-hall venue, but Pearl wanted to see the singer whose lips she had tasted in her dreams.

When Maude sauntered onto the stage singing *To Be There*, Pearl's heart ignited. It was a revelation. Maude had thrown back her head, singing lustily and shaking her hips. To Pearl, it had seemed that Maude looked only at her, skewering her soul. Maude was reaching out with imploring arms up to Pearl, who sat rigid, struck, fingernails digging into the soft cushion.

Thinking back, Pearl cringed with embarrassment at clutching that wilting red rose so tightly the thorns had pierced her skin. But as Pearl gazed at Maude, haloed in the light of the stage door entrance, the two women recognised a hunger in each other's eyes. Pearl walked towards her, as if in a trance, and thrust the bouquet at her idol. Maude gave a throaty laugh and took Pearl by the arm. 'Fancy a drink, darling?'

Lying naked in Maude's bed at the Queen's Hotel in the early hours of the morning, Pearl had rolled over to look at the singer. 'How did you guess, could you tell?'

Maude ran a hand through her blonde tresses, now lying loose around her shoulders. She kissed Pearl's breast. 'It was obvious. You looked at me like a love-sick calf. I've seen that look before. My close friend Amy Levy used to gaze at me like that. She'd recite her poetry to me:

'I see how your dear eyes grew deep,
'How your lithe body thrilled and swayed,
'And how were whiter than the keys
'Your hands that played . . .

'Little did I know she was whispering the same bloody poem to another woman as well! But I learned a great deal from her.' Maude drew Pearl close.

As the sun reached its zenith, the two women reluctantly dressed. Maude gave Pearl a long, lingering kiss. Then she sighed. 'If it wasn't for these damn rehearsals, I'd stay in bed with you all day.'

She traced Pearl's face with her little finger. 'Come and see me after the show?' They kissed again. Just before Maude opened the bedroom door, she hesitated. 'Pearl, this is new for you, and I wouldn't go showing your feelings for me in public. Not everyone will understand. Keep it between the two of us.'

At Pearl's crestfallen look, Maude laughed and chucked her under the chin. 'Cheer up, sweetheart. It's just a bit of fun for us girls, ain't it?'

During Maude's run in Portsmouth, the two women spent every night together. But Maude was at pains to warn Pearl that there were to be no demonstrations of affection or intimacy shown between them when they were out. 'You've got to stop staring at me like that,' Maude had said.

Pearl's first flames of desire were being doused in chilling water, the realisation dawning on her that this was just a dalliance for Maude. But for Pearl, it meant everything. There was no future for them and those tumultuous feelings she had for Maude were destined for her interior world, a taboo subject never to be spoken of. Her passion for Maude had to be kept in the shadows in shame and secrecy.

Would there always be heartache when a woman was involved, Pearl wondered now, as she meandered along the cobbled streets back towards the Fragrant Blossoms, loneliness biting at her heels. And then a thought crept in. What if she were to look up her old flame and see if they could rekindle their passion? That would teach Mei.

17

Pearl scrubbed the bedroom floor with a pent-up energy. Her mind kept replaying the kiss with Mei, the press of her body. She wondered if Mei felt it too. Pearl often had no idea what Mei was thinking. At times she wanted to shake Mei, to get a reaction. Pearl treasured the rare occasions when she was rewarded with a tantalising smile, a special look, just for her. But perhaps she was just imagining such moments, yearning for them to be real. She couldn't stop thinking about Mei. Was this love?

The anguish in Mei's eyes had melted Pearl's heart. The ghostly spectre of Ah Sim hovered over everything, and Pearl wanted to help release his spirit. If she could solve his murder, then Mei would be grateful, and perhaps pull Pearl into her arms, making her tremble all over again.

The water in the bucket had chilled, her fingers starting to wrinkle in the soap suds. She was so preoccupied with unattainable fantasies that she couldn't even complete the simplest tasks. Pearl twisted the washcloth, heartsore for even dreaming about a love that could never be.

She knew there was one way to ease her pain and disappointment. The one that had never let her down – the best friend who offered oblivion. She locked her bedroom door, then rattled the handle, making sure no one would disturb her. Scrambling on hands and knees, Pearl pulled up a floorboard underneath the bed. In the recess, her hands closed around the smooth edges of the opium package she had stolen from Lizzy, caressing the orange silk fabric.

The opium had been calling to her gently, its voice growing louder and more insistent. Her body ached for it. She hungered for the delicious languor the drug gave, taking away the despondency and boredom, and propelling her into a realm of exquisite bliss, where nothing and no one could hurt her.

In Portsmouth, Tommy had often bought several pipes' worth from Lascar sailors just off the ship from India, and the two of them had spent many evenings lost in a haze of daydreams, floating on the aurora borealis.

The sickness afterwards was purgatory. The sweating and tremors after a night on the poppies was dreadful, and every time Pearl would fervently swear never again. But she longed for it still, in the deepest recesses of her being. Then, with the shock of Tommy's death, opium's grip on her had abated. She thought she could do without, until this opportunity.

The opium packet was fat and comforting. Was it the right time to give in to her need for release? The impulse was like a tidal wave; if only she could resist this temptation for the sake of Mei, and keep focused on the murder investigation. Ah Sim was either smoking the opium, selling it or both. Whichever way, it had probably got him killed. Mei vehemently denied that Ah Sim was involved in drugs, but she could be wrong. After all, how close were sister and brother? There were many secrets Pearl kept close to her heart, and would not have shared with anyone.

She looked at herself in the mirror, admiring the dark purple gown given by Mei. How kind Lizzy had been to offer this to her employee. It showed her childhood friend still had some generosity, so different to the harsh side Pearl had seen at The Dragon Inn restaurant. There was a lingering scent of Mei's perfume on it, an earthy sandalwood. Pearl inhaled deeply and again relived their passionate kiss, the feel of Mei's body responding; a surge of heat rising up between them. But then Mei drew back, the fire replaced with ice.

The woman's mercurial moods were hard to fathom. Pearl carefully unwrapped the orange silk fabric to caress the opium. To her, it smelt of vanilla spice, while she knew others thought it had a tang of the earth, rich and loamy, or a deep toffee aroma. She turned the package over in her hands, and a card fell out. A Chinese blue willow drawing of a man in a boat, two birds in flight above his head. She had seen the image before, but couldn't remember where. She turned the card over and over in her hand, searching for a memory that stayed just out of reach.

Reluctantly, Pearl replaced the opium package underneath the floorboard. She would forgo her own desire to escape the world for now. Keeping the promise to help Mei came first.

At six o'clock that evening, Pearl decided to visit Inspector Crowley and show him Ah Sim's bloodied handkerchief, which Mei had given her to take to the police station as evidence. Pearl also brought the money package taken from Lizzy's office, proving that she had known Ah Sim would be at Wapping Old Stairs. Perhaps Old Jake and Lizzy were mixed up in this together. Old Jake may well be the Blue Man. On the day of the murder, he had been quick to point the finger, instead insisting it was local gangs from outside the area. And then later, he'd incriminated Lizzy.

The station waiting room was filled with a dozen youngsters, barefoot and dressed in rags; all of them grey-faced and emaciated. Every one of them had a look of bleak despair as they slouched on the floor. Pearl recognised one of the gang who had attacked her near Ma Jennings' on Pennyfields. She hadn't quite forgiven him, but he looked even thinner and sicker than the last time she had seen him.

Sergeant Knox held the boy by the ear, twisting it viciously. The child screamed in pain.

'Is that necessary, Sergeant? He can't be more than ten years old.'

Knox looked round. 'Oh it's you again, Miss. Don't be fooled by these ruffians. They're mean as they come. Caught this gang stealing coal down at Limekiln Dock. With a good judge, they'll be sentenced to breaking up stones. That'll teach 'em.'

'I need to see Inspector Crowley urgently.'

But the policeman was not at the station, Sergeant Knox informed her. 'Got called away to Scotland Yard on important business,' he said pompously. 'This matter with the Whitechapel murders is in all the papers, causing quite a ruckus. All hands on deck. You can try again later, but he could be gone hours.' Knox settled back to scrutinise the racing pages.

Pearl waited at Scotland Yard. It took more than three hours for Inspector Crowley to appear. He looked her up and down, noting the purple gown with frank suspicion. 'Mrs Fitzgerald, what are you doing here?'

'You wouldn't believe it, but there are men around here who mistook me for a fallen woman. If you are seen with me, what will people think? And you, a religious man!'

Crowley swallowed hard. He quickly raised a hand to hail a hackney carriage. 'Allow me to offer you a carriage back to Limehouse. We are advising all respectable women to stay indoors as the Whitechapel killer is still at large.'

He helped Pearl inside the coach, looked around nervously, then hopped in. Crowley had eluded her so far, but was now a captive audience as they trundled towards Limehouse.

'I've been asking around and discovered evidence that points to a possible suspect.' Her eyes shone with the fervour of a recently converted Evangelical Christian.

With a flourish, she pulled out the blood-stained handkerchief. 'I found this in Old Jake's room, one of my father's best friends and my late husband's uncle. It belonged to Ah Sim. These are his initials, embroidered in Mandarin, and as you can see, it has blood on it. Evidence of foul play, I'm positive. Surely this is something you should be looking into?'

At first, Crowley's face was impassive, then he smiled, although his eyes were remote. A sliver of pink meat was trapped between his two front teeth. No doubt he'd had a good lunch at Scotland Yard. 'You broke into the gentleman's room? Well, you are full of surprises, Mrs Fitzgerald. Let's discuss this back at the station.' His Dorset accent was soft as butter.

They said no more until they were inside his office. The inspector motioned for her to sit on a hard-backed chair opposite his desk, while he settled himself into a comfortable leather Chesterfield.

Putting his hands together as if in prayer, Crowley smiled, revealing large, uneven teeth. The meat was still there.

'Show me that handkerchief again.'

Pearl handed it over to the inspector. He inspected it gingerly between forefinger and thumb. The red stains had turned dark brown, looking even more hideous than before.

'There could be any number of reasons why Ah Sim's handkerchief was in Old Jake's room.'

Pearl felt he was playing with her, an amusing game that she did not fully understand.

'It is a lead, as I believe you call it. Surely this points to Old Jake being the killer.'

The detective's gaze was piercing. His hawkish eyes travelled disapprovingly over her tangled, messy hair, which had escaped from the pincer-like grip of hairpins as she rushed, pell-mell, on the long walk to Victoria Embankment. He opened his arms expansively. 'We are well advanced in our investigations,' he said, keeping his voice light and even.

'I do understand, Inspector. But I think I can be of some use. I was raised and grew up here, people might tell me things they wouldn't come to you with.'

The inspector sat down behind his desk and glanced at his gilt-edged bible sitting atop it, as if seeking divine guidance. He placed a hand on the dark brown leather cover, the hairs on the back of his hands a very pale blonde, the nails manicured.

'Yes, of course. I completely understand your eagerness to be of assistance. I have come across women who are excited by acts of violence before.' He regarded her as such a specimen.

Pearl was stung by his words but decided to ignore the insult. She would show him. 'I've heard from separate sources that the possible culprit is someone they call the Blue Man. Have you questioned him?'

As soon as the words were out, Pearl knew she had the inspector's attention. She was about to continue when Crowley held up a hand to stop her from speaking further, leaning forward in his chair.

'How do you know about the Blue Man? He is in our sights. One of my sergeants told me about him and we are investigating further.'

Pearl was pleased that her Uncle Peter had passed on the information and the police were looking into the man as a suspect.

'And Mrs Fitzgerald, are you telling me you went to Old Jake's place of abode unaccompanied, and have taken, nay, stolen, an item that may well belong to him?'

Pearl quickly decided not to mention Mei's presence at Old

Jake's room, keen to keep her out of harm's way. 'Yes, I was alone, and that handkerchief certainly does not belong to my father's friend. I think Old Jake is an accomplice of the Blue Man – or even the Blue Man himself. He stole the handkerchief from Ah Sim, and I believe he kept it as a souvenir of the terrible crime – or to sell later.' Pearl's voice grew louder, hoping this would convey conviction.

The inspector's face was grim. He paced up and down the room for several minutes. Pearl couldn't stand the silence. She pulled out the money packet taken from Lizzy's office with a flourish. 'I also have proof that Mrs Soo Chow is involved in opium smuggling, and Ah Sim, the murdered man, was in her employ. This note shows Lizzy knew Ah Sim was to be at Wapping Old Stairs that day. She might even have paid Old Jake to kill Ah Sim.'

Pearl felt a pang of guilt for pointing the finger at Lizzy, but quelled the thought. She didn't owe her anything. So much had changed in the intervening years. Besides, she could hardly recognise her old childhood friend anymore. And if she was involved in the killing of Ah Sim, Pearl owed it to Mei to do all she could.

Crowley took the envelope from Pearl, turning it over and over in his hand. He eventually placed it carefully on his desk. 'All this shows is that Mrs Soo Chow is engaged in the sale of drugs – which we already know. Although I thank you for this piece of tangible evidence. And so what if Ah Sim was working for her? It proves nothing. Merely that he was doing her bidding.'

'But what about Old Jake?' Pearl was stung by the inspector's lack of concern.

'Come with me. I have something to show you, which I'm sure will be of great interest.' He ushered her out of the room and then marched down the corridor, Pearl following behind.

'I have another piece of evidence linking Old Jake to the crime.

I found his silver-topped cane on the foreshore very close to where Ah Sim's body was discovered. It might be an important clue, and is another sign that he is indeed involved. What do you think, Inspector?'

Crowley didn't reply. On and on they walked, passing along hallways and turning past a warren of narrow alcoves, until Pearl had lost her bearings. This police station was much larger than she had thought. The pleasant smell of polished floors was replaced by something much more sinister, acrid and putrid.

After a sharp left, they came to a stone staircase. Gone were the gilt-framed portraits of past chief inspectors. Instead the walls were streaked with dust and dirt. The floor was sticky underfoot and spiralled downwards. As they descended, the temperature grew colder and Pearl's stomach tightened as she realised they were heading for the underground prison. The shouts of inmates locked up in the cells echoed around them, a moaning crescendo of obscenities, entreaties to their mothers and incoherent ramblings of the insane.

Behind a row of iron-grille gates, arms reached out, fingers splayed and reaching up to the heavens. 'Help me, Miss! For the love of God!' Unthinking, Pearl turned to the direction of the voice. A mass of matted hair framed a face caked with filth. But the man's eyes were bright with cunning. As soon as Pearl turned to face him, he leered at her, saliva dribbling from the corner of his mouth. 'Come here, darlin'. If I could get my hands on you, I'd tear you limb from limb!' He cackled maniacally and Pearl hastened away.

They came to a large, wooden door, which the inspector pushed open. Crowley took Pearl's arm and led her in. They were in the icy chill of the morgue. The smell of formaldehyde burned in her nostrils.

On a marble-topped table lay the naked, greyish-white corpse of Old Jake. Pearl screamed. Crowley nodded in satisfaction. Old Jake's eyes were half open and his face contorted in a petrified grimace. He did not have an easy death. There was a large gash in his abdomen, from which his intestines were curling out. Pearl tried not to gag.

The inspector put a hand on Pearl's shoulder. 'His death is most unfortunate as he was due to come in and give a statement. Now we'll never know what he was going to tell us. But what we do know is that you were the last person to see him alive, and have admitted to breaking into his home and stealing an item belonging to him. Perhaps there was a scuffle and you got the better of him? He is an old man after all, and you are a fit young woman.'

'That's not true. How can you believe that?' Pearl was bewildered and confused.

'Mrs Fitzgerald, I'm deadly serious. I am sure you mean well, but I will not tolerate anyone interfering in police business. Sergeant!'

There was the clatter of hobnailed boots as Sergeant Knox rushed into the room. He must have followed them down to the mortuary and was listening to their conversation just outside the door.

This was not at all how she had thought Crowley would react. 'Please, Inspector, I'm completely innocent,' she protested. 'Old Jake was involved somehow, I'm sure of it. You've got to believe me.'

Crowley stared at her and exhaled loudly in irritation. 'If he was indeed the Chinaman's killer, which I don't think is the case, then I am afraid Old Jake is beyond our jurisdiction and his guilt or innocence is a matter that can only be decided by God Almighty now. I'm locking you up for the night on suspicion of breaking and entering. Sergeant Knox, take Mrs Fitzgerald to the cells. I will decide in the morning whether I need to question you further about the murder of Old Jake. For now, let this be a lesson to you not to interfere in police business.'

18

Something slithered in the corner. Strange sounds echoed hollowly, while amorphous shapes squirmed to and fro. Something was coming towards her, writhing on its stomach, a malevolent presence seeking her out. It was out to do her harm. A snake was rearing up at her, its fangs bared. Pearl screamed in terror, starting awake. The full, true horror of where she was came flooding back.

The prison cell was icy. She shivered and pulled the thin blanket close around her shoulders, but quickly threw it off when she felt myriad tiny creatures weaving in and out of the material, crawling onto her skin. An infestation of lice was the last thing she needed.

The only light was coming in from a tiny window high up on the wall, criss-crossed with a wrought-iron grille. When Pearl was first thrown in here, she had felt around, like a blind person, bumping into the wash stand and the narrow iron frame of the bed. Tentatively, Pearl sat down on the bed. She realised her terrifying situation; alone in this prison cell, with no one knowing where she was. The straw mattress was so thin, Pearl could feel every lump and bump of the wire frame below.

To keep her mind off the bed bugs, Pearl closed her eyes and tried to organise her thoughts on what she knew so far about Ah Sim's murder. The man had been struck down by a ferocious blow. Pearl shuddered at the memory of the gaping wound in his belly and his terrified expression, a rictus grimace of agony. Then there was the discovery of the blood-stained handkerchief in Old Jake's room. How had it come into his possession?

It was likely that the old sea dog was present when Ah Sim was murdered, and picked up the handkerchief as a macabre memento, or for the second-hand clothes market. Mei had told her it was made from the finest Belgian linen, a present from Lizzy. Old Jake was involved in a fight over opium or gambling – or both. He could have killed Ah Sim before being killed himself. They were all connected. The mystery was how.

Rose must surely know more. If Ah Sim had taught her several Cantonese phrases, they must have spent a fair bit of time together. Could they have been lovers? The matchgirl had been scared out of her wits when asked about Ah Sim, running away like a scalded cat. To react like that . . . Rose had seen something.

There also lurked the mysterious phantom of the Blue Man. If it wasn't Old Jake, then Jeremiah was still a possible suspect. Ah Sim owed gambling debts to the indigo dye worker, and Jeremiah had threatened to kill him. Pearl thought for a moment. Could Ah Sim and Old Jake have been killed by the same person? And if so, what linked the two of them – opium? A spider's web of drugs, gambling, or even a fight over a woman came to mind. It felt like too much of a coincidence for the two murders to be unrelated, which meant she was seeking a double murderer. Could it even be the man who was killing the women in Whitechapel and Spitalfields? No, his targets had so far all been female, and he'd not yet struck in Limehouse, as far as she knew. Also, Ah Sim had been dealt a terrible blow to the head, which was a different modus operandi.

Pearl sighed and shook her head. Despite the inspector's bravado, it seemed clear that the police were no closer to finding the

Blue Man than she was. She wondered about Soo Chow, Lizzy's husband. Another person of interest, but how, Pearl had no idea. And Lizzy? What of her?

An image of Ah Sim's tortured face flashed before her again. Whoever killed him was possessed of a crazed fury. She thought again of the card that came in the opium package, wracking her brains over where she had seen the blue willow pattern illustration before, but it remained stubbornly at the edges of her memory.

Pearl bitterly regretted not staying home and smoking the opium taken from Lizzy's office. If she had, she wouldn't be in this terrible situation, but instead lying in her own comfortable and warm bed, drifting in and out of fantastical dreams.

She thought back on the nights spent smoking with Tommy. He had laughed at her desire for it, always wanting more and more. 'Not too much, now. If you get too fond of the poppy, it will be the death of you,' he'd warned.

She could do with an opium pipe now, to make her forget how badly things had gone wrong. Pearl smacked her hand against the filthy mattress in frustration. She really needed to visit the opium den above The Dragon Inn restaurant to see if there was any more information about Ah Sim. How long had he been paid by Lizzy for opium delivery, and could he have been stealing from her, which then got him killed? Another look at Lizzy's meticulous records would reveal more. But there was very little she could do from a prison cell. Hopelessness overwhelmed her as she belatedly realised her peril. She was in prison on suspicion of murdering Old Jake. If Crowley decided on a trumped-up charge, she faced the death penalty.

Pearl took in shallow, quick gasps, not wanting to inhale the foetid air. The walls were black and dripping. The cell was deathly cold. A panic assailed her. She would never get out of here alive.

'Pa! Please help me!' It was so long since she had said those words. The last time was when a gang of schoolmates surrounded her, pulling their eyes into slits and chanting in a singsong voice: 'Ching chong! Yellow devil! Half-caste!' She ran home and PJ had taken her up in his arms, softly singing a lullaby. The image vanished. He was dead. Gone forever. They would never speak again, but Pearl fervently wished she could have one last conversation with him, to say sorry for running away.

She had never felt so friendless. She had no one and nothing to call her own. She cursed herself for promising to help Mei. The vainglory of it all! There was no way she was cut out for this life. All bravery had vanished. Who did she think she was? Certainly not a brave warrior woman. All her dreams of sailing the seven seas and becoming a swashbuckling adventuress, just like the Chinese heroine Mulan, seemed laughable. The furthest Pearl had ever travelled was a port city on the Southeast coast of England.

'Mother! Please come to me.' But again, she was reaching out to a wraith, an illusion, a ghost. Who was she even asking for? Someone she had no memory of. Pearl had asked her father so many times for stories of Jai Li. Stories of softness and care, a maternal image to hold on to. There was just the one time her father had relented, offering Pearl a morsel, much revisited. 'Just before your mother died, she cradled you in her arms and looked at you with love. I've never seen such a tender moment.'

More often than not, Pa was transported back to his youth, recalling tales of the early days with his first love. When PJ first tried to kiss Jai Li, she had stamped hard on his foot. 'That's when I knew she was the gal for me,' he'd told Pearl through a throaty laugh. 'Never met a woman with more fire – apart from you.'

It was one of the last times father and daughter had been together; the night before her sixteenth birthday. PJ was in an affable mood that night, pleased that Pearl would now be of age, ready to take on the role of pub landlady.

Pearl shuddered as a cockroach crawled up her leg and gave a slight scream as she flicked it off. It landed on its back, its many legs wriggling grotesquely on the prison cot. Other women in the adjoining cells were screaming and moaning, caught up in a nightmare world of their own, despairing for their own uncertain futures.

'Please God, have mercy on my soul. If you let me out of here, I'll never do anything bad ever again.'

Even The Sailor's Arms had been taken from her. She had spent her childhood running from it, but now the tavern was the only place left in the world that was hers. A last link with her father.

She threw herself at the door, kicking and screaming. 'Let me out! Let me out! I've done nothing wrong.'

Finally giving up, she curled up on the hard, unforgiving bed, a raw ache in her throat and gave herself over to despair in the coal-black chasm of the night.

As her eyes fluttered shut, she was back in Portsmouth. The dockyard was teeming with women, a highly unusual sight. Many were crying and wailing, cradling babies in their arms. Word had got round.

Pearl fought her way to the water's edge, looking out at sea. She had been waiting anxiously for news, but *The Colossus of Rhodes* had not berthed. It was several days late. A chatter rippled around the wharves. Pearl turned round to see the dockmaster standing on a barrel. He looked sombre, the corners of his mouth turning down.

'Listen up, ladies. I have some very sad news. *The Colossus of Rhodes* capsized somewhere in the Indian Ocean, location unknown. There were no survivors.'

Screaming echoed around the dock, rising to an ear-splitting lamentation. Several women collapsed on the cobblestones, beating their breasts, tearing at their hair. Pearl's insides twisted in agony. He was gone. Tommy was gone.

The door clanged open and hobnailed boots stomped into the cell. A pale light filtered through. 'Wakey, wakey, Sleeping Beauty. Rise and shine.' Sergeant Knox shook Pearl awake. 'You're a lucky girl. Your Uncle Peter got wind you'd been banged up. He had a word with Inspector Crowley, said he'd vouch for you, so we've decided to let you go for now. But keep out of trouble.'

Pearl shuffled out of the room after whispering a feeble thank you to the sergeant. Every bone in her body ached from the freezing cold and constant shivering. She had never felt so miserable, not even when she was told that Tommy had perished, his bones dissolving in a far-off ocean, thousands of miles away. How desolate she had felt then. But her current situation was different. She had been humiliated by that cruel Inspector Crowley and she despised herself for appearing weak in front of him. Pearl was desperate for her own bed. She was a coward and as skittish as a mewling kitten.

Shuffling away from Thames Police Station, Pearl lifted her head. There was at least one person on whom she could vent her anger.

19

The Sailor's Arms looked even more ramshackle than the last time Pearl had been here. It was obvious that her father's bedroom hadn't been cleaned in months. Clothes, old bottles and piles of dirty plates, festooned with flies, were strewn all over the floor. Betty's cleaning habits had not improved with the years. Pearl wrinkled her nose as she sorted through a heap of soiled petticoats and jackets, going through the pockets, determined to find her father's will, if indeed there was one. It was the one thing that had kept Pearl going during the horrors of the night before. She'd die before letting Betty take The Sailor's Arms from her.

Next to the bed was a chest, the padlock firmly fastened. Pearl looked around for something to break it open. She picked up a rusty old barrel opener and started battering away at the lock. It smashed open on the sixth strike. Flinging it open, Pearl rifled through its contents of old newspaper clippings, jewellery and trinkets. At the very bottom was a tattered scroll, tied up with a red ribbon. She unfurled it, scanning quickly.

The last will and testament of Patrick John O'Dwyer.
I bequeath my pub and all its
contents to my beloved wife Elizabeth Jane Sullivan.

Signed *Patrick John O'dwyer*

Pearl blinked rapidly. Had her father really left the pub to Betty? She looked closer at the writing. The signature looked nothing like her father's handwriting. He was proud of his elegant penmanship. 'The Jesuits might have beaten me to a pulp but at least they taught me how to write with a good hand,' he'd said.

Then Pearl laughed out loud: her father's second name was James, not John. Betty had made a serious error.

'What the bloody hell are you doing in here?' Betty stood in the doorway, hands on hips. 'I told you before and I'm telling you again, get out and stay out!' Betty grabbed a handful of Pearl's hair.

Pearl held on tight to the will and they began grappling with each other, vying for purchase. 'You won't get away with this, Betty.'

'It's mine! Give it back to me!' Betty screamed.

'That's not my father's signature – and his second name was James, not John,' Pearl shouted back.

'You can't prove it. It's my word against yours.' Betty was clawing at Pearl's arm.

The two women were wrestling on the ground, each trying to beat the other into submission. But Pearl was younger and stronger. A powerful shove sent Betty backwards, crashing into the iron bedstead. She slumped to the floor, grunting in pain.

Pearl arrived back at the Fragrant Blossoms; at least one thing was going her way. The forged will was proof that Betty would go to any lengths to steal The Sailor's Arms pub. And now Pearl knew that PJ hadn't forgotten her. She felt in her heart that he had always meant to bequeath The Sailor's Arms to his only daughter.

The sounds of lodgers chattering to each other in Cantonese was soothing after the horrendous night in prison. She was relieved that there had been enough rice porridge for their evening meal, even if it was cold.

She was greeted by Xianfan, who had looked at her bedraggled, filthy appearance with alarm. 'We were worried when you did not appear for dinner last night. Are you unwell, Miss Pearl?'

She shook her head and ran up the stairs to the bedroom, desperate for solitude. Looking round her little sanctuary, she hugged herself, trying to get some warmth into her bones. She took off the purple dress Mei had given her. It was ruined; Pearl doubted the stains and smell of the prison could ever be removed. She placed it in a bag outside the door, not wanting to infect her other garments with lice. Washing herself thoroughly with water from the nightstand, Pearl felt clean for the first time in what seemed like months.

Her eyes were bloodshot and still wide with shock at the ordeals of the last twenty-four hours.

Breathing raggedly, she reached under the bed. As she lifted the floorboard, there it was – her drug of heavenly euphoria. If there was one thing that could obliterate what she had been through, it was black spice. She needed to blot out her humiliation at the hands of Inspector Crowley, the ghastly night in the cells – and deeper than that – her shame and desire at wanting to touch Mei's naked body. Small wonder opium was called God's own medicine.

She rummaged at the back of the wardrobe. It must be somewhere. Yes, it was here, the dark-coloured bamboo opium pipe, a gift from Tommy.

She could remember how to prepare a pipe as if it were yesterday. She broke off a piece of the fragrant brown resin and placed it in the brass bowl of the pipe, shaped like half a pigeon's egg. Using a thin silver toothpick, she took a small quantity of opium and carefully warmed it in the flame of a candle until it became the substance of molten treacle and released its fragrant aroma.

Pearl inhaled deeply, sucking greedily; the smoke filling her lungs. The drug was good; pure and clean. Her eyes closed, giving herself up to the delicious release. The tension left her body as a wonderful lassitude flooded Pearl's tingling limbs.

She lay back on the bed and watched in wonder as a rainbow-coloured phoenix swooped and fluttered around the room until it finally settled on top of the wardrobe. A better quality opium certainly produced more spectacular visions. Between the slats in the wooden floorboards, flowers were sprouting, their stems gargantuan, with luscious lilac petals, translucent and shimmering, which opened up to reveal the stamens as thick clouds of pollen powdered the air. From the centre of the blooms emerged a beautiful woman.

She wore a diaphanous gown and moved closer to Pearl, her scarlet lips breathing along Pearl's neck, making her shiver and shake. The woman was saying something but it was in a language that Pearl couldn't understand. Suddenly, the woman changed into a snarling sea serpent, sharp fangs clawing at Pearl's body. The apparition screamed again, an anguished cry and then disappeared.

A deep voice thundered around the room. 'You should have stayed with me. Look at you now, my darling daughter.' PJ O'Dwyer was towering over her, his beard intertwined with long strands of seaweed. His features were bloated but she knew it was him. His smell was all around her, the brand of tobacco he smoked, male sweat, furniture polish and the aroma of sweet cherry brandy. She was sobbing now, crying out for her father. She looked at his face, which was dissolving, melting like a church candle. And then it reformed and transformed into the grotesque face of Old Jake, his mouth wide in agony, screaming out to her as the large gash in his belly gushed blood.

The room bucked and swayed as a wave of nausea hit, and Pearl vomited down the side of the bed. Her stomach spasmed, and after a few dry heaves, she sank into unconsciousness.

There was a terrible pounding in her head. Her eyelids felt like they were stuck together with ground glass. She struggled to open them and then shut them immediately against the brilliant sunlight. There was that banging again. How could she make it go away? It was incessant, reverberating in her skull. Then there was a knock on her bedroom door. If she kept completely still, maybe it would stop.

'Pearl! What happened to you?' The figure of Mei Tan looked down on her. Dear Lord, this was the last thing she wanted. She could feel Mei's eyes travel around the room, taking in the opium pipe, and the room in its chaotic disorder. Most of all, Pearl could feel Mei's gaze, looking at her whey-coloured face, her dishevelled nightdress, stained with vomit down the front. The sickly sweet smell of opium hung heavy in the air, making Pearl want to heave again, although her stomach clenched and roiled over.

'How did you get in?' It was all Pearl could say. There was a taste in her mouth like month-old mutton. She was desperately thirsty.

'Xianfan let me in. He was worried about you. How long have you been smoking opium?' Mei's voice was cold, questioning and accusatory.

'I've not done this for a long time.' Then she felt angry at Mei's gaze, contemptuous and hard. 'Don't you dare judge me!'

'But why now? I needed your help, and you promised we could find Ah Sim's killer together. I have no one else to turn to but you.'

'It's too much for me. I've been locked up in prison overnight. I never ever want to go back there again.' Pearl's eyes were lowered as she shuddered at the experience. 'I don't want any more trouble,

Mei. All I want is to get my pub back and to be a good landlady at the Fragrant Blossoms. I can't help you anymore.'

'I beg you not to give up. If not for me, then for the spirit of your mother. Don't forget you are the daughter of a wild Canton spirit. Her blood runs through your veins. You have more courage than you know.'

Pearl shook her head. 'I'm sorry to let you down, Mei.'

'Is that all you have to say?' Mei shook her head. 'One night in prison and you're prepared to let a killer go unpunished. You could do so much with your life but instead you take refuge in the poppy and hide. I've known people like you. They crave the poppy more than life itself.' Her voice dripped with disappointment.

Pearl closed her eyes to stop the room spinning.

'My grandfather spent years on the opium couch until he was nothing but a skeleton. Our whole family suffered because of his selfishness. I thought you were different. I had hoped you cared for me. But the only person you care about is yourself.' Mei's voice was a harsh whisper. She slowly walked out of the room, quietly closing the door.

Pearl groaned and pulled the covers over her head.

20

Her body was wracked with spasms, mouth as arid as the Gobi desert. Pearl fought to keep down the congee, which was like sour sludge in her mouth. If only Ma Jennings was here. The house seemed so much quieter and Pearl sorely missed Ma's gales of laughter and continuous chatter. Ma would have offered words of comfort. Pearl was still cut to the quick by Mei's harsh words and condemnation at dropping her investigation into Ah Sim's murder.

Lizzy was up to her neck in this, but Pearl's thoughts also kept returning to Jeremiah. She needed to find out more. Ah Sim owed the indigo dye man a lot of money, so it could have been a quarrel that turned deadly. Xianfan had warned her that Jeremiah was a dangerous man and to keep away from him. But with precious little else to go on, Pearl pulled on her most comfortable brown dress, grabbed her purse and headed out for the West India Docks. Everything else could wait.

The wharves were a mass of swarming bodies; the deafening sound of sledgehammers striking metal made everyone roar at the tops of their voices. Some of the dockers were running up and down the gangplanks of ships with large sacks on their shoulders, others were rolling down large barrels, laden with spices and coffee. The aromatic smell of rum and sugar was heavy in the air. Pearl made her way to the shop selling the screeching green parakeets and looked down the side alley, where the indigo dye men had their gambling table.

Jeremiah was sitting opposite a short, squat man – Soo Chow, Lizzy's husband. Pearl remembered him from the restaurant. Both were frowning at the cards they held. Pearl flattened herself against the alley wall, and peeked out cautiously. Suddenly, the indigo dye man threw down his hand and laughed triumphantly. There was a snort of anger from Soo Chow, who grabbed hold of Jeremiah's coat. But Jeremiah was stronger and larger. He caught Soo Chow by the throat, squeezing hard.

'You know what I do to people who can't pay up,' the indigo dye man snarled. Then he laughed and shoved Soo Chow roughly away. 'Another game? Double or quits. It will give you a chance to win back some money before your wife finds out.'

'You're going to kill someone if you carry on like that, if you haven't already.' Soo Chow scowled and took a step towards Jeremiah. Then he smirked. 'Your luck won't hold. This time I will win.' He sat down again and shuffled the cards. 'OK, we play again.'

Pearl walked towards the men, who were so engrossed in their game they didn't notice her. 'Got space for a third player?'

The men looked at her, annoyed at the disruption. 'Private game,' Soo Chow said, looking at her closely. 'My wife told me all about you. She doesn't like you.' He laughed unpleasantly.

'It's a shame Lizzy can't let go of the past. But I came here to see Jeremiah.'

The indigo dye man looked vexed.

'We didn't finish our conversation the last time we met,' Pearl said. 'You ran off in a hurry when the peelers came. Is there any more you can tell me about Ah Sim? It seems he had a habit of annoying people. Anyone in particular?'

Jeremiah shrugged. 'I already told you. I didn't know him well.'

Pearl took a chance. 'Maybe, but he owed you money. Did you quarrel with him?' She was pushing, but it suited her mood. She felt wretched and ill-tempered from the night of opium.

Jeremiah's nostrils flared. 'You've got a nerve! What would I have to gain? I wanted my money back, and there'd be no chance of that if he were dead.'

There was a snigger from Soo Chow. 'Remember that fellow who beat you at cards last year? You cut him up something nasty!'

Jeremiah shot him a look. 'That was different.'

Soo Chow chuckled. 'Best keep on the right side of him, Missy. He's the indigo dye traders' best knife thrower. Won a competition for it.'

Jeremiah looked ready to throttle Soo Chow. Pearl stepped in between them. She pressed on while the indigo dye man was rattled.

'Did you know someone called Old Jake? The poor man was killed recently. My uncle's a copper and looking around for tip-offs.' She tried another tack, keeping her tone light. 'There might be some money in it if you have any information.'

'I'm no police informant! I've never heard of that man. Look, I'm just an ordinary worker, minding my own business. You have the wrong idea about me.' There was a sheen of sweat on Jeremiah's upper lip.

Out of the corner of her eye, Pearl caught Soo Chow lean over the table to sneak a look at Jeremiah's cards. 'Hey! This man's cheating!' she called out loudly.

Soo Chow stood up, knocking over the cards. 'Keep your mouth shut. Or I'll give you a good slapping.' He moved to leave. 'This woman is bringing me bad luck.'

Pearl sneered at him. 'The last man who tried to get the better of me truly regretted it.'

There wasn't anything more to be gained here from the venomous looks of the two men, so Pearl started to walk back towards Pennyfields. But after a few minutes, a voice called out: 'Mrs Fitzgerald! Let me speak with you.' Jeremiah had caught up with her.

'Don't go making trouble by giving any tittle tattle to the police about me. The last thing I need is for them knocking on my door. They don't like indigo dye men. Got it in for us. I can't afford to lose my job. Just to prove I'm no villain, I'll help you. Xianfan told me how upset Ah Sim's sister is. I feel sorry for her, losing her brother like that. If you want to know who killed him, you should talk to his boss.'

Pearl looked up at him. 'You mean Mrs Soo Chow?'

'One of my mates who works for her told me Mrs Soo Chow found out Ah Sim was stealing from her.' Jeremiah glanced around nervously. 'I've said too much already. I've told you where to look, now leave me alone.'

The tall frame of the indigo dye man receded from view, disappearing behind a line of dockers unpacking large wooden crates of tea destined for the warehouses. A fragrance of jasmine filled the air. As Pearl watched the men working, she mulled over what Jeremiah had told her. All roads were pointing in the direction of Lizzy. But it would be difficult to get into The Dragon Inn without drawing attention to herself. Pearl's heart sank at the thought of crossing her childhood friend again, but there was no alternative if answers lay behind that restaurant door. After Mei's bitter disappointment in her the last time they met, Pearl desperately wanted to make up for the poor choice she had made.

21

'But I know Xianfan. He works here. He's a very good friend of mine,' Pearl tried again, speaking in Cantonese.

A stocky man with shoulders as muscular as a charging bull barred the entrance to The Dragon Inn restaurant. He stood with his arms folded in front of him.

'I know who you are,' he grunted at her. 'Mrs Soo Chow told me not to let you in.'

The door slammed shut in her face. She hammered at it in frustration, then nursed her sore fist. Downhearted and wandering aimlessly away from Castor Street, she paid no heed to where she was going until a horse reared up in front of her, its hooves narrowly missing her head.

'Watch it, Miss! Get off the bleedin' road!' an angry drayman shouted at her, pulling on the reins to calm his unsettled horse and then galloping off. Pearl leaned unsteadily on a lamp post, taking in deep, ragged breaths. From a nearby pub, she could hear the strains of *She Has a Sailor for a Lover.*

A memory came to her of Maude Kingsley belting out the tune, warming up her voice in the Portsmouth Theatre Royal dressing room. She'd sing to Pearl, kiss her, and then they'd twirl round in a fast and frenetic waltz. Those were sultry summer nights, when sleep was the last thing on their minds. Pearl remembered the poster she'd seen the other day, advertising Maude's latest engagement in London.

Maude could get into any restaurant or theatre she wanted, now that she was the toast of the town. Maybe she could help Pearl get into The Dragon Inn. Looking round, she caught sight of a hackney carriage across the street. She made a run for it, holding on to her bonnet. Shouting up to the driver she said: 'To the Alhambra, Leicester Square, as fast as you can.'

As the two Moorish minarets and dome of the theatre came into view, Pearl hoped that she was still fondly remembered by Maude; she couldn't bear it if she'd forgotten their previous intimacy.

The Alhambra was a sparkling palace, with each window brilliantly lit by candles. A steady stream of carriages was pulling up outside, disgorging the finely dressed theatregoers. *Maude has really hit the big time,* Pearl thought, proud that the first woman she had ever loved was achieving success on the West End stage.

Walking around to the side of the building, she headed for the stage door where a number of girls were laughing gaily, squinting to light their cigarettes and puffing out long streams of smoke into the mild night air. Pearl walked purposefully to the doorway and was just about to get past, when the stage doorman shouted out: 'Can't go back there, Miss. Artistes only.'

She smiled at him, eyes wide. 'My, that's the most wonderful moustache I've ever seen. Quite the finest.'

The stage doorman smoothed the ends of his whiskers. 'Thank you, Miss. Takes a lot of time and effort to look this good. I wax and comb it every morning and night.'

'And hasn't that paid off? I'm so sorry to trouble you, but Miss Maude Kingsley is an old friend of mine. She told me to visit whenever she was in town. Could you be a treasure and see if she is free?'

'What did you say your name was? I'll see if Miss Kingsley is in her dressing room.'

As he walked off, Pearl watched the scantily clad chorus girls who filed past. She averted her gaze and peered at the tattered old posters of stars gone by. Most were long dead, either worn out by the gruelling tours or fallen to the temptations of the liquor bottle. The stage doorman stomped back, a scowl drawing down the corners of his gleaming moustache.

'Says she's never heard of you. Off you go.'

Pearl's face reddened, especially when one of the chorus girls who had lingered in the corridor started tittering at Pearl's attempts to gain entry into the star's dressing room. Ignoring the mockery, Pearl took a shilling from her purse and placed it in the doorman's hand. She could scarcely afford it, but couldn't back down now.

'Must have slipped Miss Kingsley's mind. If you wouldn't mind telling her "The summer of 1885 at The Rose Suite, Royal Marine Club, Portsmouth," there'll be another shilling for you when you come back – whether she remembers or not.'

He huffed, then took the shilling without a word and started off down the hall again. Pearl tugged at her sleeves, trying to regain composure.

The doorman returned, all smiles, accompanied by the music-hall singer herself. 'Pearl, my darling! What a delightful surprise! I'm so sorry I didn't catch your name before, but I get so many admirers it's hard to keep up. It's wonderful to see you. We've so much to catch up on.'

Maude motioned Pearl into the dressing room, closed the door and drew Pearl into a warm embrace. 'When the doorman mentioned The Rose Suite, some naughty memories came back. What sport we had!'

Pearl looked around at the bouquets of sweet-scented flowers covering every surface, especially lilies, which were Maude's favourite. The aroma of gardenia perfume was overpowering. Costumes hung on hooks covered every inch of the walls; beautiful satin brocade ball gowns, tight-fitting and revealing bodices, even a tattered private's uniform for one of Maude's novelty acts, where she strutted up and down the stage as The Wounded Soldier, down on his luck. Back in the day, it so shocked the Methodist church in Portsmouth that they stood outside the theatre brandishing placards warning of unnatural vices. Maude had just laughed, saying it brought her even bigger audiences, keen for a whiff of scandal.

They held each other at arm's length. 'It's funny, I was just thinking of you,' Maude said. 'You always had a special place in my heart. I remember I was the first to love you, my darling Pearl, lying on those satin sheets, the fire in your eyes. It is something I will never forget. Come, sit with me while I get ready for the show.' Maude smiled. 'You were so young and I was almost five years older than you. What a wonderful time we had.'

Pearl didn't say anything, but reckoned Maude must be at least fifteen years older than her, if not twenty. Her exact age was a well-guarded secret.

In the first days of their secret romance, the singer would sip absinthe, encouraging Pearl to drink with her. Pearl had agreed, but it reminded her too much of The Sailor's Arms, and besides, Pearl was already floating on dream street. She didn't want anything to cloud her memory. They would lie panting and spent, until the dawn light crept in, the windows wide open, the sea breeze swirling the curtains in Maude's rooms.

When the music-hall singer left for her next theatrical engagement in Glasgow, Pearl held on as if she would never let her go. Maude had to prise Pearl's fingers from her waist. There were tears in the actress's eyes as she murmured against Pearl's throat: 'I am in agony to leave you. *Au revoir*, my luscious one. *À la prochaine*.' It was an affectation of Maude's to use French phrases whenever she could. Something she claimed to have learned from the duc d'Orléans, one of her first titled lovers.

Pearl's first awakening was dashed upon the rocks, the realisation dawning on her that it was just a dalliance for Maude. But for Pearl, it had meant everything. Sadly, there was no future for them and those tumultuous feelings she had for Maude were destined for the shadows, never to be spoken of in public. In spite of it all, it was a time Pearl would always cherish.

An older and wiser Pearl now walked around Maude's dressing room, which was much fancier than before. She gestured to the soldier's outfit, hidden at the back. 'Do you remember when you took me into the alleyway dressed as The Wounded Soldier?'

Maude giggled. 'I don't do that act anymore. Got to be respectable now that I am a big star, I can't go fooling around with young fillies.' She playfully smacked Pearl's behind. 'Besides, I have a new lover who keeps me very busy these days. And he is incredibly jealous.' She gave Pearl a sideways glance and waited. 'Well, aren't you going to ask me who he is?'

Pearl was used to these games. Melodrama was Maude's middle name. 'Do tell. Who is your latest beau?'

In answer, Maude flung herself on the velvet divan in the corner of the room, groaning as if in torment. She placed a finger on her rouged cheek. 'I have been sworn to secrecy, but since you pressed me so hard, I will tell you. It's Bertie.'

Pearl looked at her blankly. 'A very nice name, I'm sure. And is he good to you?'

'Oh, my sweet thing. You are so unsophisticated. That's what I love about you. His name is Albert Edward, Prince of Wales. Eldest son of Queen Victoria.'

Pearl whistled. She always knew Maude was ambitious. 'Saints preserve us, you really have landed the biggest catch. Royalty!' But a part of her also felt hurt; it was yet another reminder that she had been nobody special to Maude, just another lover to while away lonely evenings on a provincial tour. A clandestine titillation.

Maude was looking very pleased, patting her luxuriant golden curls. Pearl always had a suspicion that the abundance was due to artifice. She hoped the servant girl singled out for her magnificent mane had been paid handsomely for the missing locks.

'He's a darling and completely adores me.' Maude stretched back languidly on the divan.

The prince's reputation with his many mistresses was the talk of the town and Pearl was tempted to reveal what had been said about Queen Victoria's son in The Sailor's Arms, but instead said: 'That is the most fantastic news, Maude. And I have a splendid idea. Why don't you invite Bertie to The Dragon Inn restaurant, the finest in the East End? It serves the most wonderful Chinese cuisine, and there is an opium den upstairs. Top quality stuff. I'm sure he would love it.'

Maude shook her head. 'Oh, I don't think so. He can't be seen in such places. If his Mama heard about it, Bertie would be in terrible trouble.'

Pearl nodded. 'That is true, but what a shame. He is, after all, a prince. Anyway, I'm sure you keep him very entertained. Probably best to stay away from places of vice. No doubt he would be horrified at visiting such a disreputable establishment, even if it is the talk of the West End. It's the latest place to be seen.'

The music-hall singer's interest was piqued. 'Really? Is it really that wicked? I suppose we could sneak him in incognito for a few hours. Bertie hates to be bored. He might find it amusing.' Maude looked at Pearl's shapeless brown frock, curling her lip. 'Now there's a problem.'

Maude caressed Pearl's shoulders. 'I've never understood why such a lovely girl would hide that gorgeous form under the most unattractive dresses. Let me choose some suitable attire for the evening. You will be the belle of the ball. Apart from me, of course.'

Pearl was about to object, but thought better of it. This might be her only way into The Dragon Inn restaurant. She wondered what Mei would think of her flirting with an old lover, if she might be jealous. But what was there between them? They had kissed once, only for Mei to push her away and retreat into a remote silence.

'I give myself over to you, Maude; make a prize chump out of me,' she said. With a triumphant whoop and expert fingers, Maude unhooked Pearl's dress.

22

A glowing red lantern swayed above The Dragon Inn's portico. Sitting in the hackney cab with Maude, Pearl shifted uncomfortably in a yellow satin gown that Maude had picked out for her. It was even tighter than the gown Mei had lent her, and she could scarcely breathe. Maude had whistled appreciatively at the transformation. Pearl wasn't used to showing off her bare shoulders. She felt half-naked and marvelled at how Maude could be so unselfconscious in her daringly low-cut frocks.

The carriage stopped in front of the restaurant and Pearl stepped out, ungainly as a new-born foal. She felt so awkward beside the grace of Maude, who alighted from the carriage in one effortless move. Pearl was also beginning to doubt whether coming to the restaurant would bring her any closer to Ah Sim's killer. It might only serve to annoy Lizzy, although she would undoubtedly be highly entertained by Pearl's new outfit.

A row of hansom carriages pulled up, and a group of ladies and gentlemen dressed in their finery spilled out; the men in top hats, starched white collars and tails, the women in vividly coloured dresses, skilfully manoeuvring their voluminous bustles.

'Quite a top-notch crowd here tonight,' Maude said, looking over the group with a critical eye. 'Come on, I really want you to meet Bertie.'

They were greeted at the front door by fawning waiters who ushered them in. Pearl was relieved there was no sign of the bovine doorman from before, and thankfully no sign of Lizzy. As they walked further into the restaurant, the aroma of roast duck was making her mouth water.

At the largest table at the centre of the room sat a group of men in evening dress. They were all paying attention to a portly man with pale blue eyes, a drooping moustache and full beard. His florid face was perspiring profusely, the hair plastered down in greased curls. Pearl recognised him as Albert Edward, Prince of Wales, from pictures in the *Illustrated London News*.

'There's been a breakdown of law and order in the East End. I will make sure that every criminal here is hunted down and imprisoned. Better policing on the streets. It will be my mission once I am King,' Queen Victoria's son was talking with his mouth full of noodles. His cronies nodded sycophantically.

Maude walked over to the Prince Regent, planting a kiss on the top of his head. She then perched daintily on his knee. 'Bertie, my darling, you came early! Have you been waiting long for your little pussykins?' She playfully tugged his whiskers.

Pearl looked away in disgust. Was this simpering creature really the woman she had been so deeply in love with?

'I was hungry, heard this place served the best noodles,' he said in a deep voice, quite the poshest Pearl had ever heard. The prince's gaze landed on Pearl.

'And who is your little friend?'

'This is Mrs Pearl Fitzgerald. We met in Portsmouth when I was just a young star. She kept me company in that godforsaken town.'

The Prince of Wales grunted as he struggled to push himself out of the chair. He was a small, squat figure, almost twice as wide as the gaunt Chinese waiters who scurried about carrying tureens of soup.

Albert took Pearl's outstretched hand and kissed it. 'Delighted to make your acquaintance, my dear.' He breathed against her palm, leaving a greasy patch where his lips had been.

'Maude, be a darling and fetch me some more dumplings while I feast on *this* little dumpling.' Bertie sniggered at his own joke, still keeping hold of Pearl's hand.

Maude looked pleased that her current and past lover were getting on so well. She hurried away to a long table against the back wall with large platters of lobster, oysters and sea bass.

Prince Albert took Pearl's elbow and guided her to an adjacent room where a small orchestra was playing; several couples were dancing to a lively polka. Albert enveloped Pearl in his arms and twirled her around the room. He pressed himself tightly against her. 'So, are you a music-hall artiste as well? You're a lovely dancer. What a fine mover you are!' Pearl was twisting and turning in an ungainly wriggle in an attempt to evade his wandering hands.

The room was spinning and Bertie twirled her faster and faster, his hands straying lower. Pearl moved his hand further up her back, but the prince gripped her all the tighter. 'What a sparky little gal,' he murmured in her ear.

Pearl forced herself to give a schoolgirl giggle. 'Your Royal Highness, you are too kind. I beg you for a favour. I heard you talk earlier about hunting down criminals. If an injustice has been done, there is no higher authority than you in the land.'

'A favour, eh? And what do I get in return?' He spun her faster and gripped even more tightly.

'In Limehouse, a friend of mine's brother was horribly killed. The local police haven't found the culprit yet. They need more assistance as they are overstretched with trying to find the Whitechapel killer. Might you be able to have a word with someone at Scotland Yard, Sir?'

The prince looked interested. 'A foul fiend on the loose? Law and order are most important to me and will be a top priority when I am crowned.' He lifted his chin. 'I'll have Sir Charles Warren look into it. Known Charlie for years. And you can do a little favour for me.' Bertie tickled Pearl under the chin.

With relief, Pearl saw Maude walking towards them.

'There you are. I wondered where you'd got to.' The music-hall singer's eyes danced with delight. 'Pearl, you're such a little hussy. So glad you're getting on with Bertie.' She winked at Pearl.

'I think he's about to buy me a house in Mayfair, so be nice to him,' she whispered to Pearl. Taking hold of Bertie, Maude began a slow Viennese waltz.

From behind his mistress's back, the Prince Regent mouthed at Pearl, 'See me later.'

Pearl rubbed her smarting arms where the prince had held her. She waved gaily back at him. It might cost her a few bruises and trodden toes but if Bertie put in a word with the police commissioner, it might be worth proving to Inspector Crowley she was not someone to be trifled with.

A delicious smell of suckling pig wafted towards her. She perked up at the thought of the food on offer. In the dining room she plucked a morsel from a plate of scallops. Pearl also helped herself to some egg custard tarts, surreptitiously putting a few in her purse. She wondered whether Mei had a sweet tooth.

A waiter, dressed in a black satin robe, sounded a gong, which caused a lull in the cacophonous conversations of the diners.

'Ladies and gentlemen, the land of the lotus eaters awaits you.' Everyone started chattering excitedly. Pearl joined Maude and the Prince of Wales at the bottom of the stairs leading up to the opium room. At the end of the landing on the third floor, magnificent mahogany doors opened to reveal a lavishly decorated chamber, a resplendent riot of colours auspicious to the Chinese: bright hues of red, yellow and green, with huge scarlet and gold lanterns draped from the ceiling. Opulent silk screens hung from the walls, telling the stories of the Ming emperors, hunting and killing their way across a mountainous landscape.

Pictures of concubines in flowing robes playing melodies on a Guan, the double-reed pipe, before an audience of emperors and their families, reclining on divans. Lions, dragons and eagle-headed gryphons with the body, tail and back legs of a lion, raced and flew across the room, as one painting merged with another.

Pearl breathed in deeply, anticipating the first opium rush. But she would only have one pipe, no more, just to blend in with the crowd, and to take the edge off her nerves.

Soon everything was hushed, as if in the temple of some pagan religion. Only the contented sighs of the imbibers and the soft sucking at pipes could be heard.

Reclining ladies, clad only in chemises, were sprawled on couches and daybeds; their eyes half-closed in ecstasy. Moaning softly, they were lost in a Shangri-La; their fantastical world one could only guess at. A young woman, her long brown hair falling forward over her face, was swaying from side to side on a divan. She held the longest opium pipe that Pearl had ever seen. Fingers clenched tightly by her sides, Pearl wanted to snatch the pipe away from her. She chastised herself for being so impatient.

Serving the lounging figures was a jolly-looking man. His brown silk robes rippled as he walked back and forth in soft leather slippers, while the reed matting on the floor served to deaden any harsh sounds. On the tray he held in front of him were several pipes, a candle and small porcelain jugs.

He stood close to Pearl and she heard his stomach rumbling. She whispered to him: 'Have you had anything to eat? These egg tarts are the best I've ever tasted.' She took one from her purse and offered it to him.

He gave a broad smile. 'You are the first person who has ever offered me anything to eat,' he said under his breath. 'I've been working since dawn and haven't had any food. Thank you.' He gave a small bow, took the tart and devoured it in one bite.

Pearl smiled in sympathy. Speaking in Cantonese, she whispered back: 'I understand. I've waited upon rich people in my father's pub. They treat you like dirt. People like us are invisible to them. I'm only here because of my friend Maude Kingsley. She is a close pal of the Prince of Wales. They are treating me tonight.'

He smiled at her. 'Then you are truly fortunate.'

'You must know so much about black spice. Which type should I have? Nothing too strong but something which will relax me.' She wriggled her shoulders.

'I can see you have some Chinese blood. Mother or father from Guangdong? You speak good Cantonese, although with the English accent.'

'My mother's family is from Guangdong.'

'My name is Deng, from Liwan District. I left there as a boy, but I am so homesick for the red lychees I used to pick on the banks of the river.'

Pearl gave a little gasp. 'We are from the same district, Master Deng. We could be cousins.'

The man grinned. 'In that case, I will be honoured to help you.'

He led her over to a doorway and held aside a curtain for her to enter. Inside the small box room were several large mother-of-pearl cabinets. At the one nearest to them, he pulled out a row of drawers containing smooth, dark lozenges of opium. He took one out, rubbing the surface with his thumb. 'This is from Hainan. It gives the best dreams. The westerners love it. But too much for the brain. Some never the same again.' He twirled a forefinger against his temple.

He opened another drawer. 'From Sichuan, very good for the lovemaking.' He laughed throatily. 'Makes men very strong. But then diarrhoea.'

Pearl asked question after question, complimenting Deng on his knowledge and laughing at all his jokes. After a while, she bent closer to him, saying in a hushed tone: 'Is it getting more dangerous in the East End? I've heard about the Whitechapel murders and now the Chinese man killed on Wapping Old Stairs. I'm terrified.' She shuddered and crossed her arms tightly. 'Everyone was talking about it.'

Deng nodded. 'Yes, that's what I heard. His head was bashed in and brains came out through his nose. Throat cut from ear to ear. He was disembowelled.' News of Ah Sim's death had travelled everywhere, and the manner of his death was becoming more outlandish with every passing week.

Pearl clutched on to Deng's arm. 'No! That's terrible! Do you know who the dead man was?'

The man nodded. 'Nice fellow but very foolish. One of my friends told me he was stealing opium from the boss and selling it on.'

'He worked here? The dead man got on the wrong side of Soo Chow?'

'No. His wife is the one in charge. I heard Mrs Soo Chow shouting and screaming at Ah Sim – that was his name – threatening to kill him. She kicked him out and I never saw him again.' He whistled through his teeth. 'You don't mess with the dragon lady.'

Pearl exhaled out loudly. 'Yes, I know Lizzy. We grew up together.'

Deng's eyes grew wide, with respect or fear, Pearl wasn't sure. 'Then you understand.'

She thought again of what Old Jake had said; a woman wearing golden boots with tinkling bells, running away from the murder scene. Pearl had already searched Lizzy's office, so now might be the time to see what the bedroom revealed. Falling upon an idea, she said: 'That reminds me. I have a gift from Mrs Soo Chow's mother. She asked me to bring it. They haven't been getting along recently, and no wonder after what you've told me. But Ma Jennings wants to get back in touch. She has a lovely brooch for Lizzy, very precious and expensive.' Pearl looked around her disparagingly. 'I don't trust anyone here not to steal it. It would be so helpful if you could let me know where her bedroom is, so I could leave it there for her, as a surprise?'

A frown line appeared between Deng's eyebrows. 'It's the floor below, but if you give me the present, I can leave it in a safe place for Mrs Soo Chow.'

Pearl touched his sleeve. 'There's been such bad blood between mother and daughter, and I want to bring harmony between them. Relatives should not fight, you know that from the old country. Always nice to do someone a good turn, isn't it?'

Deng tilted his head, considering this. 'You are right, but don't worry, I will take care of it.' Pearl bit her lip, wondering how she could get rid of him and search for the bedroom on her own.

She staggered sideways, hand on her brow. 'Oh, the smell of the opium is making me quite dizzy,' she muttered.

Alarmed, he said, 'Miss is not feeling well? The drug is strong for those not used to it.'

'Is there a ladies' room? I think I might be sick.' Pearl asked in a trembling voice.

'Yes, of course. Please follow me.'

At the top of the stairs, Pearl moved falteringly, leaning heavily against Deng. He took a step back, not realising he was at the edge of the top step. He stumbled, losing his balance. Deng tried to right himself, arms flailing around wildly. He fell backwards, tumbling down two flights of stairs. He landed with a heavy thud at the foot of the stairs, right in front of Lizzy. Pearl peered down, hoping he was not too badly injured, but then stepped back, close against a tapestry, making sure she was out of sight from the lower floors.

Lizzy looked down at the groaning waiter. 'Deng, you oaf! This is a dignified establishment. If I smell alcohol on your breath, you're fired.' She snapped her fingers and two men hurried forward to haul the dazed man to his feet and out of sight.

Pearl looked down from her vantage point at the top of the stairs. Lizzy was moving quickly and confidently around the restaurant, checking on her guests and taking particular care to chat with a group of gentlemen dressed in white tie and tails. Her childhood friend wore a velvet gown of dark green, studded with red sequins and diamanté, so she shimmered and glittered like a dazzling Christmas tree.

As Lizzy bustled around the crowded dining room below, inspecting the dishes and pouring glasses of Champagne for the diners, Pearl crept away from the banister, and made her way down to the second floor. She quickly opened door after door, but they were only store cupboards and supply rooms for the restaurant. The fourth door on the right had a golden handle. Pearl slipped in and knew she had finally struck lucky. The bedroom was lit by a crystal chandelier suspended from the ceiling, sending sparkling lights darting around the room.

Just as Pearl was about to rifle through the contents of a chest at the end of a massive four-poster bed, she heard Lizzy's voice getting closer. Pearl looked around for somewhere to hide. Seconds before the door opened, she jumped into a large wardrobe, leaving the door slightly ajar. Fur coats and darkness surrounded her, the fragrance of expensive perfume tickling her nose.

The bedroom door slammed shut. Through the small crack in the wardrobe door, Pearl could see Lizzy had come into the bedroom, the tiny bells on her golden boots tinkling merrily. The footsteps became more muffled when she strode across the plush Chinese rug, decorated with snarling tigers. Lizzy lit a cigarette and took a deep drag, blowing out two long, thin, concentrated lines of smoke through her nostrils. Her husband Soo Chow had followed her in with a slow, ponderous tread. He threw himself on the bed with a grunt.

Lizzy was in a very bad mood. Tapping a red-varnished nail against her front teeth, she looked in irritation at her supine husband, his head nestled comfortably on cream silk pillows. He was reading the racing pages of a newspaper.

'Soo Chow, you lazy swine, don't think you can get out of helping sort this mess, otherwise we'll end up in the rookeries.'

'Whatever you want, I will do.' Soo Chow looked up from his paper and blew Lizzy a kiss.

She ignored his affectionate gesture. 'And don't you dare go gambling as soon as my back is turned.'

Lizzy continued marching up and down the bedroom. Then in a move copied from the actress Sarah Bernhardt, whom Pearl remembered Lizzy greatly admired, Lizzy sashayed and swished her long skirts around in one deft move. She leant down over him. 'Something's up, my sweetie, no doubt about it, and we've got to take action. My men have told me there's a rival gang trying to set up in my area. I pay them plenty to hear the local chatter, but get precious little back from them. But they did tell me about the Wild Eyed Boys who are new in town, and their leader, the Blue Man. Have you heard of him?'

Soo Chow grunted in reply. 'There's talk, but you worry too much.'

'You know how much it costs to pay off the dock superintendent and all his cronies.'

Lizzy was now standing directly in front of the wardrobe. 'Whoever this gang is, they haven't reckoned with me. I've worked too long and hard.'

Pearl didn't dare breathe.

'We own this part of Limehouse,' he said decisively.

'Yes, my petal. We need to impress this on the lowlifes and stamp it out. Show them I'm in charge around here.'

Pearl's legs were beginning to cramp from bending low in the wardrobe, her ribs aching from the tightness of her dress. She wondered how much longer she could stay there.

Lizzy lit another cigarette and then began barking orders at Soo Chow. 'You need to get ready. We've got a large shipment of opium coming into the West India Docks next Friday at midnight, on the *Sir Lancelot.* Get the men ready to go down to the docks. And keep your ears open for any mention of the Wild Eyed Boys. I want names. I want to know who I am dealing with and exactly where they are based. And then we hit them hard.'

'Do I need to do it now?' her husband whined. 'I haven't had my dinner yet.' Pearl was realising that Soo Chow was slow to action, unlike his wife.

'Another thing. From what you told me, Pearl Fitzgerald is snooping around your pal Jeremiah. I told you not to gamble with him as you always lose. But it's good she's looking at him, as I don't want her asking us any more questions about Ah Sim. That bastard! He got what he deserved. No one double crosses me. My dear childhood friend has been talking to the police and getting very cosy with Mei. We can't afford her poking around in our business. But I've got a plan. A nice little stool pigeon to throw to the police. A shame really, but it can't be helped. All our problems will disappear.'

There was the sound of rustling and grunting. Pearl peeped out to see Soo Chow wrestling with Lizzy on the bed.

'Not now, Soo Chow, get off me. We need to get back to work. If you're a good boy, I'll give you a treat later.' Lizzy gave him a sharp kick. Pearl caught a glimpse of a golden heel.

'You said that the last time,' whined her husband, his voice receding as they both walked out of the bedroom.

Pearl felt even more certain that Lizzy was responsible for Ah Sim's death. Betrayed by a pair of gold boots, because who else in Limehouse would have the audacity to wear such expensive footwear on the manure-laden streets of Limehouse? Vanity would be her downfall. Yes, Lizzy had the means, motive and opportunity to kill Ah Sim. Pearl counted to a hundred before opening the wardrobe door and slipping out into the corridor and running down the stairs.

Maude's booming voice stopped her in her tracks. 'There you are! Sweetheart, I've been looking for you. The party's just started. Bertie can't get enough of that special brand of opium. Come and try some.'

Pearl hesitated. She knew she should leave now, but the call of the drug was difficult to resist. What would be the harm in imbibing just one pipe? She'd earned it, now that there was a positive lead in Ah Sim's murder. Catching hold of Maude's hand, they ran back into the opium room. The last thing she remembered was giggling hysterically and asking the prince if he thought the police commissioner would come to Limehouse for a pint at The Sailor's Arms, and give Inspector Crowley a good talking to. A lassitude washed over her limbs as she fell into unconsciousness against Maude's breast.

OCTOBER

23

'Extra! Extra! Read all about it! Police make an arrest in the Limehouse Chinaman killing!' Pearl rummaged around in her purse for a farthing to pay for the *East London Advertiser.* Her vision blurred and she shut her eyes tight before opening them to read the front page:

CHINESE LAUNDRESS ARRESTED FOR MURDER IN LIMEHOUSE

Tuesday 2nd October 1888

> Mei Tan, of Pennyfields, was last night charged with stabbing her brother Ah Sim Tan on Wapping Old Stairs in Limehouse. Eyewitnesses have come forward to say they saw the Chinese laundry worker quarrelling with her brother and stabbed him, causing a fatal wound to the stomach. It is believed brother and sister were part of a triad gang, dealing in opium.

Pearl dropped the newspaper in the street and a gust of wind fluttered the pages into the sky like pigeons scattering from the sounds of gunshot. What could have happened? A week had passed since she'd last seen Mei, the time spent lost in a haze of opium, smoking pipe after pipe in her bedroom at the lodging house.

Pearl desperately needed to see Mei.

At the police station, Sergeant Knox looked Pearl up and down. 'You've scrubbed up nice and proper.'

Pearl realised she was still wearing the tight yellow gown, given by Maude. She smiled and curtseyed low.

'How lovely to see you, Sergeant Knox. I'd appreciate your help. I'd like a moment with Miss Mei Tan. I'm her only friend here, she has no one else to look out for her.'

Knox puffed up his chest. 'Glad you've found your manners, Mrs Fitzgerald. Much as I would like to oblige, I'm afraid you cannot see the prisoner. That woman is accused of a very serious crime and the inspector is busy questioning her. She'll confess sooner or later. You can leave a message and I will pass it along.'

Pearl was seething, frustrated with this buffoon for thwarting her attempts to see Mei. As she turned her back, Sergeant Knox whistled loudly. 'See, you can dress like a lady when you want to.'

Pearl rested on a park bench, massaging her feet. Her ribs ached from the tight restriction of the gown, the whalebone stays gripping her in a skeleton's embrace. She thought about her uncle, maybe he could help with access to the cells. But there had been no word of him since they had met at the Ten Bells when he was undercover.

On and on she trod, growing more desperate with every step. It was now evening, and the bells of Christ Church Spitalfields chimed eight. The thought of Mei in a dank and verminous prison spurred her on. Pearl felt crushed at the thought of that free spirit, the high-wire acrobat whose natural habitat was the sky above the crowds, now trapped in a six-foot holding cell. And the injustice of it all, when Pearl knew that Lizzy was up to her neck in this.

She remembered that O'Dwyer had said he would be in the

Three Crowns in Shoreditch if she needed to contact him, a notorious dive, frequented by bawds and sneak-thieves. Anxiety quickened her breath as she walked across the threshold of the pub.

She could barely see through the thick fog of cigar smoke. The shouts of merriment were deafening. Sitting by the pianoforte was a familiar figure. Cuddled up on his lap was a woman with curly brown hair, abundantly flowing around her shoulders. The woman's head was tilted back, singing lustily:

'And should my partner squeeze my hand
'I know what I'm about
'If it pleases him, it don't hurt me
'I'm the merriest girl that's out.'

The man threw his head back. Pearl knew that high-pitched chuckle from her childhood days. She fondly recalled falling asleep to that sound, curled up in a corner of the snug bar in The Sailor's Arms. She stepped forward and gently touched the man on his shoulder.

O'Dwyer looked up. 'Pearl! You in trouble?'

The concern in his eyes touched Pearl and tears welled up in her eyes. O'Dwyer stood up abruptly, much to the annoyance of the woman who had been sitting in his lap. She looked sulkily at Pearl and stalked off towards the bar.

'Come outside. I'm still undercover,' he muttered.

In the alleyway, he awkwardly patted Pearl's arm. 'Dry those tears now, Petal. Nothing can be that bad.'

Pearl wiped her cheeks. 'You're the only one I've got left, now that my Pa's gone. Please, Uncle Peter. I'm asking for a friend who's locked up in the nick. She's innocent and I want to see her. But Inspector Crowley and that damned Sergeant Knox are keeping me out. I'm sure they've arrested the wrong person.'

'I'd love to help you, darlin', but I can't interfere; it's not my case.'

Pearl's shoulders heaved. 'I understand. I'm sorry to ask you.' But she wasn't completely averse to pulling at the heart strings when necessary; that was the O'Dwyer in her. 'I'll go to All Saints church and light a candle for dear Auntie Kathleen's soul.'

The policeman's cheeks paled. 'Good of you to remember my poor, sainted wife. She suffered terribly, God rest her soul.'

'You old hypocrite.' The woman who had been on his lap was at the doorway, listening. She barked out a laugh and stomped back to the bar.

'Please, Uncle Peter. I've no one else to turn to.' She wondered what would sway him. 'My father's dying words were about you. He told me to say that you were the dearest, best brother he ever had, apart from the business with Betty,' she added hastily. 'After all, family is everything.'

He wiped his forehead with a handkerchief. 'Let me see what I can do. Never liked that Crowley. He's new, not from this area. One of those educated fellows that Scotland Yard brought in. Trying to teach us what we already know. And muggins Knox owes me a favour.'

'Oh, Uncle Peter, bless you! I'm sure my father and Auntie Kathleen are smiling down on you.' Pearl kissed him lightly on the cheek. 'You are the bravest of men. I knew I could count on you.'

O'Dwyer growled. 'Never mind that. Don't go making a nuisance of yourself. Sit tight and I will be in touch.'

24

Pearl sucked the blood from a cut on her finger. She had been staring distractedly out of the kitchen window while chopping up vegetables. It had been days since her uncle had promised to help her see Mei, and there was still no word. Every muscle in her body yearned to do something, but she had promised to wait. Out of the corner of her eye, she saw a rat gnawing at a potato peeling that had fallen on the floor. Pearl threw a rolling pin at it and missed.

With an exasperated sigh, she threw the vegetables to one side and shrugged on her coat. She wasn't sure how to proceed but staying indoors would drive her to the lunatic asylum.

She paused for a moment. What would her father do? Just barge his way in and demand the truth. No beating about the bush, just square up and force Lizzy to confess to setting up Mei. She had heard Lizzy telling Soo Chow she was going to find a stool pigeon, but never imagined Mei would be the target. Maybe she should have gone to the police immediately. No, this was not the time to admonish herself. It was time to see how much of her old man's bluster and daring she had inherited.

Newell Street was crowded with draymen and their wagons rattling along the road. The ginger beer maker gestured to her, offering a glass of refreshment for her to buy. Even though she was parched, she ignored his pleas, anxious to reach The Dragon Inn restaurant.

Pearl thought longingly about the opium den on the third floor, palms starting that old familiar itch, but she was still mortified about the last time she had imbibed. A horrible vision of herself, the prince and Maude laughing hysterically together. She quickly pushed the embarrassing memory aside. She needed a clear head to talk to Lizzy.

At the side entrance, several men were sitting around a makeshift table, playing cards. She recognised the game as Fan Tan, a favourite with her lodgers. A cadaverous-looking man was drawing deeply on a cigarette.

'Do you know where Deng is? Got some business with him.' She raised her eyebrows.

The man laughed and nodded. 'Downstairs eating. Maybe afterwards, you go with me?' He eyed her up and down, trying to get a good look down her cleavage.

'Thank you, my little honey-sop. I'm sure I'll have time for you later.' She kicked up her heels, now thankful she was still wearing the tight canary-yellow gown.

She managed to get halfway up the stairs before there was a shout behind her. Two burly men were coming up fast. 'Hey you! Not allowed in here.'

She had about a ten-second head start before they caught her. Heart thumping, Pearl ran up the first flight of the stairs and dashed down the long corridor. She remembered that Lizzy's office was the second room along the hallway and pushed open the red door.

'You just can't keep away from me.' Lizzy was standing by the window, arms folded.

Two guards ran in, panting.

'No, no, leave it. But the next time you're caught off-guard by this woman, you'll be on the next boat back to Shanghai. Clear off now,' Lizzy ordered.

Lizzy's eyes travelled slowly over Pearl's body. 'Where did you get that dress? From some penny gaffe tart? It's really not your colour. Makes you look sallow. The way you go striding about. So unfeminine. Not at all ladylike.'

A rush of shame shot up Pearl's insides. Lizzy unerringly knew where to aim.

'Since when have you been bothered with how I dress? But nice of you to care,' Pearl said, keeping her voice light.

'You've been busy, getting up to all sorts. My people have had quite a time with your comings and goings. Soo Chow's been keeping tabs on you. Getting cosy with my mother, are you? Suppose it's because you've never had one.' She gave Pearl a pitying look. 'You're welcome to her, even though she's a poor substitute.' Lizzy placed a cigarette in a long ebony holder and lit it. 'And Mei. You two are quite the chums.'

'You've been following me?' The room suddenly seemed airless. It made sense now, the constant feeling of being watched.

'Of course. I know everything that's going on in Limehouse. My spies are everywhere.'

Lizzy sat down behind her desk and started slitting open envelopes. The letter opener had a beautiful jade handle. She deftly twirled it around in her hand and then pointed it at Pearl.

'This was a wedding gift from Soo Chow. The jade is a thousand years old. It's a dagger that once belonged to an emperor. He was said to have cut a hundred of his enemies' throats with it. The blade is extremely sharp.'

'Charming story,' Pearl said. 'But I've come to ask you about Mei. Why did you turn her in to the police for killing her brother? It beggars belief. You know she's innocent. What could she possibly have done to you to deserve that?'

'What do you know of Mei? She was in my employ and I know

her much better than you do. That one's a dark horse. And families don't always get along.' Lizzy ground out her cigarette in a large crystal ashtray.

'I'm sure she couldn't do anything like that. Don't force me to do this, Lizzy, but I will. You had something to do with Ah Sim's murder. I've seen proof that you paid him to work in your opium business. And people have told me you threatened to kill him. Before Old Jake was killed, he more or less told me he saw you that morning at Wapping Old Stairs. I'll go to the police and tell them what I know. Don't forget my uncle is a copper. But drop your accusation against Mei and I won't say anything.'

'How dare you threaten me!' Lizzy's throat was a blotchy red, staining her porcelain skin. 'Don't take me for a half-wit.' Lizzy thrust the letter opener's point under Pearl's chin. Its razor-sharp edge pierced her skin.

She grabbed Pearl's arm, squeezing tightly. 'I could slit you from ear to ear. You stole from me when you were last in my office. I've got a packet of merchandise missing, and I account for every single one. Acquired a taste for black jade, have you? That stuff will kill you.' She jabbed the letter opener again at Pearl's neck. A trickle of blood oozed.

Pearl breathed out slowly. 'Let's calm down and talk about this. Tell the police you were mistaken and I won't say a word to them about what I found in your office – the packets of opium, the note to Ah Sim – and now you attacking me. Lizzy, please, could you really live with yourself for sending Mei, an innocent woman, to the gallows?' She paused. Lizzy's face was unreadable, but she withdrew the dagger.

A mocking sneer was Lizzy's answer. 'You've no idea about Mei. She's a sweet thing. Very affectionate. And loves presents.' Lizzy raised her eyebrows and smiled, licking her lips.

'She is a good person. Better than any of us.' Pearl fought to keep her voice steady.

Lizzy's lips twitched. 'Let me tell you something. I know everyone's sordid little secrets. Especially yours. Did you really think I wouldn't know what the two of you were up to in her bedroom, under my roof, that I paid for? Panting over each other? There's a spyhole in the door. Such an adorable scene.'

Pearl's mouth was dry.

'She's a spicy little minx. I know you're itching to touch her. But *I* am her special friend. She is very grateful to me for the lovely gowns I buy her. Just like that purple one she so foolishly gave to you. Gets free board and lodging with me. As I said, *very* affectionate. Especially after a few glasses of Champagne. We were in our cups, and one thing led to another. She is quite the saucepot. And that acrobat's body! So strong and supple. I worked her up into such a frenzy. Soo Chow likes to watch from the spyhole, so we're all happy.'

Lizzy pushed back a flame-coloured curl from her forehead.

An agonising pain was throbbing at Pearl's temple. Lizzy and Mei. Together. How could that be possible? Pearl's head was spinning. The room went in and out of focus.

She swallowed down tears, suppressing the urge to hurl insults at Lizzy. The very least she could do was try to maintain her dignity. 'I felt sorry for you.' Pearl nodded grimly at Lizzy's questioning look. 'When we were kids, I knew you were unhappy at home, you were always looking for an excuse to be out. That's why I let you stay with me at The Sailor's Arms whenever you wanted. You've changed so much from that sweet little girl I once knew. What happened to her? All this hatred has turned you into a monster.'

'Don't speak of those times!' Lizzy's face turned deathly pale.

'It's not too late, Lizzy. Let's go to the police and tell them you made a terrible mistake about Mei.'

Lizzy stood up, knocking the ashtray to the floor. Cigarette stubs and burning embers scattered across the rug. Her eyes were glistening. She took another cigarette, lit it and took a long, ragged drag. She spoke calmly. 'Soo Chow and a couple of my workers have told the police they saw Mei on the foreshore that morning. She had a fight with her brother about money and she killed him. I went with them to interpret. Soo Chow likes to pretend he doesn't speak English. Less bother, he says. My husband will do anything I tell him to do. Besides, did you know that Mei had stabbed a man to death in China, stuck a knife deep in his belly? Very skilful with a blade. She's done this kind of thing before. The police were very interested to hear about it.'

'I don't believe you!' A terrible pressure was building up behind Pearl's eyes.

'You were never a good judge of character. Mei's dangerous. That's why I was drawn to her, but she started to get airs and graces – and I don't put up with that from anybody. So yes, I gave Mei up to the police to stop them poking about in my business. And who knows? Maybe she did kill Ah Sim. She's very strong, you know.' Lizzy raised an eyebrow.

'You're wrong. Mei loved her brother. And what about Old Jake? Did you kill him just like you killed Ah Sim?' Pearl looked at the knife in Lizzy's hand. 'That temper of yours will get you into trouble.'

Lizzy threw back her head and laughed. 'That's the funniest thing I've heard in ages. If I wanted anyone dead, I'd order one of my men to do it. I wouldn't get my dainty hands soiled. Might ruin my nails.' She jabbed the dagger again, the point pressing urgently against Pearl's throat. 'I just like toying with people.

'Nobody cares, not me and certainly not the coppers. They don't care if they nab the wrong person, as long as someone swings for it. Those peelers are all in my pocket. I keep 'em sweet with trinkets and tarts.' Lizzy paused for a moment to let that land. 'I'll spread it about town what you and Mei have been up to, and your reputation will be as filthy as the sewers that overflow in Limehouse Hole. You go making trouble and with one word from me, those mutton shunters will lock you up – again. Oh yes, I know all about the first time you were banged up by Crowley. The next time won't be so pleasant. Nice bit of fresh meat like you will go down a treat if the crims get their hands on you. Now get out before I tell my boys to give you a good thrashing.'

25

Her hands were red raw from scrubbing the dress clean and the soap suds had turned from pearly white to sludge brown. Tears streamed out of Pearl's eyes and into the washing tub; a dull ache in her throat.

Bad luck clung to her like a rancid smell. Ever since she could remember, people had abandoned her. First, her mother. She had never known the warmth of a maternal caress, or had someone gently wipe away her tears, apart from her father with his clumsy, harsh hands.

Then Tommy, who had promised he would always be true. Gone these seven years, his body vanishing in the rhythm of the ocean's depths.

Her father. Her closest living relative, until she had pushed him away. She bitterly regretted it now. If only she could have him back – just for a day. There was so much she wanted to say to him. Only now did she have the words, but it was far too late. Why did he not know she yearned for a very different life from the one he had wanted for her? And now, when The Sailor's Arms was rightfully hers, it had been snatched away. She still needed to find a lawyer to contest Betty's forged will, but helping Mei had overtaken everything else.

She thought of the fleeting, intense moments with Mei. In her dreams, she dared to hope that something might flare and kindle between them, some lasting attachment. Her stomach had flipped over as if plummeting from the top of a Ferris wheel when they had kissed. She would gladly have sacrificed so much for Mei; she had already put her life in danger for this woman.

Now, she felt like such a fool. Mei didn't care for her at all – and how much did Pearl really know of her? Being with Lizzy like that! All the signs were there. Mei pulling away, always speaking well of Lizzy, full of admiration for the kindness of her employer, perhaps even in love with her. Accepting expensive gifts, the Belgian linen handkerchiefs, the fine gowns. Pearl cursed herself. And what of Lizzy? Kissing Mei, and much more. Images kept flashing in Pearl's mind. She closed her eyes tight. Lizzy had never shown any sign of being sexually interested in women when they were growing up. But then Pearl had kept her own thoughts buried. Or was it for her husband Soo Chow's benefit? Who knew what went on behind closed doors.

And could Mei really have killed a man back in China? Pearl's mind was as murky as the soap suds in front of her, her heart curdling. It occurred to her that she'd never asked Mei where she was on the morning that Ah Sim was killed.

Lizzy and Mei could have been in cahoots all along and have planned the murder together. Maybe it was an accident that got out of hand. Lizzy had twirled around that razor-sharp letter opener, revealing she knew Ah Sim was stabbed in the belly. Was it a lucky guess or had she let that slip in her boastfulness? The specific details of the wounds inflicted hadn't been revealed to the public – as far as Pearl was aware, only herself and the police knew. She had kept from Mei the details of how Ah Sim had suffered, his painful death, to spare her feelings. But Mei could have found out those details from the police. Jealousy corroded her skin, insistent and sinuous. Pearl's desire for Mei might have clouded her judgement, but now doubt was creeping in.

She tugged at her hair, torturing herself with sordid imaginings; visions of Lizzy and Mei lying together naked kept replaying in her mind. The chilled water in the washing tub wrinkling her hands and fingers. And what of the Blue Man, where did he fit into all of this? He might be an elusive phantom, a stranger prowling in shadows, with a lust for murder . . . or just another wild goose chase the police were wasting their time on.

She was alone in the world with no one to turn to. The only thing left was to throw herself into the Thames. Pearl wondered how many seconds it would take for a blissful unconsciousness to overcome her in the shock of the ice-cold river.

A loud rapping on the front door disturbed her reverie. 'Go away,' she muttered, then closed her eyes to conjure up a picture of grey-green ripples in the Thames that would bring a welcome release from all her suffering.

The banging continued, accompanied by a loud voice. 'Pearl Fitzgerald, I didn't come all this way just to stand outside in the rain, bawling at you. Come here right now and let me in!'

Uncle Peter. She had completely forgotten about him in her abject misery. Feeling as if she was dragging a hundredweight of coal on her back, Pearl shuffled to the door. O'Dwyer took in Pearl's tear-streaked face and puffy eyes.

'Hmmm. Looks like I'm here just in the nick of time.'

He bustled around the kitchen, getting cups and saucers ready for a strong brew, and sneakily adding a large splash of rum from a hip flask, while she haltingly described the awful confrontation with Lizzy – leaving out the revelation about Mei – and the confirmation that it was Lizzy who had accused Mei of killing her brother.

O'Dwyer scratched his thick sideburns. He looked at the painting on the wall of an enormous-fanged golden lion, its claws gripping on to a young lamb. 'So you're ready to walk away from a friend in need on the word of Limehouse Lizzy, who you don't trust no more? Something wrong with that picture.' He stood close to the lion painting and traced its mane with his little finger. He copied its fierce growl and turned to Pearl, baring his own teeth. Involuntarily, she laughed.

'It's complicated, Uncle Peter. Lizzy said some things that seriously made me doubt Mei.'

'Like what?' O'Dwyer continued his scrutiny of the lion, this time curling his own fingers into an approximation of claws.

'Lizzy hinted that Mei could be dangerous, and I should be careful.' Pearl knew she was being evasive, but couldn't tell her uncle the true nature of her feelings. He wouldn't understand, and she feared his disapproval. She couldn't take another blow like that.

She sighed, struggling to find the words to explain. 'I trusted Mei and now I have doubts about her that I can't get out of my mind.'

The policeman finally drew his eyes away from the roaring lion. He gently took Pearl's hands in his. 'You're a bright girl. What does your heart tell you? I might seem like a blundering old fool, but I know about people, and I know you. Trust your instincts. It seems like Mei needs your help and if you think she is innocent of killing Ah Sim, then find out for sure. Keep your eye on Limehouse Lizzy. That one's tricky.'

'Do the police have any suspects for Old Jake? I keep thinking it might be the same person who killed both of them. He and Ah Sim were both stabbed in the belly.'

'Don't go jumping to conclusions. Old Jake was most likely killed in a drunken fight. You know how he was always up for a brawl, drinking and bragging. Forget about him and focus on your friend. But more importantly, take care of yourself.'

O'Dwyer poured himself another generous splash of rum. 'Been meaning to ask, have you sorted things out with The Sailor's Arms?'

Pearl made a face. 'Betty's not budging. But I did find a will in my father's room, and I suspect it's a forgery. Here, take a look.' She opened a kitchen drawer and handed her uncle the document.

O'Dwyer squinted at it. 'That doesn't smell right to me.' He took hold of Pearl's shoulders. 'You've got to fight for what's yours. PJ wanted you to have that pub, I know it. You're his kin. Like I told you before, go and see a lawyer to straighten things out. The law is on your side.' He touched the sergeant's stripes on his upper arm proudly.

'I don't have the money to pay for a lawyer, and where on earth would I find one? I don't know any.'

O'Dwyer tapped the side of his nose. 'I happen to know a lady lawyer. She takes an interest in helping out women in need of legal advice. Go and see Miss Eliza Orme on Chancery Lane. Tell her I sent you.'

He looked closely at the cut on her neck where Lizzy had nicked her with the knife. 'Scrapping again? Let me clean up that cut before it gets infected.'

O'Dwyer dabbed some rum from his hip flask onto a handkerchief and wiped Pearl's neck.

'Jesus, Uncle Peter! That really smarts!'

He laughed. 'Not feeling so clever now, eh? Listen, I've found a way to get you into the jail. That's what I came to tell you. Taken a big risk for you. Do you want to go on with this or not?'

Pearl hesitated and then slowly nodded at her uncle.

O'Dwyer tilted his head and then frowned. 'If Crowley hears about what I'm doing, I'll be joining your friend Mei in prison. So go and see her to find out the truth for yourself. Now, I've got a real task on my hands of getting Knox well and truly drunk. He's got hollow legs.' O'Dwyer drew her into an enormous bear hug.

'I'll be keeping a beady eye out. The last thing I want is PJ coming back and haunting me, saying I'm not looking out for his only daughter. I'll be at the nick to greet you. Come to the station the day after tomorrow at dusk.'

26

Two gentlemen in long black gowns and powdered wigs strode along the wide streets flanked by red terracotta buildings. Pearl looked in awe as they talked earnestly to each other, white collars flapping in the wind, not understanding a word they said. They ignored everyone in the thoroughfare, only nodding at others in the legal profession. Pearl knew nothing about the world of lawyers. She craned her head, looking up at centuries-old buildings, with twisted, church-like spires looming high up into the skies.

Sandwiched between the west and east ends of London, Chancery Lane was a stark contrast to her own world, although it was only half an hour's walk from Limehouse. Clean streets, well-dressed folk and the drawling, over-enunciated vowels cultivated at Eton, Oxford and Cambridge. She gazed up at the Maughan Library, with its neo-Gothic Clock Tower, ornamental pepper-pot towers, spires and arched windows, which made it look like a mediaeval church. It was one of the most magnificent buildings she had ever seen. Pearl didn't belong here; she was self-conscious of her scruffy clothes, intimidated amongst these learned folk, talking so earnestly to one another of important matters.

Rather than kicking her heels waiting around for word from her uncle, Pearl had decided to visit the lawyer he had suggested. Following his directions, Pearl walked down a series of narrow lanes until she found herself in front of an office building with a brass plate on the door, inscribed with the names 'E. Orme' and 'M. E. Richardson'. Pearl pushed open the heavy door and climbed up the stairs. The office on the first floor was a hive of activity. Two women were talking earnestly to a mother with three bawling infants, and a young errand boy carrying a large sheaf of papers scurried past Pearl and ran down the stairs, on his way to carry out deliveries.

Every wall had bookcases stacked with law reports, leather-bound volumes and large box files. Papers were overflowing everywhere – onto the floor and several tables. There was a poster for a Liberal Party meeting propped up against a wall; a lopsided stack of 'Votes for Women' leaflets next to it.

At the largest desk in the room sat a woman wearing pince-nez glasses, scribbling furiously on note paper. She was so absorbed in her work that she didn't notice Pearl approaching her desk. Her hair was a wavy mid-brown, very neatly tucked up into a bun at the top of her head. She wore little jewellery, apart from a silver chain attached to a large watch, which was fastened to the collar of her severe black silk dress.

She picked up a cigar that had been gently smouldering on an ashtray and took a puff. Pearl gave a little cough. Finally the woman looked up. Inquisitive blue eyes stared directly into Pearl's. Taking another drag on her cigar, the woman asked abruptly in an imperious tone: 'Do you know how much barmaids earn?'

Pearl was about to answer, but the woman continued earnestly. 'The working conditions of women really need to be addressed. They work such long hours, sometimes more than one hundred hours a week, and at pay far less than a man's – of course. Things need to change!' She took another deep drag of her cigar. 'Their health suffers from chronic fatigue, swollen legs and feet, and varicose veins. Someone needs to commission a survey on this.'

Pearl nodded. 'Yes, the hard work is punishing. I should know. I was brought up in a pub.'

'Well, then. You understand,' the woman's brow unfurrowed and she smiled. 'Now, what's the reason you've come here today? Do you have an appointment?'

'I'm sorry, no. But this is a matter of great urgency. My name is Mrs Pearl Fitzgerald and I'm looking for Miss Eliza Orme. My uncle sent me as he said I should consult a lawyer.'

The woman lifted her chin. 'You've found her. But I'm not a lawyer.' Eliza Orme's voice grew solemn. 'Women are not admitted to the bar.'

'Oh, I do beg your pardon. I was misinformed by Sergeant O'Dwyer.' Pearl was disconcerted by this woman and her abrupt manner.

'So, O'Dwyer is your uncle? Peter is one of the best coppers on the beat. A bit too fond of the drink, but treats fallen women with great sympathy.' Eliza stood up, leaning both hands against the desk.

'Just because men are refusing women admission to the bar, doesn't mean we are giving up. We do very well for ourselves in spite of the obstacles. I devil for about a dozen conveyancing counsel who keep me busy on drafts they want done in a hurry.'

'What do you mean by devil?' Pearl worried that she had come into some bizarre religious cult.

'To devil means I prepare written legal work for a more senior barrister. I am qualified to do this service, for which I get paid half of what a man does.' Eliza shrugged her shoulders. 'Annoying, but that's how it is for now. I am still well compensated and there is plenty of work for me and my colleagues. I specialise in wills, property transactions, settlements and mortgages. Miss Richardson also works here and Miss Reina Lawrence.' Eliza Orme's voice softened at the mention of the last name.

She gestured over to a woman who was seated at the second largest desk in the far corner. 'Reina, did I tell you I have to see a woman tonight who has been thrown out by her husband?'

The other woman, upon hearing her name, walked over to Eliza, laying a hand on her shoulder. 'You work far too hard,' Reina said. 'We must get away for a few days so you can get over that chest cold. You might be the first woman in England to earn a law degree from University College London, but you are not invincible.'

Pearl watched them both with keen interest.

'You work just as hard as I do, perhaps even more.' Eliza smiled fondly at Reina, then became aware of Pearl staring at them. Her manner changed and she was all business. 'Is there an issue I can help with, Mrs Fitzgerald?'

'Please call me Pearl. If I could explain, Miss Orme. My father passed away recently. He always said he would leave The Sailor's Arms pub to me, but I have been away for several years. Now, his lady friend, Betty Sullivan, says she is married to my father and has a will in which he named her as the beneficiary. I've got hold of the will, but it looks like a forgery to me. It incorrectly has his middle name as John, not James, as it should be. I know this but Betty obviously doesn't.'

Eliza tapped the pince-nez glasses against her teeth. 'Inheritance claims can be very tricky. Do you have the document with you? I'd like to see it. And please call me Eliza.'

Pearl handed the will over to the lawyer who read it carefully.

'Hmmm, he could have been of infirm mind when he wrote it, explaining the error. But if you have several examples of your father's signature, we could compare them and make a case that this one is a forgery, including the name error.'

'I've brought along some birthday cards and letters that my father gave to me. The signature is so different. What do you think, Eliza? If we can prove it is fake, am I the rightful owner of the pub? My father always promised it to me, his only child. My uncle can vouch for that.'

'Possibly. But your father's signature could have changed the older he became. Of more concern is if Betty Sullivan is indeed your father's legal spouse. Then she would most likely inherit as his next of kin. The new spouse would be entitled to inherit most, or potentially all, of his estate, leaving nothing for any children from a previous relationship.'

'Betty claims she can't find the marriage certificate and I suspect it's because there isn't one. Betty is a thief, she knows it's rightfully mine. This is a nightmare.' Pearl's voice grew louder, giving vent to her fury.

'Please calm yourself. Sometimes, these legal issues can drag on for a long time, so you need to be patient. But don't worry, we will sort this matter out.' Eliza's mouth twitched slightly, amused at Pearl's sudden outburst. 'You need to prove your father and Betty were never married. If there was a formal wedding, there should be documentation at the local record office. I suggest you find out if there is a legal testament of their marriage. I think that's at Limehouse St Anne.'

'I doubt it. St Anne's is an Anglican church. It's more likely to be the Catholic church at St Mary and St Michael's on Commercial Road.' Pearl was disappointed. 'I was rather hoping you would be able to do that for me?'

The lawyer smiled at her patiently. 'Forgive me if I am mistaken and speak out of turn, but not everyone is able to cover my full fees, so I often suggest people attempt the first part themselves. Perhaps you could visit St Mary and St Michael's and see if you can find the marriage certificate there. But do come back to me if that proves unsuccessful. I can then make a legal argument to see if we can register the pub in your name.'

Pearl nodded a thank you, feeling more than a little embarrassed. These posh women always made her feel dim-witted and inadequate. 'Thank you for your advice, Miss Orme,' she said stiffly. 'I'm afraid I can't pay you at the moment, but once my inheritance is settled . . .'

'Of course. We can defer payment until this matter is resolved. I am more than happy to assist you. Especially in these cases where there is some skulduggery afoot. If it's illegal, I will make it my business to find out. The underdog needs a champion.' Eliza looked pointedly at Pearl.

'That's why I studied the law – so I could explain to women their rights from a legal point of view. Now, contracts are my particular favourite. Consider a situation where a testator specifies their only daughter is the sole beneficiary of their estate in their inheritance contract. Other important issues to consider are freedom of testation, beneficiaries' rights and right to fair process.' Eliza's eyes had a faraway look, savouring the words like a delicate cream puff.

'And there is also the possibility of claiming the will invalid due to the testator's lack of capacity. You also need to look at intestacy laws, or other beneficiaries named in previous valid wills.'

Pearl's head was spinning; she had no idea what Eliza was talking about. She stood up hastily. 'I am most grateful to you. Please don't let me take up any more of your valuable time. There is just one other matter I wanted to enquire about.'

Eliza tilted her head. 'What else can I do for you?'

'My friend has been wrongly imprisoned for murder. Someone has stitched her up. Could you represent her?'

'Regretfully, that's outside the realm of my expertise. I wish I could help.' Eliza's brow creased. 'I would advise that you hire the best criminal lawyer you can afford. Forgive me for saying this, but if someone has given evidence against your friend, she is in grave danger of being sent to the gallows.'

27

Pearl pushed open the glass swing doors at Thames Police Station with perhaps more vigour than was necessary, as it banged with a loud clatter against the wall. Moving swiftly to the sergeant's desk, the beaming face of her uncle greeted her. He gave a thumbs up and hiccupped.

'Come on, duck. Sergeant Knox won't wake up for hours yet. My word, can he drink! And I gave him a right earful for locking you up that night. Creepy Crowley had better watch out now, I've got my eyes on him. Luckily one of the coppers on the beat told me what was going on. Anyways, I'm guessing you know where the cells are. Mei is in the third one down on the left. I've got my young pal Constable Brannigan to keep watch if you need anything.'

Pearl kissed her uncle on the cheek and hurried towards the cells. She remembered her way down these dank corridors; the air was clammy and foetid; a feeling of despair clung to the air like a mourning shroud. She rubbed the back of her neck, feeling both sick and excited at the thought of seeing Mei. Constable Brannigan, a fresh-faced country boy from Cork, ushered her down to the cells. He had told Pearl she didn't have much time with Mei, and he would come and collect her shortly.

The cell door swung open, revealing a wraith-like figure in

prison grey sitting on the bed. Pearl wasn't prepared for the change in Mei. Her skin was now a greyish colour, eyes huge with dark shadows pooling underneath. Her hair was matted, face caked with a layer of black soot. Prison had already taken its toll on Mei. Pearl almost wept at the sacking cloth dress that hung off her like tattered rags. She knew how much pride Mei took in her neat and clean appearance.

'How are you?' Pearl winced inwardly at the inane question as she stood awkwardly in front of Mei. There was no other furniture in the room on which she could perch.

A ghost of a smile played on Mei's cracked lips. 'Hungry. They don't serve ha gao dumplings here.'

Pearl wanted to reach out and comfort her, but then an image of Lizzy kissing Mei's breasts flashed in Pearl's mind. Any sympathy Pearl had trickled into the gutter along with her shredded heart.

'I went to see Lizzy the other day. I believed she was the one who killed your brother, and I wanted to get her confession.' Pearl tried to keep her voice steady as she paced up and down.

'What? Are you sure? I can't believe it was Liz!' Mei's face now had a greenish tinge. 'She killed my brother?' As Mei gripped the edges of the bed, Pearl could see the muscles tensing in her jaw. Neither spoke for a long time. There was just the drip, drip, drip of a leak, oozing a malevolent black slime out of a large crack in the wall.

In a monotone voice not at all like her own, Pearl said: 'You must be shocked to hear that your lover murdered Ah Sim.'

Mei put a trembling hand over her eyes. Pearl continued, trying to keep the hurt out of her voice. 'Imagine my surprise when Lizzy told me that she had been intimate with you. That she had lain with you in your bed many times.' Pearl's fingernails dug into her palms, producing sparks of pain. The putrid air of the cell filled her nostrils. 'Is it true?' Her voice cracked.

Mei was bent low, shaking her head wearily. 'How little you understand the world, Pearl. You, who have never gone without a meal in your life. You had a father who loved you, and – I suspect – plenty of suitors who desired you, and you desired them in return.'

She looked at Pearl defiantly. 'Yes, I was flattered by Liz. She was kind to me, very generous and caring. I felt special. Liz can be charming. She was my first, and we grew close, two lonely people offering each other comfort.'

'Oh, it's Liz now, is it? How sweet! You had me duped!' Pearl felt murderous.

Mei's chin went up. 'You have no right to say whether I was right or wrong to take her as a lover. Once it started, how could I refuse? I was caught. Liz was my employer. She could have taken away my job. She threatened to throw me onto the streets when I tried to end it. And I had Ah Sim to think of. He was also working for Liz.'

Pearl said nothing, an agonising ache in her throat.

She dropped to her knees in front of Mei, regardless of the filthy floor. 'Why didn't you tell me? And to think I had fallen for you,' Pearl said in a rush, the words spilling out before she could stop them.

Mei smiled sadly. 'Yes, I could see it in your eyes. And I was feeling the same. Every time we met, I wanted to be close to you, even though I tried to push you away. For the first time, I knew this was true love. So I told Lizzy we could not continue. She was angry with me and I saw her true nature. She said she'd tell the police that I killed Ah Sim. I was no use to her anymore. But I risked all – for you.'

Mei reached out to take her hand but Pearl snatched it away. 'I don't believe you. Lizzy told me that you killed Ah Sim. Handy with a dagger, was what she said, and that you had already stabbed a man to death in China.'

'How can you believe that I would kill my own brother? And yes, I did kill a man in China, but it was self-defence. I barely escaped with my life. Whatever you think, listen to what I have to say.' Mei looked anxiously at the prison cell door. 'I might never have the chance again to say this if I am sent to the gallows. There is not much time. I couldn't bring myself to talk of Liz for fear of what you would think of me. I have such feelings for you, my precious Pearl, born of the east and the west. My heart breaks with love for you. I am glad we met, even if we never see each other again.' Mei covered her eyes.

The cell door clanged open, making both women jump. 'Oi, look sharpish. Time's up.' The anxious face of Constable Brannigan peered in.

Mei looked intently at Pearl, holding her gaze. 'You have to believe I am innocent. Are you really going to listen to Liz and not me?'

Pearl sighed, shaking her head. 'I don't know what to believe. But I am going to try and find out the truth of what happened to Ah Sim. I owe him that much.'

Mei sighed. 'I loved my brother. His killer is still out there. Promise me that you will continue searching, so Ah Sim's spirit can finally be avenged.'

Outside the police station, Pearl looked up at the sky and breathed deeply. Mei loved her! But Pearl was torn between jealousy and joy. She walked in a dream-like haze back along the river, ignoring the shouts of the fruit sellers, weaving her way among the barrows. She stopped by a lamp post, a decorative serpent coiled around its column. She pressed her flaming cheek against its iron dorsal fin. Pearl's mood darkened like the eddying, swirling black ripples of the Thames. That incredibly strong undertow could bring down even the strongest of swimmers.

28

Someone was shaking her awake. Pearl had a crick in her neck from sleeping all night on a hard wooden bench at the police station. 'Mrs Fitzgerald. You have to stop coming here and making a nuisance of yourself. It's five o'clock in the morning.' Pearl looked blearily into the face of Crowley. He did not look happy.

'Inspector! I've been waiting for you all night. Please listen to me, I beg of you; Miss Mei Tan is innocent of murder.' She put a hand on his arm.

'You are wasting my time yet again. I thought you would have learned a good lesson from your last visit.'

'Please, Inspector. Throwing me in the cells won't deter me in the slightest.'

'That is apparent,' Crowley said through gritted teeth. 'You are trying my patience, but you have five minutes of my time. It's lucky Sergeant O'Dwyer is a respected copper round here and vouched for you.'

As soon as they were in Crowley's office, Pearl faced him. 'I'm sure Mrs Soo Chow is involved in Ah Sim's murder. I heard her say she was glad he got what was coming to him. He was stealing from her. She even threatened me with a dagger when I confronted her. You know she's involved in opium smuggling. You took the note from me that I found in her office, with money for

Ah Sim to collect opium. The note paper has the stamp of The Dragon Inn restaurant, with Lizzy's signature on it. The opium den is above the restaurant. One of her own employees told me she threatened to kill Ah Sim. A lot of people are pointing the finger at her.'

The inspector shook his head. 'We have eyewitness accounts of what happened that morning.'

'I know that information comes from Lizzy. But she is throwing you off the scent because she is involved. Before Old Jake died, he told me he saw a woman wearing tasselled gold boots on Wapping Old Stairs that morning. He said the boots had little bells that tinkled as she ran away. Only Lizzy wears distinctive boots like that in Limehouse.'

The detective glanced at her, his face grim. 'As I've told you before, he can no longer make a statement, so we have no way of verifying your claims. Miss Tan is in custody as she is a person of interest, and we will keep her in as long as we need to for further questioning. It was not just Lizzy who gave us Mei's name. Several witnesses saw her arguing with Ah Sim at Wapping Old Stairs. We believe brother and sister were both part of a Chinese Triad gang.'

'And what about the blow to Ah Sim's head?'

Crowley shrugged. 'There is uncertainty as to whether this was caused by a deliberate strike by an assailant or the result of the victim falling and hitting his head on rocks.'

'That's nonsense! And what about the Blue Man? He is prowling the streets of Limehouse, and might be the killer of those women in Whitechapel. You've got more on Lizzy and the Blue Man than you have on Mei Tan.'

Crowley shook his head. 'I'm not at liberty to say any more.' He made a move to usher Pearl out of his office.

She was on the verge of being thrown out. Then it came to her.

The conversation at The Dragon Inn. 'You will want to hear this, Inspector. I overheard Lizzy and Soo Chow talking about a large shipment of opium and contraband goods coming into the West India Docks. On Friday at midnight, aboard the *Sir Lancelot.*'

She had his attention. 'Now this *is* of interest. You must tell me everything you know. We need to stamp out these thefts as well as deal with the opium smuggling. The port authorities are losing a great deal of money through pilfering. Do you mean tonight, Mrs Fitzgerald?' Crowley was on alert, like a greyhound straining at the leash.

Pearl frowned. Lack of sleep and having spent the night waiting at the police station had dulled her sense of time. 'Of course, today is Friday! Yes, Inspector. Forgive me, I do indeed mean tonight.'

Crowley ground his teeth. 'Are you sure this isn't a cock and bull story?'

'Can you afford not to believe me, Inspector? What if you ignore my information and miss out on catching the criminals in the act?'

'Give me all the details you remember and I will have my men investigate – if there is indeed any truth to what you say.'

'I will tell you, but I must come with you.'

'That is completely out of the question; I cannot bring a woman.'

'I know the location of where the opium will be coming in, and I know who is behind it. I am only willing to give you the information if you take me with you.'

Crowley was silent. Pearl waited a few moments and then added softly: 'This could lead to a promotion for you, Inspector. And put you in good stead with the West India Committee.'

'Give me one reason why I should believe you,' he said.

'You don't have to believe me. Instead put your faith in the Good Lord.' Pearl looked at the bible on his desk. From her previous meetings with Crowley, she knew he was a religious man.

Hands behind his back, the detective walked over to his bible. He opened the gilt-edged book tenderly, running a loving finger down the page and then suddenly stopped.

Looking down, he read aloud where his finger had halted: *'Ask, and it shall be given you; seek, and ye shall find; knock, and it shall be opened unto you; For every one that asketh receiveth; and he that seeketh findeth; and to him that knocketh it shall be opened.'*

He turned to look at a crucifix on the wall, the ivory skin of the Christ lacerated with open wounds, the edges jagged with dirt. The crown of thorns around the neck dripped blood onto his chest, forming a ruby necklace.

'You are invoking the Divine Lord, Mrs Fitzgerald, and I must trust you as a good Christian woman. I always ask for divine guidance for the course I need to follow. Now the Holy Father has spoken, and I must obey that voice.

'You need to tell me now where this opium is coming in. But if this is mere tomfoolery, I suggest you start praying for your soul. Old Testament vengeance is swift and unmerciful. If you are giving a policeman false information, there will be a severe penalty from which your uncle won't be able to save you.'

Pearl looked at him, her eyes never wavering from his. 'Throw me in jail again, if you wish. I swear to you on my father's grave that what I say is the complete truth. But I will only reveal what I know if I am there with you.'

29

Crowley looked at her with barely concealed irritation. There was little cover at the West India Docks to shelter from the chilly night. He pulled out a handkerchief to dab at his nose and then sneezed loudly. He had dispensed with his usual policeman's attire of bowler hat and smart suit in favour of a sailor's cap, woollen pea coat and heavy hobnailed boots.

Pearl shushed him to keep quiet, but it was doubtful she'd be heard above the rattling of the ships' sails and rigging. The wind was howling, shrieking like a widow in the first paroxysms of grief. A powerful gust was buffeting at Pearl's skirts and petticoats. Her shawl billowed wildly around her, unfurling like a flag, and slapped into Crowley's face.

The clock clanged midnight and still there was no sign of anyone approaching. Pearl, Crowley and two police constables were crouching uncomfortably close together behind an enormous coil of rope and some large barrels. No protection from the elements but enough to keep them hidden from view. There was a clap of thunder and it started to rain heavily.

'Are you sure this is the right place?' snapped the detective. 'I'm beginning to think you're making a prize idiot out of me.'

Pearl put a placatory hand on his arm. 'Please, Inspector, be patient. They will be here soon. The wind is kicking up, so things might have been delayed.' She was playing for time, her nerves ragged. Mei's life was on the line. What if the plan had changed, or she had misheard the details when hiding in Lizzy's wardrobe?

An hour later, Crowley had run out of patience. 'Right, that's it. You're done. Come on, this caper is ending now.' He grabbed Pearl's arm and marched her towards the iron gates at the entrance to the West India Docks. Pearl had to admit that the ship was not coming in. The information had been false. She had to think of something, fast.

She resisted him, and then swayed, placing a trembling hand to her breast. She was shaking all over, stumbling over the uneven cobblestones. 'Please, Inspector. Let me catch my breath.' She would have fallen to the ground but Crowley just managed to catch her in his arms.

'Mrs Fitzgerald, are you feeling unwell?' he said, shaking her gently by the shoulders. 'Really, you are not as strong as you think you are,' he muttered under his breath.

'My heart is not good. I would feel much better if I had something to revive me.' Pearl moaned faintly. 'Forgive the frailties of a woman. Would you be so kind as to accompany me to the Railway Tavern? Perhaps I could have a brandy to steady my nerves and dry off from the rain. It is not far.'

If Pearl managed to persuade Crowley to wait at the pub, it would buy her time to come up with another plan. It now seemed likely the shipment wasn't coming in at the allocated time. Pearl knew the Railway Tavern was a favoured haunt of sailors and dockers. She could talk to them and see if they had any information on the *Sir Lancelot*.

Crowley looked at Pearl warily. 'As you wish. We shall go to this hostelry to seek shelter from the elements. But only for a short time until you recover.'

He awkwardly held out his arm to Pearl and they walked down the wharves until they came to the Railway Tavern on the corner of Garford Street and West India Dock Road. The pub was a meeting place for all sorts of seafarers. Coming from all four corners of the globe, they drank deeply, gossiping to while away the hours before news of their next ship. As usual, it was a swarm of sailors, chin-wagging with their fellows, telling tall tales and renewing old acquaintances.

Pearl wriggled her way to the saloon bar, followed by Crowley. She did a quick scan of the crowd. Almost by a sixth sense, she could tell the mood of a rowdy gathering of sailors and dockers, something only someone born and bred in a pub would understand, to be able to gauge whether the punters would burst into song or start a fist fight. Tonight there was an air of celebration; ships had come in and the sailors were keen to spend their earnings.

'Why, if it ain't the Fitzgerald girl!' shouted a man in a gaudily embroidered waistcoat from behind the bar. 'Got a kiss for 'ole Clarence Wilberforce?' The landlord leapt over the counter and drew her into a bear hug. When he held her at arm's length, his grey eyes watered.

'Heard about your old dad, Pearl. One of a kind, he was. Anyways, what's up with you? Lookin' a bit peaky, my girl. You up the duff or summat?' He wheezed with laughter and then looked at Crowley who was standing beside Pearl, clearly uncomfortable in these surroundings, shuffling from foot to foot. Wilberforce jabbed a saveloy-shaped finger at the detective's bony chest.

'You the daddy?'

The detective drew in his chest and backed away. A blotchy flush suffused his cheeks. 'No, I most definitely am not,' he bristled.

'Didn't think so. Not enough good spunk in yer, methinks. And yer not good enough for PJ O'Dwyer's pride and joy, neither. So you'd best keep your hands off this lady here. Odd-looking cove.' His shoulders lowered as he stared menacingly at Crowley.

'Don't worry, Clarence, he's a gentleman and I can vouch for him.' Pearl nearly laughed out loud at the thought of being romantically involved with the inspector. Pearl put a comforting hand on Crowley's arm and winked at him. He reddened and averted his eyes.

Then, she rather belatedly remembered her role as the delicate lady on the verge of collapse. She tottered unsteadily on her feet and hoped Maude would approve of her approximation of a damsel in distress. Wilberforce looked concerned, his brow wrinkling as he put out a hand to support her. 'You don't look so good, Petal. I'll just get you a drop of Grant's Morella. That'll fix you up in no time.'

Wilberforce shoved some protesting sailors off a table and motioned for Pearl and Crowley to sit. He watched approvingly as Pearl downed the glass of brandy he had placed in front of them. She gave a slight shudder. The publican's voice softened as he patted Pearl's hand.

'Must be hard for you without a husband. Sailed on *The Colossus of Rhodes*, and went down somewhere in the Indian Ocean, didn't he? Poor sod. Some of his old mates are here, just in from Jamaica. Fancy a chat with 'em, to see if they can tell you what happened? I'm sure they would like to pay their respects to his widow. They was just raising a glass to absent friends and mentioned Tearaway Tommy. They used to have bets on how fast he could shin up a rigging. I'll call 'em over.'

Pearl laughed, remembering Tommy showing off his athleticism in scampering up the ship's ropes, quicker than any monkey. She remembered cheering him on as he waved down from the crow's nest. Then her smile faded. She'd have to face his mates as Tommy's widow, endure their pitying looks.

Once Wilberforce had disappeared from sight, Crowley leaned over to Pearl and said firmly: 'You seem to be better, Mrs Fitzgerald. It is time we were leaving.' Pearl hesitated, but this was an opportunity to find out if Tommy's mates knew anything of the *Sir Lancelot* and why it had failed to berth in the West India Docks. Before she could reply, Wilberforce returned with two sailors. The Jack Tars were swaying from side to side, as if still rolling with the ocean's swell at sea.

Crowley stood up. He was growing more agitated, his jaw twitching and clenching with frustration. He was just about to speak when one of the sailors put an arm around the detective, howling with delight.

'How ya been, Jonesy? Haven't seen you for ages. You just back from India or New Zealand?' He squinted blearily at Crowley. 'God, but you've aged. If I was you, I'd lay off the drink.' Pearl was amused at Crowley being mistaken for a Jack Tar. The sailor was about to plant a moist kiss on the outraged detective when he caught sight of Pearl. He shoved Crowley out of the way and reached out for Pearl's hand, removing his cap.

'Mrs Fitzgerald! I'm Jim. Sorry about old Tommy. What a lad he was. Let's get some more drinks in for a toast. And if there is anything I can do to help, just ask.'

'Much obliged, Jim.' As Pearl watched the sailor's retreating figure, she wondered what he knew; sailors on shore leave were always up on what was happening on the docks, including which ships were coming in and out.

Pearl rose slowly. 'Please excuse me just for a moment, Inspector. I need to speak with that man, I will only be a moment.' She hurried off without waiting for an answer, following the sailor.

She tapped him on the shoulder at the bar. 'Jim, I wanted to ask, do you know which ships were coming in this evening at midnight? We were down at West India Docks earlier, waiting for the *Sir Lancelot*, a shipment coming in from Shanghai.' She raised her eyebrows at him. 'You know what I mean – contraband stuff. We waited for hours but it never docked. Does anyone know why it didn't show up? I've got a lot at stake on that ship.'

The sailor shook his head, tugging the scarf around his neck. Pearl pressed on further. 'For the sake of Tommy, gone these many years? I need the money, Jim, otherwise I could be out on the streets. You know what it's like for sailors' widows.'

He blew out his cheeks. 'Didn't know you was that hard up. Be careful, Pearl, there's a lot of dangerous folk out there, and they'd do anything for a sovereign or two. But I did hear about the *Sir Lancelot*. Thought I'd ask if they needed any men on board when they leave the docks.'

Crowley had followed them over and caught the tail end of their conversation. 'This is most important, Sir. You would do well to help us.'

'Jonesy! When did you change your accent and go all proper? Thought you was East End born and bred!' The sailor winked roguishly. 'You and Mrs Fitzgerald up to no good? Carrying on like that, I wouldn't have thought you had it in you.' He gave Crowley a hefty slap on the back, who staggered at the blow.

'You have mistaken me for someone else . . .' spluttered the policeman.

Pearl leaned into Crowley and whispered: 'Give him a shilling.'

The detective looked outraged, but Pearl kicked him in the shins. Wincing and exhaling noisily, he took out his wallet and drew out a shilling, offering it to the sailor.

Jim took the coin and bit it between his teeth. The seaman grinned broadly and tapped the side of his nose. 'You're in luck. Got some information for you. Fingers Freddy was in here earlier for a quick sup. Said he couldn't stay long because there was a consignment from Shanghai coming in. Should have been in earlier, but they got a tip-off that the private guards at West India Dock were on to it. He said it was coming into East India Docks instead. He was cursing and swearing about the change of plan.'

'What time is it due in?' Pearl was frantic that they might have missed the shipment. She prayed that they could still be in time. This was her best chance of getting Mei out of jail and it was slipping away.

She grabbed hold of the sailor before he could answer her question. 'Jim, for the love of God and all the sailors drowned at sea, please tell us the quickest way to get there.'

The sailor thought for a moment. 'Go down to the East Gate, walk right down to the end. There's a large patch of ivy on the wall. Push that aside and there's a small door. Knock four times, then three, then four again, and say: "How goes the good ship *Sylph*?" But remember to say those exact words.'

Crowley was looking pleased. He puffed up his chest. 'I'll organise my men. Mrs Fitzgerald, if you are still feeling unwell, I suggest you stay here.'

'Not bloody likely,' she told him.

Pearl ran after the detective, who was already at the door. Once outside, he blew sharply on his police whistle. After two minutes, Crowley blew again. This time, a constable came running up to him, puffing and wheezing with the exertion.

'What took you so long? Get five men from the station. The youngest and fittest,' ordered Crowley. 'Go down to the Grand Gate at East India Docks and prepare for the fight of your lives.'

The detective turned to Pearl. 'If you insist on coming, follow me, but you need to stay well back.' He moved surprisingly fast and Pearl had a painful stitch in her side by the time they were running towards Naval Row, and then along South Quay.

The last time she'd been here was with Tommy. They'd come on a secret rendezvous to get away from the prying eyes and sly whispers at The Sailor's Arms. He'd been so excited about their future life together. How different her life was now. Tommy would have howled with laughter to see what Pearl was up to – and with a police inspector in tow.

At the East Gate, Pearl and Crowley walked along the wall until they came to a large patch of ivy. After much pulling around at the thick vegetation and refusing Pearl's help, Crowley eventually found the hidden gate. He rapped sharply on the door in the sequence given to them by Jim. Crowley impatiently tapped his foot and knocked again. There was still no answer. The inspector was about to bang at the door again, when it creaked open and a weather-beaten face peered out. 'Watcha want? You're mad as hops banging on the door like that. Gonna wake the dead with all the racket.'

'Come on, my good man. You know what we are here for. Let us in immediately.' Crowley was itching to get in and tried to shoulder his way past the man who raised his fists menacingly.

'Got no idea what you're talking about. Now on your way.' The man started to close the door.

Pearl quickly scooted in front of Crowley. 'Freddy!' she said in her warmest voice. 'And how goes the good ship *Sylph*? Jim sent us over. I'm sure you remember Tommy Fitzgerald, he had a reputation for shinning up the rigging faster than anyone. He was my husband, may the saints preserve his soul. Jim told us that the *Sir Lancelot* is due in. There's a Shanghai shipment on board, and we were supposed to be there to meet it. They must have forgotten to tell us the change of plan.'

Freddy pursed his lips and started to close the door.

'A widow's got to live somehow,' Pearl said hastily. 'I'm sure you understand. My friend will show you his appreciation.' She kicked at Crowley's shins again.

The detective winced and looked indignantly at Pearl. 'Please stop doing that.'

She could sense his intransigence, so tugged hard on his jacket. 'Come on, give him some dosh, Jonesy.'

The policeman resignedly reached into his wallet, taking out a shilling.

Fingers Freddy tossed the coin in his hand. 'Don't be so stingy. I'm taking a big risk letting you in.'

Crowley reluctantly handed over a sovereign to Freddy, who nodded.

'Let's go on with it,' the inspector snarled.

They followed Freddy along a narrow passageway. 'We got word the *Sir Lancelot* was coming in here late,' the watchman said. 'Go down to the far end, next to the *Lady Gallicia.* She should be coming in within the hour.'

Pearl and Crowley walked along the quay, lined with ships moored for the night. They crouched behind a large crane near the water's edge where Freddy had told them the *Sir Lancelot* would be berthing. The minutes ticked by slowly and Pearl was becoming increasingly jumpy.

In agitation, she rifled through her pockets. Her fingers closed around a card. She took it out, wondering what it could be. She looked down at the card, decorated with a blue willow pattern picture. A man in a boat with two birds flying overhead. It had been in the opium package she had stolen from Lizzy. She'd kept it with her, hoping to remember why the image had stayed with her. With a jolt, Pearl realised where she had seen it before. It was identical to the signage board hanging above The Dragon Inn restaurant. She guessed this was Lizzy's opium den calling card. And could it be possible . . . What if the Blue Man didn't refer to a person, but a place, a location – The Dragon Inn? It was another link to Limehouse Lizzy, tying her to the murder.

Pearl was about to tell Crowley what she had discovered, but decided to wait until the drugs shipment had arrived. When they were back at the station, she could explain her theory, and the inspector would have to listen to her. The evidence was stacking up against Lizzy. So many things now pointed to Pearl's former friend.

A short, squat man was walking in their direction, holding a lamp before him. Pearl recognised the simian-like gait of the dockmaster, Mr Armstrong, who had unsuccessfully tried to withhold Xianfan's wages. What a crook the man was, cheating and involved in every intrigue at the docks!

Armstrong moved towards a slatted iron gate set in the thick walls of the dock, just a few feet away from where they were hiding. Crowley looked at Pearl and put a finger to his lips. The dockmaster selected a large key from the bunch hanging at his waist and unlocked the door. The rotund figure of Soo Chow, Lizzy's husband, slunk in.

Soo Chow nodded a greeting at the dockmaster and handed him a small parcel. Armstrong quickly stowed the packet inside his jacket and hurried away back to his office. Soo Chow then turned and waved in the direction of the gate. After a moment, ten black-clad men slipped in. To Pearl's eye, they seemed very small and undernourished, some limped along, others suffered under bowed backs.

She recognised some of them as waiters from The Dragon Inn. Others were probably Chinese sailors stranded in the docks. Once the ships had berthed, they often had no money to pay for the return journey back to Shanghai, and were forced to sleep rough in the arches and narrow alleyways that surrounded the docks. They seemed like the most raggle-taggle gang she'd ever seen. She felt sorry for them, having to do the dirty work of their employers. Pearl wondered how Lizzy could be so uncaring as to use these destitute men. And now Pearl was responsible for them being apprehended and thrown in jail. Perhaps she could persuade Crowley to let them go once they had caught the real villains.

The wind was a howling gale, its vicious chill needling through Pearl's skirts. She shot a quick look at Crowley, hoping he would remain patient. Pearl could just make out his eyes, glittering as he stared out at the water. He was silent, a muscle twitching in his jaw.

And then the outline of the *Sir Lancelot* clipper gradually came into view, the sound of creaking sails and clinking rigging growing louder. As the ship docked, Pearl and Crowley grinned excitedly at each other, even as the rain soaked them.

Soo Chow's men crowded together at the wharf's edge. Despite their lack of physical stature, they all moved with practised ease. They formed a human chain at the clipper's edge and started passing large wooden crates to each other down the gangplank.

Pearl wondered if Jeremiah would turn up, but there was no sign of him. She was disappointed that her hunch he was involved in some way had so far come to nought.

Crowley raised a whistle to his lips. A shrill peal rent the air and five policemen rushed in from the side door, where they had been waiting for Crowley's command.

Despite the raw-boned appearance of Soo Chow's gang, the men lashed out at the coppers with fists and well-aimed kicks. There were roars and shrill cries as the two sides fought. One gang member swung an iron bar at a policeman's head. It made contact with a sickening crunch, and the copper dropped like an anchor at sea.

Pearl watched the fight from behind the crane, unsure of who was gaining ground in the skirmish. After several more minutes of fierce fighting, a few of Soo Chow's men seemed to lose heart. They turned tail and ran, followed by the policemen. Crowley's orders to bring the fittest men had clearly been ignored as some of the policemen puffed and panted, struggling to keep up with Soo Chow's men, who melted into the night. Pearl was relieved to see them go.

Crowley was shouting at a couple of constables who were breathing laboriously, hands on knees. 'You blithering idiots, get after those men!' The inspector moved forward to grasp one gang member who was trying to limp away. Crowley punched him hard on the side of the head.

A slight movement caught Pearl's eye. Soo Chow was inching towards the side door. Once there, he would almost certainly evade capture. She hitched up her skirts and pelted after him, bonnet flapping behind her. 'Come back here!'

Soo Chow stood up and turned to face her, his dark eyes flashing dangerously. He had a slight smile on his face as he lunged forwards and unleashed a backhander. Pearl staggered backwards, blood spurting from her nose. An image of Mei locked up in prison flashed through her mind. Pushing past the pain, she stumbled after Soo Chow who was nearly out of sight. There was no way in hell that he was getting away from her.

She launched herself upon him, leaping on his back and sinking her teeth into his neck. He bellowed with pain and fury, trying to shake her off. Her mouth tasted the salt of his sweat, mixed with an iron tang. She wasn't sure whether the blood filling her mouth was Soo Chow's or her own.

Fists punching wildly, she attacked every part of him she could reach. Pulling and twisting at his ears, sticking her fingers up his nose, thumbs gouging his eyes. He was shrieking even more loudly, howling and bellowing, but Pearl didn't care. She was in a fury. All the frustration of the past few months was pouring out of her.

Someone was dragging her off Soo Chow. 'Enough. We've got him,' Crowley yelled.

She sank to the ground, exhausted.

30

Pearl peered at Soo Chow through the eyelet in the police interrogation room door. His clothes were ripped and filthy from the fight at East India Docks. With a badly bruised hand, he dabbed at the corner of his mouth with a handkerchief and tried to stem the blood running from a large cut above his left eye. Pearl wondered whether the handkerchief was one that Mei had washed and starched. Soo Chow was running his tongue along his teeth, as if counting they were all still present and correct. His right eye was puffy and he had a huge lump on his forehead.

Limehouse Lizzy's husband had now been questioned for several hours. He was refusing to say anything, other than: 'No understand.' Pearl knew Soo Chow could speak fluent English, but was playing the ignorant foreigner, hoping it would be to his advantage.

Inspector Crowley was growing increasingly irate, pacing and slamming doors. Sergeant Knox was standing next to Pearl, trying to edge her out of the way to sneak a look at Soo Chow. Since Pearl had brought Knox a bottle of porter and a pork pie to combat his hangover, after his whiskey-fuelled night with Sergeant O'Dwyer, he was now treating her like a favoured daughter.

'Ole Creepy Crowley is fit to bust. We've caught a large shipment of contraband goods and the biggest haul of opium we've ever seen, with a few of the gang members, too. The port authorities are very pleased. But he can't get the Chinaman to say nothing,' Knox whispered to her. He seemed gleeful at the detective's lack of progress.

Pearl had insisted on staying at the police station. She was desperate for Soo Chow to reveal more details about his wife's opium dealings – and link Lizzy to Ah Sim's murder. It was clear to Pearl that the drugs gang was led by the husband and wife team; Lizzy the brains and Soo Chow the brawn. Surely that would explain the Blue Man connection and lead to the release of Mei.

Inspector Crowley was adamant that she leave, promising to inform her if there were any developments in the case. But at the stubborn look on Pearl's face, together with her loud and continued protests of how Crowley would never have gone to the docks without her help, he had begrudgingly shown her into his office. His manner towards Pearl was softening; the night at the docks had forged a bond between them.

Pearl looked around the inspector's office, keen to find out if there was anything she could use to her advantage in gaining his trust. The picture of the Virgin Mary, a vision in aquamarine, hands clasped in prayer, stared sorrowfully down at her from a gilt-framed painting above the inspector's desk. Bored with waiting, she trailed her finger along the teak desk and pulled open a drawer.

Her eyes alighted upon a black-edged card with a photograph of a young girl, perhaps thirteen years of age. She was an English rose, with alabaster skin and appeared to be in a deep slumber, her head on a pillow and long tresses of honey-blonde hair fanning out on white linen. But there was something about the rigid stillness of the figure. Pearl realised she was not sleeping, but dead.

She felt a pang of guilt at reading the inspector's private papers, but pushed it aside, the need to find out more about him quelling her misgivings. Pearl opened the card and read the message:

Sept 1887

My darling son,

I was very glad to receive your letter, and I understand that police business kept you away from attending your beloved sister's funeral. Please know that your little one is safe from all the sin and sorrow in the world. But oh, my poor boy, how we miss her. She was sweetness personified. The house was filled with people on the day of her funeral, and everyone said she was the most perfect girl that ever lived. She was as lovely in death as she was in life. I count the days until I meet her in heaven again.

Take care of yourself, my sweet Archibald.

Your heartbroken mama

Pearl placed the card back in the drawer, feeling contrite for snooping. Her attitude towards the detective was mellowing now she knew of his private sorrow. His irascible nature hid a profound grief.

The door opened and Crowley marched in, mopping his brow. His shoulders were hunched up around his neck. He brightened slightly upon seeing her. 'How are you feeling, Mrs Fitzgerald? Surely you must be tired. Your assistance with the investigation has been invaluable, but I'm afraid that damn Chinaman is not talking. Please excuse my language.'

Pearl nodded, thinking that the reason was more likely the detective's lack of interrogation skills. She had seen the inspector's technique of shouting and shaking his fist at Soo Chow, who had looked back at the policeman with an insolent sneer.

Pearl gathered her belongings and walked towards the door. Her mind was racing; she needed to get into that interrogation room with Soo Chow. She would do whatever it took to get Mei out of prison, even if it meant resorting to using Crowley's religious devotion.

She stopped in front of the picture of the Virgin Mary and crossed herself. 'Blessed Mary, full of grace, please hear my prayer for little Jane, my sweet baby who died six years ago, aged just four months. May the good Lord rest her sweet, innocent soul.' Pearl bent her head, hands clenched tightly in front of her.

Crowley put out a hand to clasp hers. 'My dear Mrs Fitzgerald. I had no idea. My condolences to you on the loss of your daughter, who was without sin.'

'Thank you, Inspector.' Pearl offered a silent prayer to God to forgive her for telling such a falsehood, but she was doing her best to stop Mei, an innocent soul, from being hanged on the gallows.

Crowley swallowed audibly. He dabbed at his nose. Clearing his throat, he said: 'If there is anything I can do to help alleviate your pain, please let me know. We are united in sorrow.'

She said quickly: 'Then accept my help. I have already offered my services to you as interpreter to talk to Soo Chow in his mother tongue. Please, Inspector, might I try? I can speak to him in Cantonese and ask about the opium shipment, and also what he knows about the murders of Ah Sim and Old Jake.'

The inspector shook his head. 'I appreciate the offer, but it won't do much good.'

Pearl reached out to touch his arm. 'Of course. But surely we should try everything possible before giving up?' She looked beseechingly into his eyes.

Pearl followed meekly behind Crowley towards the interrogation room.

'Stick to my lead and say we have him for smuggling opium and also bribing an official of the docks. Ask him to name all of the people in charge and connected with the smuggling operation. If he doesn't cooperate, tell him that we will assume he is the leader of the gang and he will be deported back to China – or sentenced to hard labour.'

Pearl hesitated. 'Perhaps we should start by asking him some easier questions.'

The inspector bristled. 'Do you have the temerity to think you know better than I do when conducting a police interview? Mrs Fitzgerald, kindly do exactly as I ask.'

She bowed her head in acquiescence.

The prisoner was sitting at a desk, arms folded across his chest. He looked at Pearl sourly. 'What are you doing here? I'm not speaking to anyone – and certainly not you,' he said in Cantonese.

Crowley looked questioningly at Pearl.

She spoke to the prisoner in his mother tongue. 'I am here to act as translator, although I know you speak good English. It won't help you by stalling the police. Not talking isn't going to work. I know you don't trust me, but who else do you have? I can help you get out of here.'

'What I want,' he snarled back in Cantonese, 'is for you to lie on your back so I can see what a half-Chinese cunt looks like.'

Keeping her expression neutral, she said: 'From what the local girls say, you're all talk and as well hung as the eunuchs in the Forbidden City. Now keep quiet. Just listen to what I have to say.'

Soo Chow's face was sullen as he eyed her dubiously, weighing up his options.

Crowley ran a hand under his collar. 'What did you say to him? This isn't getting anywhere.'

'Inspector, please give me some time. I was explaining to Soo Chow that I am here to translate and that you are a very important man. I understand the ways of Chinese men, and they don't trust English police.'

'Very well. But continue cautiously.'

'I could start by asking him something we know the answer to, so we can test to see if he is telling the truth. What do you suggest?'

'Ask him where he lives and who he resides with.'

Pearl repeated the question to Soo Chow. 'What is this? You know I live with Lizzy at The Dragon Inn,' the prisoner said sullenly.

Crowley was growing impatient. 'I understood the gist of that. Ask him about the opium shipment.'

'Please forgive me, Inspector. We speak different dialects, so it is taking us a while to navigate the language, but we are getting there.'

She stood in front of Soo Chow, gripping the sides of the desk. 'The policeman asked you that question as a trick. He knows who your wife is because she is in a basement cell right here in this station. She has already made a statement to the police that you are the boss of the drug smuggling gang, and she knows nothing about it.' She was trusting that Soo Chow trusted no one, not even his wife. It was the only way her deception might prove successful.

Soo Chow's eyes narrowed. 'Lizzy would never do that. My wife is completely loyal to me,' he said in a loud voice.

'Please try to stay calm when I talk to you, otherwise the policeman will know I have said something I shouldn't have. Believe me, it is in your best interests to listen to me. The police are trying to put all the blame on you.'

'Why should I trust you? You're working with the police, you two-faced bitch!'

'Mrs Fitzgerald! What has made him react like that?' Crowley was growing testy. 'You need to tell me what is being said. May I remind you that you are only here as an interpreter. Don't do or say anything rash.'

'I don't know what made him so angry. I asked him who he lived with and he shouted at me that he wouldn't say a word against Lizzy. Let me ask him to stay calm and answer more of your questions.'

She turned to face Soo Chow. 'I can go now, if that is what you wish. But I know things the police won't tell you. The inspector will charge you, whether you did it or not, and you're going to be in prison for the rest of your life. Do you want to be breaking rocks for ten years? You won't last long in these cold and damp cells. They might even hang you. Now nod like you are agreeing with me.'

Soo Chow's eyes grew wide, and then he slowly nodded. Crowley picked up on the cue. 'Thank you, Mrs Fitzgerald. Tell him we know that he lives with Limehouse Lizzy, nee Jennings, at The Dragon Inn restaurant on Castor Street. Is that the headquarters of the opium gang?'

Pearl looked at Soo Chow and asked how much he understood of what Crowley had said. 'Most of it, although he speaks very quickly. But I know he mentioned my wife's name and the restaurant.'

'Lizzy also informed the police you were smuggling in large shipments of opium.' Pearl kept her voice steady. 'Your wife has pointed the finger at you. She is throwing you to the wolves to save her own skin.'

Soo Chow ground his teeth. 'I can't believe she would do this to me!'

'I know what Lizzy's like, ready to turn on her friends,' Pearl said. 'How do you think the police knew where to find you at the docks, and the exact time the opium shipment was coming in, even after the location was moved?'

To Crowley, she said: 'He has confirmed that The Dragon Inn is the base for the opium gang.'

She turned to Soo Chow. 'Nod your head, as if you are agreeing with me.'

Satisfied, Pearl said: 'Lizzy has told the police you are the drug dealer and the inspector wants you to confess to all of it. Lizzy also said that you murdered Ah Sim and Old Jake.'

Soo Chow jerked his head up. He screamed: 'This is all a lie! I haven't killed anyone.' His hand reached out to Pearl. 'Tell the policeman. I'm not hanging for this.' He stood suddenly, overturning the table.

Crowley shoved him down hard. 'You will stay seated!' he barked.

'What did he say about Ah Sim and Old Jake?' Crowley asked.

'He knows something about the murders. Can I ask him about it?'

'Find out what he knows.'

Pearl turned to Soo Chow, his face now slick with sweat. 'Don't worry, I'm on your side. But I have to tell you that Lizzy has been poisoning the inspector's mind. They questioned her first and she saw it as a chance to get out of this without a charge. She is a white woman, after all. You are a foreigner in this country.'

Soo Chow shook his head. 'I'm not going to take the blame for her. Tell him Lizzy is the one behind it all. She is in charge of the drug dealing, said it was good money. I was happy with just the restaurant and laundry business. The opium was all her idea. Thought it would bring in business from the West End.'

'How can you prove it is her in charge of the operation and not you?'

'I know where she keeps the ledgers. She writes it all down by hand – she keeps everything. I have nothing to do with it, I just do what she says. All I wanted was a quiet life.' His voice was whining now, all bravado evaporating.

Pearl nodded. 'Inspector, Soo Chow has named his wife as the boss in charge of the opium smuggling. He can provide proof – written evidence – and all the names involved. Can I continue?'

'That's exactly what we need. Carry on, Mrs Fitzgerald.'

Pearl continued her questioning. 'What about the killings of Ah Sim and Old Jake? You need to provide evidence about that, otherwise you are going down for it. Is Lizzy behind all this? You must give us proof so that the police believe it is Lizzy and not you.' Pearl's fists were bunched tight, unsure whether Soo Chow would give up his wife. Smuggling was one thing, but this was double murder.

He watched her closely. 'Hmmm . . . She was angry with Ah Sim. I've never seen her so furious. Said he'd been cheating her out of money and that she'd kill him. The next day he turned up dead. I'm not sure about the other man. But my wife has a vicious temper, always beating the staff.'

'Are you willing to give evidence against Lizzy? Let me speak to the inspector. He might be able to do a deal with you.'

'I am saying nothing unless I get out of here. Nothing.'

Pearl turned to Crowley. 'Inspector, Soo Chow says he will give evidence that Lizzy killed Ah Sim and Old Jake. He is willing to give you information that will put an end to the opium gang and solve the murders. He will testify in court, but only in exchange for his freedom.'

Crowley was striding up and down. 'Let me deal with this now.'

He grabbed Soo Chow by the collar and shouted in his face: 'Did Lizzy kill the Chinaman and Old Jake?'

Soo Chow's eyes were wide with fright. He nodded wildly, looking at Pearl.

'He has admitted it, Inspector!' Pearl was flooded with relief. Soo Chow was a broken man and would agree to anything now.

Pearl stood in front of Soo Chow. 'And will you retract your statement that you saw Mei Tan kill her brother?' He nodded again.

Crowley looked from Pearl to Soo Chow and back. 'I'd need him to be a police informer from now on. Not just for these crimes but also for those in the future. It would be useful to have a Chinaman on the inside telling me what's going on in their community. Soo Chow needs to come with me to The Dragon Inn restaurant and show me where the evidence is. If it all stacks up, we'll arrest Limehouse Lizzy.'

As they walked back to the inspector's office, the tension in Pearl's neck was easing. She hoped she had done enough to save Mei.

'Perhaps the Blue Man is not a person but a location, referring to The Dragon Inn. Lizzy's calling card for the opium den has a picture of a blue man in a boat. It's the same as the sign above the restaurant. What do you think?'

'Mrs Fitzgerald, I think we can wrap this all up. I have managed to rid the East End community of this fiendish opium gang and solve two murders.' Crowley straightened his tie, and then to Pearl's astonishment, he took her hand and kissed it.

'Many thanks for your help.' He cleared his throat and looked deep into her eyes. 'When I first met you, I thought you were the most annoying woman I had ever met. Interfering and, at times, most unladylike.'

She was about to object but Crowley interjected. 'Please, let me finish. I have to admit that the hours I have spent with you have been some of the most exciting in my life. Infuriating, yes, but enjoyable as well. My experience with the fairer sex is limited, I admit. I was unused to ladies of the modern age behaving in such a forward fashion. But Mrs Fitzgerald, or if I may take the liberty of calling you Pearl, I do feel deeply drawn to you. Would you do me the honour of having luncheon with me on Sunday afternoon? Perhaps we could attend mass afterwards.'

Pearl was astonished. She decided not to remind him that he had thrown her in jail for a night. Torn between amusement and embarrassment, Pearl bit the side of her mouth to stop laughing. She could scarcely believe it was possible that Crowley would come a-courting. The excitement of securing a conviction must have gone to his head.

'That's very kind of you, Inspector. I would love to accept your invitation. As you know, I am still grieving for my beloved father. If I may give your offer some consideration . . .' Her voice trailed off, affecting a melancholy tone.

'Yes, yes of course. Please take as long as you need.' The detective released her hand and Pearl couldn't decide whether he was disappointed or relieved that his hasty invitation hadn't been outright rejected. Crowley's voice was gentle as he extended his arm to lead her out of his office. 'Once again, many thanks for your assistance.'

'Before I leave, there is just one more request I have, Inspector. Miss Mei Tan was wrongfully imprisoned for these crimes and is still in the cells. Since Limehouse Lizzy, the real culprit, has been identified, would you be so kind as to release Mei?'

31

Pearl hopped from foot to foot at the back door of the police station where the prisoners were let out. It had been at least two long hours and she wondered if the coppers did this on purpose, to prolong the agony for those waiting.

While she was pacing, she suddenly shivered. Down a side alley adjacent to the police station, a man was watching her, his features obscured by a cloud of tobacco smoke from his pipe.

But then the back door of the prison inched open and Mei came walking tentatively down the stairs, holding on to the rail for support. Her eyes blinked rapidly, unused to the bright glare of daylight after weeks incarcerated in a dark prison cell. Her dress hung off her slim frame.

Pearl thought that Mei would look for her, run to her. But Mei simply raised her face to the sky, enjoying the warmth of the sun. She stared up at the clouds, taking in their beauty. She breathed in the fresh air. Then she saw Pearl and smiled, walking slowly towards her. They collided, holding on to each other fiercely. Breast to breast, thigh to thigh.

'Take me home with you,' Mei said.

Pearl knew there was a hunger in her eyes as she grabbed Mei by the hand and led her to the bedroom. She threw Mei on the bed, took a key from her own cleavage and locked the door. She lay on top of Mei, pinning her to the bed, ripping feverishly at her prison dress.

'Wait,' Mei said. 'Let me wash first. My dress is filthy.'

'That's how I want you.' Pearl was pulling down Mei's dress, nuzzling her breasts. She kissed her erect nipples and bit her neck. 'I've been wanting to do this to you. For months.'

Mei laughed. 'I love that you can't wait, but I really need a bath. That prison cell was full of all kinds of nasty creatures.'

To Pearl, it seemed to take an age to boil hot water for the tin bath, the waiting an agony. But Mei was determined to wash off the filth from the jail, and stripped off her filthy clothes. Kneeling next to Mei, Pearl slowly soaped her back. She sucked at Mei's earlobe, breathing hard. 'Tell me you like it like this,' Pearl whispered against Mei's neck.

'Slow down, I can hardly breathe,' Mei laughed again.

'I can't stop.' Pearl kissed her lips gently, then probed deep inside Mei's mouth with her tongue.

Mei lay back in the tin bath, her body responding, quivering.

'I want you,' she said, her breath ragged and coming in gasps.

Pearl caressed Mei's breasts, hands travelling downwards. Mei arched her back and moaned softly.

'You're so wet.' Pearl withdrew her fingers and circled around Mei's labia.

'I want to fuck you until you come. But not yet.' Pearl led Mei to the bedroom and they fell on the bed.

'Don't stop, don't stop,' Mei whispered, feverishly thrusting her hips to seek out Pearl's fingers. Pearl entered her again and continued thrusting hard in a frenzy. She pushed three fingers inside Mei. They were bucking and writhing, almost fighting each other until Mei came in loud groans. Pearl put a hand over Mei's mouth to muffle her cries.

After a few moments, Mei slid on top of Pearl, pushed her legs apart and kissed her arms, her breasts, her stomach, her hips. Pearl allowed the slow seduction of her body, breathing in the tenderness and hunger of her lover. Mei's mouth moved against Pearl's cunt, her tongue exploring the folds and crevices of Pearl's labia before she began rhythmically licking her clitoris, her Pearl. And Pearl let go, roaring her pleasure, forgetting the outside world existed.

Mei rolled off Pearl, panting and giggling. 'You were so loud I think the whole household has woken up.'

They both reluctantly sat up and started to get dressed, then Mei pushed Pearl against the wall. 'I want you again.'

The next few days passed in a haze of tangled limbs and deep caresses. Pearl would awake at dawn, body still trembling from Mei's touch. She watched Mei sleeping next to her, listening to her breathing, afraid to wake her. Then Mei's eyes would open, a teasing smile on her lips. This was a fresh beginning, and in this new-found delight, Pearl pushed all thoughts of Lizzy aside. Finding one another was lifting Mei's sorrow at Ah Sim's tragic death, at least for a few precious moments.

As they lay in bed one morning, Mei murmured against Pearl's throat: 'I meant to ask you. Did you do as that lawyer suggested and find out if Betty really is married to your father?'

'She suggested I go to the church and look in the marriage register, but I've had other things on my mind.' Pearl kissed the pulse beating at Mei's neck.

Mei took Pearl's face in her hands. 'This is your inheritance, your birth right. It's also worth a great deal of money. It could make a difference to your life. You could give employment to others. Do you know how many people would be so grateful for what you have? We must go. Besides, I'm curious. I've never been inside a Roman Catholic church. Is it true they drink blood?'

The church of St Mary and St Michael was freezing cold inside, but then it had always felt frigid, even at the height of summer. The memories came back to Pearl, all those gloomy Sundays sitting on hard wooden benches, the hours trickling by so slowly. She looked at Mei, who was gazing in wonder at the large stained-glass window at the far end of the church, the multicoloured light streaming in, a rainbow of reds, greens, blues and yellows.

Then Mei looked to the right, at the large crucifix. Her eyes widened in alarm at the naked body of Christ hanging on the cross, blood oozing from the thorn of crowns that punctured his head, the vivid gash on the abdomen. She clung on to Pearl. 'Why is there a statue of a man in agony?'

Pearl shook her head. 'It would take me years to explain. I'm not sure I understand it myself. Come on, we've got to find the priest. I haven't been here for years, so Father Kelly might have moved parish, or even passed away.'

They walked along the nave of the church, their heels echoing on the tiled stone floor. The incense was pungently strong, and Pearl's heart plummeted. The smell brought back memories of the hours listening to sermons, the priest droning on and on, preaching hell and damnation to those practising unnatural vices. Pearl never dared speak in confession of her confused yearnings for music-hall actresses or admit to kissing Maude Kingsley's poster. After mass, her father would often be in a rare, pious mood, forbidding any frivolities. Sundays were not for running around on the streets of Limehouse, when there were floors to sweep for a clean, God-fearing home, he'd said.

Just past the pulpit was a small door, which opened as they

approached it, a young man hurrying out. Pearl approached him. 'Excuse me, Father, I wonder if you could help me. I have come to find my father's marriage certificate. Are the records kept here? Perhaps Father Kelly could assist me.'

The priest looked just out of his teens, judging by the pimply rash that covered his cheeks. He shook his head. 'Father Kelly passed away two years ago.' The young man made the sign of the cross. 'I took over from him. Father McCarrick's my name. The register is back here,' the priest gestured to the room he had just come from, 'but we had a flood a while back, and some of the books didn't survive. You are welcome to take a look.'

Inside the room, Father McCarrick led the two women to a glass-panelled bookcase and unlocked it, releasing a cloying smell of mildew. He gestured to a row of leather-bound books. 'These are the records for the last ten years. Everything before that was destroyed. I hope you find what you're looking for.' He smiled kindly then frowned. 'Now, I have to prepare a sermon.' He paused to consider for a moment. 'I was thinking of Psalm 23:4, "Even though I walk through the valley of the shadow of death, I will fear no evil, for you are with me; your rod and your staff, they comfort me."' He nodded to himself, as though the matter was decided.

Mei shuddered as she watched him leave the room. 'This is a very strange religion. Why is it all about death and dying? My Buddhist faith believes in meditation for a calm and peaceful mind.'

'That sounds preferable, but I doubt you will change the minds of Catholics around here.' Pearl wondered about Mei's beliefs. There was so much more to find out about this woman. But now was not the time. 'Let's start looking for the marriage certificate.'

A moth flew out of the first book Pearl opened. It smelt of damp and several silverfish swarmed along its spine. A few of the names were legible, but there were large sections where the ink had faded so much it was impossible to read.

The book Mei was searching through had begun to disintegrate in her hands. Painstakingly, they searched through all the remaining books, but none revealed the names of PJ O'Dwyer and Betty Sullivan.

This was a disappointing setback. There was no proof that PJ had got hitched to his fancy woman, but also the evidence was so hard to decipher that they couldn't be sure the records weren't in their hands but illegible. All Pearl was left with was more questions, all pointing to lengthy and expensive legal action if she was to win her inheritance.

They walked back along the river, their silence broken by the piercing voice of the paperboy, who was holding up a stack of *Weekly Heralds* almost bigger than himself. 'Extra! Extra! Read all about it!' he screeched. 'Limehouse Lizzy found guilty for murder of Chinaman!'

Inspector Crowley hadn't wasted any time in making public the biggest case of his career. Pearl gave the boy a penny and scanned the front page:

LIMEHOUSE WOMAN GUILTY OF BRUTAL DOUBLE MURDER

Wednesday 24th October 1888

After a week's trial at the Old Bailey, Mrs Elizabeth Soo Chow, nee Jennings, was convicted of the killing of Jacob McGowan, known as Old Jake, a former sailor, and Ah Sim Tan, a Chinese labourer in her employ.

"I thank the local people who have come forward with

> information," said Inspector Crowley, who was in charge of the murder investigation. "We are pleased that the culprit of these two vicious killings will feel the full might of the law."
>
> Known locally as Limehouse Lizzy, the convicted killer is the owner of The Dragon Inn restaurant in Castor Street, and a laundry servicing West End hotels.
>
> Mrs Soo Chow faces execution by hanging. She is currently being held at Newgate Prison. Miss Mei Tan, sister of victim Ah Sim Tan, who was previously arrested for the murder, has been released from custody, without charge.

Back at the lodging house, both women were lost in their own thoughts. Pearl tried to lighten the mood. 'Where's my sweetheart? I haven't had a kiss for at least an hour,' she called out.

Mei shushed her. 'Not so loud, the lodgers might hear you.'

In reply, Pearl pulled her close. 'We can go into the larder and shut the door.' But Mei was distracted, re-reading the newspaper article.

Pearl looked over her shoulder. So Lizzy was facing the gallows. To see it in black and white made her blood run cold. How had it come to this? She felt sick but could summon little sympathy for her childhood friend. Lizzy had committed murder, and Pearl could never forget holding Ah Sim until the life faded from his eyes.

Mei was silent, her brow furrowed. 'I am glad they have caught her. Ah Sim's spirit will finally be able to rest. But the blade has two sides. The laundry is closed, so I will have to look for another job and somewhere to live.'

Keen to keep thoughts of Lizzy out of her mind, Pearl put her arms around Mei's waist. 'You don't have to look very far. You belong here with me at the lodging house. You can have your own room, for decency's sake and to stop people asking questions. But you will spend your nights with me.' They kissed softly, and Pearl moved her hand to Mei's breast but was playfully slapped away.

'You will have to wait until tonight.'

Walking to the kitchen, Pearl hummed a music-hall ditty as she lit the stove to brew a large pot of tea. It had slipped her mind, but some new lodgers had arrived and were sitting in the hallway. Tseng and Fung Yeen were two brothers, relatives of Xianfan. She greeted them in Cantonese and told them to have some food, showing them where the bowls and spoons were kept. Tseng and Fung Yeen slurped at their congee broth, answering questions Pearl asked them about where they had come from in China. She tried to concentrate on the answers, but her thoughts kept straying to Mei's light footsteps upstairs and the night ahead.

Lying close to one another the next morning, Mei's voice was soft and low as she regaled Pearl with stories of her days at the Shanghai circus. Pearl imagined Mei flying through the air, arms aloft. 'I'm thinking of you in a tight acrobat's leotard. Maybe you could do some of your tricks, just for me.'

Mei laughed and shook her head. 'I'm completely out of shape, too old and a lot heavier than in my circus days.'

Pearl caressed Mei's thigh. 'Think of the money you'd make as a street acrobat.' She stroked Mei's hair. 'You could get back into practice, only you'd have to stop eating so many egg custard tarts.'

Pearl ducked under the bed covers to avoid a slap. In a muffled voice she said: 'I think that was the moment I fell in love with you, seeing you shin up the drainpipe at Old Jake's place; such strength and grace, and the way you kicked that man in the face . . .'

'And I couldn't take my eyes off you in that tight purple frock I lent you!'

But at this, Pearl felt a buzz of irritation. Lizzy had given Mei that dress. She said nothing as she slid out of bed.

'Where are you going so early?' Mei asked, also getting up.

'I'm going to the fishmonger. He promised me a good price if I get there early.'

'Hmmm. As long as you're not stepping out with anyone else.'

They both reluctantly dressed and went downstairs. In the kitchen, Mei lifted Pearl in her arms, whirling her around. They both laughed, out of breath.

There was a faint rattling at the front door. 'Let's not answer,' Pearl whispered.

'Temptress! If I am to be a good housekeeper here, I must get on with my washing.' Mei smiled, then ran back up the stairs.

Pearl sighed, pulled her hair tighter into a bun and smoothed down her skirts. As she walked down the corridor, the front door slowly opened. It was Ma Jennings.

32

The two women stood facing one another. In the turmoil of recent events, Pearl hadn't even thought about Ma Jennings – or what she was going through. With a feeling of dread, Pearl wondered whether Ma was coming back to stay at the lodging house permanently. She must have heard news about Lizzy, to arrive so suddenly and without notice at the Fragrant Blossoms.

Recovering herself, Pearl put an arm around Ma and led her down the corridor and into the parlour. 'Where are my manners? Please, come in. I'm so sorry I haven't written to you. I hope you have been receiving the monthly payments. It's not much but . . .' Her words trailed off.

'Don't you worry about that, my love. I'm sure you must have been busy.' There was a tightness in Ma's voice as she patted Pearl on the arm.

Mrs Jennings took in the parlour, the gaily coloured walls in cheerful pinks, greens and yellows, so different from the stale brown hues from her tenure as landlady. The tables were laid out with red-and-white starched tablecloths, and there were sparkling silver jugs on the sideboard, a present from Inspector Crowley for Pearl's help in the recent investigations. Sturdy crockery was ready for the lodgers' evening meal. Ma looked admiringly at the paintings of the Nuorilang waterfall, with swallows tumbling and turning in misty skies, a gift from departing lodgers.

Ma gave out a sigh and sat down on the divan by the fireside, grimacing slightly. Pearl looked at her more closely and realised how much weight the former landlady had lost. Her light blue eyes were bloodshot and her previously plump cheeks were now wrinkled sails, lying slack on a windless day.

Ma smiled, screwing up her rheumy blue eyes to look at Pearl. 'You're looking just peachy, my girl. This life is suiting you. I have to confess I had my doubts at first, you not having the first inkling about the ways of the business. But you've done a first-class job.'

Pearl squeezed Ma's hand. 'I was taught by the best.'

The older woman winked at her. 'You caught on quick enough.'

There was an awkward silence. Pearl cast about for something to say and how to bring up the subject of Lizzy. 'How about a nice cup of tea?'

'That would be just the ticket.'

Ma watched Pearl move around the parlour before saying: 'Might as well spit it out why I'm here. I wish I could say this is just a social visit, but I need to ask a favour. I'll be quick, as I don't have much time left. I'm ailing. Not long for me on this Earth now, and there's one thing I must do before I die.'

Pearl's heart constricted. Ma held up a hand. 'Got to get this off my chest,' she said in a rush. 'I want you to take me to see Lizzy. I've sent her letters, but she hasn't replied. You must help me. I need to see my daughter before I pass on – or she does.'

Pearl's mouth dropped open. 'Ma, I'm so sorry. But there is something I need to tell you.'

At the older woman's questioning look, Pearl knew she'd have to tell her everything. She sat down beside Ma and took her hand. It trembled slightly, like a wounded bird. The thick bluish-green veins stood out against her translucent skin, the fingers knotted with arthritis.

'I'm so sorry. It was me who gave the police information about Lizzy. I promised Mei I would find her brother's killer, and that's what I've done. I hope you can forgive me.'

There was no cry of outrage from Ma, just a small nod. 'Yes, I know. Sergeant O'Dwyer wrote a letter telling me everything. Probably to save you from telling me. You turned on your old pal. I know there was bad blood between you, but there should be loyalty.' Ma paused, closing her eyes, taking in short breaths. Pearl suspected Ma was conserving her energy. The journey from Ramsgate must have exhausted her.

'I'm sure you had your reasons. But you are wrong about my girl, and I come here so you can put that right.' Ma looked steadily at Pearl. 'Lizzy couldn't kill no one. Get someone else to do her dirty work? Yes. I've no illusions about her, but I do know this: she hides it well, but underneath she's a good Catholic, terrified that her soul will descend into hell and suffer for eternity. Many times I've heard her screaming with nightmares when she was a child.'

'It's understandable that you would want to protect Lizzy. But you have no idea what she's done.'

'That may be, but not murder. Lizzy would never do anything like that. I'm begging you. Are you sure she done it? There's no doubt in your mind?'

Pearl was torn up inside. She looked at Ma Jennings, her eyes brimming. She had been so kind to Pearl, offering comfort in her bereavement. And now Ma was asking for help. But this would be a betrayal of Mei, whose brother had died at the hands of Lizzy. And an injustice for Ah Sim, who had died in Pearl's arms.

'I'm so sorry. It must be terrible for you. But I have done what I thought was right. It is in the hands of the law now.'

Ma stood, the tremor in her hands now more visible. 'Will you not grant a dying woman's wish? I was there when you needed me.'

'I wish I could help, but I have no doubt that Lizzy committed those crimes. She's about as innocent as the Devil.'

This was said with more vehemence than Pearl intended, and from the stricken look on Ma's face, she had gone too far, but she crossed her arms mutinously.

Ma Jennings sat down on a chair by the parlour fire. 'As you wish. I will stay here until you change your mind.'

There was a slight movement in the doorway. Mei was standing there, watching. How long she had been there, Pearl had no idea. Mei's face was impassive as she turned and went into the kitchen, bracing her hands against the sink as she stared out of the window. Pearl followed and stood closely behind her.

'You must help her,' Mei said. 'No matter how you or I feel about it. You will never forgive yourself when Liz is hanged, knowing you refused Ma's final request to see her. She is wrong about her daughter being innocent, so what harm can it do?'

Mei moved to the cupboards and took out ingredients for a hot broth stew. She began chopping up carrots and potatoes.

'I can't do it. I don't want to see Lizzy ever again,' Pearl said loudly, everything now rushing out. 'What about you? She murdered your brother – and you still have feelings for her? I hate it when you call her Liz.'

Xianfan was talking with some new lodgers who had just arrived in Limehouse from a long sea voyage and were playing cards in a corner of the room. The men glanced up, and then continued with their game.

'Keep your voice down,' Mei muttered. 'Of course I want her to pay for killing Ah Sim. But this is for Ma Jennings. She was there for both of us when we had no one.'

Pearl whispered furiously: 'Why should I help, after everything Lizzy has done? I've kept quiet, but you know how I feel about that woman. After what she did to your brother. After what she did to you – with you!'

Pearl picked up a pot of tea and hurled it with all her might. Mei ducked; it narrowly missed her head and shattered against the wall. Dark brown stains cascaded down the painting it had hit. Porcelain shards skittered across the floor, like frozen white teardrops.

Finally, Mei spoke. 'Just for once, put aside your own feelings,' she said harshly. 'Ma Jennings is dying. She needs to see her daughter one last time. Help her, otherwise you're not the person I thought you were.'

Mei walked out of the lodging house, the front door closing with a quiet click. Pearl stalked up and down the kitchen. She turned to face the mirror. 'How dare she talk to me like that!' she said to her reflection, her face a grimace of fury.

Pearl thought of the play she had been reading aloud with Mei: *'It is the green-eyed monster which doth mock the meat it feeds on.'* How true that was. Her insides were dissolving as if dipped in prussic acid. The tea continued to drip down the wall, the stains spreading across the wallpaper that Pearl and Mei had just finished putting up. She'd have to clean it soon so it wouldn't leave a permanent mark.

As the evening drew on, her anger subsided, replaced with a gnawing concern, which grew with every minute that Mei was missing. The hours ticked past and the light was fading as dusk descended; the air thick and suffocating. It was dark now. She was aware Ma Jennings was still waiting in the parlour, and that the fire must be low. Grudgingly, Pearl carried some wood from the kitchen and stoked the fire. The elderly woman looked at Pearl, but no words were spoken.

Pearl opened the front door, looking up and down the street, hoping to see Mei, but there was no sign of her. There was only the shadowy figure of a man, leaning against a low brick wall. She couldn't see his face, only the sailor's cap pulled low over his brow. He seemed to look her way, but then greeted another man and they walked off together.

What if Mei had been attacked? A woman out on the streets alone made for easy prey, particularly with the Whitechapel killer still on the streets. Perhaps the woman she loved was lying injured in a ditch. What if Mei disappeared and Pearl never found her again?

Rushing out without her coat, Pearl ran down empty alleyways and courtyards, determined to search all night if necessary. Then a woman came towards her. Pearl recognised that graceful walk and her heart lurched painfully.

'Where did you go?' Pearl grabbed hold of Mei, hugging her tightly.

'I went to see Rose and Polly. They had asked me round for tea and to show them some *Shŏubó* moves to defend themselves against the police on their marches.'

'Forgive me,' Pearl whispered.

In the parlour, Ma Jennings was snoring gently. Pearl's heart constricted as she noticed the wrinkled, withered face, the shadow of death in the sunken eye sockets, and a horrible wheezing coming from the chest. She whispered gently to the sleeping woman: 'I'll do what you ask, Ma. I'll take you to see your daughter.'

33

Ma Jennings' breath was rattling as they walked to Thames Police Station and Pearl marvelled at the determination of her friend. What occupied Ma's thoughts Pearl could only guess. Maybe she wasn't thinking of anything but simply concentrating on staying alive long enough to see her daughter. Pearl tried to remember Lizzy as the sweet little girl with ginger curls from childhood days. How close they had been. Was a little sympathy creeping in?

No. Every time she thought of Lizzy and Mei together, a hot, searing hate consumed her.

Pearl held tightly on to Ma as they passed The Sailor's Arms, and she looked up to see multi-coloured bunting swirling around a crudely scrawled sign haphazardly fastened above the front door:

Under New Manigement Of Betty Sullivan

Pearl ground her teeth.

Inspector Crowley was waiting for them as they approached the side entrance of the police station. Pearl had paid a visit to the policeman, saying that she would be delighted to take up his offer of high tea with him. He had looked surprised, then delighted, suggesting a visit to The Savoy in the West End the following week. After accepting, Pearl asked if Ma Jennings could visit her daughter. He demurred, but then, upon seeing Pearl's crestfallen look, agreed, saying it was only fitting for family to pay a final visit to the condemned prisoner.

At the staircase down to the cells, Crowley excused himself, saying he had urgent interrogations to conduct. 'Until next Sunday,' he whispered, bending to kiss her hand. 'I will leave Sergeant Knox to take you to see Lizzy.'

Pearl grinned at him, trying to imagine his reaction when she brought Mei, along with the matchgirls Rose, Polly and Gerty Connolly to The Savoy. Not quite the outing he was likely hoping for.

Knox was waiting at the bottom of the stairs, swinging a large bunch of keys attached to his belt, and walked them to the jail cell at the end of the corridor. He inspected each key, his mouth pursed in concentration, shaking his head and frowning slightly. Pearl tapped her foot, biting back a terse request for him to hurry up.

'Got so many keys here it always takes an age to find the right one. Shouldn't be too long now.'

She gave Knox a quick, tense nod.

At last he gave a satisfied grunt, selecting a key he had looked at several times before. Knox pushed the key into the lock and turned until, with a sharp squeak, the door unlocked. Then he twisted the knob and pushed. Nothing happened.

He looked at Pearl and gave a shrug of his shoulders. 'Sometimes it sticks in the cold and damp down here,' he grunted.

The policeman motioned the two women out of the way. He walked back several steps and then hurled himself at the door, slamming into it with the force of a charging bull. The heavy prison door flew open and Knox barrelled into the room. Pearl gently took the older woman's hand in hers and they walked inside the cell together.

Knox was sprawled on the stone floor, his arms and legs wriggling, like an enormous cockroach on its back. The prisoner was watching from the bed. 'Well, that's a most amusing pantomime.' Lizzy took a cigarette from a large ebony box and lit it, watching the hapless Knox stagger to his feet.

Lizzy slowly stood. She was wearing a silk orange gown, the colour of glowing coals in a brazier. A fur wrap was draped around her shoulders. She looked radiant. Her eyes lazily flicked to Pearl. 'Come to have a good gawk at me banged up in the nick?'

Pearl shook her head. 'Looks like you've brought your own personal wardrobe with you. Much more becoming than the prison garb. How much did you have to pay the guards?'

Lizzy was about to reply when Ma Jennings limped forward, arms outstretched, as if to warm herself on Lizzy's fiery energy. 'My darling daughter,' Ma whispered. But there was no answer from Lizzy. Ma continued to chatter away, as if they were at home on a dull Sunday afternoon. 'I should have brought you some more clothes. Are you hungry? What would you like to eat? I should have brought your favourite, a nice plum pudding with lots of cream.'

Lizzy's eyes widened a fraction. Her expression was impassive, although a muscle spasmed in her jaw. Ma carried on, this time with more urgency, her voice coming quick and hoarse.

'I needed to see you. You might not want to speak to me, but I've got things to say to you. It's my last chance. I'm dying. You don't deserve this, you don't deserve to be hanged. But listen, all that you went through when you were a nipper, we never spoke of it. I am truly sorry, but I . . .'

Lizzy stood in front of Ma Jennings, toe to toe.

'How dare you!' Lizzy's voice was a venomous hiss. 'I'll be glad when you're dead. Best news I've heard in a long time. It's the least you deserve, and I hope your innards rot 'til you stink like a beached whale.'

Ma staggered back as if she had been struck. Pearl caught her before she fell to the floor. Ma's voice was weak and shaky, her face taut with pain. 'How could I have hoped for anything other than you hating me. I didn't protect you. I had no idea what those men were doing to you. I didn't know at the time, only later, when Mrs Smith, that busybody next door, told me that all these men were talking about you in such a terrible way . . .'

Pearl screwed her eyes shut, mind reeling. She almost put her hands over her ears. All that time she'd feared something awful had been happening to Lizzy, but she had refused to accept the gossip and filthy whisperings Tommy had been feeding her. She'd hoped it was false. And now the truth was out, Pearl couldn't ignore it, admitting to herself that she hadn't helped Lizzy either. The most she'd done was offer a bed for the night, a brief respite from the horrors that awaited her friend.

Lizzy snorted impatiently at her mother. 'Enough with your lies. Of course you knew what was happening. You just didn't want to know. Didn't want to stop the money coming in. Men were paying twice as much for my young cunt than they were for your sour parts.'

Ma Jennings whispered: 'I'm so sorry they done those things to you.'

Pearl felt sick. Not only was it true, but Ma had known it was happening to Lizzy all along. She couldn't bear to look at Ma.

'I don't want your sympathy and lies. What use are they to me now? Just get out. I hope you burn in hell.'

'I was being used by those men as well, I couldn't manage . . .'

Pearl turned away, holding on to the filthy prison wall for support. Her childhood friend had suffered unimaginable terrors, and Ma was still trying to defend herself.

'I was a child!' screamed Lizzy. 'Now leave before I rip the heart right out of you.' Lizzy raised her hands in front of her, claw-like, as if ready to strike her mother down.

Pearl moved forward, standing between the two women. 'Just listen to your mother for a moment,' she said quietly, trying to find some compassion for Ma.

Lizzy turned to look at Pearl. 'It's none of your damn business. This is between me and her. And how's that little trollop of mine? You had her yet? Tell Mei I've been missing her. She screams like a Banshee. "Fuck me again," she used to beg me. I think of the long nights we spent together. They give me so much pleasure all alone in my cell, imagining her between my thighs.'

Pearl bit her lip hard, tasting blood.

Lizzy's old swagger had returned. She stood up and started humming. Swaying from side to side, with hands on hips, she began singing in a piercing vibrato:

'Ta-Ra-Ra Boom-De-Ay!
'A smart and stylish girl you see,
'Belle of good society
'Not too strict but rather free
'Yet as right as right can be!
'Never forward, never bold
'Not too hot, and not too cold
'But the very thing, I'm told,
'That in your arms you'd like to hold.'

Waltzing with an imaginary partner, Lizzy moved this way and that, gracefully managing to avoid any physical contact with Ma Jennings in the tiny cell. Then she stopped abruptly in front of her mother.

'You thought I'd forgive you,' Lizzy sang in the same melody as the music-hall song. 'Well, I never will.' Her voice changed to a low whisper, thick with menace. 'I bear the burden of what happened to me every day of my life. You are not my mother. You stopped being my mother the day you let the first man have his filthy way with me and you just took the money. Now get out.'

Ma's eyes rested unwaveringly on her daughter. 'Alright. I wanted to spare you, but here's the truth. My ruined girl, the child prostitute. At least if the men went with you, I'd have a night off. I was in a torment of my own, drinking too much after your father died and no money in the house. How was I to clothe and feed us both, keep a roof over our heads? So shout and curse at me until it's all out. Kill me, if that will make you feel better. I know I did wrong, but the past is the past. I can't do nothing about it now.'

Lizzy breathed out a long, ragged breath. For the first time she looked uncertain. She walked the four steps it took to cross the room and sat back down on the bed. 'Now we're getting somewhere. At last you're speaking the truth I've been waiting to hear. Of course you wait until we are both facing death. I knew you were ashamed of me, couldn't bear the sight of me. You knew exactly what those bastards were doing with me. Fucked morning noon and night by punters. You could hear my screams, night after night, and yet you did nothing. Where were you?'

Lizzy's screech was so full of pain and misery. Pearl stared at the bars on the prison window, furry with cobwebs and dust. She fought to keep down the bile that rose in her throat. All those times Lizzy had come to her, bruised and tearful . . .

Lizzy was screaming and screaming, an unearthly sound that echoed piercingly around the walls. Then she stopped as suddenly as she began, slowly wiping the spittle from her mouth. 'If you really want to atone for your sins, Mother dear, do something useful and get me out of here. Find out who the real killer is.' She turned to jab a thumb at Pearl. 'I know you think I did it, but you're wrong. I've been set up for killing Ah Sim and Old Jake good and proper. I never done it.'

'You might feel better if you confess to your crimes, Lizzy,' Pearl said gently. 'I'm truly sorry for what happened to you back then, but you can't blame that on your actions now. I know you are a killer, going by the name of the Blue Man. I've worked it all out. The sign above The Dragon Inn, the same as the drawing on your calling card, the blue man in the boat. It all makes sense.'

Lizzy looked at Pearl as if she was speaking in tongues. 'What are you gibbering about?'

Just as Pearl was about to reply, the cell door opened and Sergeant Knox poked his head in. 'What a racket! Keep the bleedin' noise down. You've set off all the other women. I'm not getting in trouble for the likes of you. One more minute and then out.' The door clanged shut.

Mother and daughter seemed to have forgotten Pearl's existence as they faced each other. 'Do something that can help me instead of this maudlin reunion.' Lizzy jutted her chin at Ma Jennings. 'I heard tell of a rival gang. The Wild Eyed Boys. It's something to do with them. And I'm not the Blue Man, so spend your last days proving my innocence.'

Walking down the corridor, Pearl did her best to shut out the screaming of the female prisoners and the deafening noise of their tin cups and plates clanging against the walls. Ma Jennings was weeping in earnest now. Pearl tentatively patted her on the back, but she couldn't shake the creeping revulsion that Ma was complicit in her daughter's suffering, and had stayed silent about it for all these years.

* * *

The horses reared up on their hind legs, whinnying madly, foaming at the mouth. There were screams as passengers jumped out of the way, the mare's hooves narrowly missing a small boy's head who was cleaning up horse dung, gravel spraying in every direction. The coach to Ramsgate had arrived.

Pearl found a seat for Ma Jennings and helped her in.

'May God never forgive me. My poor Lizzy.' Ma coughed so hard she was unable to catch her breath.

Pearl didn't envy the passengers' journey ahead, sitting on hard wooden benches for hours, the wind coming in from the broken windows.

'It'll be good for you to get away from here. Some sea air will perk you up,' she said to Ma, struggling for something to say. She still found it hard to meet the gaze of the other woman.

'Thanks, pet. I know you've already told me you can't help, but I will ask you one more time.' She squinted at Pearl through watering eyes. 'Is there any chance she is innocent? I beg you to find out if there is any truth in what Lizzy says, so I can rest easy, knowing I've done all I could.'

'Lizzy is guilty. I'm sure of it,' Pearl said.

'In that case, please attend Lizzy's hanging. I can't bear for her to be alone. You were once best friends, and I need to know how she was in her final hours. And bless you. You've been the best daughter I could ever have asked for. Take care of yourself and treasure Mei.'

Pearl looked away, a heat creeping up her neck.

'Stay true to where love takes you. Now, will you write to me when you've seen Lizzy at the end?' Ma opened her arms wide for a last hug, but Pearl stiffened, hesitating a moment before accepting the embrace.

The carriage door slammed shut, the coachman lashed his horses and Pearl stood waiting until it disappeared into the distance.

34

An elfin girl stood in the doorway. It was Polly, the matchgirl from the lodging house down the street. The suppurating wound on her cheek looked even larger than the last time Pearl had seen her. Pearl was stricken with remorse that she had neglected to leave the leftovers from supper on the matchgirls' doorstep, as she usually did. They came home so tired from work that they often went straight to bed without dinner.

Pearl held out her hand to Polly. 'Come in out of the rain and have some bread and butter,' she said, opening the door wide for the girl to come in. Polly appeared all too conscious of the odour coming from the pus oozing from her gum, as she wrapped a scarf closer around her face, hiding the disfigurement.

'Thank you kindly, Mrs Fitzgerald, but I can't stop now. Got to get round the whole neighbourhood. There's a meeting down at Goulston Street Hall in Whitechapel tonight about the Women Match Makers Union. We've got over 666 members now. Clementina Black from the Women's Trade Union League is coming to give us advice. The lady lawyer, Miss Eliza Orme, might be coming as well. She is so clever. Do come along if you can make the time. And if you could help towards our fund? I know you've been most kind already, but . . .' Polly rattled her tin expectantly.

'I've met Eliza Orme. She is a force of nature. I'd love to hear her speak publicly.' Pearl was impressed that Eliza would even think of taking time out of her busy schedule to help the matchgirls. 'It was so encouraging to meet a woman in the legal profession. Perhaps it is a sign of things changing. Anything I can do to help, let me know.' Pearl took out her purse and handed Polly a few pennies. The matchgirl's face brightened. 'That's ever so good of you.' Then she hesitated before saying: 'If it's not too much trouble, do you have any spare bread and butter to bring to the meeting? Some of the girls haven't had a decent meal for nearly two days.'

'And how about some jam and marmalade? I'll bring the sandwiches along later.'

'Oh, Mrs Fitzgerald, that'd be right grand!'

After Polly had left, Pearl sat at the kitchen table, thinking about Eliza Orme's zeal. Pearl wished she could summon up the same drive for her own legal predicament, but her thoughts kept returning to Ma Jennings. What kind of mother was she? No longer the jovial woman Pearl had always thought her to be, always ready with a maternal hug, but revealed instead as heartless, ready to throw her own daughter to the wolves. The truth had haunted Pearl in the days that followed, as she carried out her daily tasks, trying to make sense of it all.

The front door opened with a clatter as Mei came rushing in, arms full of brightly coloured papers and cartons to decorate the lodging house common rooms. After nuzzling Pearl's ear, Mei looked curiously at the large stack of half-made sandwiches on the table.

'Does housework really make you that hungry?' she teased. 'You've got enough there to feed the Xin army.'

Pearl sighed. 'I promised to make Polly some sandwiches for the matchgirls, but it's taking me an age. I said I would go to Goulston Street Hall, but I think I'll just drop these off and then come home.'

'Oh, we must go.' Mei seized the knife out of Pearl's hand and started vigorously spreading butter on the bread. 'I know you've been in low spirits recently, but the matchgirls need our help. They are our neighbours. They are organising a march later and we must support them.'

'It will be dangerous. You could be arrested.'

'I'm going, even if you won't come.' Mei took out a muslin cloth to cover the sandwiches.

'Don't think for a minute you're going alone. I need to come along and protect you.' Pearl flexed her biceps.

Mei whistled. 'My hero! No villain would dare come near me. If we leave now, we can catch up with the girls on the way to Whitechapel.'

The crowd outside Goulston Street Hall was so dense that Pearl and Mei had to push through with their precious parcels of sandwiches. 'What a crush! I can't believe there's so many people.' Pearl looked at the women around them, who were chattering excitedly with each other, handing out banners and placards. She felt lifted by the energising force of these women. It was such a welcome relief from her tortured feelings about Ma and Lizzy. The memory of them screaming at each other kept replaying in her mind every night.

Mei noticed Pearl's drooping shoulders and squeezed her arm. 'There is hope, my love. I know you are troubled that Ma Jennings has asked for help with her daughter.'

There was a quiver in Pearl's voice when she spoke. 'It breaks my heart to say no to her when she is dying, but I simply can't.' She also couldn't bear to tell Mei about the horrendous exchange of words between Ma and Lizzy in the prison.

'Try not to think about that now. Let's enjoy being here and helping these women.'

Rose waved at them from the stage. 'You are a godsend, Mrs Fitzgerald. Have to keep rattling the tins while we're out on the streets,' she said once they had weaved their way towards her. A group of smiling young women bobbed their heads and took the packages with squeals of appreciation before disappearing into the kitchens behind the stage.

'How are you, Mei? Lovely to see you and thanks so much for the smashing food,' Polly said, grinning, her usual self-consciousness fading. 'Stand by the side of the stage here and you'll get a good view of the speakers tonight. And you're in luck. Gerty Connolly is on first.' Polly's eyes shone with the fervour of the newly converted Salvation Army cadet.

'Gerty's speaking in front of this packed crowd?' Pearl couldn't believe that wisp of a girl was involved in politics.

'Oh, our Gerty is bloody marvellous. You know she stood up to the bosses when some of the women were poorly, asking for them to be taken back to work when they was sacked? Once she speaks, you'll forget everything else. Watch out now, here she comes.'

Gerty Connolly walked confidently to the middle of the stage. She wore a bonnet similar to the one Pearl had seen her wear several months ago, this one with four long ostrich feathers in a brilliant shade of red. The plumes shivered and shook with every animated turn of her head.

A ripple of expectation ran through the crowd, which gradually fell away into silence. Gerty strode up and down the stage, waving and smiling at faces in the audience. Holding up her hands, as if drawing the crowd to her bosom, she began to speak.

'I want to thank you all for coming out on a Sunday when you could be snug at home. I know some of you have walked six miles to get here when you're already tired.' Her voice was high and shrill, but rang out clearly, all the way to the back of the hall. 'Think of your sister workers what got the sack, just for dropping a match on the floor. It could easily have been you. Or the times when it's been your turn to get a clout from the foreman for no good reason other than he's got a sore head from too much booze.'

There were nods and shouts of assent from the crowd.

'A shame the journalist Mrs Besant can't be here tonight. But then she never did want us walking out of the factory. What's the point of boycotts she's argued, claiming that ain't going to get us anything. But we can't go on being fined for going to the lav or having dirty feet, or whatever the bosses decide, just so they can get out of paying us a full day's wages. That's why we need a union – to stop those things ever happening to us again.'

'That's right you tell 'em, Gerty!' The crowd was swaying, shouts going up, brought on by Gerty's fervour.

On the stage, Gerty's alert brown eyes flashed with fury. 'You know I'm there with you lovely gals. Every step of the way. Wasn't I there with you when they put up that blasted statue of Gladstone in the main courtyard of the factory, paid for with our own wages – not that we asked for it? I climbed on top of the plinth and cut my arm, letting my blood flow upon the marble. When they pulled me down, I cried: "Don't you dare stop me. We paid for it with our blood, sweat and tears!"'

Gerty pulled up the sleeves of her dress to show burns, scars and cuts where she had been injured over the years by faulty machinery.

Cries of 'Shame!' went up around the hall. The ardour of the crowd was catching. Gerty might be small and of tender years, but her power was sweeping through the crowd like a tenement fire. Mei was also listening intently, nodding vigorously and jumping up and down.

The room grew hushed again as Gerty carried on speaking. 'But that ain't the worst of it. We're dying because we have to use the white phosphorus, 'cos the bastards won't pay for the dearer red stuff, even though they know it's causing Phossy Jaw. How many of us have black gums and suffer agonies as our teeth fall out?'

With tears now streaming down her face, her hands entreating the women, Gerty said in a tremulous voice: 'We've all puked our guts up, feeling so sick and queasy. Fairfax Road is filled with pools of our bile that glow bright green in the dark. That ain't right.'

Pearl tensed. She pushed quickly through the crowds to reach Rose, who was spellbound by the speaker on stage.

'What's Gerty talking about? Tell me about this glowing green puke,' Pearl shouted in her ear.

Rose answered absently, eyes still gazing upon the stage. 'We don't get a lunch break and there's no separate kitchen, so we eat our lunch at the workstations. The phosphorus is all over our hands and gets into our stomachs. Makes you feel right sick. Just outside the factory gates the pools of vomit shine brighter than gaslight. Makes our clothes glow in the dark, as well.'

Of course! The glowing green pool of liquid at Wapping Old Stairs near the dead body. Pearl grabbed Rose's arm. 'Tell me about Ah Sim. You were with him at Wapping Old Stairs the morning he was killed, weren't you?'

Rose put a hand over her mouth, aghast at what she had let slip and began to back away from Pearl.

But Polly, who had been listening to their conversation, nudged her sister. 'Tell Miss Pearl. She's a good friend and deserves to be told the truth. If you won't tell her, I will. Nothing to be ashamed of.' She turned to Pearl. 'She doesn't talk about going a-courting with Ah Sim 'cos the old boys don't like local girls stepping out with Chinamen. Think they'll kidnap us and sell us into slavery. But Rose has got something to tell you, something you ought to know.' She gave her sister another nudge.

Pearl took Rose to one side and held her shoulders. 'You puked your guts up when you saw what was done to him.'

Rose wrenched herself out of Pearl's grip. 'I never . . . I don't know nothing!'

'What did you see? You must have seen who did that to Ah Sim.'

'Don't know what you're talking about.' Rose's mouth was quivering as she pulled away and joined the crowd of women who were shouting and yelling, getting ready for the march.

On stage, Gerty Connolly was now screaming at the top of her high, thin voice, the sound cutting through Pearl's fractured thoughts. 'Always hold your head up. Remember you're as good as anyone. Now let's get our placards ready, link arms and march on Westminster. Show them toffs we mean business! Support the Union of Women Match Makers!'

Mei fought her way through the crowds towards Pearl. 'Where have you been? Come on, we're marching to the Houses of Parliament. I've never been there before!' Pearl caught hold of Mei's hand and they walked together, heading west.

They were jostled on both sides, so great was the throng of women who chattered and laughed as they walked down Goulston Street. Pearl asked Polly: 'What's the plan for the march?'

'First off, we're going to *The Link* newspaper offices in Bouverie Street to see Mrs Besant and ask if she'll join us. Then we'll go on to Parliament and shout at the MPs in Westminster. That's always good for a laugh. And then, if the coppers don't run us in, we'll take them for a right merry dance along the Embankment.'

Polly's scarf had slipped from her face, revealing the weeping abscess on her jaw, the flesh rotting away. Polly's chin lifted at seeing Pearl's pitying gaze. 'I might be a little 'un but I've got a loud voice and I can run fast,' she said, winding the scarf more firmly across her cheeks.

When they reached Annie Besant's office, a haughty-looking woman was peering out from a first-floor window. 'That's Mrs Besant,' said Polly.

'Go home,' Mrs Besant called down in an aggrieved tone, waving her hand as if shooing away pigeons. 'Withdrawing your labour is not the answer. This will do you no good. And you're blocking up the street.'

'Whatsamatter, love? Frightened of getting kicked by a peeler's hoss? You stay indoors where it's safe and warm and write another article. We'll do all the hard work,' Gerty shouted up to the journalist, giving her a middle-finger salute. The only answer she received was a sharp click of the latch as Mrs Besant firmly shut the window.

The women marched slowly on to Westminster and entertained themselves by chanting slogans: 'Better conditions for workers!' 'Reform Now! Join the Union!'

The hour it took to walk to the House of Commons passed by quickly in amiable chatting and joking with the women around them, who seemed particularly fascinated with Mei, asking her to say words in Cantonese.

'You can say *wǒ ài nǐ* to your sweetheart, which means "I love you",' Mei said, giving Pearl a covert glance. The women started laughing raucously and all were repeating the phrase when a shrill whistle rent the air.

'Watch out, it's the coppers!' Polly cried.

Hobnailed boots clattered on the cobblestones as a phalanx of policemen charged at the women, grabbing their hair, twisting arms behind backs and bodily picking them up, before hurling them across the street. Women caught by blows from the police let out blood-curdling screams. Pearl saw a woman dragged along the ground by a constable, while another was pinned down, her face in the dirt.

The matchgirls fought back ferociously. Removing long hat pins from their bonnets, they brandished them like sabres, deftly jabbing at the policemen.

Mei had also been caught in the melee, a policeman squeezing her throat. Face contorted with agony, Mei struggled for breath. She seemed to collapse downwards, but then with a twist of her hips she threw the policeman over her back and then thrust her elbow upwards, jabbing him in the nose. He gave a sharp gasp of pain before he fell to his knees. The copper was immediately surrounded by women, who stabbed him in the backside with their hat pins. Pearl gave a triumphant whoop, while a group of matchgirls watching nearby cheered. 'What a girl! Teach us how to do those Chinese tricks and them thugs will never lay hands on us again.'

Mei laughed and waved at her admiring crowd. What she didn't see was an enormous figure bearing down on her. Pearl picked up a rock and threw it with all her might at the policeman's head. Mei's would-be assailant staggered back, holding his head, blood trickling from his scalp. Pearl rushed forward to grab Mei's arm as more policemen and hired thugs ran at them.

Then a more dangerous threat appeared. Police horses had moved in and were surrounding the women, edging closer and closer. Mei was shouting at one mounted policeman, trying to grab hold of the reins.

'Fuck off, you bitch!' he said as he swung his truncheon down upon her. It hit her arm with a sickening crunch. Pearl ran forward to help Mei, who was hunched over with pain.

'Let's get out of here before we're nabbed,' Pearl said.

In the panic and swarming crowd, Rose and Polly had become separated, Rose slipping further and further away from the protective band of matchgirls, and closer to the police line. A surge of police horses galloped towards the women and Pearl saw that Rose was too close to the horses. She leapt towards her, pushing the matchgirl out of the path of a charging horse. A second later, Rose would have been trampled under its hooves. Pearl and Rose lay in a crumpled heap on the cobblestones, bloody and shaken. Polly and Gerty rushed to their aid, half-carrying them down a side road, out of sight from the police.

Subdued, the women made their way back to Limehouse, exhausted from the long hours at the march. They were a filthy, bedraggled bunch; Pearl limping, while Mei gingerly held on to her injured arm. Was it all worth it, Pearl wondered, if the matchgirls still failed to gain better working conditions? As they passed the Captain Kidd pub, Pearl wondered if her Uncle Peter was drinking there tonight, and what he would say about his fellow coppers' vicious treatment of the matchgirls.

Something made Pearl turn around just then, and her gaze landed on a man who was looking her way, dimly illuminated in the glow of the street's gaslight. She could feel his eyes burning into her, and as Pearl looked straight at him, and caught a glimpse of his profile, she stopped dead in her tracks.

'What's the matter?' Mei was looking at her.

'Nothing, I . . .'

Pearl turned back to where the phantom had been standing, but the doorway was as dark and empty as a hag's mouth.

35

The day after the march, Pearl visited the matchgirls' lodgings to check in on them, bringing soup and cakes.

'How is Rose feeling? I'm glad you two managed to get back safely.'

Polly was on her hands and knees, scrubbing at Rose's dress in a bowl of murky water. 'Looks like she has some broken ribs. She's still ailing.'

The matchgirls' room was about the size of a prison cell and Rose was lying motionless on a small bed that the two sisters shared. A thin blanket covered her. The windows were pasted over with layers of newspaper in an attempt to keep the wind and rain out. A chair with two dresses, a shawl and a nightdress on it was the only other item of furniture in the room.

'I don't mean to intrude while she's recovering, but I need to talk to Rose. It's really important.'

Polly looked doubtful but then nodded.

Pearl sat on the bed, and shook Rose's shoulder gently. The girl stirred, slowly opened her eyes, and smiled at Pearl. 'Thank you for pulling me from them horses' hooves. You saved my life.'

'I'm glad I was there to help. And now I'd appreciate you helping me, Rose. Tell me about the morning Ah Sim died.' Pearl held Rose's hand.

'I'm scared. I don't want to end up like he did. I ain't told nobody. If I tell you, you must promise to keep my name out of it.'

'I promise, no one will know your identity.'

'I don't think I can.'

'It's time to get it off your chest. Surely you want your man's killer brought to justice?'

Rose's breathing was slowed. 'Alright, yes, I was there. I wish to God I'd never gone.' She paused, thinking back. 'Ah Sim was in high spirits. He took me down to Wapping Old Stairs to show off. He wanted me to think he was a man about town, a real catch. Bragging about getting well paid from the stuff he was selling. I didn't believe him at first, and he wanted to prove it to me. Told me to hide behind this old cart on the foreshore and watch his biggest deal yet. And then . . .' Rose's voice faltered.

'Go on. You'll feel better if you share the burden.'

'Two men rowed up to the shore and started talking to Ah Sim. Then there was shouting. They started punching him. Calling him a thieving bastard. I was so scared I couldn't move.'

Pearl interrupted her. 'Two men? Are you sure one of them wasn't a woman, wearing gold boots?'

'No, it was definitely two men. One was an old geezer, waving around a big stick, with a silver handle.'

That had to be Old Jake. It made sense, and reinforced Pearl's earlier suspicion that Jake was trying to distract from his own role in the crime by accusing Lizzy.

Pearl's heart began to beat faster in panic. 'Maybe the other person you saw was a tall woman? About five feet ten in height?'

'I didn't see no lady. The older man hit Ah Sim with his stick and then the other one stuck a dagger in Ah Sim's belly. It was the most terrible thing I ever laid eyes on. I'll never forget it as long as I live.' Tears began to stream down the girl's face.

'As soon as the men went off, I went to Ah Sim, but he was in a terrible state, blood all over him. I threw my guts up and then ran for it. I was scared for my life. I'll never forgive myself for not staying and helping him, but I thought he was dead.'

'Of course. But think again about what you saw. Two men and not a woman?' Pearl's mouth was dry, an unease rising. Surely the matchgirl must have been mistaken in the horror of the moment.

'Well, you asked me, Mrs Fitzgerald. Are you calling me a liar?' Rose turned her face to the wall.

'Of course not,' Pearl rushed to reassure the young girl, but it was clear that the conversation was over.

Walking back from Rose and Polly's room, Pearl turned over in her mind what Rose had said. She desperately wanted the matchgirl to have seen Lizzy in the act of killing Ah Sim, to prove that she was right, that Lizzy deserved to face the gallows. But now a whisper of doubt was growing like a canker inside her. Try as she might, she couldn't ignore it. She had been wrong.

Lizzy's words came back to her: 'I've done plenty, but I am innocent of the crime I have been convicted of.' Ma was convinced that a strong Catholic faith and the threat of perpetual damnation in purgatory would stop Lizzy from committing murder. That it was more her style to get others to do the dirty work.

Pearl was so lost in thought that she had automatically walked back towards The Sailor's Arms. She was curious to see a large crowd gathered outside. It hadn't been this packed since the celebrations for Queen Victoria's Golden Jubilee. Several policemen were pushing back the mob. Pearl spotted Sergeant O'Dwyer among them and squirmed through the crowd to speak with him.

She caught hold of his sleeve. 'What's going on, Uncle Peter?'

He ushered her past the police cordon, to the side door of

the pub. 'Bad business, Pearl. There's been another murder, and we suspect it's the same assailant as done the killings here in Limehouse – your Chinese feller and Old Jake. Similar method.'

'Who is it?'

O'Dwyer hesitated, his head jerked up towards Pearl's old bedroom.

Pearl ran for the stairs before her uncle could stop her. 'Don't be going in there,' he said in a hoarse whisper.

From the doorway of the attic bedroom, Pearl could see a figure lying on her old bed. The eyes and mouth were stretched wide in terror, the face blanched, the bedsheets a deep crimson. A dagger was sticking out of the woman's belly. Betty Sullivan.

Pearl's knees went weak. Sergeant O'Dwyer's arms went round her. 'Steady, girl, steady.'

'What happened?'

'She was found here by Mr Matthews.'

Pearl shuddered. 'Are you sure it's the same killer? Ah Sim had a blow to the head.'

'But they were all stabbed deep in the belly. Might be some differences, but the wound is very similar in all of the cases. A large cut in the abdomen, so deep the intestines were coming out.'

Pearl sat down quickly.

'Now, you need to get out of here sharpish.' O'Dwyer was trying to help Pearl out of the room, but her legs refused to move.

'Why?'

'Betty's been boasting all over Limehouse that she owns The Sailor's Arms lock, stock and barrel, and kicked you out. Now Betty's dead, you inherit the pub. That makes you a prime suspect in her murder.'

Was it possible the same person had killed Ah Sim, Old Jake and Betty? Pearl remembered what Rose had only just told her. '*It was definitely two men . . . The older man hit Ah Sim with his stick and then the other one stuck a dagger in Ah Sim's belly.'*

Lizzy's strident voice kept coming back. *'I've been set up for killing Ah Sim and Old Jake good and proper. I never done it.'*

Pearl quickly left by the side door, the awful realisation that she was responsible for sending an innocent woman to the gallows hitting her hard. What was happening to her? Doubling over and bracing her hands on her knees, she took in slow breaths. As she did so, something caught her eye across the road – a man at the window of the warehouse opposite. The dirt on the glass obscured his features, but he was smiling down at Pearl. She blinked and when she looked again, the stranger had vanished.

Inspector Crowley greeted her with a genial smile at the police station front desk. 'So good to see you, Pearl. Please come and sit down.' He led her gently by the elbow to sit on his Chesterfield armchair, and the leather groaned as she sank into it. It was still the most uncomfortable chair she had ever come across.

'How have you been keeping? I am so looking forward to our visit to The Savoy on Sunday.' At first, Pearl couldn't think what he was referring to. Then she quickly recovered herself.

'Oh, yes of course, it will be such a treat. But I actually came to speak to you about another urgent matter, Inspector.'

Crowley waited, inclining his head to her.

'I have made a terrible mistake. I no longer believe Lizzy Soo Chow is guilty of murder. I've just heard that Betty Sullivan has been murdered in exactly the same way as Old Jake and Ah Sim. I also have information that strongly suggests Old Jake was one of Ah Sim's two killers. I did try to tell you he was involved. Perhaps you have heard of the Wild Eyed Boys? I remember now that at my father's wake Old Jake told me he belonged to the gang.'

Crowley was looking at her, perplexed.

'And now an eyewitness to Ah Sim's murder has come forward with important information, saying that she saw two men kill him, and not a woman. I implore you, Inspector, please believe me. If an innocent woman is wrongly incarcerated, we need to keep investigating the case.'

Crowley nodded soothingly, cupping her elbow. 'You are overwrought, my dear. It is in your tender nature that you do not want to feel responsible for sending a woman to the gallows. But fear not. This was a thorough police investigation, and we have the right person behind bars.'

Pearl shook her head vehemently. 'The killer is still out there—'

Crowley interrupted her. 'As your friend,' here he smiled kindly at her, 'I advise that you must keep your distance in the matter of Betty Sullivan's murder. As you are in line to inherit the pub and would materially benefit from her death, you will inevitably be asked questions during her murder inquiry. I will do my best to protect you, but it's best to stay away.'

'But you don't understand, Inspector Crowley. I think the wrong person is in jail and I helped put her there.'

'A woman's heart and her overwrought emotions are why the fairer sex will never rise within the ranks of the police. A logical brain is needed. That's why you will never see a female Commissioner of Police of the Metropolis. Pearl, please go home. Let the matter rest with us.'

Walking out of the police station, Pearl shivered, goosebumps pimpling her skin upon realising that she was the link between all of the killings. She had found Ah Sim dying on the foreshore, Old Jake was her husband's uncle, and now Betty, her father's common-law wife. Could she be the next victim?

36

Pearl took off her coat and carefully hung it on the rack in the hallway, next to Mei's. She walked into the kitchen and put the kettle on the stove for a pot of strong tea. As she waited for it to boil, she sat down dejectedly on a kitchen chair.

Mei pulled her into an embrace. 'What has happened?'

'Betty Sullivan has been killed.'

'Oh, my goodness. She was a wicked woman, but I would not have wished her dead.'

'I think the same person murdered Ah Sim, Old Jake and Betty. May God forgive me, but I don't think Lizzy did it. I've done her a terrible wrong. I went to see Inspector Crowley, but he doesn't believe me. I need to look at the evidence again. If there is the slightest chance Lizzy didn't kill your brother, I must find out.'

She looked at Mei for reassurance but Mei was staring at her with disbelief. 'Did you ever think of my feelings? I thought I knew Liz well – and then to find out she killed Ah Sim . . . I will never forgive myself for being close to her – or forget what she did. She deserves to pay for her crimes.'

Pearl reached for Mei's hand. 'My darling, you don't understand. Rose told me everything. She was there—'

'No, *you* don't understand,' Mei snapped. 'Do as the inspector says and let the matter drop. You looked into it because of Ma Jennings, but now it's time for us to move on.'

'You encouraged me to do what Ma asked. Why have you changed your mind now?'

'That was to honour the request of a dying woman, not because I believed Liz was innocent.'

The two women faced each other, intransigent. Mei's face was rigid. 'The spirit of my brother is avenged. Ma wants you to attend the hanging, and I'm coming with you.'

'Please don't. It's a sickening business, and it won't bring Ah Sim back.'

Mei's face contorted with anguish.

'I know that.' Mei pounded on her chest. 'I want *vengeance*. That woman killed my brother and for that I want to see her suffer. I'll never see him again, listen for his footsteps, hear his special knock at the door, see the way he smiled at me when I was cooking his favourite dishes. It's the only way I will find peace.' She broke into deep sobs, her whole body shaking. There was nothing for Pearl to do but hold Mei in her arms and stroke her hair. They stayed like that for a long time.

The days crawled by slowly, but there was plenty to do, with the upkeep of the lodging house, shopping, cooking for their lodgers and an endless list of repairs. Pearl did everything and anything to keep her mind from thinking about the possibility of Lizzy's innocence. But the nagging feeling was developing into an avalanche that threatened to engulf her. In an attempt to lighten the mood, they managed an occasional trip to the music hall. They went to see Dan Leno at the Forester's in Mile End. But even though Leno was billed as 'The Funniest Man on Earth', he failed to raise a smile between them.

There was a yawning chasm between them now, and Lizzy's execution was hovering over them. Pearl would look at Mei, struck dumb with desire, wanting to touch her, hold her, comfort her. But when Pearl opened her mouth to speak, the words evaporated on her tongue. She would place rose petals on Mei's pillow, buy little treats of sherbet lemons, leave love notes for her to find in the pockets of her coat. But Mei was silent, as unreachable as a shipwreck on the Cape of Good Hope.

Pearl had even asked her uncle if there was any way to postpone the execution and continue the investigation so they could uncover fresh evidence. He had shaken his head and tutted.

'Have the sense to let it go, Pearl.'

'But there are other suspects still out there.'

'We've cleared up two murders as well as the drug smuggling racket. Bosses at Scotland Yard are very pleased with the division, and our Inspector Crowley. No need to rock the boat.'

Finally, Pearl went in search of Soo Chow, who knew more about Lizzy's business than anybody else. She'd persuaded him to give evidence against Lizzy, and at the time, she had believed that what she was doing, manipulating him, was the only way to get to the truth. But now she wanted to hear if there was another version of events – preferably the truth. She wanted to ask him if he knew where Lizzy was that morning. If Lizzy was at The Dragon Inn, there would be plenty of eyewitnesses who could testify as to her whereabouts.

With a growing queasiness in the pit of her stomach, she realised that Soo Chow could have been the other man who was with Old Jake, taking part in killing Ah Sim. It would explain why he was quick to point suspicion at his wife and make a deal with the police.

The front door of The Dragon Inn was nailed shut, wooden boards criss-crossing the front. The blue willow pattern sign had fallen off, and now lay scattered on the ground. Walking around to the side door, all was completely deserted. No hint of Soo Chow anywhere.

Pearl cast about for other possible suspects. Who could have been the man Rose saw with Old Jake that morning? What about Jeremiah? He'd been nagging at the back of her mind. She needed to look at him again. After all, there was a chance that the indigo dye docker could still be the Blue Man. Ah Sim was in debt to him; things could have turned violent.

If Pearl could link Jeremiah to Betty Sullivan's killing, she might be able to persuade Inspector Crowley to take a look at him. She knew it was tenuous, but she just needed enough suspicion for Lizzy's case to be re-opened. Pearl headed for the West India Docks.

Ignoring the stares and catcalls from bored sailors wanting a bit of sport, she marched on towards the place where she and Xianfan had found the indigo dye men. There he was, playing whist at his usual spot.

She greeted him warmly. 'How are you, Jeremiah? Can you spare a moment to speak with me?'

He narrowed his eyes. 'What do you want?'

'It won't take long. Please, it's important.'

Reluctantly, Jeremiah got up from the card table. His mates nudged each other and sniggered as he stalked towards Pearl. Jeremiah looked back. 'No looking at my cards, now,' he warned them.

They walked along the quayside. 'Excuse the intrusion, Jeremiah, but there's been another murder. Betty Sullivan, a close friend of my father, was killed. She may have been done in by the same person who did Ah Sim. I'm asking around the docks for information. Do you know anything? Were you acquainted with her?'

'Accusing me again! I don't know any Betty Sullivan. Never heard of her. I've been away in Canterbury this past week. Ask anyone, I got back this morning. Stop pestering me with these damn fool questions. And don't go sticking your nose in my business, if you know what's good for you.' He leaned in close, so close she could see the tobacco stains on his teeth, then stomped back to the card game.

Another dead end. Jeremiah wasn't the killer.

She walked back along Wapping High Street and stopped in front of The Sailor's Arms. Her heart sank as she looked at the pub's derelict state. It looked desolate; no stragglers or sailors on its doorstep. The pub belonged to her now, but that was of little comfort, only sorrow and regret.

A large padlock was securely fastened to the front door. Perhaps her Uncle Peter had arranged that. She walked down the side alley; the passageway door was ajar. She pushed it open and walked up the stairs.

Noises were coming from her father's bedroom. She crossed the corridor, picking up a coal shovel and brandished it in front of her. The startled face of Mr Matthews whirled round as she barged into the room.

'Mr Matthews! What are you doing here?'

'You trying to give me a heart attack?' He clutched his chest. 'Guess you'll be taking over here now. Just packing up a few of my things and Betty's. Not the same without the old girl.' He dabbed a handkerchief to his nose and blew loudly. 'Terrible business. I can't get out of my mind how I found her.'

Pearl considered for a moment. 'You needn't leave, Mr Matthews. I'll need someone to help me here, and you know this place inside out. Get some of the old customers back in. You know all of them.'

His face brightened. 'Do you really mean that?'

'You can start by sorting out what stock we have in the cellar.'

While Mr Matthews was in the basement itemising the caskets and stacks of bottles, Pearl walked around the saloon bar. It was an awful mess. An atmosphere of abandonment and loss shrouded the stagnant air. She made herself go back into her father's bedroom, images of him clinging on to life in the crumpled sheets coming back to her unbidden.

She opened drawers, cupboards, searching thoroughly. On a high shelf in the wardrobe, she found what she was looking for. The title deeds to The Sailor's Arms. Pearl would take the documents to Eliza Orme and see if she could get everything settled so she was the sole and legal owner of the public house. For once, things were going her way. She rushed out onto the street and into the fresh air.

At last it came. The day she was dreading. Mei hadn't mentioned Lizzy's execution at all, but on the evening before, she said: 'If we're going to be up early, we should get some rest.'

'Are you sure about going? It will be horrendous.'

Mei's mouth was set in a hard line. 'It's what I must do.'

Lizzy was hanging from a rafter, swinging violently to and fro. Her tongue was purple and distended, eyes popping out of their sockets as she pointed a claw-like hand at Pearl. 'You did this to me,' she rasped.

Pearl sat bolt upright in bed, soaked in sweat. She put a hand to her own throat and drew in a deep breath. She looked over at Mei, who was soundly sleeping. When the church clock struck six bells, Pearl decided to get up; there was no more rest to be had for her. The darkness of the night had terrified her, shadows dancing across the ceiling like monsters from the abyss. She had listened to

Mei's laboured breathing throughout the night and grew alarmed at how feverish her lover felt, her nightdress drenched with sweat.

She gently shook Mei. 'Your body is burning up. Stay in bed and rest.'

Mei murmured and rolled over. 'Wake me in half an hour. I'll get dressed then.' She fell back into a deep slumber.

Pearl crept downstairs. All was quiet apart from the snoring of her lodgers, who would be up soon and off to the docks. She lit a fire and filled the kettle so it would be ready for their tea. Then she placed a large pot containing congee on the warming stove. The hot rice porridge would set them up for the day. She wondered if she should eat a little, but the thought of it made her stomach churn.

Pearl returned to the bedroom to check on Mei but she was still fast asleep, a light sheen of perspiration covering her face. Mei shouldn't come to the hanging if she was poorly.

A thought crossed Pearl's mind. Perhaps she didn't need to go herself after all. She could spend the day looking after Mei. Maybe she could visit Uncle Peter or treat herself to just one pipe of opium – she had hidden a small quantity where Mei would never find it – or perhaps take in the latest show at Wilton's Music Hall. But no. Her nightmare, her unconscious, was calling to her. Pearl needed to face up to her mistake; Lizzy was guilty of many things, but Ah Sim's murder was not one of them. She needed to stop the hanging; she didn't want Lizzy's blood on her hands.

Pearl pulled on her black cloak, bonnet and gloves last worn at her father's funeral, and walked quickly in the direction of Thames Police Station.

37

Pearl hammered at the door of Inspector Crowley's office. Her hair was as wild and unkempt as her thoughts.

He looked displeased. 'I waited for you at The Savoy. You never turned up.'

Contrite, she remembered. 'I'm so sorry, but this is urgent. I'm asking you one last time. No, I'm begging you. You need to stop the execution.' She looked at the clock above his desk. 'The hanging is in three hours. There's not much time left.'

He shook his head. 'You must calm yourself. Justice needs to be done.'

'If you can't help, I will find someone who can.'

Sir Charles Warren! The conversation she'd had with the Prince of Wales at the opium den came back to her. If there was one person who could get Lizzy a stay of execution, it had to be the Commissioner of Police. And didn't Bertie say he was old pals with Warren? She needed Maude to take her to Bertie.

Pearl raced out into the road. A hackney cab was clattering by and she stood in front of it. 'Stop!' she cried, holding both hands in front of her, as if she had supernatural powers to halt the carriage in its tracks. The horse reared on its hind legs, whinnying, mouth flecked with foam.

'Are you bloody mad! I could have killed you!' The cab driver was apoplectic with rage. He shook a meaty fist at her, his bowler hat askew from the sudden stop.

'This is an emergency. Take me to 139 Piccadilly. There's a good tip if you hurry.' Pearl clambered in without waiting for a reply. Muttering about imbecilic women crossing the roads, the cab driver whipped his horse and took off.

The West India Dock Road was at a standstill, a long line of carts, carriages and trams blocking the way. Pearl shouted up to the cab driver. 'What's holding us up?'

'Accident ahead. Looks like a horse and carriage rammed into the back of another.'

'Can't you go another way?' Pearl was leaning at a perilous angle out of the carriage.

'Not much I can do. You just sit tight.' The cab man settled more comfortably in his seat and lit a briar pipe. Pearl pounded the side of the carriage and let out a yell of frustration. All through the hour-long journey she fidgeted, willing with all her might for the cab to move faster.

When they eventually reached Mayfair, Pearl was in a state of high agitation. She had little time to marvel at the imposing Mayfair mansion that Bertie had installed Maude in, although the singer had boasted it was the former home of the notorious Lord Byron. She dashed up the front stairs and rapped on the brass door knocker. She didn't let up until a footman opened the door an inch. She pushed past him and shouted from the bottom of the stairs. 'Maude! Maude! I need to see you. It's urgent.' Pearl paced up and down the hallway, suspiciously observed by the footman.

Several minutes later, Maude tottered down the stairs in a translucent negligee. 'Blimey, you're making such a bloomin' racket.'

Having just woken up, the accents of the Canning Town girl were all too apparent.

'I need you to take me to see Bertie. A friend of mine is about to be hanged and I need Bertie to talk to Sir Charles Warren and stop it,' Pearl gabbled.

'What are you on about? I've a punishing headache.' Maude put a hand to her temple . 'Bertie and me had a frightful row last night. He's taken up with some young floozy. Told me we were finished.'

'Please, Maude. For the sake of our friendship, we need to see Bertie. He promised to help me when we last met.' The footman had followed Pearl and was watching keenly.

'What friendship? It was years ago. And one night out in an opium den ain't gonna make us all best pals. I shouldn't even be associating with the likes of you. I'm respectable now.' She looked at Pearl as if she were a piece of effluvia floating in the Thames.

The footman, at Maude's command, slammed the door in Pearl's face. Maude's rejection stung but the fear of the consequences was worse for Pearl, and even worse for Lizzy.

Frantic, Pearl headed towards Old Bailey Street. The hours were passing by so quickly. It was now nearly eight o'clock in the morning, and yet the skies were still dark, mottled with glowering, rain-filled clouds. The flower girls, watercress sellers and the costermongers were preparing for the day, setting up their stalls, while others made their way towards the City to sell their wares in wicker baskets slung over one arm. They were laughing gaily and chattering as if today was just like any other.

Pushing past the crowd, Pearl was stopped by a young girl. She looked to be around ten years old. Barefoot, her tough little soles were impervious to the sharp cobbles and stones on the pavement. She had a perfectly round face and rosy complexion, which was probably due to the chill wind coming off the river, rather than evidence of a strong constitution. At the top of her voice she shrieked at Pearl: 'Two bundles a penny, primroses! Sweet violets, penny a bunch!'

'Not now, sweetheart, maybe later.'

The girl smiled, showing greyish gums and three little black teeth.

'I'll give you another bunch for a penny?' she persisted, her eyes fixed on Pearl in a sad smile.

Relenting, Pearl said: 'I'll take three bunches of primroses, please.'

The girl looked happy with the tuppence Pearl had given her, hopeful that it would keep her from starving for at least another week.

Pearl noticed the three bunches of primroses in her hand were wilting already, the stems cold and clammy. The delicate pink petals were stained with brown at the edges and curled inwards as if trying to stay alive.

The fortress-like walls of Newgate Prison were stained black with soot; a massive crowd of people had gathered outside, numbering in their thousands. The air was fizzing with excitement. It could have been a king or queen's coronation the gathering had come to see.

There were so many people here, and most of them would not see the actual execution. Only a select few, who paid for the privilege, would be invited inside the walls of the prison to watch the gruesome spectacle.

An organ grinder was standing on a wooden crate, playing a lively ditty. He had with him a gibbering monkey, its fur bald in patches, chattering and screeching along with the melody. Several women were dancing wildly, kicking up their heels, and watched admiringly by a group of young swells. The men had dressed in their finest, puffing up their chests to show off embroidered waistcoats.

They grinned and play-punched each other, before turning to ogle at the dainty ankles of the women who were prancing and whirling each other around in a frenzy. Pearl couldn't understand how a hanging could be seen as a time for merriment. She would never have dreamt of coming to watch the sordid event if it hadn't been for Ma's request. The engorged bloodlust of the crowd unsettled her, and she was relieved that Mei was not witnessing this. Pearl was continually jostled by the crowd, who were impeding her way forward towards the prison gates.

A long queue was forming around the meat pie seller, as Pearl tried to elbow her way past. The hanging had awakened a ravenous appetite in the crowd, although the smell and sight of the greasy liver and pork pies was causing waves of nausea in Pearl's stomach. The pie man's apron was seeped in grease, forming a large shiny patch around his belly.

He scratched his gargantuan backside, picked his nose and then chose a juicy suet pudding for a waiting giggling girl who was holding out a penny. She grabbed it from him and took a large bite out of the pie. A sliver of fat slopped wetly onto the ground. It was quickly licked up by a mangy dog with pink and grey patches on its back, a weeping bite wound across its snout. *Not the victor of many fights,* thought Pearl, feeling sorry for it. She bent down to stroke the mongrel but hastily withdrew her hand from its snapping, snarling jaws.

A young man, top hat perched on the back of his head, walked with his arm clamped around a young girl. They couldn't have been much older than sixteen. 'Why can't we go in, Charlie? There's nothing to see here,' she whined. The woman's shiny pink bonnet looked new and Pearl wondered if she had bought it especially for the occasion.

'We coulda seen it about twenty year ago, when they done the last public hanging, but they've stopped it for the likes of us who can't pay,' the young man was saying. 'Only toffs and lucky sods who can afford a few sovereigns are allowed to witness hangings now.'

'Count yourself lucky you can't see it,' Pearl couldn't help herself from saying to them. 'You watch someone die in that horrible way, and it will haunt you for the rest of your life.' They looked at her as if she was an escapee from Bedlam.

Pearl knew that the courting couple would be envious of her ability to pay a large sum to see someone suffer so gruesomely. Ma had left a pile of coins on the kitchen table before she left the lodging house, and Pearl suspected it was her life savings. She would gladly exchange places with the courting couple, but she needed to do as Ma requested. Of course Lizzy must be punished for her crimes – and Pearl wanted to fulfil her promise to Mei to find her brother's killer – but Lizzy had spoken with such conviction when she claimed that she was not guilty for Ah Sim's murder, and Pearl now had significant evidence that she was innocent. Pearl was desperate to get a stay of execution and to continue the investigation, despite the jealousy that still constricted her heart. Let them send Lizzy to prison for life, or pack her off on a ship bound for Australia, rather than forcing her to face the gallows.

The crowd was growing ever larger, undulating and rippling, like a large ocean swell, with Pearl edging closer to the prison gates, with agonising slowness.

'I'm bored, Charlie,' the young woman whined.

'I can think of something to put a spring in your step.' Her beau hugged her more tightly, making the woman squeal with delight. 'But before I do, let me tell you the dreadful things that are going to happen soon.' Charlie looked serious and removed his hat in mock solemnity. 'Once they hang the prisoner, they'll hoist a black flag on the pole above the main gate, just there,' he said, pointing as he lowered his voice. His girl looked at him, eyes big as dinner plates.

Pearl watched the two lovebirds distractedly. How on earth could they think that waiting outside the location of an execution was suitable for a romantic outing? She couldn't understand the wish to see someone die, the ability to hear the crack of the broken neck and derive pleasure from it.

'Then the prison bell will toll, and a chill will go right through you. That's to say the condemned man, or in this case woman, is a goner. And the crowd will be screaming and crying and laughing, kissing and hugging each other. It's like the end of the world has come.'

The crowd suddenly divided as a carriage came through at speed, opening up a pathway for Pearl to run down. She could now see the side entrance Uncle Peter had instructed her to go to. Banging on the brass knocker, there was a lengthy wait until the door opened slowly and a prison guard's head peered out.

'Officer Jenkins? Sergeant O'Dwyer sent me.' He nodded and stuck out his palm. Pearl placed three sovereigns on it. 'Come now, Mrs Fitzgerald, your uncle said you'd be good for four. I've got a wife, a mother-in-law and five young babes to feed.'

'Uncle Peter told me that you'd agreed on the price earlier.'

'Didn't realise this one would draw such a distinguished crowd. Got nobility wanting a look. I can easily sell your place to another punter.' Pearl rummaged in her purse and placed another sovereign on the guard's outstretched palm, quelling an urge to curse him for profiting from the execution.

A cacophony of shrieking and screaming knocked Pearl back as soon as she entered the prison courtyard. Pearl looked up at the arch windows criss-crossed with bars and could see the pale arms of prisoners behind the iron grilles waving scraps of white cloth. Their cries of lament merged into such a crescendo that at first Pearl couldn't make out what they were saying. Each convict had their own phrase, which they repeated again and again like an unholy chorus, their hysteria at fever pitch on the day of an execution.

'May God forgive me and watch over my children!'

'I'm innocent!'

'Pray for my soul!'

Pearl tried to blot out the tortured voices of the prisoners as Officer Jenkins ushered her and a group of smartly dressed gentlemen in top hats towards a tall shed with a slanted roof, abutting the far corner of the yard. They gathered outside the door and waited.

Looking towards the large wooden shed, she began trembling. Several important-looking men were standing at its entrance, talking quietly to each other.

'We call it Cold Meat Shed, where they do the hangin'. You'll get a good view of the action, don't you worry. Time to go in now,' Officer Jenkins said to her.

Pearl looked around anxiously. 'Can you direct me to the person in charge? I need to speak with him immediately.'

'No chance of that, Miss. The guvnor's got to make sure everything's right. Now do you want in or not?'

Pearl nodded, realising that Jenkins was unlikely to help, despite her pleadings. Her best chance of talking to the prison governor would be to approach him as soon as she set eyes on him.

Inside the shed, Pearl's eyes grew accustomed to the gloom. It smelt of stale sweat, sawdust and terror. She joined a small crowd gathered close to the gallows, which stood on a wooden podium. They were talking in subdued voices. There was no laughter but an air of febrile anticipation. One of the ladies fluttered her fan in the coquettish manner of an opera singer, complaining of the heat and swishing the hem of her silk brocade dress impatiently.

The gentlemen in morning dress beamed and nodded at each other, puffing away on fat cigars. It could have been a day at the races, rather than watching the spectacle of someone being deliberately put to death. At least the baying crowd outside the walls of Newgate Prison were more honest in their lust for blood. Pearl again regretted needing to be here. This was unlikely to bring any solace to Ma Jennings or closure for Mei. But maybe, just maybe, she could still save Lizzy's life.

Officer Jenkins' voice grew respectful. 'See that gentleman in the corner? That'll be your man, Her Majesty's executioner, Mr James Berry.'

Pearl turned to look at a fellow with a well-tonsured beard and moustache. A worried-looking chap, Mr Berry was engaged in a heated exchange with a squat man who was pointing to a gold pocket watch. The executioner was gesturing animatedly, and Pearl wondered what could have caused the tension between them.

Jenkins bent towards her conspiratorially. 'Looks like the hangman's having another barney with Governor Smithson, but we're running late. Mr Berry's got the frights about the drop. Up in Norwich, the prisoner was given too long a drop and his head came clean off. The Chaplain fainted dead away.

'There was the devil of a row afterwards and fingers were pointed. Mind you, too short a drop and they dangle there gasping for breath, like a landed carp, flapping and struggling.' Pearl winced at the thought. Jenkins continued: 'Berry don't want to get it wrong again. Could end up relieved of his duties.'

Pearl noticed the hangman disappearing behind some curtains.

She jumped in alarm at a loud bang. Silence and then more banging, again and again. Pearl turned to the prison guard. 'What on earth?'

'That'll be Berry testing the trap door,' explained Jenkins. 'Don't want it sticking.'

The tension was building in the crowd and their chattering grew quieter. The shed's stuffiness and the odour of musty clothes, heated by palpitating flesh, was overpowering. She suddenly spotted Governor Smithson, wondering whether she could get to him. Just then an electrified ripple ran through the crowd.

From an alleyway across the courtyard, a tall figure emerged, her hands bound and shackled between two brawny women warders. Lizzy somehow managed to move elegantly, even though she was in chains. But then, she had always cut a dashing figure. Despite the horrors that awaited her, Lizzy was in high spirits.

The three women walked as nonchalantly as if they were on a Sunday stroll in the park. They passed close enough for Pearl to catch their conversation.

Lizzy was chuckling with one of the warders. 'You should cook him a nice pork stew, Bertha. That's the quickest way to a man's heart.'

Then she turned to the other warder. 'She ran off without paying? The nerve! I'd have dealt with that nasty business. A good beating would teach her.' All three women roared with laughter at the thought.

Lizzy was putting on a good show with her calm demeanour, acting without a care in the world. Almost in slow motion, she glided towards the scaffold. The shed fell silent as everyone stopped moving, their eyes riveted on the condemned prisoner.

'It's time.' Governor Smithson was still nervously playing with his pocket watch.

Berry nodded his assent. 'Everything's ready.'

The gentleman next to Pearl rubbed his hands vigorously. 'What we've all been waiting for. Should be worth seeing.' He smiled at her, eyes twinkling. She looked at him aghast, realisation dawning on her that this was actually happening, and there was nothing she could do about it. She was paralysed, unable to get through the constricting crowd to reach the governor or Lizzy. The horror was about to unfold.

The executioner gave the signal, and with a firm grasp, the two prison warders helped Lizzy to climb the steps up to the gallows platform, her chains clanking.

'Prisoner – do you have any final words?' Governor Smithson said.

Lizzy spoke in a strong, calm voice. 'If you've all come to hear me repent for my sins, then you've come to the wrong place. Chaplain, don't bother praying for me. I'll be meeting my God soon enough. I don't regret anything. I've had more larks and earned more money than any of you could ever dream of. Eaten the finest food, smoked the choicest opium and had the wildest couplings.

'So look your fill at me. Watch and gawp and get all hot as I go for the drop. See if I care! I hold my hands up to the crimes I've committed, but no murders. Let it be known, I did not kill anyone, as the Lord Almighty is my witness.'

Lizzy scanned the crowd. 'I know you are here, Pearl Fitzgerald! This is all your doing! You know I'm innocent!' And then her eyes found Pearl. 'I see you. You haven't heard the last of me. I'll be back to haunt you until the last trumpet sounds.'

Pearl's face was scalded by Lizzy's fierce stare.

Lizzy then closed her eyes and began praying:

'Hail, Mary, full of grace,
'the Lord is with thee.
'Blessed art thou amongst women
'and blessed is the fruit of thy womb, Jesus.
'Holy Mary, Mother of God,
'pray for us sinners,
'now and at the hour of our death.
'Amen.'

'This is all wrong! Stop the hanging!' Pearl shouted. Shoving and pushing through the crowd with all of her strength, she managed to grab hold of Governor Smithson. 'I beg you. This is a terrible miscarriage of justice.' She was screaming, voice raw, clutching at him.

'Get this woman out of here, Officer Jenkins!' Governor Smithson was apoplectic. Before Pearl could say another word, Jenkins ran over, threw her over his shoulder, and marched to the far side of the room.

The prison clock tolled nine. 'Do it now, Berry!' ordered Governor Smithson.

The executioner carried Lizzy to the centre of the platform and pulled a white hood over her head. Then he took a step to the side of the trap door. Berry tugged the lever and Lizzy plunged down towards the brick-lined pit below. Pearl braced herself for the sound of a sharp crack, like a branch snapping, as the neck broke. Instead she heard a horrible gargling sound.

'Bloody hell!' Berry called out. 'Not again. Smithson, I warned you.' He ducked under the trap door. The crowd was agog with excitement. There was a shout for smelling salts as a lady collapsed to the ground.

Muffled sounds were coming from behind the curtain concealing the trap door.

'What's he doing?' Pearl cried at Jenkins, who had put her down but was still restraining her.

'Too short a drop. Berry's gone to pull on the legs – to finish the job off – otherwise they'll be twisting and turning for several minutes before finally copping it.'

Pearl staggered towards the prison exit. She couldn't turn around. She couldn't look. Behind her, she could faintly hear Jenkins' voice calling to her.

'Don't worry, Miss, your first time always takes some getting used to. Come back inside when you're ready for a gander. The body's going to be left on the rope for at least another hour before they bury her.'

She retched into the nearest gutter. With eyes streaming, she leant against a horse trough and whispered: 'It's over, Ma. I tried to stop it, really I did.'

Pearl was still holding on to the flower girl's wilted primroses as she walked trance-like along the street. She heard footsteps running fast towards her, but when she whirled round in panic, no one was there.

At the Shanty Emporium, a tea shop on Cheapside that she and Ma had once visited, Pearl ordered a cup of tea. It grew cold as she stared out of the window, her eye catching on the silhouette of a man, something familiar about him. Was he following her? Or was it her overwrought imagination?

Taking out note paper and pen from her handbag, she hastily scrawled a note with a shaking hand. She had to do it now, and then do her best to forget this dreadful incident.

Dear Ma,
I hope you arrived safely back in Ramsgate and my best wishes to your sister. I did as you wished and attended Lizzy's hanging. Lizzy behaved with dignity and courage.

She died quickly and I'm certain she felt no pain. I hope you will be relieved to hear this, and to know that Lizzy has gone to a better place.

Faithfully,
Pearl

She placed the missive in an envelope, eager to put an end to this business. Lizzy was dead, and there was nothing more Pearl could do, except push down the gnawing guilt constricting her heart.

38

Pearl lay in bed, motionless, listening to the muffled voices of her lodgers, the scraping of the chairs as they moved around the parlour, and the click-clack sound of their ivory Mah Jong tiles. Mei came in with a bowl of soup, but Pearl turned away.

'Do you want me to call the doctor? You haven't been out of the house for days now.' Mei sat down on the bed next to Pearl, smoothing the rumpled covers.

'No, I'm fine.'

'We handed out leaflets and collected money last night. Polly, Rose, Gerty and all the girls were asking after you. Even Rose wished you better and was grateful for the shilling. There was a bit of a scuffle with the police on Fairfax Road, where we were picketing at the match factory gates. But Gerty put up such a fight, we were able to make a run for it. Maybe you will decide if you can get out of bed for the meeting on Friday night? Everyone is going despite the long hours they've been working.' Mei's voice was light, trying to engage Pearl in conversation.

As the minutes passed by in silence, Mei let out a cry of exasperation and pulled at the bed covers. 'Why won't you tell me what happened at the execution?'

'There's really nothing to say. Lizzy is dead, and I don't want to talk about it anymore.' Pearl couldn't bear telling Mei she had tried in vain to stop the hanging, and that her guilt was a festering lesion. It would widen the growing rift between them.

Mei left the room without saying another word. Alone, the sounds and the sights of Lizzy's final hours kept replaying in Pearl's head. Particularly haunting were the ghastly noises of Lizzy choking on her last breaths. And when she least expected it, these images were replaced by Betty sprawled on the bed in her old room at The Sailor's Arms, blood seeping from the hideous wound in her abdomen. Pearl was tortured by the growing fear that the real killer was still out there. The uncertainty was eating away at her. Could she have done more to save Lizzy?

Towards evening, Mei came in again, asking if she wanted anything to eat. Pearl remained mute.

'What have I done?' Mei cried out. 'Do you want me to leave here?'

'No, of course not.' Pearl's reply was muffled by the bed clothes.

'You've been so different since Lizzy's hanging. Are you ashamed of me and what we are to each other? Have you changed towards me? I should go away.'

Pearl reached out to pull Mei close. 'I couldn't bear it if you left me. I'm nothing without you.'

A few hours later, they lay naked, entwined in each other's arms. Against Pearl's breast, Mei murmured: 'We should get up. If we're to keep the lodgers we've got, I need to make their dinner. They should be home soon from the docks.'

Pearl protested, reluctant to let go. 'Just one more kiss,' she whispered. The women grudgingly arose from bed and hurriedly dressed.

The kitchen was a flurry of activity as Pearl fried vegetables and Mei stirred a large cauldron of wonton broth. The oven was fiercely hot, the ginger and lemongrass fish stew bubbling within.

Pearl was a competent cook, but Mei was in her element, creating a wonderful array of delicious treats. She bent over the stove, tasting soups and sauces, tilting her head, adding a little more spice here and there to the dishes until finally uttering a smack of satisfaction.

Tseng and Fung Yeen, Xianfan's relatives, trooped in wearily from a day on the docks and greeted the two women, bowing respectfully. Pearl and Mei bowed in return, greeting them like long-lost friends. The lodgers fell upon the dishes prepared for them as if they hadn't eaten in months. From the appreciative sounds and the empty bowls proffered for second helpings, Tseng and Fung Yeen were delighted to have such a good cook who prepared dishes they were homesick for. They chattered animatedly in Cantonese to Mei, asking after her health, and offering condolences for Ah Sim.

Pearl greeted Xianfan, who was sitting in a corner. 'Miss Pearl, good that there are more lodgers here.' He smiled. 'You are a much better landlady than Ma Jennings.' He paused and looked away. 'I am sorry, but can I pay rent later? There has been no work for me these last few days. No one wants to employ an old man.' He lowered his eyes and voice as he added: 'And now The Dragon Inn is closed. Everyone gone.'

'Don't worry, Xianfan. Would you consider taking on the handyman tasks here at the Fragrant Blossoms that Ah Sim used to do? And you are so good with the lodgers, always going down to the docks to see if any of the Chinese sailors need a lodging house to stay in. That's worth a lot of money to me.'

Xianfan smiled brightly. 'It would be an honour, Miss Pearl.'

'Helloooo!' The smiling face of Gerty Connolly was at the front door. 'Come to bring back the pot Mei lent us. That was a super leek and potato pie.'

'Come in and have a brew.' Pearl opened the door wider.

'Lovely. I popped in to say we're celebrating. Those buggers Bryant & May have agreed to all our conditions, recognition of the union, stopping the unfair fines, and we can have our meals in a separate room, away from that bloody phosphorus.'

'Wonderful news! Makes it worth getting trampled on by police horses and battered by peelers. I'm so pleased for you.'

'Us girls wanted to thank you for your help. We're going out next week to see the boxing at Sebright Music Hall, and after that we'll go dancing. Our treat.'

'That's very kind of you, but I think I'll miss out on the boxing. I've had years watching men laying into each other at The Sailor's Arms. I'd love to meet you after for the dance though.' Pearl was thinking about holding Mei closely in her arms, in public.

'But this is not the same as two drunk sailors getting batty fanged. There is a skill to boxing – the feinting, the power, the movement around the ring, the outwitting of opponents. I've got to be quite the expert. Polly's favourite, Ching Hook, is on the bill; he's sparring twice a night every night this week at eight p.m. and ten p.m.' Gerty gave a wink.

'It's not only boxing but lots of other entertainers. There's the lady wrestlers, with Miss Connie Mathias. A gold medal prize to any woman or man under nine stone six pounds who makes the best show against her. There's also the Sisters Briggs, such lovely warblers, and Tom Murray the whistling wonder. Oh, and Ching Hook is fighting the Sapphire Stevedore. You wanted to know when he was on.'

NOVEMBER

39

Ching Hook stepped into the ring at Sebright Music Hall, the Hackney crowd greeting him with tumultuous applause. The boxer raised his arms aloft, grimacing at the crowd. The muscles on his chest stood out in carved relief and Pearl was reminded of the marble statue of Hermes she'd seen in the British Museum. Men cheered and the women whooped at his antics. Pearl took advantage of the crowd's attention being focused on the boxers to stroke Mei's hand and gaze into her ebony-dark eyes.

Hook strutted around the canvas, nodding at the crowd and thumping on his chest with padded gloves. George Belmont, Sebright's promoter, entered the ring. 'Welcome ladies and gents,' he bellowed. 'To my right is Ching Hook, black champion of the world!'

He gestured to his left. 'And his opponent tonight is the Sapphire Stevedore.' There were boos and hisses from the audience.

'Ching should do well tonight. He's a welterweight and the Sapphire Stevedore is a lightweight.' Gerty cupped her hands around her mouth to shout at Pearl and Mei.

Pearl was staring at the Sapphire Stevedore's torso. He was indeed covered in blue ink. The largest illustration was of a naked lady, hand coyly covering her breasts on the front of his chest, surrounded by garlands, stars and flowers. The arms and every inch of his torso was covered with palm trees, an eagle's wings and the face of a cheerful-looking woman, with MOTHER inscribed underneath. He was wearing a turquoise mask, entirely covering his face, with tiny eye slits and nostril holes.

In the intense heat of the packed house, the two opponents circled each other. The place was crammed to suffocation. Ching Hook had turned his head, momentarily distracted by a woman blowing kisses at him and the Sapphire Stevedore took his opportunity and landed several punches on Ching Hook's face and neck. There were yells at this unsportsmanlike behaviour, but Ching Hook, enraged at being caught out so early on in the match, powered into a series of blows, finishing off with a punch to the solar plexus, and then a vicious uppercut. Amid the roars, the Sapphire Stevedore stood stock still like a huge tree for a moment, then felled, toppling backwards with an almighty crash. He was out cold.

A torrent of objects were thrown onto the stage: beer bottles, rotting cabbages, hats and other missiles. A group of men at the front started jostling each other and then throwing punches. The fighting was spreading from the ring to all four corners of the crowd, and the entire hall became a maelstrom of seething bodies.

Pearl was pushing her way forwards, wanting to get nearer to the ring. This was her chance to speak to the Sapphire Stevedore, once he was conscious, and find out if there was somehow a chance he could be the mysterious Blue Man. But Mei was tugging on her arm. 'Come on, let's get out of here. You're taking me dancing.'

Pearl hesitated. She might not get another chance to find this man again. But Mei's sparkling eyes, and the anticipated thrill of waltzing with her, was too tempting. Pearl took one last look at the stage, then followed Mei and her companions off to the Mile End Road.

The Paragon Music Hall was an imposing building, topped by

a wide arch with 'Theatre of Varieties' proclaimed in glittering letters on the architrave. The balustraded balcony was lined with gentlemen smoking and ladies fluttering fans, looking down on the throng down below, hoping to gain entrance. Every window was aglow with light, its illumination amplified by enormous wall mirrors, gaslights and chandeliers. A formidable-looking woman was standing on the staircase in front of baize-covered doors, beadily looking at everyone waiting.

'Management here want to make sure they don't get no lowlifes and undesirables in,' Gerty was saying to Pearl, once they were all inside and looking around them. 'Don't want ladies coming in looking for business. Mind you, those poor gals got to earn a living somehow.'

'I've been wanting to ask you about the Sapphire Stevedore, Gerty. Do you know if he's dangerous? I think he could be the Blue Man. Local talk say he's Ah Sim's killer. What do you think? Could it be him?'

Gerty threw back her head and laughed. 'Nah, couldn't be. I remember that day. Third June, wasn't it? Everyone agog at the killing. But it wasn't my boxer. Spent all night with him. Best birthday I've ever had!'

Mei's mouth opened wide in wonder at the gaudily decorated interior of the music hall. 'I've never seen anything so magnificent,' she murmured. The hangings of rich-coloured velvet stretched from ceiling to floor. Murals of elephants, mermaids, harps and angels covered the proscenium arch and front panels of the private balconies. The large domed ceiling of the auditorium was awash with dancing Moorish figures holding Indian draperies suspended from the centre.

An orchestra of around fifty musicians was seated in the gallery at the furthest end of the dance hall. The conductor was attired in full evening dress, as were the rest of the band. At the first wave of the baton, the sounds of a Viennese waltz filled the room.

Rose and Polly sat at a side table, sipping on sherry wine, while a man in a brightly chequered suit bowed before Gerty and asked her to dance. The matchgirl and her partner immediately started whirling wildly, careening around heedless of the music's tempo, and colliding with an elderly couple who were moving in slow, sedate circles.

'Come on, let's join them.' Pearl led Mei onto the floor.

'But I don't know this dance,' Mei said, looking worried.

'I'll teach you, it's easy. My father taught me and we had plenty of impromptu parties at The Sailor's Arms. I'm a good dancer.'

Pearl tenderly took Mei's hand. 'Just hold me close and follow. One, two, three, one, two, three. Keep in time to the music.'

Mei had a good sense of rhythm and quickly picked up the pace. 'I knew you'd be a wonderful dancer.' Pearl drew Mei closer and caressed her lower back. A man approached and asked Mei to dance. Mei glanced at Pearl, smiled, and shook her head at the man as they quickly twirled away.

At two o'clock in the morning, Pearl was ready to leave, worn out from having twirled around to every waltz, polka and quadrille. Plus, she had trodden on Mei's toes several times, and was more than a little miffed to find that Mei was the better dancer. Mei hadn't wanted to leave the Paragon, but Pearl lured her away with the promise of one last dance in their bedroom.

As dawn's light curled slowly into the room, Pearl was falling into a delicious drowse, thighs wrapped around Mei's. Her heart hadn't felt so light in weeks.

'That dance hall is the most stunning building I have ever seen.' Mei was wide awake and chattering excitedly. 'We could decorate

The Fragrant Blossoms in the style of the Paragon. We'd be famous for miles around. It could help with getting us more business.'

'More like infamous, known as the gaudiest lodging house in Limehouse,' Pearl muttered sleepily.

Mei gave such a shove, Pearl nearly fell out of bed. 'You have no imagination. This place is so drab, we need brighter colours.'

'My beloved, if that is your heart's desire, pray, carry on. Now, this is my heart's desire . . .' Pearl drew her closer.

Pearl soon regretted giving Mei free rein, but could see how much joy it gave her lover. Mei's requests for any decorative items and artefacts their lodgers had brought with them was received with great enthusiasm and she attacked every room with gusto, giving them each a complete transformation.

'What do you think?' The bandana wound around Mei's head was covered in dust and paint, but she was looking very pleased with herself.

Every wall was painted a brilliant crimson and covered with scrolls in gold Chinese script wishing health, wealth, long life and happiness. There were huge porcelain vases decorated with scenes of emperors, courtiers and ladies dancing in flowing gowns, sleeves bunched around their delicate wrists.

A nest of paper lanterns in a range of eye-popping shades of red, yellow and blue hung down from the ceiling, the fringing swaying and weaving with the slightest breeze.

There was even a tiny elephant, a replica of the one they had seen at the Paragon Music Hall. Where on earth Mei could have purchased that from was a mystery.

'How much did all of this cost?' was all Pearl could think of to say.

'Oh, don't worry about that,' Mei said breezily. 'Xianfan and the others put word around that we were looking for some things to liven up this place. It's amazing how much they brought with them from China. So generous, they say it reminds them of home. If only Ah Sim were here. He would have loved it all so much.'

All the elation in her face evaporated as she thought of her murdered brother. Pearl put an arm around her shoulder. 'I'm so sorry,' she whispered, watching the tears roll from Mei's eyes. All the dancing, making a home together and even the nights of love could only keep the grief and horror at bay for so long, before it was back to tinge their world a sombre grey.

'I would gladly do anything to make you happy. What can I do?'

But Mei shook her head sadly and stared out of the kitchen window, which she could barely see out of now it had been decorated with a menagerie of vividly coloured toy dragons, serpents, firebirds, lions and griffins.

There were long periods of silence, with Mei holding on to her sorrow like a child's well-worn blanket. And nights when Pearl wouldn't go to bed, but instead paced the kitchen, afraid to sleep in case she dreamed again of Lizzy pointing an accusing finger at her. Each of them isolated in their own torment.

There was a loud crash and Pearl startled awake, heart thumping. She guessed it was nearly three o'clock in the morning. Someone was moving about in the kitchen. The heavy tread of hobnail boots sounded unfamiliar. The lodgers never went down to the kitchen in the middle of the night. She looked over at Mei, but she was a sound sleeper. Pearl put on Mei's turquoise robe and crept out of the bedroom, slowly inching her way down the stairs. As she got to the last step, it creaked loudly. She stopped, holding her breath. After a few moments, Pearl tiptoed into the kitchen. At the door, she picked up a hammer, left there by Xianfan, who had been doing some repairs.

The outline of a broad-shouldered man was silhouetted in the moonlight. Pearl was ready to strike the intruder, but something stilled her hand. He was singing *The Black Velvet Band* in a beautiful, baritone voice.

A voice Pearl recognised.

A paralysis crept up her body as the man turned around. His weather-beaten face was badly scarred, but he smiled at her as he pushed his peaked cap far back on his forehead, revealing a mass of curly locks. He gave an appreciative whistle as his sharp eyes travelled lazily over her dressing gown, as though sensing she was naked underneath.

'My Peking Pearl, you're looking fine and dandy. Still the prettiest girl I ever set eyes on in all my days.' Pearl's vision blurred as all air was sucked from her body. Her limbs were heavy and she stood rooted to the spot as she stared at the figure in front of her. The room was swimming before her eyes. His face was coming in and out of focus. Could it really be him? Or was this some terrible nightmare?

She squeezed her eyes shut and then opened them wide. The man was still there. She opened her mouth to speak, but only a faint squeak came out. This could not be happening. This must be a hallucination. Pearl shivered convulsively, clutching at the table to steady herself. She felt Mei come silently up behind her and look questioningly at the stranger in the kitchen.

The man walked around the room. He picked up the Royal Doubloon crockery, which Pearl had taken from The Sailor's Arms, the silverware on the sideboard, and took in the number of tables set out for the lodgers. 'Nice, very nice,' he murmured.

It really was him. Pearl's tongue felt too large for her mouth. As if from very far away, she turned to Mei and said: 'This is Tommy Fitzgerald, my husband.'

40

The silence seemed to go on forever, as the three looked from one to the other. Pearl sneaked a glance at Mei, who was staring at Tommy. Pearl tried again to speak, but nothing came out. Tommy finally broke the spell. He sat down at the kitchen table. 'Fetch me a cup of tea, my treasure. I'm home at last.' He sighed contentedly.

'How, what . . . How can you be so calm?' Pearl was incredulous. 'I thought you were dead. Why didn't you come back? Why didn't you send word to me?' She couldn't stop talking now. She felt a sick anger, the room spinning around her. She was going to faint. Pearl rubbed her temples, trying to take in deep breaths.

'Sweetheart, the ship went down and I managed to cling on to a life raft. A schooner picked me up and I travelled to the Caribbean. Quite an adventure, I'll say. I wanted to make my fortune before coming back to you. Only thing was, I got into a bit of trouble with the law and needed to lie low for a while. Did some business then caught a clipper back to London.' Tommy gave her that naughty schoolboy grin she knew so well.

She was trying to order her scrambled thoughts.

'How long have you been in Limehouse?'

His eyes slid to the side, always a sign he was lying. 'Not long. Had a few errands to sort out.'

'How dare you!' She was shouting now, pacing up and down

the kitchen. 'You just left me in Portsmouth all alone. I had no money. I nearly ended up in the workhouse. I thought you had drowned and now you show up here – alive – as if nothing has happened.'

Mei took a step towards Pearl, putting a hand on her back, continuing to stare at Tommy. Ignoring Mei, Tommy stood up and took a couple of steps towards Pearl, touching her shoulder.

She shook him off, arms folded. 'I still can't believe it. Is it really you?' He looked much older and careworn, but Pearl knew that face anywhere.

He walked over inquisitively to the larder, then leaned against the door, one leg crossed at the ankle. 'My sweet darling. We married so young and I wanted to see the world. To prove what I was made of. Now I'm back, and I want to make a fresh start with you. Besides, I've not been well. I need a place to rest, with some good home cooking.'

'Why, what's wrong with you?' His skin was sallow and pock-marked, marred with a dark brown rash. Pearl looked more closely at him. Several encrusted sores lined the edges of his mouth. Not at all like the fresh-cheeked boy she'd grown up with.

He shrugged. 'Caught something when I was abroad. I've been poorly, but the doctor says I'll be fine if I take my medicine and get some rest. No more seafaring for me.' He looked around the kitchen, taking everything in. 'You've done well for yourself, girl. Must make a pretty penny.'

He turned to her with a wolfish grin. 'And I hear you're coming into an inheritance. The Sailor's Arms is yours, now that the old bastard is dead.'

'Don't speak like that about my father. And how do you know all this?'

'As I said, I've been around. Kept my ear close to the tittle tattle of this town.' He tapped the side of his nose. 'Heard that bitch Betty Sullivan's belly was slit open.'

'You're very well informed.' She was just about to ask who he had been talking to when a plate clattered into the sink. Mei had started noisily washing the pots and pans. She turned to look at Pearl, her eyes flashing with annoyance that she had been forgotten.

Pearl was mortified at having left Mei out of the conversation. She swallowed with difficulty. 'This is Mei. We've become friends and she lives and works here as the housekeeper.'

He nodded approvingly at Pearl. 'She a good cook? You. Bring me food quick. Understand? And then you can clean my boots.' Tommy gestured at Mei, moving his hands to his mouth, miming eating with a spoon.

Mei spoke for the first time in a level voice, devoid of emotion. 'I can fetch you some food, Sir, but I am no charwoman.' Her hands were clenched tightly by her sides.

'Don't speak to Mei like that! She is not a servant but a close friend of mine.'

Tommy gave a snort of laughter; he had evidently caught the tender look between Pearl and Mei. 'Oh, I see now! Up to your old tricks, Pearl? You should watch yourself, people will talk.'

She lifted her chin defiantly. 'I don't know what you mean by that.'

Her husband looked at Mei with renewed interest. 'Did you know that my wife was always having pashes on music-hall tarts in Portsmouth? Turned a blind eye 'cos at least it wasn't with any of my mates while I was away.' He blew a kiss at Pearl.

'It's really none of your business what I do anymore, Tommy.' She was furious that he still managed to rile her. 'You can't just turn up here and expect everything to go back to the way it was. You can stay for some dinner but then you have to leave.'

'Don't think you can get rid of me that easily.' Tommy's face was no longer teasing, his cracked lips thinning into a vicious line. 'I'm your husband and I'll take charge here and at The Sailor's Arms. There's a lot I can do with the business.'

'I've done well enough without you all these years. You left me, with no word. You have no right just deciding to turn up whenever you want. Don't you know that women's income is no longer the property of their husbands? The law got changed nearly twenty years ago.' Her husband had only been back in her life a few moments and was already infuriating her.

Tommy grabbed hold of her arm. 'Think you're so clever. The law don't matter. I'll take whatever I want from you. Besides, I know things, Pearl Fitzgerald, my darling wife. If the people round here got to know what you and your lady friend were up to, you'd be laughed out of Limehouse. Folk always knew you was an odd one, even when we were young. I saved you from all that by marrying you and taking you away from here.'

'You wouldn't dare!' The two were facing off against one another and Pearl summoned all her control not to throw something at him. Something heavy like a meat mallet.

'Please, Mr Fitzgerald, don't do anything hasty, I beg of you.' They both turned to look at Mei. She had been watching the fight between husband and wife. 'Sit at the kitchen table and I will fetch you a bowl of stew. You must be hungry. Please, make yourself at home.'

Pearl had never heard Mei sound so meek. The sight of Tommy had really unsettled the poor girl.

Tommy cocked his head to one side and smiled. 'At least one of you is paying me the respect I deserve. Yes, I am famished.' He sank down on a chair, took his cap off and put his muddy boots on the table.

Mei pulled open the kitchen drawers, taking out a soup spoon and a large bowl from the cabinet. Then she walked over to the stove and started stirring the stew, adding generous amounts of salt and pepper. Pearl picked up a ladle and started to help Mei with the food. She said softly: 'I'm so sorry. I can't believe he's still alive and back here. We've got to do something. I'm not taking this lying down.'

'Hush. We'll talk about this later. Not now.' Mei continued staring into the stew.

Whistling through his teeth, Tommy smirked at the two women. 'Ah, a lover's tiff. I look forward to watching the two of you making up from the waist down. But first, bring me my dinner.' He smacked his lips as Mei brought him his meal.

'Hmmm, good. I look forward to many more meals with just the three of us.' He slurped at the steaming broth. The two women stood motionless, watching him eat. Pearl could feel Mei's body tighten, but she had no words of comfort, nothing to offer her. The arrival of Tommy had sent her mind into a panicked confusion.

'Any chance of seconds?' He gave a cheeky grin. 'Haven't eaten so good in quite a while.'

'Of course, Mr Fitzgerald. Please have as much as you want.' Mei smiled sweetly at him as she took his bowl and ladled in another generous helping.

'Now, you don't need to be so formal. After all, you're an intimate friend of my wife's. Call me Tommy. I'm sure there will be plenty of time for us to get better acquainted.' He smiled, licking at a sticky dribble of gravy down the side of his mouth.

Pearl stood in front of him, fighting the urge to push his face into the stew. 'That's enough, Tommy. Keep a civil tongue in your head when you speak to Mei.'

'So touchy!' her husband mocked. 'Haven't seen you this smitten since Maude Kingsley. Remember when I caught you mooning over her poster?'

He sniggered at her flushed face. Then he yawned and stretched out his arms expansively. 'Warm house, plenty of good food. I could sleep for a week. Now where's our bedroom? I'll just go and . . .' Tommy's eyes rolled back in his head. Then he slumped forward, snoring like a bear in hibernation.

'That worked more quickly than I thought,' Mei said, looking down at the comatose man sprawled across the table.

'What do you mean?' Pearl was bewildered.

'I put laudanum in his broth. Ma Jennings left nearly a full bottle in one of the cabinets. Seems like she was partial to a drop or two. The idea just came to me. He should be out for a while.'

Pearl looked at Tommy, whose eyelids fluttered delicately as dreams chased across his imaginary world. 'How much did you give him?'

'Quite a lot. Shame he didn't finish the second bowl. It would have solved our problem if he never woke up.'

'What? You must be out of your mind! He's not worth going to the gallows for.'

'Do you want him back?' It was said so quietly, Pearl wasn't sure she had heard the question correctly. But Mei's face was stricken.

'Of course not,' Pearl said hastily. 'Don't be ridiculous.'

'Oh, it's me that's foolish, is it? Are you sure you didn't know he was going to turn up?'

Pearl breathed out slowly. 'I'm not going to argue with you about him.'

'Let's talk later. I can't stand the sight of him. How could you want his hands on you?' Mei spat out.

'Don't do this. It's not getting us anywhere. Please, let's not fight.'

They left Tommy to his slumbers in the kitchen and went up to their bedroom to make a plan.

Pearl closed the door and sat on the bed. 'I still can't believe it. Tommy has been alive all this time and never came to look for me.'

Mei was pacing the floor. She stopped in front of the dresser and opened the jewellery box. She took out a necklace and ran it through her hands. 'Who is Maude Kingsley? And am I to be discarded now your husband is back? What else haven't you told me?' She said it in a rush, and though her voice was low and even, Pearl could hear the raw hurt.

'Sweetheart, Maude was long before I met you, someone I knew in Portsmouth. It really isn't important. It's been over for years. I adore you more than anyone in the world. I think of you morning, noon and night. Please believe me.' Pearl punched a pillow. 'Trust Tommy to throw that in my face now to cause trouble between us. He's the real problem here.'

'We've got to get rid of him.'

'What do you mean?' There was a heaviness in Pearl's chest. Could Mei be capable of doing Tommy harm? She tried to shake off the thought, but Mei had killed someone before.

'I don't know yet,' Mei sighed. 'But the three of us can't live here together. I couldn't bear it.'

'But what can we do? He is my husband and if he chooses to stay with me, it will be very difficult to throw him out. And what if he does go around telling everyone what we are to each other? That will be the end of us. No one will accept us. I wanted us to share a life right here in Limehouse. I don't want Tommy to take it away.' She ran her hands through her hair, whispering to herself: 'I still can't believe he's alive.'

They sat side by side on the bed. 'Let's run away, start somewhere new. Please don't leave me.' Mei was sobbing.

Pearl stroked her head, making soothing noises. 'We are going to be together. That you can be sure of. But if we escape from here, where will we go and what will we live on? You know better than I what our fate will be. The whorehouse or the workhouse. Let's bide our time and see what Tommy does. I'm hoping he'll get bored and leave us in peace.'

'That will never happen. You saw how he looked at all our possessions. And there is something very wrong with him. Looks to me like he has the pox. Maybe we could set the police on him. He must have done something bad to come and hide out here. Ask your Uncle Peter to deal with it.'

The two women talked long into the night, each thinking up outlandish schemes to get rid of their unwelcome guest. Tommy would be asleep for a few hours yet, but they grew more desperate as the minutes ticked by, and there was still no plan to get out of this dire situation. By early light they had run out of words, and they fell asleep holding tightly on to one another, as if for the last time.

41

There was a cold, empty space beside her. Then the memory of Tommy's return came flooding back. But where was Mei? Pearl threw on her dress and raced downstairs.

Mei was standing by the kitchen table, her midnight-black hair wild and tangled, an anguished look in her eyes. She gripped a long knife so tightly her knuckles shone white, the sharp end an inch from Tommy's throat. He was snoring like a hog.

'Mei, put the knife down,' Pearl whispered. She crept towards Mei and carefully took the blade out of her lover's hand.

Mei slumped against the kitchen cabinet in surrender, the crockery rattling. 'I couldn't think what else to do. He will ruin everything for us. All we've built up, the life we have together, this place. It's over. There's nothing left.'

'We can work this out. Just be patient, let's keep our nerve and take things slowly.'

'It's no good. Your husband is back. There's no place for me. I'm not going to be his charwoman and watch you two together. I've got to leave here.' Tears streamed down Mei's face.

Pearl tenderly wiped Mei's cheeks. 'Please don't go. Stay. I can't live without you.'

But Mei pushed past her and ran upstairs.

There was a groan from Tommy. He opened one eye, looking

around him in confusion. Then he saw Pearl and grinned. 'Ah, my lovely wife, a gorgeous sight for her long-lost husband.'

He rubbed his temples. 'I've the most powerful headache, like I've gone ten rounds with Ching Hook. Fetch me something to drink. When I'm feeling this queasy, a pot of beer always settles my stomach. And add a dash of rum.'

As Pearl fetched his drink, she wondered about Mei. She had lost her heart to this alluring woman, but the stark image of her beloved holding a knife to Tommy's throat was unnerving. Desperate times called for desperate measures. Unbidden, the words of Lizzy rang out. '*How well do you really know that little trollop? She's no angel. There's things she's done that would make your hair stand on end. Handy with a dagger. Even I wouldn't turn my back on her.*'

Pearl tried to shake off her anxieties. Placing the drink in front of Tommy, she wracked her brains wondering how best to get rid of him. This man was different to the one she had known in her youth. 'You never used to drink in the mornings.'

He looked at her with narrowed eyes. 'Don't nag. I'm a sick man. This is the only thing that sees me right first thing. And I've got errands to attend to. Going down to the docks today to see a mate. I lent him money just before we eloped. Put on your finest bonnet. You're coming with me. I want everyone to see I'm back with my wife, let them know I've returned to Limehouse, a respectable businessman with a lodging house and a tavern to run.' He chuckled.

'I'm not going anywhere with you.'

His eyes were cold and distant. 'You're very fond of Mei, aren't you? Want to keep her? I could just as easily sling her onto the streets as I could make her life a living hell if she stays with us. So I suggest you start doing as I say.'

Pearl started to protest but the look on Tommy's face stilled her tongue. It might be a good idea to get her husband away from Mei – she wasn't taking any bets on who would kill the other first. She also needed some time to think and form a plan of action to get out of this impossible situation.

'Come on, darlin'. No point in staring into space. Things to do, scoundrels to see.' Tommy threw Pearl's bonnet and purse at her and headed for the door without waiting.

A greasy drizzle was settling on the cobblestones. They looked like slimy slugs, tightly wedged side by side. Tommy held fast to Pearl's arm as they walked along Limehouse Causeway. He seemed unsteady on his feet, almost slipping in the puddles between the uneven cobbles. But she knew that by gripping on to her, Tommy was showing who was in charge, making it clear that his wife belonged to him.

They were a few streets away from the West India Docks just as ten o'clock in the morning was chiming on the church bells. Pearl's heart constricted as she thought about leaving Mei on her own. She'd be concerned about Pearl's sudden departure with Tommy.

Pearl could hear and smell the docks long before they came into sight. She had always marvelled at the cacophony of noise, the dockers roaring, cursing and whistling at each other. The smell of the West India Docks was like no other. Men from all over the world gathered together, speaking in a dozen different languages: the Shanghai dialect, Portuguese, Arabic, Malay and Bengali. And if they didn't speak the same language they communicated with each other in sign language, smiles, gestures and exchanges of small gifts. The fragrance of tea, molasses, animal hides and tobacco filled the air, mixed together with the smell of the urinal. Shit, piss and vomit from a thousand dockers in a never-diminishing stench.

At seeing the massive stone gates to the docks, Tommy came

alive. He cocked his head to one side, eyes alert as he hurried forward. *He's home,* thought Pearl, remembering that the blood of generations of watermen, labourers and stevedores ran in his veins.

They snaked their way around the courtyards and alleyways that led up to the docks, lined with ramshackle tenements where the sailors and dockers lodged. And then they were in the docks themselves, a seething hub of activity, as large wooden chests containing precious cargoes from the four corners of the world were ferried from the ships to the warehouses on the backs of powerfully built men, their dirt-streaked shirts dark with sweat.

Pearl was doubtful whether Tommy could find his mate in this writhing mass of commerce, but her husband was looking this way and that, almost sniffing the air in anticipation.

'You'll never find him,' she said irritably.

'Don't you worry about that. Someone owes me money, I get 'im. There's no way you can miss Jack the Purl Man's vessel, the *Sea Witch.* It's a wonder she floats at all.'

He weaved in and out of the crowd, pushing and shoving dawdling sailors out of the way, all the while holding tight to Pearl's hand, until he was at the wharf's edge, the ships jostling on the river. Then he gave a grunt of satisfaction, his focus zeroing in on a small yellow boat next to a tea clipper. 'There's that blasted purl man.'

He cupped his hands together and bellowed down at the rickety skiff, bobbing alongside the clipper. 'Jack! Oy there, matey! Jack Wiggins, you whoreson, where's that money you owe me?'

Tommy pushed Pearl in front of him and she looked out onto the river to see a man, waddling to and fro, serving drinks from a large barrel on the boat to a group of sailors. The man was stout and wide, like a baby walrus.

He looked up in surprise and then gaped at Tommy. 'Bless me

if it isn't the biggest scallywag of them all. Fitzgerald, I thought you was long dead! I'll be with you in a jiffy, just finishing off here for the day. Go down to the South Gate, I'll pull in there and you can jump aboard the *Sea Witch*. I've only a drop of purl left at the bottom of the barrel but there's more than enough to get us scammered. You can tell me what you've been up to all these years.'

Pulling in at the South Gate, Jack helped Pearl jump aboard the boat. Tommy clambered in after her, but staggered sideways, holding on to the side of a barrel to steady himself.

'Reckon you've lost your sea legs, my lad,' the purl man jeered. 'Living soft on the land. When you was a boy, there was none stronger and quicker at loading and unloading the crates, and taking a few choice morsels for yourself, right under the noses of the foremen.'

Tommy shot him an angry look, then shrugged his shoulders. 'We're all getting on, ain't we, Jack? Anyway, d'you remember my wife, Pearl? We used to run around together as nippers before we ran off to get hitched down in Portsmouth.'

'I certainly do,' replied Jack. 'Old PJ O'Dwyer was in a towering rage. Couldn't believe you'd taken his only daughter away from him. Lucky he didn't catch you.' Jack turned to Pearl, doffing his sou'wester hat. 'Pleased to see you again, Mrs Fitzgerald. Welcome aboard. Now, how about a wee dram to keep warm in this bitter wind?'

She smiled but shook her head. Purl was such a powerful brew, no wonder sailors ended up seeing mermaids after a few tankards in the early hours of the morning. Tommy licked his lips. 'I'd be obliged for a sup. Haven't had that stuff in an age. Never known anything like a group of tars fighting for a drop of purl beer after a long voyage. Nothing slakes the thirst like it. Still the best in the London docks?'

Jack winked. 'It's all in the mix of ingredients, my secret is sea wormwood. Piping hot beer, add in the gin, sugar and ginger to give it a kick. Might be a bit rough as it's the dregs, but that's where it's strongest. A right gum tickler. Come with me and take a draught or four. Catch up on old times. It's been seven years or more, ain't it? Let's drink to life, old friends, and forget past debts.' The purl man gave a hopeful half smile.

Tommy snorted. 'Do you think I'm soft in the head and don't remember what I did for you? I gave you a start in the purl business when you was down, with not a farthing. Now I've come to collect.' He poked a finger at Jack's chest. Tommy's moods could apparently still swing abruptly. 'I want my dosh.' His voice was hushed but full of menace.

'Right you are. Didn't know you was short of cash.' Jack rubbed the spot where Tommy had jabbed him.

Tommy shook his head. 'I'm not, Jack, I've got a number of dealings bubbling away, just need some ready coins to pay my men for work done. And who better to supply those coins than someone who made a mint out of my generosity?'

Jack laughed. 'You've got me there. And I'm grateful for the start you gave me in the purl business. I'll pay you back. Just wasn't expecting to see you after all this time. We need to go to Deptford Docks. That's where I keep my dosh.'

'Well, let's be off. No time to waste.'

'Whatever you say, Tommy.'

As soon as they cleared the wharves, Jack set the skiff's nose south-east, towards Deptford. Pearl sat at the stern of the boat, watching Limehouse recede into the distance, a dull pain behind her eyes. No one knew where she was, alone with these two men, and clueless as to where they were heading. Deptford was a dangerous place, a hideout for thieves and the most feared criminals.

She was beginning to feel very afraid. Tommy's volatile moods were making her uneasy. If the purl man didn't pay up, there could be trouble.

The waves rocked the boat from side to side. Her whole life was disintegrating; the bright future with Mei that had only just started now seemed destined for failure. There was no way out, stuck as she was on the boat with Tommy. She hardly knew him now. Something must have happened in the intervening years, or had she always forgiven his scallywag ways, believing the best of him?

The wind stung her eyes. It seemed the only option was to ride it out with Tommy, to see where all this led. Perhaps Mei's suggestion was right. If they were to have any future together, they might have to run away, leaving this all behind to start again somewhere else. It meant giving up her inheritance, The Sailor's Arms and the Fragrant Blossoms, which they had worked so hard on. To be so close to happiness and now this . . . Could she give it all up for love?

Perhaps if she could appeal to Tommy, to reach the boy she once knew; the one who blushed easily and looked at her with such tenderness all those years ago.

She turned round to see Tommy wiping his mouth, drops of purl beer staining the front of his coat. His face was a mottled stain of puce. His eyes were red-rimmed and he beckoned her to come and sit next to him. Pearl pretended she hadn't seen his gesture and turned to stare in the direction of Limehouse once again, now vanished in the grey mist. She wondered how long she would have to endure this nightmare.

As more purl beer was poured out of the barrel, Tommy grunted in appreciation. She sat on the wooden slats opposite the two men, watching in dismay as their voices grew more slurred. Pearl caught snatches of conversation, Tommy boasting about all his business plans, telling Jack he had a lodging house and a tavern. All his lies and bragging! Taking credit for the back-breaking work she and Mei had put in.

She rounded on Tommy, furious. 'Why did you bring me along?' she said through gritted teeth. 'I want to go back to Limehouse.'

'You're here because I say so. You will do exactly as your husband tells you.'

The purl man shushed them. 'Now, now, don't go hammer and tongs at each other. You both need to get along for a happy marriage.'

'What do you know?' Tommy sneered. 'I need another drink.'

As Jack poured out another large tankard for Tommy, Pearl's hopes of appealing to her husband's better nature were dashed as surely as a seagull chick falling on rocks from its nest.

The choppy waves swirled around the boat as the blustery wind picked up, cutting through her thin shawl. She re-fastened the straps of her bonnet to prevent it from coming loose and blowing away into the river.

Think, think. She must think what to do. But her mind moved as turgidly as week-old porridge and failed to come up with the answers she searched for. Pearl groaned loudly as the two men started to warble old sea shanties, swaying from side to side, their arms clasped around each other's shoulders like long-lost friends.

Jack yawned loudly. He shuffled off to the far end of the skiff and lay down on a bundle of sailcloth. 'Think I'll just have a kip. Keep an eye on the tiller, Tommy. No worries, though. These winds will take us to Deptford Docks in no time at all.'

42

While Tommy continued to sing as Jack snored, Pearl gazed longingly back at the receding docks. She watched the tiny figures of lumper men running nimbly up and down the gangways, loading and unloading barrels and wooden crates. There was a tang of brine in the air, intermingled with the smell of fish entrails and sewage.

The mist had settled into a regular pea souper, mantling the river with an emerald shroud. Thoughts haphazardly chased around in her mind like a swarm of antagonised wasps. She wasn't sure how to reach Tommy. He had changed, that much was clear, but into what kind of a man, she had no idea. She didn't know him anymore. She didn't know what he was capable of.

Tommy drew near, his body close to her back. She shuddered and he pressed in closer, mistaking her reaction for desire. 'You're still beautiful,' he whispered. 'You belong on a boat, the wind in your hair. It'll always be you and me.'

'We're not sixteen anymore.' She moved away from him.

The wind was picking up and howling now, the thick fog becoming impenetrable; a chilly, light drizzle blurring Pearl's vision. To distract herself from Tommy's unwanted presence, she looked out across the water at the vague shape of a passenger paddle steamer, making a trip to Gravesend, its decks crowded with silhouettes of courting couples. She could hear their laughter, which carried on the breeze. An accordion was picking out the melody to *The Rose of Tralee.* Pearl felt a pang in her chest when she remembered singing it to Mei only the week before. They had laughed at discovering how tone deaf they both were, beguiled by finding all the things they had in common. That seemed so long ago now. In the space of a few hours, the promise of a new life was receding; her old life back to haunt her. She was back where she'd started.

She needed to reason with Tommy, to try to make him understand who she was now. He was chuckling to himself and muttering; his eyes glinting, reflecting the lights from the distant shore.

She moved to the seat opposite him, forcing herself to speak calmly. 'I'm not the same person I was back in Portsmouth or when we were young 'uns. We've both changed. A lot has happened. If you really cared for me, you'd want me to be happy. I've made a life for myself here. I finally feel at home.' She had his attention now and pressed on. 'I loved you once, really I did. But you left me all those years ago. What was I to think? I thought you were dead and so I mourned you. I let you go. Now I ask that you do the same for me. Let me go, Tommy.'

He shook his head. 'I don't care what you've been up to. I didn't think you'd become a nun when I left.' He chuckled to himself. 'We can start again.'

She fought the urge to move away as he reached over to twist a lock of her hair around his finger.

'I just can't, Tommy. It's too late for us now, but you will always be my first love, my laughing boy.' Pearl remembered him on bended knee, all those years ago, holding out a brooch to her, most likely stolen. Her father caught sight of them from the upstairs window of The Sailor's Arms and gave Tommy the beating of a lifetime. Pearl had held Tommy while he cried, cleaning the blood off his face. But those days of it being the two of them against the world were long gone.

Pearl looked at him for a long time, the lines on his face accentuated by the flickering lantern light. His once-lean jawline was softened with sagging jowls, his chin covered with patchy bristles.

She thought about the years that had passed since they had set eyes on each other, and her own ageing. She looked down at her hands, the roughened, cracked skin from the daily washing of pots and pans at the lodging house. There always seemed to be so much cleaning to do. When she combed her hair in the mornings, Pearl saw grey hairs at the temple, and the frown lines between her eyes were now more marked. Would Mei still love her now that she was no longer in the first flush of youth?

She realised Tommy was speaking. 'You must believe that I was always going to come back to you one day, Pearl. It was always you and me.' There was a slight throb in his voice.

'You've got to understand. It's over between us, Tommy. Has been for a long time. I need you to please go. Is it money you need? I'll give you what I can.'

She turned to move away but Tommy gripped her wrist, wrenching it sharply. She yelped. He didn't seem to care that he had caused her pain. A thick vein twitched just beneath his eye.

'You're not listening to me. I'm here to provide for you, my wife. And I'll take The Sailor's Arms whether you want me to or not. Remember my dreams to be a pirate? Well, I've come back with the spoils, and I want to share them with you. I've got a plan that will make us rich beyond our wildest dreams.'

She curled her lip in derision. Tommy's grip tightened, and Pearl gave another gasp of pain. 'You need to show me some respect, girl. As you say, we've both changed and I'm an important man in Limehouse now.'

Pearl frowned, bewildered. 'But I thought you'd only just got back to Limehouse? Is this more of your lies and deceit?'

'You have no idea who I am! You never truly realised what I was capable of, Pearl. Well, let me tell you. I'm the boss of the Wild Eyed Boys gang. We've been here for a while now, and finally taken over from Lizzy in Limehouse. Join me, sweetheart. We were always a great team. We'll have the Fragrant Blossoms and The Sailor's Arms to use as a base for the Wild Eyed Boys, with you and me at the helm.

'No more draughty warehouses, away from nosy peelers and layabouts wanting a cut. Think of it; such fun! Now that Lizzy and Soo Chow are out of the way, thanks to you, we'll be the richest, most feared couple in Limehouse. I'll give you everything your father never could. You'll want for nothing. You'll never have to work again. It's not too late for us to have nippers. Think of it, a young Tommy and Pearl running about.'

'What are you on about? You're in charge of a criminal gang?' She could barely get out the words. Her tongue felt thick and unwieldy. 'Oh, Tommy, no.' Water was leaking into the boat and seeping into her boots.

'Please leave me alone. Just take all my savings and go.' She struggled to free herself from his grip.

'I'm not going anywhere. 'Til death do us part, remember?'

Leaning closer to him, she hissed: 'My father was right about you all those years ago. Good-for-nothing Tommy, that's what he called you.'

Tommy's lip tightened. 'That's right. Bring up your old man. He never liked me. I could have given him the drubbing he deserved, but stayed my fists out of respect for you.'

'Don't make me laugh! He would have knocked you out cold. Now you come back here wanting to live off me. Call yourself a man? To think I loved you once. Now I just pity you. You're nothing to me.'

He pulled Pearl towards him, cupping her cheeks, like sweethearts out at a summer ball. But his caress quickly turned into a vice-like grip. His face a demonic mask. Fear surged in Pearl's body. She froze.

'Don't come all high and mighty with me, Mrs Fitzgerald. You're in this up to your eyeballs. I've been keeping tabs on you. You put Limehouse Lizzy in prison for the murder of Ah Sim and Old Jake. She was hanged at the gallows on evidence you brought to the peelers. But the bitch was innocent all along.'

43

Nausea washed over her. The boat rolled from side to side in the choppy waters. Jack the purl man muttered faintly in his sleep. A tugboat's horn sounded faintly in the distance.

'I don't understand.'

He shrugged. 'My poor, naïve Pearl. I told you I was here to do some business. I put things in motion. Lizzy might have thought she ruled the roost, but I was laying down very careful plans. She was no match for me.'

They were both standing now, unsteadily. Pearl faced him. 'You wouldn't have the nerve. You're weak. Nothing but a scrounger.'

His face tensed. 'Taunting me again?'

'What have you done, Tommy?' Pearl was breathing in short, quick gasps.

He spat into the water. 'You said it yourself, we've both changed.'

'Tell me.'

Tommy sat back against the beer barrel, reaching across Jack's sleeping form and pulling down the stopper. He poured himself a pint, the liquor slopping over the sides. He was clearly enjoying the stunned look on Pearl's face. 'I've done what I said I would always do. Think back to when we was young. I always had it in me. The courage to take chances in spite of the danger.'

A memory stirred of Tommy as a young lad, brandishing a

dagger with great deftness, in fights with rival gangs who had come into Limehouse. She felt sick at herself for how proud she had been of his prowess, basking in the reflected glory.

He took hold of the tiller and steered their path, ever closer to the lights of Deptford. The flickering lamp swinging on the mast illuminated the feverish, half-crazed look in Tommy's eyes.

'Ah Sim worked for me. That greedy son-of-a-whore was stealing from me. He was my lookout, but I found out he was double-dealing with Lizzy's lot.'

A strangled whisper came out: 'Please tell me you didn't . . . you couldn't have . . .'

'Oh, couldn't I?' Tommy held Pearl's shoulders, looking deep into her eyes. He was enjoying himself. 'Ah Sim was working for Lizzy and I wasn't going to take that lightly. There needs to be discipline in a crew. I stuck him like a pig in his belly and he died like the traitor he was. No one crosses me.' He smacked the side of the boat with his fist, making Pearl flinch.

She covered her face, avoiding his eyes to hide the horror she felt. Tommy struck a lucifer and carefully lit the lamps on each side of the boat.

Pearl fought hard to concentrate on his words. 'How did this all happen?'

Tommy considered for a moment, then nodded. 'You're right, you should know, if you're going to be by my side. My gang was ready to take over, and I needed to get rid of Lizzy. And you . . . Oh Pearl, you were magnificent. You helped me. I led you right to her. Laid you clues that she was the killer. And you picked them up as eagerly as a dog hungry for scraps.' He grinned, then spoke in a rush, bragging like a schoolboy.

'You met Deng, one of my men, at The Dragon Inn restaurant. I instructed him to tell you that Limehouse Lizzy killed Ah Sim, to take you exactly where I wanted to lead you. My Uncle Jake was feeding me information all the time, kept me in the know. And he told you about seeing a woman wearing gold boots at Wapping Old Stairs to throw you off the scent of us.' Tommy gave a hoot of laughter, wiping his eyes. 'You fell for that one. Couldn't wait to get a noose around Lizzy's neck. Priceless!' Then he grew quiet, looking at Pearl with a faraway look on his face. 'Could you ever have imagined this when we were kids together?'

Pearl doubled over, holding her stomach. 'Please tell me it isn't true.' She leaned over the side of the boat and retched. She gripped hard to the sides, splinters of wood piercing her flesh. There was a violent lurch to one side, the waves lapping at the *Sea Witch*.

Pictures flashed in Pearl's mind of the times she'd seen a man – someone resembling Tommy, she only now realised – staring at her from alleyways and pub windows. 'I've felt someone watching me since I've been back home. He had a look of you, but I thought my mind was playing tricks on me. But it *was* you.'

'I loved following you.' Tommy cocked his head to one side. 'I bided my time. Wanted to be sure that everything was in place before I came back to life. No point in a gang war when you can pick your enemies off from afar or get them to turn on each other. I'm not surprised Soo Chow squealed on Lizzy. What a cowardly rat.'

'And I caused her death – because of you?' Pearl's voice was a hoarse whisper. 'Lizzy loved you once. How could you be so callous?'

'Ask yourself the same question. She trusted you when we were nippers. You knew how she felt about me, and yet you left Limehouse without saying a word to her.' Tommy smiled and caressed Pearl's face. 'You see? We are cut from the same cloth.'

'You're wrong!' The wind was picking up, causing another rolling wave to pitch the boat to one side, foul-smelling water and seaweed sprayed them. Pearl leaned back on the wooden slats, icy water soaking her skirts.

Her father would be laughing at her now, shaking his head sadly. 'That Fitzgerald boy was a wrong 'un, not worth kissing the sole of your shoe.'

Despite wanting to scream and hurl every object on the boat at Tommy, Pearl needed to find out everything she could. She drew in a shaky breath.

'What about Old Jake? How did he die?'

'I had no choice. The old fool tried to blackmail me, wanted a bigger share of the loot. He was a witness to what I'd done to Ah Sim, and couldn't keep his mouth shut when he'd had a few. Said he'd tell the peelers if I didn't increase his money, that he was going to see Inspector Crowley, put me in it, and then he would be in charge. Dropped like a stone when I cut him. No loose ends.'

So Rose's recollection of that morning had been right all along. Two men, one with a long stick. Cold sweat broke out on Pearl's forehead. 'He was your uncle! How could you do it?'

Tommy was deranged. His sickness had affected his mind. And no one knew she was out here alone on the water with this man.

'You've turned into the Devil.'

Tommy looked surprised. 'I'm still the same boy from Limehouse. Only now I'm wiser and stronger. You need to be ruthless to get what you want. The plan was always to control the opium in Limehouse and get rid of the competition. And why don't we take over The Dragon Inn? Soo Chow has scarpered. An added bonus.'

They were far out on the river now. He staggered over to the beer barrel, clambering over Jack's slumbering form, and poured out another large measure. He gulped it down and put an arm around her shoulder. He smelt like he hadn't had a bath in months, a malodorous mix of body odour and alcohol oozing out of his pores.

The words came tumbling out. 'Did you kill Betty, too? She didn't have anything to do with the opium smuggling.'

'I did that one for you, sweetheart. I couldn't have that old witch stealing our inheritance,' Tommy continued, oblivious to Pearl's stricken expression. 'I need someone I can trust. Ah Sim and Old Jake betrayed me. But you – you have always been there for me. And I need you to look after me. I'm a sick man. Those filthy whores in Australia gave me the clap. But I'll get my strength back and be shipshape in no time.'

He put his arm around her waist. 'There now, I've no more secrets from you.' Tommy pulled Pearl close, nuzzling her hair. 'I'd forgotten how good you smell.'

She pushed him off. 'How dare you! After all you've told me, do you really think I can be with you? I can't bear to look at you. You're a monster!'

Tommy squeezed tighter, but she wrenched herself out of his grasp and scrambled to the ship's bow, waving madly at passing ships on the horizon. But they were all too far away to see her.

He looked at her with narrowed eyes. 'That's the last time you talk back to your husband.' He slapped her hard across the face. Pearl's teeth rattled from the blow, blood filling her mouth. She fell backwards, her head hitting the side of the boat.

Looking up at him, she wondered how she was going to escape. 'What's come over you? You've never laid a hand on me – ever – not even playfighting as children.'

He shrugged and lit his pipe again, puffing contentedly. 'I don't take kindly to anyone who disrespects me. You'd best remember that.'

'You've got to hand yourself in, Tommy. You're not well.'

'We could be rich. No one will ever treat us like they did when we were young.' He spoke calmly. 'Are you going to stand by me? Or are you also going to betray me?' Pearl shrank back from him, edging away, stumbling back against the rudder as Tommy came towards her.

She looked around for anything to defend herself. Her hand closed around something cold and heavy. The metal ladle for stirring the purl beer. She swung it in a wide arc, cracking his cheekbone. He yelled with pain, then sprang on top of her, his hands around her neck, squeezing hard. She couldn't breathe, hands clawing helplessly. A grey fog crept into the corners of her vision. *So this is it,* she thought. *Goodbye, Mei. I love you.*

She sensed, rather than heard, a dull thud. The pressure on her neck lessened.

Pearl opened her eyes to see Tommy slumped to one side. Jack the purl man was holding a leather sap in his hand.

'You leave your missus alone,' growled Jack. 'The racket you two were making would waken the dead. And you've made a mess of my boat.'

Quick as a flash, Tommy threw a punch at the purl man, who reeled backwards. There was a tangle of limbs, boots kicking out. Then a hand reached out, holding a large knife.

She knew that hand. It was large and powerful, but it was also once tender. And now there was nothing she could do to stop it. The ruby ring she had given Tommy on his sixteenth birthday – a family heirloom that once belonged to her grandfather – flashed on his little finger as he wielded the knife high above his head. And then in a swift motion, Tommy slashed across the purl man's stomach. Jack slumped to the deck, holding his abdomen, unable to hold back the tide of dark crimson spurting between his fingers.

Pearl gave a hoarse scream. Tommy turned towards her. He

towered over her, his face spattered with great gouts of the purl man's blood.

She shrank away from him as he laughed softly. The bloodlust was upon him. 'Looks like I'll have to find myself a new wife.'

Flailing around, trying to stand up against the rocking of the waves, her hand closed upon the handle of a beer tankard. She threw it at Tommy as hard as she could. It hit his forehead with a crack. He gave a great roar and staggered towards her. Their faces were within inches of each other. Pearl steadied herself by the boat's mast, the lantern swinging wildly. She sprang at him, pushing him backwards, scratching and clawing deep into his flesh. He pulled hard at her hair, clumps coming away, and Pearl tried to punch him in the stomach, as her father had taught her.

'Fight dirty, Pearl. Go for the low blow,' she could hear PJ urging her on. But she was no match for Tommy.

He grabbed hold of her upper arms, lifting her up, trying to push her overboard. With all of her might she clung on, thighs clasped around him. She was tearing at his clothes, ripping at his shirt. Tommy threw her back into the boat and Pearl landed awkwardly, sprawling back on the wooden slats.

He roared and tore off the rest of his shirt, flinging it into the water. He stood there, bare-chested, arms outstretched. By the light of the boat's lantern, she saw that his entire torso was covered with blue tattoos; ultramarine mermaids and sea serpents coiled around his arms. A tall ship foundering on rocks undulated on his chest and belly. The words *Pearl and Tommy forever* in a love heart were etched above his heart.

She gaped. 'The Blue Man.'

Tommy arched his back and howled like a wolf. 'I am Cú Chulainn, the great warrior-hero of Ireland, come to life.'

He had truly lost his mind. The wind was screaming now,

the waves churning around them. The boat rocked haphazardly from side to side. Suddenly it tilted sharply to one side, and as he locked her in a tight embrace, they both pitched backwards into the treacherous Thames.

She gasped as the shock of the ice-cold waves awoke all of her senses. She coughed, swallowing mouthfuls of filthy, foetid water. Tommy was no longer holding on to her; the dress's heavy fabric was pulling her down into the depths.

Flapping her arms wildly, she surfaced and managed to swim towards the side of the boat, clinging on. She had seconds before the strong tides of the Thames sucked her under. Using every last ounce of her strength, she managed to hoist herself up high enough to topple back into the boat. She lay there panting, shivering and gasping like a landed carp.

A wave of exhaustion swept over her. Shivering violently, she desperately wanted nothing more than to sleep. A faint voice called to her. 'Pearl! Help me!' She looked out and saw Tommy, his head just above the surface of the river as the rain started to lash down on them. He had never learned to swim.

Without thinking, Pearl grabbed one of the oars and pushed it out towards him. Tommy managed to cling on to it and she dragged the oar close to the side of the boat with all her might. He held out his other arm for Pearl to pull him on board. But her hand refused to move. It stayed by her side, unwilling to reach out. And when she finally managed to force her hand out to him, a strong swell swept him away.

Tommy's head disappeared beneath the waves and then popped back up again. He was coughing and spluttering but all the while staring up at her. Then a wave engulfed him and he disappeared down into the depths for good.

Pearl looked out into the darkness for what seemed like hours.

There was no sign of Jack the purl man's body. It must have gone overboard when the boat nearly capsized. A steamer passed by with a crowd out for an evening's entertainment. She could hear an accordion, the sounds of laughter and the clink of glasses.

Sodden. She was totally sodden. She rowed the boat slowly back to shore. Her body was aching all over.

Climbing the steps up the embankment, she walked with difficulty. Her dripping garments clung to her limbs like a sulky child dragging its feet. Tottering along the wharves, people were gawping at her and laughing.

'Fancied a swim, did you, darlin'?' leered one young lad. She bared her teeth at him, and he flinched, backing away from this alarming harridan. She walked on, anxious to get away from the river that had nearly claimed her life.

She staggered back towards Limehouse, heading for the Fragrant Blossoms. The streets seemed to welcome her; the calls of the costermongers, the flower sellers and the draymen bellowing at the children to get out from under the horses' hooves. Her throat tightened when she thought of running up and down the Limehouse lanes with Tommy and Lizzy when they were young. A memory of her father sprang up then, him lifting her in his reassuring arms. All three had vanished from her life and the only time she would see them again would be in dreams or nightmares. Or in heaven, but she doubted that either Lizzy or Tommy would be there.

Pearl sat down to rest on a park bench in St John's Churchyard, water dripping from her hems. She wanted a moment to look around her. All the detritus from the past had been washed clean away with the downpours. The trees had shed their leaves, the branches like skeletal fingers. She wondered what she would do now, how to cope in this strange, new life. And the answer came to her: Mei.

Pearl opened the door to the lodging house. There was a small suitcase in the hallway.

Mei was standing in the kitchen, shrugging on an overcoat. She took in Pearl's dishevelled appearance. 'Where have you been? You left no word.'

Pearl couldn't speak, even though there was so much she wanted to say to Mei.

In the continuing silence, Mei looked towards the front door. 'It would have been better if I'd gone before you returned with your husband. I'll leave now. I know you don't want me to stay.' Her voice was barely a whisper.

Pearl walked over to Mei and hugged her tight, not caring that her clothes were coated in slime. 'Please stay. Tommy's not coming back. We're safe.'

DECEMBER

44

The pub door would not budge. Pearl twisted and rattled the key, and after much cursing, the lock finally clicked open. With several hefty shoves and a growling protest, the oak double doors to The Sailor's Arms swung wide.

The smell of stale beer was fainter than before, but the tang of tobacco from a thousand pipes was still heavy in the air. A layer of dust covered every surface.

Queen Victoria's portrait, with its thick black moustache drawn on, was clinging even more precariously to the wall. The glass on the frame was now shattered. Someone had apparently taken some traitorous pot-shots at the monarch one rowdy night. One more and it would come crashing down.

The pub was in disarray; filthy, unkempt and uncared for. It looked as if it had been empty for years instead of a few short weeks. But all that was going to change now. The Sailor's Arms was hers.

This was a new beginning, and Pearl would make the pub everything she and Mei imagined. Over the last few days, the two of them, along with the matchgirls, had talked long into the night over plans. Eliza Orme and her companion Reina had also pitched in. Pearl had suggested holding English classes for Chinese, Indian, Malay and other seafarers who were adrift and friendless in Limehouse, saying they could use her father's bedroom as a classroom. Mei was keen to open a clinic for mothers and babies. Rose and Polly were hoping for a creche, allowing mothers to work. The basement could also serve as a soup kitchen for the homeless.

Pearl limped around the pub, every muscle in her body screaming in protest with each step. Stopping in front of the mirror, a face ravaged by the river and a life-and-death fight with Tommy looked back at her. This Pearl was haggard; haunted, but hopeful.

One side of her face was still terribly swollen, and a bloody scrape marked her other cheek. It would probably leave a scar, but Pearl didn't care. She surveyed the carnage. Happy and free, Pearl couldn't wait until her name and Mei's was above the lintel at The Sailor's Arms.

She looked across at Mei, standing by the bar. Nothing could stop them from being together now; they could finally start afresh with no more recriminations. The morning Pearl had returned home to find Mei with her suitcase in the hallway had been a tough reckoning. Would she stay for good? There had been tears and accusations. Mei was furious with Pearl for disappearing with Tommy, leaving no word if she would ever be back. And Pearl needed to regain Mei's trust for even considering she could kill Tommy or be in cahoots with Lizzy.

Pearl promised to tell Mei everything from now on, and that included the horrifying details of Tommy's death. It was a tragic end for the boy who had spun such tales of fame and fortune, all those years ago.

She shook herself, casting off old ghosts. A celebration was needed to mark the beginning of her life with Mei, and also her inheritance. She would throw a party for their friends and begin a new chapter at The Sailor's Arms.

The old man sitting at a corner table in the saloon bar sucked on his pipe and exhaled noisily. He eyed the group of women laughing together in the snug bar at the back of the pub with displeasure. He hawked and spat on the sawdust floor before turning to his friend, who was also staring at the women.

'There was a time when The Sailor's Arms was a good old-fashioned mariner's tavern. That was in PJ O'Dwyer's day. Can't say I hold with these new-fangled ways. And women talking politics! Not the same.' He took a deep draft from his beer tankard. 'But this has been my pub for many a year, and I'm too old to find another local. They're not going to get rid of me.'

Pearl had been watching them from behind the bar. She pulled a couple of pints and walked over to the old sea dogs, placing the drinks in front of them. 'On the house,' she said, smiling at them. 'This is still your pub, there's just a few changes round here. Not to worry, you'll be well looked after by some familiar faces.' Pearl gestured to Mr Matthews who was cleaning some glasses. He'd taken on the role of pub manager with gratitude and Pearl knew she could depend on him to keep the old timers happy. The men grunted, supped at their free beer and continued to glare at the group of women who were talking at the top of their voices in the snug bar.

One voice boomed out louder than all the others. 'Violent resistance is not the answer. That's why I disagree with the strike action.' Eliza Orme was in full stride, gesticulating wildly with a teacup in one hand and waving a slice of cream sponge cake in the other.

The Sailor's Arms had at last re-opened, and to commemorate its first week, Pearl invited some of her new pals, including the lawyer and Reina Lawrence, in gratitude for helping to secure the deeds of the pub.

Eliza had patiently explained to Pearl the intricacies of property deeds and the land registry title register. How she understood all those papers with their convoluted legal terms was still beyond Pearl's comprehension.

Reina was looking at Eliza, nodding with approval. 'I'm thinking of standing one day as borough councillor in Hampstead, as soon as women are no longer prohibited from standing for election. We need more ladies taking part in politics, and to allay men's fears that no terrible revolution will occur once we do,' she said.

Eliza nodded, becoming more animated with every bite of cake. 'I'm sure you will be a wonderful councillor. Perhaps you can persuade the trade unions that withdrawing labour is not the way forward. Economic sanctions are a far better option and accomplish much more.'

'Dear lady, it is easy for you to say,' Rose Driscoll butted in. Pearl admired the matchgirl's courage in speaking up and disagreeing with the lawyer. 'We had no choice but to go on strike. Those buggers at Bryant & May were forcing us to sign papers to say we were all happy with conditions at the factory, even though it was all lies. We needed to stand together. Fourteen hundred of us came out last year, and we showed 'em what for. And what happened? We got our demands met!'

As Pearl looked around the room, she wondered what her father would make of it all. She held his favourite shot glass, with the green four-leaf clover design. He had always wanted her to be landlady of The Sailor's Arms, but likely not in the way she was intending. Pearl doubted he would have approved of her changes, but she would make them anyway.

There were more shouts and raucous laughter from the women as Pearl walked back to the snug bar. Eliza was about to launch forth into another speech, but thankfully was interrupted by Mei, bringing in a large platter of food. Pearl came forward to help her, quickly piling a large helping onto Eliza's plate.

'Recite for us one of your favourite classic Chinese poems, Xianfan,' Pearl said hurriedly.

Her favourite lodger was sitting quietly in a corner, puffing on a clay pipe. Pearl was glad he had stayed on at the Fragrant Blossoms and was acting as a go-between, bringing in sailors from the docks, doing repairs at The Sailor's Arms and the lodging house. He nodded, stood up and cleared his throat. In a melodious voice, he began to recite *Beating the Drum*, a favourite poem of Mei's. While the others were listening, Pearl pulled Mei into the kitchen for a close embrace. She whispered in Mei's ear, reciting along with Xianfan:

'Meet or part, live or die,
'We've made an oath, you and I.
'Give me your hand I'll hold,
'And live with me till old!'

He was halfway through the poem when there was a banging on the door.

'That'll be my uncle, late as usual,' Pearl murmured against Mei's cheek.

'I hope he isn't bringing his latest fancy woman,' Mei said. 'The last one who came here tried to steal all the cutlery. She rattled all the way to the door where the knives and forks fell out of her drawers.'

Pearl was laughing when she opened the door. 'Now, Sergeant O'Dwyer. You'd better not be . . .' But it wasn't her uncle at the door. Pearl instead looked into the emerald green eyes of a handsome woman.

'Are you Pearl Fitzgerald?' the stranger said in a rush. 'I wonder if I could speak with you for a moment. Sergeant O'Dwyer sent me.'

'Of course. Do come in.' Pearl led the woman into the snug bar. The conversation stopped as everyone turned to stare at the newcomer.

The woman was taken aback. She laid a gloved hand on Pearl's arm. 'I have interrupted your evening. How rude of me. I do apologise for coming unannounced, but if I could have a moment of your time, I would be forever in your debt.'

'Not at all. Please, take a seat.' Pearl was intrigued by this strikingly beautiful visitor. 'Why did my uncle tell you to come to me?'

The woman slumped into a chair and began to weep, dabbing a handkerchief to her aquiline nose. 'I am in a desperate situation. My husband has been murdered. I need you to find his killer.'

ACKNOWLEDGEMENTS

This book started with a walk along Wapping High Street, slipping on the cobblestones beneath my feet, and peering in at intriguing pubs such as the Captain Kidd, The Grapes and the Town of Ramsgate, wondering about the characters who frequented them over a century ago. I imagined a woman running along the riverside, fighting against injustice and a place to belong in Limehouse. That publican's daughter was Pearl Fitzgerald.

I'd like to thank my amazing agent, Imogen Morrell at Greene & Heaton, who believed in Pearl and was keen to help me bring her to life. My editor Beth Wickington, who fell for Pearl and Mei, bringing added pace and depth to the story, as well as Jennifer Edgcombe, fiction editor at Headline Publishing Group.

To keep me going were my fellow scribblers in our Pen Across the Pond writers group, Jennifer (for her unwavering encouragement), Neelam, Jon, Edd, Keywanne and Frances, for their support and feedback.

Angela my partner, who has been there since the very beginning, coming up with ingenious suggestions and additions. My family, my mother Ng Tuck Heng, Corriene, Alison, Shelley, Helena, Louise, Blonnie and cousin Liz, as well as childhood family friend Jenni. I'm glad I could namecheck the Dragon Inn in honour of Jenni's father.

Part of the fun of writing historical fiction is the research and I have reached out to experts in the field, who responded with great generosity. These include Peter Clarke, a former City of London police officer, who helped me with the history of policing and crime in Limehouse. Dr Leslie Howsam, Distinguished University Professor Emerita at the University of Windsor, who wrote an incredible biography of Eliza Orme, the first woman to earn a law degree in England, from University College London in 1888.

I've always loved finding historical characters lurking at the corners, so I was delighted to find out about Ching Hook, courtesy of Sarah Elizabeth Cox's fascinating delve into boxing, *Grappling with History*.

I owe a huge debt to Louise Raw for her ground-breaking book *Striking a Light: The Bryant and May Matchwomen and their Place in History*, telling the remarkable adventures of the matchwomen, and the strike, which was first and foremost a working-class movement. Also the invaluable repositories of knowledge where I have spent many happy hours – the British Library, the helpful staff at Tower Hamlets Local History and Archive, the London Museum Docklands as well as the London Archives.

One of the best memories I have is of walking around the East End, listening to Wander East Through East, an audio tour of Limehouse Chinatown, written by Halima Khanom, part of the MA Heritage Studies programme at the University of East London. Also David Rosenberg, with his fiery and inspiring East End tours, bringing incredible detail to London's radical history.

Of great help in the early shaping of the book were Erin Kelly, Clare McGowan and Laura Wilson during my time on City University's MA in crime writing. Also my friend Shelley who was on the course, with her fantastic support. Katy Darby of City University was a colossal help keeping me on track with balancing research and literary elements. Also the Polari salon creative writing course with Paul Burston and Karen McCleod.

And I doubt any of this would be possible without the friends who helped my promises come true – John, Ellie, Kelly, Rebecca, Katherine, Gemma – and many others.

Dear Reader,

We'd love your attention for one more page to tell you about the crisis in children's reading, and what we can all do.

Studies have shown that reading for fun is the **single biggest predictor of a child's future success** – more than family circumstance, parents' educational background or income. It improves academic results, mental health, wealth, communication skills and ambition.

The number of children reading for fun is in rapid decline. Young people have a lot of competition for their time, and a worryingly high number do not have a single book at home.

Our business works extensively with schools, libraries and literacy charities, but here are some ways we can all raise more readers:

- Reading to children for just 10 minutes a day makes a difference
- Don't give up if children aren't regular readers – there will be books for them!
- Visit bookshops and libraries to get recommendations
- Encourage them to listen to audiobooks
- Support school libraries
- Give books as gifts

Thank you for reading: there's a lot more information about how to encourage children to read on our website.

www.JoinRaisingReaders.com